DOROTI

was born in 1873. The thir gentleman, from the age of seventeen she was obliged to earn her own living, which she did initially as a governess-teacher: first in Hanover, then in north London and finally in a country house. In 1895 her mother committed suicide, the family broke up and Dorothy Richardson began a new life in London as secretary assistant to a Harley Street dentist. During her years in London her friends were the socialist and avant garde intellectuals of the day. She became an intimate of H. G. Wells, who, among others, encouraged her to write. She began in journalism and for the rest of her life she lived as a writer, earning very little. In 1917 she married the young painter, Alan Odle, who died in 1948. For the whole of their married life they lived their winters in Cornwall and their summers in London. Dorothy Richardson's journalism includes scores of essays, reviews, stories, poems and sketches written and published between 1902 and 1949. Her journalism was her livelihood but the writing of PILGRIMAGE was her vocation; this long novel absorbed her artistic energy between 1914 and her death in 1957.

PUBLISHING HISTORY

FIRST EDITIONS:
Pointed Roofs (1915), *Backwater* (1916), *Honeycomb* (1917), *The Tunnel* (Feb 1919), *Interim* (Dec 1919), *Deadlock* (1921), *Revolving Lights* (1923), *The Trap* (1925), *Oberland* (1927), *Dawn's Left Hand* (1931) — all published by Duckworth: *Clear Horizon* (1935) — published by J. M. Dent & Cresset Press

COLLECTED EDITIONS:
Pilgrimage (including *Dimple Hill*), 4 vols, 1938 — J. M. Dent & Cresset Press, London: A. Knopf, New York

Pilgrimage (including *March Moonlight*), 4 vols, 1967 — J. M. Dent, London: A. Knopf, New York

Pilgrimage, 4 vols, 1976 — Popular Library, New York

Pilgrimage, 4 vols, 1979 — Virago, London
    Volume 1: *Pointed Roofs, Backwater, Honeycomb*
    Volume 2: *The Tunnel, Interim*
    Volume 3: *Deadlock, Revolving Lights, The Trap*
    Volume 4: *Oberland, Dawn's Left Hand, Clear Horizon, Dimple Hill, March Moonlight*

DOROTHY M. RICHARDSON

PILGRIMAGE

with an introduction by Gill Hanscombe

III

Deadlock
Revolving Lights
The Trap

VIRAGO

TO
J.D. BERESFORD

A *Virago* Book

Published by Virago Press 1979
in association with Mrs Sheena Odle
and Mark Paterson & Associates
This edition published by Virago Press 2002

A CIP catalogue record for this book is available
from the British Library

ISBN 0 86068 102 5

Virago Press
An Imprint of
Little, Brown Book Group
100 Victoria Embankment
London EC4Y 0DY

CONTENTS

PAGE

INTRODUCTION 4

DEADLOCK 9

REVOLVING LIGHTS 231

THE TRAP 397

INTRODUCTION

OF THE early twentieth-century English modernists, there is no one who has been more neglected than Dorothy Miller Richardson. There are several reasons for this. First, the style she forged in the writing of *Pointed Roofs*, the first volume of the *Pilgrimage* sequence, was new and difficult, later earning the nomination 'stream-of-consciousness'. *Pointed Roofs* was published in 1915 and was, therefore, the first example of this technique in English, predating both Joyce and Woolf, its more famous exponents. Secondly, the thoughts and feelings of its protagonist, Miriam Henderson, are explicitly feminist, not in the sense of arguing for equal rights and votes for women, but in the more radical sense of insisting on the authority of a woman's experience and world view. Thirdly, *Pointed Roofs* explores Miriam's sympathetic response to German culture and in 1915, when it was first published, this was an unpopular subject which contributed to the establishing of adverse critical reaction. Undaunted, however, by ambivalent response to her work, Richardson persisted in her task of completing the *Pilgrimage* sequence, a task which occupied her, intermittently, for the rest of her life.

Richardson regarded *Pilgrimage* as one novel and its constituent thirteen volumes as chapters. She regarded it, also, as fiction, even though the life of Miriam Henderson so closely resembles her own. The reason for this was that Richardson, after many attempts to write a more conventional novel, resolved finally that she must write about the subject she knew best, which was, she maintained, her own life. This is not to claim that every incident and every character in the novel add up to a photographic reproduction of Richardson's early life; but it is to claim that the genuine impulse of her work derives from the tension between her own life and that of Miriam, her fictional *alter ego*. The whole world of *Pilgrimage* is filtered through Miriam's mind alone; the reader sees what she sees and is never told what any of the other characters sees. Fiction usually means that the author invents or imagines his or her material. Richardson used the real material of her own life for her writing, and she used herself as her central character. The fictional process in *Pilgrimage* consists in how she shaped and organised and interpreted that material. There is, therefore, much in her life and personality to lend interest to her work.

She was born in Abingdon, Berkshire, on 17 May 1873, the third of four daughters. Her father, Charles Richardson, came from a family who had achieved financial success through a grocery business, but Charles longed to give up 'trade' and to become a gentleman. He sold the business and lived off the proceeds for some years. His wife, Mary Taylor, came from East Coker in Somerset, from a family whose name was listed among the gentry in local registers. When she was five years old, Dorothy Richardson was sent for a year to a small private school where she learned to read and spell and where nothing else interested her. When she was six, the family moved to the south coast, near Worthing, owing to her mother's ill health and her father's financial straits. Her school made no impression on her. In Dorothy's eleventh year, her father's investments improved and he moved his family up to London. Her life at this stage included croquet, tennis, boating, skating, dances and music; apart from musical evenings at home, she was introduced to the classics, to Wagner and Chopin and to Gilbert and Sullivan. She was taught by a governess, of whom she later wrote: 'if she could, [she] would have formed us to the almost outmoded pattern of female education: the minimum of knowledge and a smattering of various "accomplishments" . . . for me . . . she was torment unmitigated.' After this, she was sent to Southborough House, whose headmistress was a disciple of Ruskin, where the pupils were encouraged to think for themselves. Here Richardson studied French, German, literature, logic and psychology. At this point, her father, through disastrous speculation, lost the greater part of his resources, which forced Richardson at the age of seventeen, to seek employment as a teacher. Her first appointment, in a German school, later provided the material for *Pointed Roofs*.

After six months Richardson returned to England; two sisters were engaged to be married, the third had a position as a governess and her mother was near to a nervous collapse. In order to be near her mother, she took a post at the Misses Ayre's school in Finsbury Park, North London. Her impressions and experiences here provided the material for her second volume, *Backwater*. In 1893,

Charles Richardson was finally made a bankrupt; his house and possessions were sold and the family moved to a house in Chiswick, generously provided by John Arthur Batchelor, who became the husband of Dorothy's eldest sister Kate. By 1895, Richardson had moved from Finsbury Park to a post in the country as governess to two children, her experience of which is recorded in *Honeycomb*, her third volume. On 29 November 1895, while on holiday at Hastings with Dorothy, Mary Richardson committed suicide by cutting her throat with a kitchen knife.

After this, Richardson wanted a complete break: '. . . longing to escape from the world of women, I gladly accepted a post . . . a secretarial job, offering me the freedom I so desired.' She lived in a Bloomsbury attic on a salary of one pound per week. London became her great adventure. During these years she explored the world lying outside the enclosures of social life, which included writers, religious groups from Catholic to Unitarian and Quaker, political groups from the Conservative Primrose League to the Independent Labour Party and the Russian anarchists, and, through books and lectures, science and philosophy. At this time she found the philosophers 'more deeply exciting than the novelists'. These interests and activities provided the contextual material for her subsequent volumes. From working as a secretary, she gradually branched out into translations and freelance journalism which 'had promised release from routine work that could not engage the essential forces of my being. The small writing-table in my attic became the centre of my life'.

As a result of a series of sketches contributed to *The Saturday Review*, a reviewer urged her to try writing a novel. She later wrote that the suggestion 'both shocked and puzzled me. The material that moved me to write would not fit the framework of any novel I had experienced. I believed myself to be . . . intolerant of the romantic and the realist novel alike. Each . . . left out certain essentials and dramatized life misleadingly. Horizontally . . . Always . . . one was aware of the author and applauding, or deploring, his manipulations.' In 1917, at the age of forty-four, she married Alan Odle, an artist many years younger than herself. The marriage, in spite of misgivings, was a happy one, providing her with 'a new world, the missing link between those already explored'. She died in 1957 at the age of eighty-four.

A niece of Alan Odle's, who knew Dorothy Richardson and Alan Odle can add some human detail to this picture. In middle age, Richardson still had a golden heap of very long hair, piled on the top of her head; she had a 'massive' face, dark brown eyes, a clear skin, and pince-nez balanced on her nose, because she was 'always reading'. She created the impression of being tall, because she was 'so stately'. Alan Odle, in fact over six feet tall, was very thin, with waist-length hair wound around the outside of his head. He never cut his hair and rarely his fingernails, but since he had 'beautifully long elegant fingers', the image he presented was not an unattractive one. He, like Dorothy, had dark brown eyes and an ascetic face. They were very controlled together, extremely calm, always sitting side by side. Dorothy talked the most and late into the night; she seemed never to do 'anything ordinary' and had a voice 'like dark brown velvet'. She spoke very slowly indeed and was 'immensely impressive as a person'. Her life seemed to be arranged 'very very carefully' and she was 'not at all spontaneous in her actions'. She could 'only work on a certain image of herself' which was 'very cerebral'. It was hard for her to deal with ordinary people. Although she and Alan were affectionate with each other, they 'didn't touch'. Dorothy always called him 'sergeant', a joke arising from the fact that after only one day's service in the army, he had been discharged on medical grounds. Dorothy, in contrast to Alan, was 'very plump, with white creamy arms and very beautiful hands'; 'as she spoke she would screw up her eyes and slightly purse her mouth and everyone would listen'.

Charles Richardson often called Dorothy his 'son', as a compensation, it seems, for his lack of a male child. Indeed there is the evidence of Richardson's own recollections, as well as the portrayal in *Pilgrimage* of Miriam's relationship with her father, to reinforce the view that much of the original stimulus of the novel was owed to Dorothy's failure to adjust to the feminine role expected of her by late nineteenth-century middle-class society. But was it a failure? Or might it be seen as a triumph? Miriam's pilgrimage is partly the journey towards the resolution of that question. Because Richardson's father used all the family resources, it was necessary for the four daughters to make their own ways and accordingly, at the age of seventeen, Richardson answered an advertisement for an English student-teacher in a German academy for girls. *Pilgrimage* begins at

this point, a point at which, for Miriam, the beginning of economic
autonomy corresponds with the beginning of autonomous self-
consciousness. From this point until her meeting with Alan Odle,
Richardson's life is paralleled by that of her protagonist Miriam.
The parallels are numerous and strictly consistent, as Richardson's
letters and papers confirm.

Consistent with ordinary reality, also, are the descriptions of
London life at the turn of the century. And equally convincing are
the detailed accounts of households, lectures, activities and even
conversations. The precision of Richardson's memory at some twenty
to forty years distance is itself remarkable. It should not be assumed,
nevertheless, that she saw her function as a writer in traditional
autobiographical terms. On the contrary, she always insisted that her
task was truly appropriate to fiction and that *Pilgrimage* should be
judged as fiction. The mastery with which the author is able to
transform the haphazard impressions of subjective experience into a
thematically organised psychological narrative is the extent to which
this work of fiction achieves artistic integrity.

Miriam's consciousness is the subject matter of this novel. And it
seems to her that the experiences and perceptions of women have
been brutally and unreasonably discounted by men. Nor has she any
mercy for the majority of women who have, in her judgment, col-
luded with men in the suborning of their female gifts and attributes.
Such women are satirised, caricatured and eventually dismissed.
On the other hand, her stance is not topical. She does not become a
Suffragette. She does not argue for a recognition of the equality of
the sexes. She counts it a disadvantage to be a woman only in the sense
that the men who govern society refuse to recognise and to allow
women's contributions. In all other respects, she affirms, implicitly
and explicitly, the value of her own perceptions and judgments,
which by inference Richardson would have us generalise to include
an equivalent valuation of all women's experiences. The particular
virtues concomitant to such a feminism are the deliberate rejection
of female role-playing, an insistence on personal honesty, a passionate independence and a pilgrimage towards self-awareness. Its
particular vices are correspondingly stark: an inability to compromise
adequately in relationship, a tendency to categorise alternative views
as ignorance or obstinacy, a not always healthy flight from confrontation and a constant temptation to egocentricity.

These failings, however, Richardson allows Miriam to demonstrate; she is not content, in her authorial role, to idealise either Miriam's moral powers or her intellectual expertise. The qualities of intelligence Richardson most prized were not abstract rationalism and analytic empiricism, but the ability to perceive relationships between phenomena and the effort to synthesize feeling and reflection. This valuation has important consequences for her fiction, since it leads to a breaking down of the structural divisions we normally impose on experience, for example, the assumption that the external world has a finite integrity which is not influenced by subjective states and the further assumption that the division of time into past, present and future is necessary and meaningful. These major structures are, for her, simply categorisations of space and of time which our culture has developed in order to define for the individual his place in nature and in society. The subjective experience of time becomes the framework within which reality exists and the corresponding task of fiction becomes the conscious bringing into relationship of meaningful moments.

The impact on her style of this effort to delineate a female consciousness was radical. She stretched the unit of the sentence sometimes to the length of a long paragraph; she dispensed with the usual rules of punctuation, often substituting a series of full stops in place of explanation or other detail; she changed from one tense to another within a single paragraph; and she changed from the first person 'I' to the third person 'she' within a single reflection. She omitted details about people and places which readers could justifiably demand to know. Yet her feminist stance is not only evident in her uncompromising adherence to the unfolding of Miriam's consciousness and the forging of a new style. Together with her rejection of the technical conventions of the realist novel went a rejection of the values which the tradition of the English novel had attested. This rejection, however, was not formulated either from the principles of aesthetics or from a general philosophical orientation. It issued primarily from her conviction that the novel was an expression of the vision, fantasies, experiences and goals of men and that only rarely in the history of the novel could a genuine account of the female half of the human condition be found.

In *Pilgrimage*, Miriam often argues with Hypo Wilson about the male bias of the novel and in most of these exchanges the main burden of her argument is that authors seek to aggrandise themselves by constructing elaborate edifices which promise to reveal truths about life but which really reveal truths about the author. Nevertheless, like all radicals, Richardson is ambivalent at heart, recognising that a work of fiction must take its place among its predecessors. Therefore, in her own terms, she is forced to make an assessment of the tradition and to take a theoretical stand on the question of the structure and function of the novel. And because of her conviction that the traditional conventions express an overwhelmingly masculine world view, she must transform those conventions to accommodate Miriam's world view. For Richardson, therefore, words themselves become highly charged with ambivalence. The higher insights are above and beyond language.

There is in *Pilgrimage* a direct connection between Miriam's alienation from male consciousness and her distrust of language. Since style is necessary to a structured use of language, it must be acquired. However, she argues in *Deadlock*, style, because of its 'knowingness', is the property of men and of male writers in particular; men who feel 'the need for phrases'. For Miriam, the trouble with language is that it sets things 'in a mould that was apt to come up again'. The fear of things 'coming up again' can be seen as a fear of commitment, which later prompts the extravagance 'silence is reality'. That may, indeed, be true, but it is an impossible position for a writer to hold. Miriam is compelled, therefore, to rationalise her ambivalence by trying to understand how men use language.

Clearly in a work of such length, which owes less than is usual to previous models, there is bound to be some unevenness in technical control, an inevitability Richardson was fully aware of. In fact she often singled out particular sections of her text as failing to fulfil her intentions; such passages she marked 'I.R.', which stood for 'imperfectly realised'. Even so, *Pilgrimage* is a major contribution to our literature. Richardson's very original vision of female experience, together with her uncompromising experimental style, make the novel an extraordinary testament to the validity of female individuality. It is to be hoped that this first paperback edition of *Pilgrimage* to be published in England points to a new, rich and perceptive understanding of Richardson's achievement.

Gillian E Hanscombe, St Hugh's College, Oxford, 1979

DEADLOCK

CHAPTER I

MIRIAM ran upstairs narrowly ahead of her thoughts. In the small enclosure of her room they surged about her, gathering power from the familiar objects silently waiting to share her astounded contemplation of the fresh material. She swept joyfully about the room ducking and doubling to avoid arrest until she should have discovered some engrossing occupation. But in the instant's pause at each eagerly opened drawer and cupboard, her mind threw up images. It was useless. There was no escape up here. Pelted from within and without, she paused in laughter with clasped restraining hands. The rest of the evening must be spent with people. The nearest. The Baileys. She would go down into the dining-room and be charming with the Baileys until to-morrow's busy thoughtless hours were in sight. Half-way downstairs she remembered that the forms waiting below, for so long unnoticed and unpondered, might be surprised, perhaps affronted by her sudden interested reappearance. She rushed on. She could break through that barrier. Mrs Bailey's quiet withholding dignity would end in delight over a shared gay acknowledgment that her house was looking up. She opened the dining-room door, facing in advance the family gathered at needlework under the gaslight, an island group in the waste of dreary increasing shabbiness . . . she would ask some question, apologizing for disturbing them. The room seemed empty; the gas was turned dismally low. Only one light was on, the once new, drearily hopeful incandescent burner. Its broken mantle shed a ghastly bluish-white glare over the dead fern in the centre of the table and left the further parts of the room in obscurity. But there was someone there; a man, sitting perched on the sofa-head and, beyond him, someone sitting on the sofa. She came forward into silence. They made no movement; boarders, people she did not know, stupefied by their endurance of the dreariness of the room. She crossed to the fireside and stood looking at the clock face. The clock was not going. 'Are you wanting the real Greenwich, Miss Henderson?' She turned, ashamed of her mean revival of interest in a world from which she had turned away, to observe the woman who had found possible a friendly relationship with Mr Gunner. 'Oh yes I *do*,' she answered hurriedly, carefully avoiding the meeting of eyes that would call forth his numb clucking laughter. But she was looking into the eyes of Mrs Bailey. . . . Sitting tucked neatly into the sofa corner, with clasped hands, her shabbiness veiled by the dim light, she appeared to be smiling a faraway welcome from a face that shone rounded and rosy in the gloom. She was neither vexed nor pleased. She was far away, and Mr Gunner went on conducting the interview. He was speaking again, with his watch in his hand. He, having evidently become a sort of intimate of the Baileys, was of course despising her for her aloofness during the bad period. She paid no heed to his words, remaining engrossed in Mrs Bailey's curious still manner, her strange unwonted air of having no part in what was going on.

She sought about for some question to justify her presence and perhaps break the spell, and recovered a memory of the kind of inquiry used by boarders to sustain their times of association with Mrs Bailey. In reply to her announcement that she had come down to ask the best way of getting to Covent Garden early in the morning, Mrs Bailey sat forward as if for conversation. The spell was partly broken, but Miriam hardly recognized the smooth dreamy voice in which Mrs Bailey echoed the question, and moved about the room enlarging on her imaginary enterprise, struggling against the humiliation of being aware of Mr Gunner's watchfulness, trying to recover the mood in which she had come down and to drive the message of its gaiety through Mrs Bailey's detachment. She found herself, at the end of her tirade, standing once more facing the group on the sofa; startled by their united appearance of kindly, smiling, patient, almost patronizing tolerance. Lurking behind it was some kind of amusement. She had been an awkward fool, rushing in, seeing nothing. They had been discussing business together, the eternal difficulties of the house. Mr Gunner was behind it all now, intimate and helpful, and she had come selfishly in, interrupting. Mrs Bailey had the right to display indifference to her assumption that anything she chose to present should receive her undivided attention; and she had not displayed indifference. If Mr Gunner had not been there she would have been her old self. There they sat, together, frustrating her. Angered by the pressure of her desire for reinstatement, she crashed against their quietly smiling resistance. 'Have I been interrupting you?'

'No, young lady; certainly not,' said Mrs Bailey in her usual manner, brushing at her skirt.

'I believe I have,' smiled Miriam obstinately.

Mr Gunner smiled serenely back at her. There was something extraordinary in such a smile coming from him. His stupid raillery was there, but behind it was a modest confidence.

'No,' he said gently. 'I was only trying to demonstrate to Mrs Bailey the binomial theorem.'

They did not want her to go away. The room was freely hers. She moved away from them, wandering about in it. It was full, just beyond the veil of its hushed desolation, of bright light; thronging with scenes ranged in her memory. All the people in them were away somewhere, living their lives; they had come out of lives into the strange, lifeless, suspended atmosphere of the house. She had felt that they were nothing but a part of its suspension, that behind their extraordinary secretive talkative openness there was nothing, no personal interest or wonder, no personality, only frozen wary secretiveness. And they had *lives*, and had gone back into them or forward to them. Perhaps Mrs Bailey and Mr Gunner had always realized this . . . always seen them as people with other lives, not ghosts, frozen before they came, or unfortunates coming inevitably to this house rather than to any other, to pass on, frozen for life, by their very passage through its atmosphere. There had been the Canadians and the foreigners, unconscious of the atmosphere; free and active in

it. Perhaps because they really went to Covent Garden and
Petticoat Lane and Saint Paul's. . . . There's not many stays
'ere long; them as stays, stays always. A man writing; pleased
with making a single phrase stand for a description of a third-
rate boarding-house, not seeing that it turned him into a third-
rate boarding-house. Stays always; *always*. But that meant
boarders; perhaps only those boarders who did nothing at all
but live in the house, waiting for their food; 'human odds and
ends' . . . literary talk, the need for phrases.

These afterthoughts always came, answering the man's
phrase; but they had not prevented his description from coming
up always, now, together with any thoughts about the house.
There was a truth in it, but not anything of the whole truth.
It was like a photograph . . . it made you *see* the slatternly
servant and the house and the dreadful-looking people going
in and out. Clever phrases that make you see things by a
deliberate arrangement, leave an impression that is false to life.
But men do see life in this way, disposing of things and rushing
on with their talk; they think like that, all their thoughts false
to life; everything neatly described in single phrases that are
not true. Starting with a false statement, they go on piling
up their books. That man never saw how extraordinary it
was that there should be *anybody*, waiting for *anything*. But
why did their clever phrases keep on coming up in one's mind?

Smitten suddenly when she stood still to face her question,
by a sense of the silence of the room, she recognized that they
were not waiting at all for her to make a party there. They
wanted to go on with their talk. They had not merely been
sitting there in council at the heart of the gloom because the
arrival of new boarders was beginning to lift it. They had
sat like that many times before. They were grouped together
between her and her old standing in the house, and not only
they, but life, going, at this moment, on and on. They did
not know, life did not know, what she was going to prove.
They did not know why she had come down. She could not
go back again without driving home her proof. It was here
the remainder of the evening must be passed, standing on guard
before its earlier part, strung by it to an animation that would

satisfy Mrs Bailey and restore to herself the place she had held in the house at the time when her life there had not been a shapeless going on and on. The shapelessness had gone on too long. Mrs Bailey had been aware of it, even in her estrangement. But she could be made to feel that she had been mistaken. Looked back upon now, the interval showed bright with things that would appear to Mrs Bailey as right and wonderful life; they were wonderful now, linked up with the wonder of this evening, and could be discussed with her, now that it was again miraculously certain they were not all there was.

But Mr Gunner was still there, perched stolidly in the way. In the old days antagonism and some hidden fear there was in his dislike of her, would have served to drive him away. But now he was immovable; and felt, or for some reason thought he felt, no antagonism. Perhaps he and Mrs Bailey had discussed her together. In this intolerable thought, she moved towards the sofa with the desperate intention of sitting intimately down at Mrs Bailey's side and beginning somehow, no matter how, to talk in a way that must in the end send him away. 'There's a new comet,' she said. They looked up simultaneously into her face, each of their faces wearing a kind, veiled, unanimous patience. Mrs Bailey held her smile and seemed about to speak; but she sat back resuming her dreamy composure as Mr Gunner taking out his notebook cheerfully said:

'If you'll give me his name and address we'll take the earliest opportunity of paying a call.'

Mrs Bailey was pleading for indulgence of her failure to cover and distribute this jest in her usual way. She was ready now for a seated confabulation. But he would stay, permitted by her, immovable, slashing across their talk with his unfailing snigger, unreproved.

'All sorts of people are staying up to see it; I suppose one ought,' Miriam said cheerfully. She could go upstairs and think about the comet. She went away, smiling back her response to Mrs Bailey's awakening smile.

Her starlit window suggested the many watchers. Perhaps

he would be watching? But if he had seen no papers on the way from Russia he might not have heard of it. It would be something to mention to-morrow. But then one would have to confess that one had not watched. She opened her window and looked out. It was a warm night; but perhaps this was not the right part of the sky. The sky looked intelligent. She sat in front of the window. Very soon now it would not be too early to light the gas and go to bed.

No one had ever seen a comet rushing through space. There was nothing to look for. Only people who knew the whole map of the sky would recognize the presence of the comet. . . . But there was a sort of calming joy in watching even a small piece of a sky that others were watching too; it was one's own sky because one was a human being. Knowing of the sky and even very ignorantly a little of the things that made its effects, gave the most quiet sense of being human; and a sense of other human beings, not as separate disturbing personalities, but as sky-watchers. . . . 'Looking at the stars one feels the infinite pettiness of mundane affairs. I am perpetually astonished by the misapplication of the term *infinite*. How, for instance, can one thing be said to be infinitely smaller than another?' He had always objected only to the inaccuracy, not to the dreary-weary sentiment. Sic transit. Almost every one, even people who liked looking at the night sky, seemed to feel that, in the end. How do they get this kind of impression? If the stars are sublime, why should the earth be therefore petty? It is part of a sublime system. If the earth is to be called petty, then the stars must be called petty too. They may not even be inhabited. Perhaps they mean the movement of the vast system going on for ever, while men die. The indestructibility of matter. But if matter is indestructible, it is not what the people who use the phrase mean by *matter*. If matter is not conscious, man is more than matter. If a small, no matter how small, conscious thing is called petty in comparison with big, no matter how big, unconscious things, everything is made a question of size, which is absurd. But all these people think that consciousness dies. . . .

The quiet forgotten sky was there again; intelligent, blotting out unanswered questions, silently reaching down into the life that rose faintly in her to meet it, the strange mysterious life, far away below all interference, and always the same.

Teaching, being known as a teacher, had brought about Mrs Bailey's confident promise to the Russian student. There was no help for that. If he were cheated, it was part of the general confusion of the outside life. He also was subject to that. It would be a moment in his well-furnished life, caught up whenever his memory touched it, into the strand of contemptible things. He would see her drifting almost submerged in the flood of débris that made up the boarding-house life, its influence not recognized in the first moments because she stood out from it, still bearing, externally, the manner of another kind of life. The other kind of life was there, but able to realize itself only when she was alone. It had been all round her, a repelling memory, just now in the dining-room, blinding her, making her utterly stupid . . . and there they were, in another world, living their lives; their smiling patience taking its time, amused that she did not see. Of *course* that was what he had meant. There was no other possible meaning. Behind barred gates, closed against her, they had sat, patiently impatient with her absurdity. Mrs Bailey and Mr Gunner.

He had had the clearness of vision to discover what she was behind her half-dyed grey hair and terrible ill-fitting teeth. Glorious. Into the midst of her failing experiment, at the very moment when the shadow of oncoming age was making it visibly tragic, had come this man in his youth, clear-sighted and determined, seeing her as his happiness, his girl. She was a girl, modest and good. Circumstances could do nothing. There, as she stood at bay in the midst of them, the thing she believed in, her one test of everything in life, always sure of her defence and the shelter of her curious little iron strength, had come again to her herself, all her own. It was the unasked reward of her unswerving faith. She stood decorated by a miracle.

Mrs Bailey had triumphed; justified her everlasting confident smile.

She was enviable; her qualities blazoned by success in a competition whose judges, being blind, never failed in discovery.

But the miracle gleams only for a moment, and the personal life, no longer threading its way in a wonderful shining mysteriously continuous and decisive pattern freely in and out of the worldwide everything, is henceforth labelled and exposed, repeating, until the eye wearies of its fixity, one little lustreless shape; and the outside world is left untouched and unchanged. Is it worth while? A blind end, in which death swiftly increases. But without it, in the end, there is no shape at all?

The hour had been such a surprising success because of a smattering of *knowledge*: until the moment when he had said, 'I have always from the first been interested in philosophy.' Then knowing that the fascinating thing was philosophy, and being ignorant of philosophy, brought the certainty of being unable to keep pace. Philosophy had come, the strange nameless thread in the books that were not novels, with its terrible known name at last, and disappeared in the same moment for ever away into the lives of people who were free to study. But if, without knowing it, one had been for so long interested in a subject, surely it gave a sort of right? Perhaps he would go on talking about philosophy without asking questions. No matter what failure lay ahead, it might be possible, even if the lessons lasted only a little while, to find out all he knew about philosophy. It was a privilege, another of those extraordinary privileges coming suddenly and unexpectedly in strange places, books or people knowing all about things one had already become involved in without knowing when or why, people interested and attracted by a response that at first revealed no differences, so that they all in turn took one to be like themselves, and looking at life in their way. It made a relationship that was as false as it was true. What they were, they were permanently; always true to the same things. Why, being so different, was one privileged to meet them? There must be some explanation. There was something that for a while attracted all kinds of utterly different people, men and women —and then something that repelled them, some sudden revelation of opposition, or absolute difference, making one appear to have been playing a part. Insincere and fickle.

What is fickleness? He is fickle, people say, with a wise smile. But one always knows quite well why people go away, and why one goes oneself. Not having the sense of fickleness probably means that one is fickle. There is something behind the accusation and the maddening smile with which it is always made, that makes you say thank heaven. People who are not what they call fickle, but always the same, are always, in the midst of their bland security, depressed about life in general, and have 'a poor opinion of humanity.' 'Humanity does not change,' they say. It is the same as it was in the beginning is now and ever shall be. *Oooo.* And now to Godthefather . . . and they find even their steadfast relationships *dull.* They are the people who talk about 'ordinary everyday life,' and approve of 'far horizons,' and desert islands and the other side of the moon, as if they were real and wonderful and life was not. If they went there it would be the same to them; they would be just the same there; but something in the way their lives are arranged prevents them from ever suddenly meeting Mr Shatov. They meet only each other. The men make sly horrible jokes together . . . the Greeks had only one wife; they called it monotony.

But I find my daily round at Wimpole Street dull. No, not dull; wrong in some way. I did not choose it; I was forced into it. I chose it; there was something there; but it has gone. If it had not gone, I should never have found other things. 'But you would have found something else, my child.' No. I am glad it has gone. I see now what I have escaped. 'But you would have developed differently and not got out of touch. People don't if they are always together.' But that is just the dreadful thing. . . . Cléo de Mérode going back sometimes, with just one woman friend, to the little cabarets. . . . Intense sympathy with that means that one is a sort of adventuress . . . the Queen can never ride on an omnibus.

Why does being free give a feeling of meanness? Being able to begin all over again, always unknown, at any moment; feeling a sort of pity and contempt for the people who can't;

and then being happy and forgetting them. But there is pain
all round it that they never know. It is only by the pain of
remaining free that one can have the whole world round one
all the time. . . . But it disappears. . . .

No, just at the moment you are most sure that everything is
over for ever, it comes again, and you cannot believe it ever
disappeared. But again with the little feeling of meanness;
towards the people you have left and towards the new people.
If you have ever failed anybody, you have no right to speak to
any one else. All these years I ought never to have spoken to
anybody. 'If I have shrunk unequal from one contest, the
joy I find in all the rest becomes mean and cowardly. I should
hate myself if I then made my other friends my asylum.' Emerson would have hated me. But he thinks evil people are
necessary. How is one to know whether one is really evil?
Suppose one is. The Catholics believe that even the people
in hell have a little relaxation now and again. Lewes said it is
the relief from pain that gives you the illusion of bliss. It was
cruel when she was dying; but if it is true where is the difference? Perhaps in being mean enough to take relief you don't
deserve. Can any one be thoroughly happy and thoroughly
evil?

Botheration. Some clue had been missed. There was
something incomplete in the thought that had come just now
and seemed so convincing. She turned back and faced the
self that had said one ought to meet everything in life with one's
eyes on the sky. It had flashed in and out, between her thoughts.
Now it seemed alien. Other thoughts were coming up, the
thoughts and calculations she had not meant to make, but they
rushed forward, and there was something extraordinary behind
them, something that was part of the sky, of her own particular
sky as she knew it. She had the right to make them, having
been driven away from turning them into social charm for
the dining-room. Once more she turned busily to the sky,
thrusting back her thoughts; but it was just the flat sky of
every day, part of London; with nothing particular to say.

Thinking it over up here, alone in the universe, could not
hurt the facts. To-morrow there would be more facts. That

could not be helped, unless one died in the night or the house were burned down. Facing the empty sky, sitting between it and the empty stillness of the house, she felt she was beaten; too tired now to struggle against the tide of reflections she had fled downstairs to avoid. . . .

Only this morning, it seemed days ago, coming into the hall at Wimpole Street, the holidays still about her, little changes in the house, the greetings, the busy bustling cheerfulness, the sense of fresh beginnings, all ending in that dreadful moment of realization; being back in the smell of iodoform for another year; knowing that the holidays had changed nothing; that there was nothing in this life that could fulfil their promises; nothing but the circling pressing details, invisible in the distance, now all there, at a glance, horribly promising to fill her days and leave her for her share only tired evenings. Unpacking, the spell of sunburnt summer-scented, country-smelling clothes, the fresh beginning in her room, one visit to an A.B.C. and the British Museum, and everything would be dead again. No change at Tansley Street; through the crack in the dining-room door Mr Rodkin and his newspapers, Mr Gunner sitting over the empty grate waiting for nothing; Mrs Mann standing on the hearthrug, waiting to explain away something, watching Sissie and Mrs Bailey clear the table, with a smile fixed on her large well-made child's face; Mr Keppel coming out of the room with his graceful halting lounge and going on, unseeing, upstairs, upright in his shabby dreamy grey clothes as if he were walking on level ground. Lingering a moment too long, Mrs Bailey in the hall, her excited conspirator's smiles as she communicated the news of Mr Rodkin's friend and the lessons, as if nothing were changed and one were still always available for association with the house; her smiling calculating dismay at the refusal, her appeal to Mr Rodkin, his abstracted stiff-jointed emergence into the hall with his newspaper, his brilliant-eyed, dried-up laugh, his chuckling assertion, like a lawyer, that he had promised the lessons and Shatov must not be disappointed; the suspicion that Mrs Bailey was passing the moments in fear of losing a well-to-do newcomer, an important person brought in by her only good boarder; the wretched sense of being caught and linked up again in the shifts and deceptions of the bankrupt house; the uselessness; the certainty that the new man, as described, would be retained only by his temporary ignorance and helplessness, the vexatious thought of him, waiting upstairs in the drawing-room in a state of groundlessly aroused interest and anticipation, Mr Rodkin's irresponsible admiring spectator's confidence as he made the introductions and vanished whilst the little dark frock-coated figure, standing alone in the cold gaslight of the fireless room, was still in the attitude of courteous obeisance; the happy ease of explaining to the controlledly waiting figure the impossibility of giving lessons in one's own language without the qualification of study; his lifted head, the extraordinary gentleness of the white, tremulous, determined features, the child-like openness of the broad forehead, the brilliant gentle deprecating eyes, familiar handsome unknown kindliness gleaming out between the high arch of rich black hair and the small black sharply-pointed French beard; the change in the light of the cold room with the sound of the warm deep voice; the few well-chosen struggling words; scholarship; that strange sense that foreigners bring, of knowing and being known, but without the irony of the French or the plebeianism of Germans and Scandinavians, bringing a consciousness of being on trial, but without responsibility. . . .

The trial would bring exposure. Reading and discussion would reveal ignorance of English literature. . . .

The hour of sitting accepted as a student, talking easily, the right phrases remembering themselves in French and German, would not come again; the sudden outbreak of happiness after mentioning Renan . . . *how* had she suddenly known that he made the Old Testament like a newspaper? *Parfaitement;* j'ai toujours été fort interessée par la philosophie. After reading so long ago, not understanding at the time and knowing she would only remember, without words, something that had come from the pages. Perhaps that was how students learned; reading and getting only a general impression and finding thoughts and words years afterwards; but then how did they pass examinations?

For that moment they had been students together, exchanging photographs of their minds. That could not come again. It was that moment that had sent him away at the end of the lesson, plunging lightly upstairs, brumming in his deep voice, and left her singing in the drawing-room . . . the best way would be to consider him as something superfluous, to be forgotten all day and presently, perhaps quite soon, to disappear altogether. . . . But before her exposure brought the lessons to an end and sent him away to find people who were as learned as he was, she would have heard more. To-morrow he would bring down the Spinoza book. But it was in German. They might begin with Renan in English. But that would not be reading English. He would demur and disapprove. English literature. Stopford Brooke. He would think it childish; not sceptical enough. Matthew Arnold. *Emerson.* Emerson would be perfect for reading; he would see that there was an English writer who knew everything. It would postpone the newspapers, and meanwhile she could find out who was Prime Minister and something about the English system of education. He *must* read Emerson; one could insist that it was the purest English and the most beautiful. If he did not like it, it would prove that his idea that the Russians and the English were more alike than any other Europeans was an illusion. Emerson; and the comet.

Mr Shatov stood ceremoniously waiting and bowing, as on the previous evening, a stranger again; conversational interchange was far away at the end of some chance opening that the hour might not bring. Miriam clasped her volume; she could fill the time triumphantly in correcting his accent and intonation, after a few remarks about the comet.

Confronting him she could not imagine him related to Emerson. No continental could fully appreciate Emerson; except perhaps Maeterlinck. It would have been better to try something more simple, with less depth of truth in it. Darwin or Shakespeare. But Shakespeare was poetry; he could not go about in England talking Shakespeare. And Darwin was bad, for men.

He listened in his subdued controlled way to her remark and again she saw him surrounded by his world of foreign universities and professors, and wondered for a sharp instant whether she were betraying some dreadful English, middle-class, newspaper ignorance; perhaps there were no longer any comets; they were called by some other name . . . he might know whether there was still a nebular theory and whether anything more had been done about the electrical contact of metals . . . that man in the *Revue des Deux Mondes* saying that the first outbreak of American literature was unfortunately feminine. Mill thought intuition at least as valuable as ratiocination . . . Mill; he could read Mill. Emerson would be a secret attack on him, an eloquent spokesman for things no foreigner would agree with. 'Ah yes,' he said thoughtfully, 'I always have had great interest for astronomy, but now please tell me'—he lifted yesterday's radiant face. Had there been yesterday that glow of crimson tie showing under the point of his black beard and the gold watch-chain across the blackness of his waistcoat? —'how I shall obtain admission to the British Moozayum.'

Miriam gave instructions delightedly. Mr Shatov hunched crookedly in his chair, his head thrown up and listening towards her, his eyebrows raised as if he were singing and, on his firm small mouth, the pursed look of a falsetto note. His brown eyes were filmed, staring averted, as if fixed on some far-away thing that did not move; it was like the expression in the eyes of Mr Helsing, but older and less scornful. There was no scorn at all, only a weary, cynically burning knowledge, yet the eyes were wide and beautiful with youth. Yesterday's look of age and professorship had gone; he was wearing a little short coat; in spite of the beard, he was a student, only just come from being one amongst many, surrounded in the crowding sociable foreign way; it gave his whole expression a warmth; the edges of his fine soft richly-dented black hair, the contours of his pale face, the careless hunching of his clothes, seemed, in a strange generous way unknown in England, at the disposal of his fellow-creatures. Only in his eyes was the contradictory lonely look of age. But when they came round to meet hers, his head still reined up and motionless, she seemed to face the chubby upright determination of a baby, and the deep melancholy in the eyes was like the melancholy of a puppy.

'Pairhaps,' he said, 'one of your doctors shall sairtify me for a fit and proper person.'

Miriam stared her double stupefaction. For a moment, as if to give her time to consider his suggestion, his smile remained, still deferential but with the determined boldness of a naughty child lurking behind it; then his eyes fell, too soon to catch her answering smile. She could not, with his determined unaverted and now nervously quivering face before her, either discourage the astounding suggestion or resent his complacent possession of information about her.

'I should tell you,' he apologized gently, 'that Mrs Bailey has say me you are working in the doctors' quarter of London.'

'They are not doctors,' said Miriam, feeling stiffly English, and in her known post as dental secretary utterly outside his world of privileged studious adventure, 'and you want a householder who is known to you and not a hotel or boarding-house keeper.'

'That is very English. But no matter. Pairhaps it shall be sufficient that I am graduate.'

'You could go down and see the librarian; you must write a statement.'

'That is an excellent idee.'

'I am a reader, but not a householder.'

'No matter. That is most excellent. You shall pairhaps introduce me to this gentleman. Ah, that is very good. I shall be most happy to find myself in that institution. It is one of my heartmost dreams of England to find myself in midst of all these leeter-aytchoors. . . . When can we go?'

There was a ring on the little finger of the hand that drew from an inner pocket a limp leather pocket-book; pale old gold curving up to a small pimple of jewels. The ringed hand moving above the dip of the double watch-chain gave to his youth a strange look of mellow wealthy middle age.

'Ah. I must write in English. Please tell me. But shall we not go at once, this evanink?'

'We can't; the reading-room closes at eight.'

'That is very English; well; tell me what I shall write.'

Miriam watched as he wrote with a small quick smoothly moving pencil. The pale gold of the ring was finely chased. The small cluster of tiny soft-toned pearls encircling and curving up to a small point of diamond were set in a circlet of enamel, a marvellous rich deep blue. She had her Emerson ready when the writing was done.

'What is Emerson?' he inquired, sitting back to restore his book to its pocket. 'I do not know this writer.' His reared head had again the look of heady singing, young, confronting everything, and with all the stored knowledge that can be given to wealthy youth, prepared to meet her precious book. If he did not like it, there was something shallow in all the wonderful continental knowledge; if he found anything in it, if he understood it at all, they could meet on that one little plot of equal ground; he might even understand her carelessness about all other books.

'He is an American,' she said, desperately handing him the little green volume.

'A most nice little volume,' he demurred, 'but I find it strandge that you offer me the book of an American.'

'It is the most perfect English you could have. He is a New Englander, a Bostonian; the Pilgrim Fathers; they kept up the English of our best period. The sixteenth century.'

'That is most interestink,' he said gravely, turning the precious pages. 'Why have I not heard of this man? In Russia we know of course their Thoreau, he has a certain popularity amongst extremists, and I know also of course their great poet, Vitmann. I see that this is a kind of philosophical disquisitions.'

'You could not possibly have a better book for style and phraseology in English, quite apart from the meaning.'

'*No*,' he said, with reproachful gravity, 'preciosity I cannot have.'

Miriam felt out of her depth. 'Perhaps you won't like

Emerson,' she said, 'but it will be good practice for you. You need not attend to the meaning.'

'Well, ach-ma, we shall try, but not this evanink; I have headache, we shall rather talk; let us return to the soobjects we have discussed yesterday.' He rested his elbows on the table, supporting his chin on one hand, his beard askew, one eye reduced to a slit by the bulge of his pushed-up cheek, his whole face suddenly pallid and heavy, sleepy-looking.

'I am *most*-interested in philosophy,' he said, glowering warmly through his further, wide-open eye. 'It was very good to me. I found myself most excited after our talk of yesterday. I think you too were interested?'

'Yes, wasn't it extraordinary?' Miriam paused to choose between the desire to confess her dread of confronting a full-fledged student, and a silence that would let him go on talking while she contemplated a series of reflections extending forward out of sight from his surprising admission of fellowship. It was so strange, an exhilaration so deep and throwing such wide thought-inviting illumination, to discover that he had found yesterday exceptional; that he, too, with all his wonderful life, found interest scattered only here and there. Meanwhile his eagerness to rekindle, without fresh fuel, the glow of yesterday confessed an immaturity that filled her with a tumult of astonished solicitude.

'You must let me correct your English to-day,' she said, busily taking him with her voice by the hand in a forward rush into the empty hour that was to test, perhaps to destroy, the achievement of their first meeting. 'Just now you said "the subjects we have discussed yesterday." "Have" is the indefinite past; "yesterday," as you used it, is a definite point of time; passé défini, we *discussed* yesterday. We have always discussed these things on Thursdays. We always discussed these things on Thursdays. Those two phrases have different meanings. The first indefinite because it suggests the discussions still going on, the second definite referring to a fixed period of past time.'

She had made her speech at the table, and glanced up at him apologetically. Marvelling at her unexpected knowledge of the grammar of her own tongue, called into being, she supposed, by the jar of his inaccuracy, she had for a moment almost forgotten his presence.

'I perceive,' he said shifting his chin on his hand to face her fully, with bent head and moving beard-point; his voice came again as strange, from an immense distance; he was there like a ghost; 'that you are, in spite of your denials, a most excellent institutrice. Ach-ma! My English is bad. You shall explain me all these complications of English verb-mixing; but to-night I am *ree*ally too stupid.'

'It is all quite easy; it only appears to be difficult.'

'It shall be easy; you have, I remark, a more clear pure English than I have met; and I am very intelligent. It shall not be difficult.'

Miriam hid her laughter by gathering up one of his books with a random question. But how brave. Why should not people admit intelligence? . . . It was a sort of pamphlet, in French.

'Ah, that is most-interestink; you shall at once read it. He is a most intelligent man. I have hear this lectchoor——'

'I heard, I heard,' cried Miriam.

'Yes; but excuse a moment. Really it is interestink. He is one of the most fine lecturours of Sorbonne; membre de l'Académie; the soobject is l'Attention. Ah it is better we shall speak in French.'

'Nur auf deutsch kann man gut philosophieren,' quoted Miriam disagreeing with the maxim and hoping he would not ask where she had read it.

'That is not so; that is a typical German arrogance. The French have some most distinguished p-sychologues, Taine and, more recently, Tarde. But listen.'

Miriam listened to the description of the lecture. For a while he kept to his careful slow English and her attention was divided between her growing interest in the nature of his mistakes, her desire to tell him she had discovered that he spoke Norman English in German idiom with an intonation that she supposed must be Russian, and the fascination of watching for the fall of the dead-white, black-fringed eyelids on to the brooding face, between the framing of each sentence. When he passed into French, led by a quotation which was evidently the core of the lecture, she saw the lecturer, and his circle of students, and indignantly belaboured him for making, and them for quietly listening to, the assertion that it is curious that the human faculty of attention should have originated in women.

Certainly she would not read the pamphlet. However clever the man might be, his assumptions about women made the carefully arranged and solemnly received display of research, irritatingly valueless. And Mr Shatov seemed to agree, quite as a matter of course. . . . 'Why should he be *surprised*?' she said when he turned for her approval. '*How*, surprised?' he asked laughing, an easy deep bass chuckle, drawing his small mouth wide and up at the corners; a row of small square even teeth shining out.

'Ach-ma,' he sighed, with shining eyes, looking happily replete, 'he is a *great* p-sycho-physiologiste,' and passed on to eager narration of the events of his week in Paris. Listening to the strange inflections of his voice, the curiously woven argumentative sing-song tone, as if he were talking to himself, broken here and there by words thrown out with explosive vehemence, breaking defiantly short as if to crush opposition in anticipation, and then again the soft, almost plaintive sing-song beginning of another sentence, Miriam presently heard him mention Max Nordau and learned that he was something more than the author of *Degeneration*. He had written *Die conventionellen Lügen der Kulturmenscheit*, which she immediately must read. He had been to see him and found a truly marvellous white-haired old man, with eyes, *alive*; so young and vigorous in his enthusiasm that he made Mr Shatov at twenty-two feel *old*.

After that she watched him from afar, set apart from his boyhood, alone with her twenty-five years on the borders of middle age. *There* was the secret of the youthful untested look that showed in certain poses of his mature studious head. His beard and his courtly manner and the grave balanced intelligence of his eyes might have belonged to a man of forty.

Perhaps the Paris visit had been some time ago. No; he had come through France for the first time on his way to England. . . . She followed him, growing weary with envy, through his excursions in Paris with his father; went at last to the Louvre, mysterious grey building, heavy above a row of shops, shutting in works of 'art,' in some extraordinary way understood, and known to be 'good'; and woke to astonishment to find him sitting alone, his father impatiently gone back to the hotel, for an hour in motionless contemplation of the Venus, having *wept* at the first sight of her in the distance. The impression of the Frenchman's lecture was driven away. All the things she had heard of on these two evenings were in the past.

He was in England now; through all the wonders of his continental life, England had beckoned him. Paris had been just a stage on his confident journey; and the first event of his London life would be Saturday's visit to the British Museum. His eager foreign interest would carry the visit off . . . and she remembered, growing in the thought suddenly animated towards his continued discourse, that she could show him the Elgin Marbles.

The next evening, going down to the drawing-room at the appointed time, Miriam found it empty and lit only by the reflection from the street. . . . Standing in the dim blue light she knew so well, she passed through a moment of wondering whether she had ever really sat talking in this room with Mr Shatov. It seemed so long ago. His mere presence there had been strange enough; youth and knowledge and prosperity, where for so long there had been nothing but the occasional presence of people who were in mysterious disgraceful difficulties, and no speech but the so quickly acrimonious interchange of those who are trying to carry things off. Perhaps he was only late. She lit the gas and, leaving the door wide, sat down to the piano. The loose, flatly vibrating, shallow tones restored her conviction that once more the house was as before, its usual intermittent set of boarders, coming punctually to meals, enduring each other downstairs in the warmth until bedtime, disappearing one by one up the unlighted stairs, having tea up here on Sundays, and for her, the freedom of the great dark house, the daily oblivion of moving about in it, the approach up the quiet, endlessly dreaming old grey street in the afternoon, late at night, under all the changes of season and of weather; the empty drawing-room that was hers every Sunday morning with its piano, and always there at night within its open door, inviting her into its blue-lit stillness; her room upstairs, alive now and again under some chance spell of the weather, or some book which made her feel that any life in London would be endurable for ever that secured her room with its evening solitude, now and again the sense of strange, fresh, invisibly founded beginnings; often a cell of torturing mocking memories and apprehensions, driving her down into the house to hear the dreadful voices, giving out, in unchanged accents, their unchanging words and phrases.

Someone had come into the room, bringing a glow of life. She clung to her playing; he need not know that she had been waiting for him. A figure was standing almost at her side; with that voice he would certainly be musical. Its sturdiness and the plaintiveness were like the Russian symphonies; he could go to the Queen's Hall; his being late for the lesson had introduced music. . . . She broke off and turned to see Sissie Bailey, waiting with sullen politeness to speak. Mr Shatov was out. He had gone out early in the afternoon and had not been seen since. In Sissie's sullenly worried expression Miriam read the Baileys' fear that they had already lost hold of their helpless new boarder. She smiled her acceptance and suggested that he had met friends. Sissie remained grimly responseless and presently turned to go. Resuming her playing, Miriam wondered bitterly where he could have lingered, so easily dropping his lesson. What did it matter? Sooner or later he was bound to find interests; the sooner the better. But she could not go on playing; the room was cold and black; horribly empty and still. Mrs Bailey would know where he had set out to go this afternoon; she would have directed him. She played on zealously for a decent interval, closed the piano, and went downstairs. In the dining-room was Sissie, alone, mending a table-cloth.

To account for her presence, Miriam inquired whether Mrs Bailey were out. 'Mother's lying down,' said Sissie sullenly, 'she's got one of her headaches.' Miriam sympathized. 'I want her to have the doctor; it's no use going on like this.' Miriam was drawn irresistibly towards Mrs Bailey, prostrate in her room with her headache. She went down the hall feeling herself young and full of eager strength, sinking with every step deeper and deeper into her early self; back again by Eve's bedside at home, able to control the paroxysms of pain by holding her small head grasped in both hands; she recalled the strange persistent strength she had felt, sitting with her at night, the happiness of the moments when the feverish pain seemed to run up her own arms and Eve relaxed in relief. The beautiful unfamiliar darkness of the midnight hours, the curious sharp savour of the incomprehensible book she had read lying on the floor by the little beam of the night-light. She could surely do something for Mrs Bailey, meeting her thus for the first time without the barrier of conversation. At least she could pit her presence and her sympathy against the pain. She tapped at the door of the little room at the end of the passage. Presently a muffled voice sounded and she went in. A sense of release enfolded her as she closed the door of the little room. It was as if she had stepped off the edge of her life, out into the wide spaces of the world. The room was lit feebly by a small lamp turned low within its smoky chimney. Its small space was so crowded that for a moment she could make out no recognizable bedroom shape; then a figure rose and she recognized Mr Gunner standing by a low camp bedstead. 'It's Miss Henderson,' he said quietly. There was a murmur from the bed and Miriam bending over it saw Mrs Bailey's drawn face, fever-flushed, with bright wild eyes. 'We think she ought to have a doctor,' murmured Mr Gunner. 'M'm,' said Miriam absently.

'Good of you,' murmured Mrs Bailey thickly. Miriam sat down in the chair Mr Gunner had left and felt for Mrs Bailey's hands. They were cold and trembling. She clasped them

firmly and Mrs Bailey sighed. 'Perhaps you can persuade
her,' murmured Mr Gunner. 'M'm,' Miriam murmured.
He crept away on tiptoe. Mrs Bailey sighed more heavily.
'Have you tried anything?' said Miriam dreamily, out into
the crowded gloom.

The room was full of unsightly necessaries, all old and in
various stages of dilapidation, the overflow of the materials
that maintained in the rest of the house the semblance of
ordered boarding-house life. But there was something vital,
even cheerful in the atmosphere; conquering the oppression of
the crowded space. The aversion with which she had contemplated, at a distance, the final privacies of the Baileys behind
the scenes, was exorcized. In the house itself there was no
life; but there was brave life battling in this room. Mrs Bailey
would have admitted her at any time, with laughing apologies.
Now that her entry had been innocently achieved, she found
herself rejoicing in the disorder, sharing the sense Mrs Bailey
must have, every time she retired to this lively centre, of keeping
her enterprise going for yet one more day. She saw that to
Mrs Bailey the house must appear as anything but a failure,
and the lack of boarders nothing but unaccountable bad luck.
'A compress, or hot fomentations, hot fomentations could not
do harm and they might be very good.'

'Whatever you think my dear; good of you,' murmured Mrs
Bailey feebly. 'Not a bit,' said Miriam looking about, wondering how she should carry out, in her ignorance, this mysteriously
suggested practical idea. There was a small fire in the little
narrow fireplace, with a hob on either side. Standing up she
caught sight of a circular willow-pattern sink basin, with a tap
above it and a cupboard below, set in an alcove behind a mound
of odds and ends. The room was meant for a sort of kitchen
or scullery; and it had been the doctors' only sitting-room.
How had the four big tall men, with their table and all their
books, managed to crowd themselves in?

In the dining-room Sissie responded with unconcealed
astonishment and gratitude to Miriam's suggestions and bustled
off for the needed materials, lingering, when she brought them,
to make useful suggestions, affectionately controlling Mrs

III—B

Bailey's feeble efforts to help in the arrangements, and staying to supply Miriam's needs, a little compact approving presence.

As long as the hot bandages were held to her head Mrs Bailey seemed to find relief and presently began to murmur complaints of the trouble she was giving. Miriam, longing to sing, threatened to withdraw unless she would remain untroubled until she was better, or weary of the treatment. At ten o'clock she was free from pain, but her feet and limbs were cold.

'You ought to have a pack all over,' said Miriam judicially.

'That's what I felt when you began,' agreed Mrs Bailey.

'Of course. It's the even temperature. I've never had one, but we were all brought up homoeopathically.' Sissie went away to make tea.

'Was you?' said Mrs Bailey, drawing herself into a sitting posture. Miriam launched into eager description of the little chest with its tiny bottles of pilules and tinctures and the small violet-covered book about illnesses strapped into its lid; the home life all about her as she talked. . . . Belladonna; aconite; she was back amongst her earliest recollections, feeling small and swollen and feverish; Mrs Bailey, sitting up, with her worn glad patient face seemed to her more than ever like her mother; and she could not believe that the lore of the book and the little bottles did not reside with her.

'Aconite,' said Mrs Bailey, 'that was in the stuff the doctor give me when I was so bad last year.' That was all new and modern. Mrs Bailey *must* see if she could only rapidly paint them for her, the home scenes all about the room.

'They *use* those things in the British Pharmacopoeia, but they pile them in in bucketsful with all sorts of minerals,' she said provisionally, holding to her pictures while she pondered for a moment over the fact that she had forgotten until to-night that she was a homoeopath.

Mr Gunner came quietly in with Sissie and the tea, making a large party distributed almost invisibly in the gloom beyond the circle of dim lamplight. There was a joyful urgency of communication in the room. But the teacups were filled and passed round before the accumulated intercourse broke through the silence in a low-toned remark. It seemed to come from every one and to bear within it all the gentle speech that had sounded since the world began; light spread outward and onward from the darkened room.

Taking her share in the remarks that followed, Miriam marvelled. Unqualified and unprepared, utterly undeserving as she felt, she was aware, within the controlled tone of her slight words, of something that moved her, as she listened, to a strange joy. It was within her, but not herself; an unknown vibrating moulding force. . . .

When Sissie went away with the tea-things, Mr Gunner came to the bedside to take leave. Sitting on the edge of the bed near Miriam's chair, he bent murmuring; Miriam rose to go; Mrs Bailey's hand restrained her. 'I think you know,' whispered Mr Gunner, 'what we are to each other.' Miriam made no reply; there was a golden suffusion before her eyes, about the grey pillow. Mrs Bailey was clutching her hand. She bent and kissed the hollow cheek, receiving on her own a quick eager mother's kiss, and turned to offer her free hand to Mr Gunner who painfully wrung it in both his own. Outside in the darkness St Pancras clock was striking. She felt a sudden sadness. What could they know of each other? What could any man and woman know of each other?

When Mr Gunner had gone and she was alone with Mrs Bailey, the trouble lifted. It was Mrs Bailey who had permitted it, she who would steer and guide, and she was full of wisdom and strength. She could unerringly guide any one through anything. But how had she arrived at permitting such an extraordinary thing?

'Poor boy,' sighed Mrs Bailey.

'Why poor boy? Nothing of the sort,' said Miriam.

'Well, it's a comfort to me you think that; I've worried meself ill over him. I've been keeping him off for over a twelvemonth.'

'Well, it's all settled now so you needn't worry any more.'

'It's his age I look to; he's only two-and-twenty,' flushed Mrs Bailey.

'He looks older than that.'

'He does look more than his age, I allow; he never had any home; his father married a second time; he says this is the first home he 's had; he 's never been so happy.' All the time he had been halting about in the evenings in the dining-room, never going out and seeming to have nothing to do but a sort of malicious lying-in-wait to make facetious remarks, he had been feeling at home, happy at home, and growing happier and happier. Poor little man, at home in nothing but the dining-room at Tansley Street. . . . Mrs Bailey. . . . Was he good enough for her? She had not always liked or even approved of him.

'Well; that 's lovely. Of course he has been happy here.'

'That 's all very well for the past; but there 's many breakers ahead. He wants me to give up and have a little home of our own. But there 's my chicks. I can't give up till they 're settled. I 've told him that. I can't do less than my duty by *them.*'

'Of course not. He 's a dear. I think he 's splendid.' But how generously glowing the struggling house seemed now; compared with a life alone, in some small small corner, with Mr Gunner.

'Bless 'im. He 's only a clurk, poor boy, at thirty-five weekly.'

'Of course clerks don't make much; unless they have languages. He ought to learn one or two languages.'

'He 's not over strong. It 's not money I 'm thinking of——' She flushed and hesitated and then said with a girlish rush, 'I 'd manage; once I 'm free; I 'd manage. I 'd work my fingers to the bone for 'im.' Marvellous, for a little man who would go on writing yours of yesterday's date to hand as per statement enclosed; nothing in his day but his satisfaction in the curves and flourishes of his handwriting . . . and then home comforts, Mrs Bailey always there, growing more worn and ill and old; an old woman before he was thirty.

'But that won't be for a long time yet; though Polly 's doing splendid.'

'Is she?'

'Well, I oughtn't to boast. But they 've wrote me she 's to be pupil-teacher next year.'

'*Polly?*'

'Polly,' bridled Mrs Bailey and laughed with shining eyes. 'The chahld's not turned fifteen yet, dear little woman blesser.' Miriam winced; poor little Polly Bailey, to die so soon, without knowing it.

'Oh, that's magnificent.' Perhaps it was magnificent. Perhaps a Bailey would not feel cheated and helpless. Polly would be a pupil-teacher, perkily remaining her same self, a miniature of Mrs Bailey, already ·full of amused mysterious knowledge and equal to every occasion.

Mrs Bailey smiled shyly. 'She's like her poor mother; she's got a will of her own.' Miriam sat at ease within the tide . . . where did women find the insight into personality that gave them such extraordinary prophetic power? She herself had not an atom of it. Perhaps it was matronhood; and Mary hid all these things in her heart. No; aunts often had it, even more than matrons. Mrs Bailey was so splendidly controlled that she was an aunt as well as a mother to the children. She contemplated the sharply ravaged little head, reared and smiling above the billows of what people called 'misfortunes' by her conscious and self-confessed strength of will; yes, and unconscious fairness and generosity, reflected Miriam, and an immovable sense of justice. All these years of scraping and contrivance had not corrupted Mrs Bailey; she ought to be a judge, and not Mr Gunner's general servant. Justice is a woman; blindfold; seeing from the inside and not led away by appearances; men invent systems of ethics, but they cannot weigh personality; they have no individuality, only conformity or nonconformity to abstract systems; yet it was impossible to acknowledge the power of a woman, of any woman she had ever known, without becoming a slave. Or to associate with one, except in a time of trouble. But in her deliberate excursion into this little room she was free; all her life lay far away, basking in freedom; spreading out and out, illimitable; each space and part a full cup on which no hand might be laid . . . that little man was just a curious foreign voice, which would presently rouse her impatience . . . and just now he had seemed so near. . . . Was she looking at him with Mrs

Bailey's eyes? Mrs Bailey would say, 'Oh yes, I think he's a
very nice little man.' Beyond his distinction as a well-to-do
boarder, he would have, in her eyes, nothing to single him out.
She would respect his scholarship, but regarding it as a quality
peculiar to certain men; and without the knowledge that it was
in part an accident of circumstance. She would see beyond it;
she would never be prostrate before it.

But the distant vision of the free life was not Mrs Bailey's
vision; there was something there she could not be made to
understand, and would, in any way there were words that tried
to express it, certainly not approve. Yet why did it come so
strongly here in her room? The sense of it was here, somewhere in their intercourse, but she was unconscious of it.
Miriam plumbed about in the clear centre—where without
will or plan or any shapely endeavour in her life, she was yet
so strangely accepted and indulged. Mrs Bailey was glancing
back at her from the depths of her abode, her face busy
in control of the rills of laughter sparkling in her eyes and
keeping, Miriam knew, as she moved, hovering, and saw the
fostering light they shed upon the world, perpetual holiday;
the reassuring inexhaustible substance of Mrs Bailey's
being.

'It's Sissie I worry about,' said Mrs Bailey. Miriam
attended curiously. 'She's like her dear father; keeps herself
to herself and goes on; she's a splendid little woman in the
house; but I feel she ought to be doing something more.'

'She's awfully capable,' said Miriam.

'She is. There's nothing she can't turn her hand to.
She'll have the lock off a door and mend it and put it on again
and put in a pane of glass neater than a workman and no mess
or fuss.' Miriam sat astonished before the expanding accumulation of qualities.

'I don't know how I should spare her; but she's not satisfied
here; I've been wondering if I couldn't manage to put her into
the typing.'

'There's isn't much prospect there,' recited Miriam, 'the
supply is bigger than the demand.'

'That is so,' assented Mrs Bailey; 'but I see it like this;

where there's a will there's a way and one has to make a beginning.' Mrs Bailey had made up her mind. Quite soon Sissie would know typewriting; a marketable accomplishment; she would rank higher in the world than a dental secretary; a lady typist with a knowledge of French. That would be her status in an index. No doubt in time she would learn shorthand. She would go capably about, proud of her profession; with a home to live in, comfortably well off on fifteen shillings a week; one of the increasing army of confident illiterate young women in the city. No, Sissie would not be showy; she would bring life into some office, amongst men as illiterate as herself; as soon as she had picked up 'yours to hand' she would be reliable and valuable. Sissie, with a home, and without putting forth any particular effort, would have a place in the world.

'I'll make some inquiries,' said Miriam cheerfully. Mrs Bailey thanked her with weary eagerness; she was flushed and flagging; the evening's work was being cancelled by the fascination which had allowed her to go on talking. She admitted a return of her neuralgia and Miriam, remorseful and weary, made her lie down again. She looked dreadfully ill; like someone else; she would go off to sleep looking like someone else, or lie until the morning, with plans going round and round in her head, and get up, managing to be herself until breakfast was over. But all the time, she had a house to be in. She was Mrs Bailey; a recognized centre. Miriam sat alone, the now familiar little room added to the strange collection of her inexplicable life; its lamplit walls were dear to her, with the extraordinary same dearness of all walls seen in tranquillity. She seemed to be responding to their gaze. Had she answered Mrs Bailey's murmur about going to bed? It seemed so long ago. She sat until the lamp began to fail and Mrs Bailey appeared to be going to sleep. She crept out at last into the fresh still darkness of the sleeping house. On the first floor there was a glimmer of blue light. It was the street lamp shining in through Mr Shatov's wide-open empty room. When she reached her own room she found that it was one o'clock. *Already*, he had found his way to some horrible haunt. She wrapped her evening round her, parrying the thought of him. There should be no lesson to-morrow. She would be out, having left no message.

When she came in the next evening he was in the hall. He came forward with his bearded courteous emphatically sweeping foreign bow; a foreign professor, bowing to an audience he was about to address. 'Bitte, verzeihen Sie,' he began, his rich low tones a little breathless; the gong blared forth just behind him; he stood rooted, holding her with respectful melancholy gaze as his lips went on forming their German sentences. The clangour died down; people were coming downstairs, drawing Miriam's eyes as he moved from their pathway into the dining-room, still facing her with the end of his little speech lingering nervously on his features. He was in his frock-coat, and shone richly black and white under the direct lamplight; he was even more handsome than she had thought, solidly beautiful, glowing in shapely movement as he stood still and gestureless before her, set off by the shapelessly moving, dinner-drawn forms passing into the dining-room. She smiled in response to whatever he may have said and wondered, having apologized for yesterday, in what way he would announce to her the outside engagement for this evening for which he was so shiningly prepared. 'Zo,' he said gravely, 'if you are now free, I will almost immediately come up; we shall not wait till eight o'clock.' Miriam bowed in response to the sweeping obeisance with which he turned into the dining-room, and ran upstairs. He came up before the end of the first course, before she had had time to test, in the large overmantel, the shape of her hair that had seemed in the little mirror upstairs, accidentally good, quite like the hair of someone who mysteriously knew how to get good effects.

'I have been sleeping,' he said in wide cheerful tones as he crossed the room, 'all day until now. I am a little stupid; but I have very many things to say you. First I must say you,' he said, more gravely, and stood arrested with his coat tails in his hands, in front of the chair opposite to hers at a little table, 'that your Emerson is *most*-wonderful.'

Miriam could not believe she had heard the deep-toned emphatic words. She stared stupidly at his unconscious thoughtful brow; for a strange moment feeling her own thoughts and her own outlook behind it. She felt an instant's pang of disappointment; the fine brow had lost something, seemed familiar, almost homely. But an immense relief was surging through her. 'No—Ree—ally; most-wonderful,' he reiterated with almost reproachful emphasis, sitting down with his head eagerly forward between his shoulders, waiting for her response. 'Yes, *isn't* he?' she said encouragingly and waited in a dream while he sat back and drew little volumes from his pocket, his white eyelids downcast below his frowning brow. Would he qualify his praise? Had he read enough to come upon any of the chills and contradictions? However this might be, Emerson had made upon this scholarly foreigner, groping in him with his scanty outfit of language, an overwhelming impression. Her own lonely overwhelming impression was justified. The eyes came up again, gravely earnest. 'No,' he said, 'I find it most difficult to express the profound impression this reading have made on me.'

'He isn't a bit original,' said Miriam surprised by her unpremeditated conclusion, 'when you read him you feel as if you were following your own thoughts.'

'That is so; he is not himself philosophe; I would call him rather, poète; a most remarkable quality of English, *great* dignity and with at the same time a most perfect simplicity.'

'He understands everything; since I have had that book, I have not wanted to read anything else . . . except Maeterlinck,' she murmured in afterthought, 'and in a way he is the same.'

'I do not know this writer,' said Mr Shatov, 'and what you say is perhaps not quite good. But in a manner I can have some sympa-thaytic apprysiacion with this remark. I have read yesterday the whole day; on different omnibuses. Ah. It was for me *most*-wonderful.'

'Well, I always feel, all the time, all day, that if people would

III—*B

only read Emerson they would understand, and not be like they are, and that the only way to make them understand what one means would be reading pieces of Emerson.'

'That is true; why should you not do it?'

'Quotations are feeble; you always regret making them.'

'No; I do not agree,' said Mr Shatov devoutly smiling, 'you are wrong.'

'Oh, but think of the awful people who quote Shakespeare.'

'Ach-ma. People are, in general, silly. But I must tell you you should not cease to read until you shall have read at least some Russian writers. If you possess sensibility for language, you shall find that Russian is *most*-beautiful; it is perhaps the most beautiful European language; it is, indubitably, the most rich.'

'It can't be richer than English.'

'Certainly it is richer than English. I shall prove this to you, even with dictionary. You shall find that it occur, over and over, that where in English is one word, in Russian is six or seven different, all synonyms, but all with *most* delicate individual shades of nuance . . . the abstractive expression is there, as in all civilized European languages, but there is also in Russian the most immense *variety* of natural expressions, coming forth from the strong feeling of the Russian nature to all these surrounding influences; each word opens to a whole aperçu in this sort . . . and what is most significant is, the great richness, in Russia, of the people-language; there is no other people-language similar; there is in no one language so immense a variety of tender diminutives and intimate expressions of all natural things. None is so rich in sound, or so marvellously powerfully colourful. . . . *That* is Russian. Part of the reason is no doubt to find in the immense paysage; Russia is zo *vast*; it is inconceivable for any non-Russian. There is also the ethnological explanation, the immense vigour of the people.'

Miriam went forward in a dream. As Mr Shatov's voice went on, she forgot everything but the need to struggle to the uttermost against the quiet strange attack upon English; the double line of evidence seemed so convincing and was for the

present unanswerable from any part of her small store of knowledge; but there must be an answer; meantime the suggestion
that the immense range of English was partly due to its unrivalled collection of technical terms, derived from English
science, commerce, sports, 'all the practical life-manœuvres,'
promised vibrating reflection, later.

But somewhere outside her resentful indignation, she found
herself reaching forward unresentfully towards something very
far off and, as the voice went on, she felt the touch of a new
strange presence in her Europe. She listened, watching intently, far off, hearing now only a voice, moving on, without
connected meaning. . . . The strange thing that had touched
her was somewhere within the voice; the sound of Russia. So
much more strange, so much wider and deeper than the sound
of German or French or any of the many tongues she had heard
in this house, the inpouring impression was yet not alien. It
was not *foreign*. There was no barrier between the life in it
and the sense of life that came from within. It expressed that
sense; in the rich, deep various sound and colour of its inflections, in the strange abruptly controlled shapeliness of the
phrases of tone carrying the whole along, the voice *was* the very
quality he had described, here, alive: about her in the room.
It was, she now suddenly heard, the disarming, unforeign thing
in the voice of kind commercial little Mr Rodkin. Then there
was an answer. There was something in common between
English and this strange language that stood alone in Europe.
She came back and awoke to the moment, weary. Mr Shatov
had not noticed her absence. He was talking about Russia.
Unwillingly, she gave her flagging attention to the Russia
already in her mind; a strip of silent sunlit snow, just below
Finland, St Petersburg in the midst of it, rounded squat square
white architecture piled solidly beneath a brilliant sky, low
sledges smoothly gliding, drawn by three horses, bell-spanned,
running wildly abreast, along the silent streets or out into the
deeper silence of dark, snow-clad wolf-haunted forests that
stretched indefinitely down the map; and listened as he drew
swift pictures, now north, now south. Vast outlines emerged
faintly, and here and there a patch remained, vivid. She saw

the white nights of the northern winter, felt the breaking through of spring in a single day. Whilst she lingered at Easter festivals in churches, all rich deep colour blazing softly through clouds of incense, and imagined the mighty sound of Russian singing, she was carried away to villages scattered amongst great tracts of forest, unimaginable distances of forest, making the vast forests of Germany small and homely . . . each village a brilliant miniature of Russia, in every hut a holy image; brilliant colouring of stained carved wood, each peasant a striking picture, filling the eye in the clear light, many 'most-dignified'; their garments coloured with natural dyes, 'the most pure plant-stain colours,' deep and intense. She saw the colours, mat and sheenless, yet full of light, taking the light in and in, richly, and turned grievously to the poor cheap tones in all the western shops, clever shining chemical dyes, endless teasing variety, without depth or feeling, cheating the eye of life; and back again homesick to the rich tones of reality. . . .

She passed down the winding sweep of the Volga, a consumptive seeking health, and out into the southern plains where wild horses roamed at large, and stayed at a lodge facing towards miles and miles of shallow salt water, sea-gull haunted, and dotted with floating islands of reeds, so matted and interwoven that one could get out from the little shallow leaky fishing-boat and walk upon them; and over all a crystal air so life-giving that one recovered. She heard the peasants in the south singing in strong deep voices, dancing by torchlight a wild dance with a name that described the dance. . . .

Throughout the recital were vivid words, each a picture of the thing it expressed. She would never forget them. Russia was *recognizable*. So was every language. But no foreign sound had brought her such an effect of strength and musical beauty and expressiveness combined. That was it. It was the strange number of things that were together in Russian that was so wonderful. In the end, back again in England, sitting in the cold dilapidated room before the table of little books, weary, opposite Mr Shatov comfortably groaning and stretching, his eyes already brooding in pursuit of something that would presently turn into speech, she struggled feebly with a mournful uneasiness that had haunted the whole of the irrevocable expansion of her consciousness. A *German*, not a Russian ethnologist, and therefore without prejudice, had declared that the Russians were the strongest kinetic force in Europe. He proved himself disinterested by saying that the English came next. The English were 'simple and fundamentally sound.' Not intelligent; but healthy in will, which the Russians were not. Then why were the Russians more forceful? What was kinetic force? And . . . mystery . . . the Russians themselves knew what they were like. 'There is in Russia, except in the governing and bourgeois classes, almost no hypocrisy.' What was kinetic. . . . And religion was an 'actual force' in Russia! 'What is ki——'

'Ah, but you shall at least read some of our great Russian authors . . . at least Tourgainyeff and Tolstoi.'

'Of course I have heard of Tolstoi.'

'Ah, but you shall read. He has a most profound knowledge of human psychology; the most marvellous touches. In that he rises to universality. Tourgainyeff is more pure Russian, less to understand outside Russia; more academical; but he shall reveal you most admirably the Russian aristocrat. He is cynic-satirical.'

'Then he can't reveal *anything*,' said Miriam. Here it was again; Mr Shatov, too, took satire quite unquestioningly; thought it a sort of achievement, worthy of admiration. Perhaps if she could restrain her anger, she would hear at least in some wonderful explanatory continental phrase, what satire really was, and be able to settle with herself why she knew it was, in the long run, waste of time; *why* the word satirist suggested someone with handsome horns and an evil clever eye and thin cold fingers. Thin. Swift was probably fearfully thin. Mr Shatov was smiling incredulously. If he went on to explain, she would miss the more important worrying thing. Novels. It was extraordinary that he should. . . .

'I don't care for novels. . . . I can't see what they are about. They seem to be an endless fuss about nothing.'

'That may apply in certain cases. But it is a too extreme statement.'

'It is extreme. Why not? How can a statement be too extreme if it is true?'

'I cannot express an opinion on English novelistic writings. But of Tolstoi it is certainly not true. *No*; it is not in general true that in fictional representations there is no actuality. I have read with my first English teacher in Moscow a story of your Myne-Reat. There was in this story a Scotch captain who remained for me most typical British. He was *very* fine, this chap. This presentation made me the more want what I have want always since a boy: to come to England.' Was Mayne Reid a novelist? Those boys' stories were glorious. But they were about the sea; and the fifth form . . . 'a noble three-bladed knife, minus the blades' . . .

'There's a thing called *The Ebb-Tide*,' she began, wondering how she could convey her impression of the tropical shore; but Mr Shatov's attention, though polite, was wandering, 'I've read some of Gorki's short stories,' she finished briskly. They were not novels; they were alive in some way English books were not. Perhaps all Russian books were.

'Ah, *Gorrrki*. He is come out direct from the peasantry; very powerfully strange and rough presentations. He may be called the apostle of misère.'

. . . the bakery and the yard; the fighting eagles, the old man at the prow of the boat with his daughter-in-law. . . . All *teaching* something. How did people find it out?

'But really I must tell you of yesterday,' said Mr Shatov warmly. 'I have made a Schachpartei. That was for me *very good*. It include also a certain exploration of London. That is for me, I need not say, most-*fascinatink*.' Miriam listened eagerly. The time was getting on; they had done no work. She had not once corrected him, and he was plunging into his preliminary story as if their hour had not yet begun. She was to share.

'There was on one of these many omnibuses a gentleman who tell me where in London I shall obtain a genuine coffee. Probably you know it is at this Vienna Café, in Holeborne. You do not know this place? *Strange*. It is quite near to you all the time. Almost at your British Museum. Ah; this

gentleman has told me too a most funny story of a German who
go there proudly talking English. He was waiting; ach, they
are very slow in this place, and at last he shouts for every one
to hear, "Vaiter! Venn shall I become a cup of coffee?"'

Miriam laughed her delight apprehensively. 'Ah, I like
very much these stories,' he was saying, his eyes dreamily
absent, she feared, on a memory-vista of similar anecdotes.
But in a moment he was alive again in his adventure. It was
at London Bridge. I have come all the way, walkingly, to this
Café. It is a strange place. Really *glahnend*; Viennese; very
dirrty. But coffee most excellent; just as on the Continent.
You shall go there; you will see. Upstairs it is most dreadful.
More dirrty; and in an intense gloom of smoke, very many
men, ah, they are dreadful, I could not describe to you. Like
monkeys; but all in Schachparteis. That shall be very good for
me. I am most enthusiastic with this game since a boy.'

'Billiards?'

Why should he look so astonished and impatiently explain
so reproachfully and indulgently? She grasped the meaning
of the movements of his hands. He was a chess-player, 'a
game much older—uralt—and the most mental, the only true
abstractive game.' How differently an English chess-player
would have spoken. She regarded his eager contained liveliness. Russian chess players remained alive. Was chess
mental? Pure tactics. Should she declare that chess was a
dreadful boring indulgence, leading nowhere? Perhaps he
would be able to show her that this was not so. Why do the
Germans call two people playing chess a chess-party? 'I have
met there a man, a Polish doctor. We have made party and have
play until the Café close, when we go to his room and continue
there to play till the morning. Ah, it was most-beautiful.'

'Had you met him before?'

'Oh no. He is in London; stewdye-ink medicine.'

'St*uddy*ing,' said Miriam impatiently, lost in incredulous
contemplation. It could not be true that he had sat all night
playing chess with a stranger. If it were true, they must both
be quite insane. . . . The door was opening. Sissie's voice, and
Mr Shatov getting up with an eager polite smile. Footsteps

crossing the room behind her; Mr Shatov and a tall man
shaking hands on the hearthrug; two inextricable voices; Mr
Shatov's presently emerging towards her, deferentially, 'I
present you Dr Veslovski.' The Polish doctor, gracefully
bowing from a cold narrow height, Mr Shatov, short, dumpy,
deeply-radiant little friend, between them; making a little
speech, turning from one to the other. The Polish head was
reared again on its still cold grey height; undisturbed. . . .
Perfect. Miriam had never seen anything so perfectly beautiful. Every line of the head and face harmonious; the pointed
beard finishing the lines with an expressiveness that made it
also a feature, one with the rest. Even the curious long narrow
capless flatly-lying foreign boots, furrowed with mud-stiffened
cracks, and the narrowly cut, thin, shabby grey suit shared the
distinction of the motionless reined-in head. Polish beauty.
If that were Polish beauty, the Poles were the most beautiful
people in Europe. Polish; the word suggested the effect, its
smooth liquid sheen, sinuous and graceful without weakness.
The whole word was at home in the eyes; horribly beautiful,
abysses of fathomless foreign . . . any kind of known happenings were unthinkable behind those eyes . . . yet he was here;
come to play chess with Mr Shatov, who had not expected him
until Sunday, but would go now immediately, with her permission, to fetch his set from upstairs. She lingered as he
hurried away, glancing at the little books on the table. The
Emerson was not among them. The invisible motionless
figure on the hearthrug had brought her a message she had
forgotten in her annoyance at his intrusion. Going from the
room towards his dim reflection in the mirror near the door,
she approached the waiting thought—Mr Shatov's voice broke
in, talking eagerly to Mrs Bailey on the floor below. From the
landing she heard him beg that it might be some *large* vessel,
quite voll tea; some drapery to enfold it, and that the gazz
might be left alight. They were going to play chess, through
the night, in that cold room . . . but the thought was gladly
there. The Polish. doctor's presence had confirmed Mr
Shatov's story. It had not been a young man's tale to cover
an escapade.

CHAPTER II

SHE hurried through her Saturday morning's work, trying to keep warm. Perhaps it was nervousness and excitement about the afternoon's appointment that made her seem so cold. At the end of her hour's finicking work in Mr Hancock's empty fireless room, amongst cold instruments and chilly bottles of chemicals, she was cold through. There was no one in the house but Mr Leyton and the cousin; nothing to support her against the coming ordeal. Mr Leyton had had an empty morning and spent it busily scrubbing and polishing instruments in his warm little room; retiring towards lunch time to the den fire with a newspaper. Shivering over her ledgers in the cold window space, she bitterly resented her inability to go out and get warm in an A.B.C. before meeting Mr Shatov in the open. Impossible. It could not be afforded; though this morning all the absolutely essential work could be finished by one o'clock. It was altogether horrible. She was not sure that she was even supposed to stay for lunch on Saturday. The day ended at one o'clock; unless she were kept by some urgent business, there was no excuse. To-day she must have finished everything before lunch, to keep her appointment. It could not be helped; and at least there was no embarrassment in the presence of Mr Leyton and the boy. She would even lock up and put on her outdoor things and go down in them. It would not occur to them that she need not have stayed to lunch. Her spirits rose as she moved about putting things in the safe. She dressed in Mr Leyton's warm room, washing her hands in very hot water, thawing, getting warm. The toque looked nice in his large mirror, quite stylish, not so home-made. Worldly people always had lunch in their outdoor things, even when they were staying in a house. Sarah said people ought always to wear hats, especially with evening

49

dress. Picture hats, with evening dress, made pictures. It was true, they would, when you thought of it. But Sarah had found it out for herself; without opportunities; it came, out of her mind through her artistic eyes. . . . Miriam recalled smart middle-aged women at the Corries', appearing at lunch in extraordinary large hats, when they had not been out. That was the reason. It helped them to carry things off; made them talk well and quickly, with the suggestion that they had just rushed in from somewhere or were just going to rush off. . . . She surveyed herself once more. It was true; lunch, even with Mr Leyton and the cousin, would be easier with the toque and her black coat open showing the white neckerchief. It gave an impression of hurry and gaiety. She was quite ready, and looked about for entertainment for the remaining moments. Actually; a book lying open on Mr Leyton's table, a military drill-book of course. No. *What* was this? *Lovely Woman*, by T. W. H. Crosland. Why so many similar English initials? A superfluity of mannishness. An attack of course; she scanned pages and headings; chapter upon chapter of peevish facetiousness; the whole book written deliberately against women. Her heart beat angrily. What was Mr Leyton doing with such a book? Where had it come from? She read swiftly, grasping the argument. The usual sort of thing; worse, because it was colloquial, rushing along in modern everyday language and in some curious way not badly written.

Because some women had corns, feminine beauty was a myth; because the world could do without Mrs Hemans's poetry, women should confine their attention to puddings and babies. The infernal complacent cheek of it. This was the kind of thing middle-class men read. Unable to criticize it, they thought it witty and unanswerable. That was the worst of it. Books of this sort were read without any one there to point things out. It ought to be illegal to publish a book by a man without first giving it to a woman to annotate. But what was the answer to men who called women inferior because they had not invented or achieved in science or art? On whose authority had men decided that science and art were greater than anything else? The world could not go on until this question had been answered. Until then, until it had been clearly explained that men were always and always partly wrong in all their ideas, life would be full of poison and secret bitterness. Men fight about their philosophies and religions, there is no certainty in them; but their contempt for women is flawless and unanimous. Even Emerson . . . positive and negative, north and south, male and female . . . why *negative*? Maeterlinck gets nearest in knowing that women can live, hardly at all, with men, and wait, have always been waiting, for men to come to life. How can men come to life; always fussing? How could the man who wrote this book? Even if it were publicly burned and he were made to apologize; he would still go about asquint . . . lunch was going to be late, just to-day, of course.

'I *say*.'

'*What* do you say?' responded Miriam without looking up from her soup. Mr Leyton had a topic; she could keep it going with half her attention and go restfully on, fortifying herself for the afternoon. She would attack him about the book one day next week.

'I *say*. What say you, George?'

'Me? All right. I say, I say, I say, anything you like, m'lord.'

Miriam looked up. Mr Leyton was gazing and grinning.

'What's the matter?' she snapped. His eyes were on her toque.

'*Where* did you get that hat? Where *did* you get that tile?' sang the cousin absently, busy with his lunch.

'I made it, if you *must* know,' said Miriam. The cousin looked across; large expressionless opinionless eyes.

'Going out in it?' What *was* the matter; Mr Leyton had never noticed anything of hers before; either it was too awful, or really rather effective and he unconsciously resented the fact of her going about in an effect.

'Why not?'

'Well; looks rather like a musical comedy.'

'Cheek,' observed the cousin; 'I do call that cool cheek; you're balmy, Leyton.' Mr Leyton looked no more; that was his genuine brotherly opinion; he thought the toque showy. It was the two wings, meeting in the middle of the front; he meant pantomime; he did not know the wings were cheap; he was shocked by the effectiveness; it *was* effective; cheap and hateful; but it suited her; pantomime effects were becoming. Where was the objection?

'That's all right. I'm glad. I like musical comedies.'

'Oh; if you're satisfied. If you don't mind looking risky.'

'I say, look here old man, steady on,' blushed the cousin.

'Well. What do you think yourself? Come on.'

'I think it's jolly pretty.'

'*I* think it's jolly *fast*.'

Miriam was quite satisfied. The cousin's opinion went for nothing; a boy *would* like pantomime effects. But the hat was neither ugly nor dowdy. She would be able to tear down Oxford Street, no matter how ugly the cold made her feel, looking *fast*. It would help her to carry off meeting Mr Shatov. *He* would not notice hats. But the extraordinary, rather touching thing was that Mr Leyton should trouble at all. As if she belonged to his world, and he were in some way responsible.

'All right, Mr Leyton; it's fast; whatever that may mean.'

'Old Leyton thinks hats ought to be slow.'

'Look here, young fellow-me-lad, you teach your——'

'Great-grandfather not to be rude.'

'I fail to see the rudeness; I've merely expressed an opinion, and I believe Miss Henderson agrees with it.'

'Oh, absolutely; ab-so*lute*-ly,' chanted Miriam scornfully. 'Pray don't worry about the pace of my millinery, Mr Leyton.' That was quite good, like a society novel.

'Well, as I say, if you're *satisfied*.'

'Ah. That's another matter. The next time I want a hat I'll go to Bond Street. So easy and simple.'

'Seen the paper to-day, George?'

'Paper? Noospaper? No time.'

'Seen the *B. M. J.*?'

'No, sir.'

'And you an aspiring medico.'

'Should be an expiring medico,' yodelled George, 'if I read all those effusions.'

'Well. More disclosures from Schenck.'

'Who's he, when he's at home?'

'You know. Schenck, man; *Schenk. You* know.'

'Oh, sorry; all right. What's he babbling about now?'

'Same thing; only more of it,' giggled Mr Leyton.

'If it's half past I must go,' announced Miriam peremptorily. Two watches came out.

'Then I advise you to hook it pretty sharp; it's twenty to. You'd better *read* that article, my son.' Miriam folded her serviette.

'Righto. Don't worry.'

'*Why* all this mystery? Good morning,' said Miriam departing.

'Good morning,' said the two voices. Mr Leyton held the door open and raised his voice to follow her up the stairs. 'We're discussing matters somewhat beyond your ken.'

She could not stay. She could not have tackled him if she had stayed. Anger was perhaps as funny as embarrassment. He would have been shocked at the idea of her quietly considering the results of Schenck's theory, if it proved to be true; beyond her ken, indeed. It was hateful to have to leave that; he *ought* to be robbed of the one thing that he imagined gave him an advantage in the presence of women. The women in his world *would* be embarrassed by the discussion of anything to do with the reproduction of the race. *Why?* Why were the women embarrassed and the men always suggestive and facetious? If only the men could realize what they admitted by their tone; what attitude towards life.

It was a bitter east wind; the worst kind of day there was. All along Oxford Street were women in furs, serene, with smooth warm faces untroubled by the bleak black wind, perhaps even enjoying the cold. Miriam struggled along, towards the cruel east, shivering, her face shrivelled and frozen and burning, her brain congealed. If she were free, she could at least have a cup of coffee and get warm and go into the museum and be warm all the afternoon. To meet a stranger and have to be active and sociable when she was at her worst. He would be wrapped in the advantage of a fur-lined coat, or at least astrakhan, and be able to think and speak. He would wonder what was the matter; even his careless foreign friendliness would not survive her frightful appearance. Yet when a clock told her the appointed time was past, the torment of the wind grew sharper in the thought that she might miss him. There was the Holborn Library, as he had described. There was no one there, the pavement was empty; he had given her up and gone; had perhaps never come. She was relieved. She had done her best. Fate had saved her; her afternoon was her own. But she must show herself, perhaps he might be sheltering just inside the door. The doorway was empty. There was a man leaning against the lamp-post. She scanned him unwillingly, lest he should turn into Mr Shatov; but he produced only the details of the impression she had taken before she glanced, a shabby, sinister-looking Tottenham Court Road foreign loafer, in yellow boots, an overcoat of an evil shade of brown, and a waiter's black-banded grey felt hat; but she had paused and glanced and of course his eye was immediately upon her, and his lounging figure upright as she swept across the pavement to gain the road and flee the displeasing contact. He almost ran into her; trotting . . . 'ah, I am glad' . . . it *was* Mr Shatov.

Looking like that, she was now to take him in amongst the British Museum officials, and the readers she knew by sight and who knew her; introduce him to the librarian. She scanned him as he eagerly talked, looking in vain for the presence she had sat with in the drawing-room. The eyes had come back; but that was all, and she could not forget how brooding, almost evil, they had looked just now. They gleamed again with intelligence; but their brilliant beauty shone from a face that looked almost dingy in the hard light; and yellowish under the frightful hat peaked down, cutting off his forehead. He was gloveless and in his hands, grimed with walking in the winter streets, he held a paper bag of grapes which he ate as he talked, expelling the skins and flinging them from him as he walked. . . . He looked just simply disreputable. Even his voice had gone; raised against the traffic, it was narrow and squeaky; a disreputable foreigner, plunging carelessly along, piercing her ear with mean broken English. She shouted vague replies in French; in yelled French his voice was even more squeaky; but the foreign tongue gave a refuge and a shape to their grouping; she became a sort of guide; any one could be that to any sort of foreigner.

In the cloak-room were the usual ladies comfortably eating lunch from sandwich tins and talking, talking, talking, to the staff moving endlessly to and fro amongst the cages of hanging garments; answering unconsciously. The mysterious everlasting work of the lunching ladies, giving them the privilege of being all day at the museum, always in the same seats, accepted and approved, seemed to make no mark upon them; they bore themselves just as they would have done anywhere, the same mysteriously unfailing flow of talk, the mysterious basis of agreement with other women, the same enthusiastic discussions of the weather, the cases in the newspapers, their way of doing this and that, their opinions of places and people. They seemed to have no sense of the place they were in, and yet were so extraordinarily at home there, and most wonderful of all, serene, with untroubled eyes and hands, in the thin stuffy heat of the cloak-room.

These thoughts came every time; the sense of Mr Shatov, busy, she hoped, washing his face and hands down beyond the stairs leading to the unknown privacies at the other end of the corridor, could not banish them; the bearing of these ladies was the most mysterious thing in the museum. In this room she was always on her guard. It was jolly, after roaming slowly across the courtyard towards the unfailing unchanging beauty of the great grey pillars, pigeon-garlanded, to wander through the out-branching hall to where the lame commissionaire held open the magic door, and fly along the passage and break in here, permitted, cold and grimy and ruffled from the street, and emerge washed and hatless and rested, to saunter down the corridor and see ahead, before becoming one of them, the dim various forms sitting in little circles of soft yellow light under the high mysterious dome. But in one

unguarded moment in this room, all these women would turn
into acquaintances, and the spell of the museum, springing
forth perhaps for a while, intensified, would disappear for ever.
They would turn it into themselves, varying and always in the
end, in silence, the same. In solitude it remained unvarying
yet never twice alike, casting its large increasing charm upon
them as they moved distant and unknown.

In the lower cloak-room, there was always escape; no sofas,
no grouped forms. To-day it stood bare, its long row of
basins unoccupied. She turned taps joyously; icy cold and
steaming hot water rushing to cleanse her basin from its revealing relics. They were all the same, and all the soaps, save
one she secured from a distant corner, sloppy. Surveying,
she felt with irritated repugnance, the quality, slap-dash and
unaware, of the interchange accompanying and matching the
ablutions. A woman came out of a lavatory and stood at her
side, also swiftly restoring a basin. It was *she*. . . . Miriam
envied the basin. . . . Freely watching the peaceful face in the
mirror, she washed with an intense sense of sheltering companionship. Far in behind the peaceful face serene thoughts
moved, not to and fro, but outward and forward from some
sure centre. Perfectly screened, unknowing and unknown,
she went about within the charmed world of her inheritance.
It was difficult to imagine what work she might be doing, always
here, and always moving about as if unseeing and unseen.
Round about her serenity any kind of life could group, leaving
it, as the foggy grime and the dusty swelter of London left her,
unsullied and untouched. But for the present she was here,
as if she moved, emerging from a spacious many-windowed
sunlight-flooded house whose happy days were in her quiet
hands, in clear light about the spaces of a wide garden. Yet
she was aware of the world about her. It was not a matter of
life and death to her that she should be free to wander here in
solitude. For those women she would have a quiet unarmed
confronting manner, at their service, but holding them off without discourtesy, passing on with cup unspilled. Nothing but
music reached her ears, everything she saw melted into a background of garden sunlight.

She was out of sight, drying her hands, lighting up the corner of the room where the towels hung. . . . If Mr Shatov were on *her* hands, she would not be regretting that the afternoon could hold no solitary wanderings. She made no calculations; for she could not be robbed. That was strength. She was gone. Miriam finished her operations as though she remained, drying her hands unhurriedly, standing where she had stood, trying to survey the unforetellable afternoon with something of her sustained tranquillity.

He would probably be plunging up and down the corridor with a growing impatience. . . . There he was, unconcernedly waiting; his singing determined child's head reared hatless above the dreadful overcoat, the clear light of the corridor upon its modest thought-moulded dignity . . . distinguished . . . that was what he was. She felt unworthy, helplessly inadequate, coming up the corridor to claim him. She was amongst the people passing about him before he saw her; and she caught again the look of profound reproachful brooding melancholy seated in his eyes, so strangely contradicting his whole happy look of a child standing at a party, gazing, everything pouring into its wide eyes; dancing and singing within itself, unconscious of its motionless body.

'Here we are,' she said avertedly as he came eagerly forward.

'Let us quickly to this official,' he urged, in his indoor voice.

'All right; this way.' He hurried along at her side, beard forward, his yellow boots plunging in long rapid strides beneath his voluminously floating overcoat.

She resented the librarian's official manner; the appearance of the visitor, the little card he promptly produced, should have been enough. Stud. Schtu*dent*, how much more expressive than *stew*dent . . . to be able to go about the world for years, so-and-so, stud . . . all doors open and committed to nothing. She asserted herself by making suggestions in French. Mr Shatov responded politely, also in French, and she felt the absurdity of her eager interference, holding him a prisoner, hiding his studious command of English, in order to flourish forth her knowledge. 'We are not afraid even of Russian, if Mr Shatov prefers to use his own tongue,' said the librarian.

Miriam flashed a suspicious glance. He was smiling a self-conscious superior English smile. It soured into embarrassment under her eye.

'It is no matter,' said Mr Shatov gently, 'you shall immediately say me the requisite formules which I shall at once write.' He stood beautiful, the gentle unconsciously reproachful prey of English people unable to resist their desire to be effective. They stood conquered, competing in silent appreciation, as he bent, writing his way into their forgotten library.

'Now I am pairfectly happy,' he said, as he passed through the swing doors of the reading-room. His head was up radiantly singing, he was rushing trustfully forward, looking at nothing, carrying her on, close at his side, till they reached the barrier of the outmost catalogue desk. He pulled up facing her, with wide wild eyes looking at nothing. 'We shall at once take Anaka*ray*ninna in *English*,' he shouted in an enthusiastic whisper.

'We must choose seats before we get books,' murmured Miriam. There was plenty to do and explain; the revelation of her meagre attack on the riches of the library need not yet come. Were they to read together? Had he reached his goal 'midst all those literatures,' to spend his time in showing her Tolstoi? He followed her absently about as she filled in the time while they waited for their book, by showing all she knew of the routine of the library. 'There shall of course,' he said in a gruff explanatory tone, arresting her near the entrance to the central enclosure, 'be a quite exhaustive system of catalogue, but I find there is too much *formalities*; with all these little baskets.' 'Ssh,' begged Miriam, leading him away. She drifted to the bookshelves, showing him the one shelf she knew on the south side; there was a reader on a ladder at the very shelf. 'Carlyle's *French Revolution* is up there,' she said confidently. 'Na, na,' he growled reproachfully, 'this is a most purely unreliable fictional history, a tour de force from special individual prejudices. You should take rather Thiers.' She piloted him across to her shelf on the north side to point out the *Revue des Deux Mondes* and the *North American Review*. He paused, searching along the shelves. '*Ah. Here* is books.'

He drew out and flung open a heavy, beautifully printed volume with wide margins on the pages; she would show him the clever little folding arrangements to hold heavy volumes; 'You do not know these?' he demanded of her silence; 'ah that is a great pity; it is the complete discours de l'Académie francaise; you shall immediately read them; ah, they are the most *perfect* modèles.' She glanced at the open page beginning 'Messieurs! Le sentiment de fierté avec laquelle je vous'; it was a voice; exactly like the voice of Mr Shatov. He stood with the heavy open volume, insisting in his dreadfully audible whisper on wonderful French names prefixed to the titles of addresses, fascinating subjects, one of them Mr *Gladstone*! He looked French as he spoke; a brilliantly polished Frenchman. Why had he not gone to France? He was German too, with a German education and yet with some impatiently unexplained understanding and contempt—for Germany. Why was he drawn towards England? That was the mysterious thing. What was the secret of the reverence in this man for England and the English? He was not an anarchist. There he stood, Russian, come from all that far-away beauty, with German and French culture in his mind, longingly to England, coming to Tansley Street; unconsciously bringing her her share in his longed-for arrival and its fulfilments. She watched as he talked, marvelling at the undeserved wealth offered to her in the little figure discoursing so eagerly over the cumbrous volume. And at this moment the strange Russian book was probably waiting for them.

It was a big thick book. Miriam sat down before it. The lights had come on. The book lay in a pool of sharp yellow light; Tolstoi, surrounded by a waiting gloom; the secret of Tolstoi standing at her side, rapidly taking off his overcoat. He drew up the chair from the next place and sat close, flattening out the book at the first chapter and beginning to read at once, bent low over the book. She bent too, stretching her hands out beyond her knees to make herself narrow, and fastening on the title. Her anticipations fell dead. It was the name of a woman. . . . Anna; of all names. Karenine. The story of a woman told by a man with a man's ideas about people.

But Anna Karenine was not what Tolstoi had written. Behind the ugly feebleness of the substituted word was something quite different, strong and beautiful; a whole legend in itself. Why had the translator altered the surname? Anna Kar*a*yninna was a line of Russian poetry. His word was nothing, neither English nor French, and sounded like a face-cream. She scanned sceptically up and down the pages of English words, chilled by the fear of detecting the trail of the translator.

Mr Shatov read steadily, breathing his enthusiasm in gusts, pausing as each fresh name appeared, to pronounce it in Russian and to explain the three names belonging to each character. They were all expressive; easy to remember because of their expressiveness. The threefold name, giving each character three faces, each turned towards a different part of his world, was fascinating. . . . Conversation began almost at once and kept breaking out; strange abrupt conversation different from any she had read elsewhere. . . . What was it? She wanted to hold the pages and find out; but Mr Shatov read on and on, steadily turning the leaves. She skipped, fastening upon the patches of dialogue on her side of the open page, reading them backwards and forwards, glancing at the solid intervening portions to snatch an idea of the background. What was the mysterious difference? Why did she feel she could hear the tone of the voices and the pauses between the talk; the curious feeling of things moving and changing in the air that is always there in all conversations? Her excitement grew, drawing her upright to stare her question into the gloom beyond the lamp.

'Well?' demanded Mr Shatov.

'It 's fascinating.'

'What have I told you? That is Tols*toi*,' he said proudly; 'but this is a most vile translation. All these *nu* and *da*. Why not simply *well* and *yes*? and boszhe moi is, quite simply, my God. But this preliminary part is not so interesting as later. There is in this book the self-history of Tolstoi. He is Layvin, and Kitty is the Countess Tolstoi. That is all most wonderful. When we see her in the early morning; and the picture of this wedding. There is only Tolstoi for those marvellous touches. I shall show you.'

'Why does he call it *Anna Karayninna*?' asked Miriam anxiously.

'Certainly. It is a most masterly study of a certain type of woman.'

The fascination of the book still flickered brightly; but far away, retreated into the lonely incommunicable distance of her mind. It seemed always to be useless and dangerous to talk about books. They were always about something else. . . . If she had not asked, she would have read the book. without finding out it was a masterly study of Anna. Why must a book be a masterly study of some single thing? Everybody wisely raving about it. . . . But if one never found out what a book was a masterly study of, it meant being ignorant of things every one knew and agreed about; a kind of hopeless personal ignorance and unintelligence; reading whole books through and through, and only finding out what they were about by accident, when people happened to talk about them, and even then, reading them again, and finding principally quite other things, which stayed, after one had forgotten what people had explained.

'I see,' she said intelligently. The readers on either side were glancing angrily. Miriam guiltily recalled her own anger with people who sat together murmuring and hissing. But it felt so different when you were one of the people. The next time she felt angry in this way, she would realize how interested the talkers were, and try to forget them. Still it was wrong. 'We must not talk,' she breathed. He glanced about and returned to his shuffling of pages.

'*Heere* it is,' he exclaimed in a guttural whisper far more distinct than his mutterings; 'I shall show you this wonderful passage.'

'Ssh, yes,' murmured Miriam firmly, peering at the indicated phrase. The large warm gloom of the library, with its green-capped pools of happy light, was stricken into desolation as she read. She swung back to her world of English books and glanced for comfort at the forms of Englishmen seated in various attitudes of reading about the far edges of her circle of vision. But the passage was inexorably there; poison dropping from the book into the world; foreign poison, but translated

and therefore read by at least some Englishmen. The sense
of being in arms against an onslaught already achieved, filled
her with despair. The enemy was far away, inaccessibly gone
forward spreading more poison. She turned furiously on
Mr Shatov. She could not disprove the lie; but at least he
should not sit there near her, holding it unconcerned.

'I can't see anything wonderful. It isn't true,' she said.

'Ah, that is very English,' beamed Mr Shatov.

'It is. *Any* English person would know that it is not true.'
Mr Shatov gurgled his laughter. 'Ah, that is very naïve.'

'It may be. That doesn't make any difference.'

'It makes the difference that you are inexperienced,' he
growled gently. That was true. She had no experience.
She only *knew* it was not true. Perhaps it was true. Then
life grew bleak again. . . . It was not true. But it was true
for men. Skimmed off the surface, which was all they could
see, and set up neatly in forcible quotable words. The rest
could not be shown in these clever, neat phrases.

'But I find the air here is most-evil. Let us rather go have
tea.'

Astonishment melted into her pride in leading him down
through the great hall and along the beloved corridor of her
solitary pacings, out into the gigantic granite smile of the Egyp-
tian gallery, to the always sudden door of the refreshment room.

'If I got locked into the museum at night I should stay in
this gallery,' she said unable to bear companionship in her
sanctuary without extorting some recognition of its never-failing
quality.

'It is certainly impressive, in a crude way,' admitted Mr
Shatov.

'They are so absolutely peaceful,' said Miriam, struggling
on behalf of her friends with her fury at this extraordinary
judgment. It had not before occurred to her that they were
peaceful, and that was not enough. She gazed down the vista
to discover the nature of the spell they cast. 'You can see
them in clear light in the desert,' she exclaimed in a moment.
The charm grew as she spoke. She looked forward to being
alone with them again in the light of this discovery. The chill

of Mr Shatov's indifferent response to her explanation was buried in her private acknowledgment that it was he who had forced her to discover something of the reason of her enchantment. He forced her to think. She reflected that solitude was too easy. It was necessary, for certainties. Nothing could be known except in solitude. But the struggle to communicate certainties gave them new life; even if the explanation were only a small piece of the truth. . . . 'Excuse me I leave you a moment,' he said, turning off through the maze of little figures near the door. The extraordinary new thing was that she *could* think, untroubled, in his company. She gratefully blessed his disappearing form.

'I 'm going to have toast and jam,' she announced expansively when the waitress appeared.

'Bring me just a large pot of tea and some kind of sweetmeat,' said Mr Shatov reproachfully.

'Pastries,' murmured Miriam.

'What is *pastries* ?' he asked mournfully.

'Pâtisseries,' beamed Miriam.

'Ah no,' he explained patiently, 'it is not that at all; I will have simply some small things in sugar.'

'No pastries; cake,' said the waitress, watching herself in the mirror.

'Ach bring me just *tea*,' bellowed Mr Shatov.

Several people looked round, but he did not appear to notice them and sat hunched, his overcoat coming up behind beyond his collar, his arms thrust out over the table, ending in grubby clasped hands. In a moment he was talking. Miriam sat taking in the change in the feeling of the familiar place under the influence of his unconcerned presence. There were the usual strangers strayed in from the galleries, little parties, sitting exposed at the central tables near the door; not quite at home, their eyes still filled with the puzzled preoccupation with which they had wandered and gazed, the relief of their customary conversation held back until they should have paid, out of their weary bewilderment, some tribute of suitable comment; looking about the room, watching in separate uneasiness for material to carry them past the insoluble problem. They were unchanged. But the readers stood out anew; the world they had made for her was broken up. Those who came in twos and sat at the more sequestered tables, maddening her with endless conversations at cross purposes from unconsidered assumptions, were defeated. Their voices were covered by Mr Shatov's fluent monologue and, though her own voice, sounding startlingly in the room, seemed at once only an exclamatory unpractised reproduction of these accustomed voices, changing already their aspect and making her judgment of them rock insecurely in her mind, it was threaded into his unconcerned reality and would presently be real.

But the solitary readers, sitting in corners over books, or perched, thoughtfully munching and sipping, with their backs to the room, on the high stools at the refreshment counter, and presently getting down to escape untouched and free, through the swing door, their unlifted eyes recovering already, through its long glass panels, the living dream of the hugely moving galleries, reproached her for her lost state.

Mr Shatov's dreaming face woke to prevent her adding milk to his tea, and settled again, dwelling with his far-off theme. She began listening in detail, to screen her base interest in her extravagant fare. 'It is a remarkable fact,' he was saying, and she looked up astonished at the sudden indistinctness of his voice. His eyes met hers severely, above the rim of his cup, 'but of almost universal application,' he proceeded thickly, and paused to produce between his lips a saturated lump of sugar. She stared, horrified. Very gravely, unattained by her disgust, he drew in his tea in neat noiseless sips till the sugar disappeared . . . when he deftly extracted another lump from the basin and went on with his story.

The series of lumps, passing one by one without accident through their shocking task, softened in some remarkable way the history of Tourgainyeff and Madame Viardot. The protest that struggled in her to rise and express itself was held in check by his peculiar serenity. The frequent filling of his cup and the selection of his long series of lumps brought no break in his concentration. . . . Above the propped elbows and the cup held always at the level of his lips, his talking face was turned to hers. Expressions moved untroubled through his eyes.

When they left the tea-room, he plunged rapidly along as if unaware of his surroundings. The whole museum was there, unexplored, and this was his first visit. He assented indifferently to her suggestion that they should just look at the Elgin Marbles, and stood unmoved before the groups, presently saying with some impatience that here, too, the air was oppressive and he would like to go out into the freshness.

Out in the street he walked quickly along brumming to himself. She felt they had been long acquainted; the afternoon had abolished embarrassments, but he was a stranger. She had nothing to say to him; perhaps there would be no more communications. She looked forward with uneasiness to the evening's lesson. They were both tired; it would be an irretrievable failure to try to extend their afternoon's achievement; and she would have to pass the intervening time alone with her growing incapability, while he recovered his tone at the dinner-table. The thought of him there, socially alive while she froze in her room, was intolerable. She, too, would go in to dinner . . . their present association was too painful to part upon. She bent their steps cheerfully in the direction of home. 'Excuse me,' he said suddenly, 'I will take here fruits,' and he disappeared into a greengrocer's shop, emerging presently munching from an open bag of grapes.

Supposing books had no names . . . Villette had meant nothing for years; a magic name until somebody said it was Brussels. . . . Lucy Snowe was impressed by St Paul's dome in the morning because it was St Paul's. That spoilt the part about the journey; waking you up with a start like the end of a dream. St Paul's sticking out through the text; someone suddenly introduced to you at a gathering, standing in front of you, blocking out the general sense of things; until you began to dance, when it came back until you stopped, when the person became a person again, with a name, and special things had to be said. St Paul's could not be got into the general sense of the journey; it was a quotation from another world; a smaller world than Lucy Snowe and her journey.

Yet it *would* be wonderful to wake up at a little inn in the city and suddenly see St Paul's for the first time. Perhaps it was one of those journey moments of suddenly seeing something celebrated, and missing the impression through fear of not being impressed enough; and trying to impress your impression by telling of the thing by name. Everybody has that difficulty. The vague shimmer of gas-lit people round the table all felt things without being able to express them. . . . She glowed towards the assembled group; towards every one in the world. For a moment she looked about in detail, wanting to communicate her thought and share a moment of general agreement. Everybody was talking, looking spruce and neat and finished, in the transforming gaslight. Each one something that would never be expressed, all thinking they were expressing things and not knowing the lonely look visible behind the eyes they turned upon the world, of their actual selves as they were when they were alone. But they were all saying things they wanted to say. They *did* express themselves, in relation to each other; they grew in knowledge of each other, in approval or disapproval, tested each other and knew, behind their strange immovable positive conversations about things that were all matters of opinion perpetually shifting, in a marvellous way each others' characters. They also knew, after the first pleasant moment of meeting eyes and sounding voices, when one tried to talk in their way, that one was playing them false. The glow could live for a while when one had not met them for some time; but before the end of the meeting one was again condemned, living in heavy silence, whilst one's mind whirled with the sense of their clear visions and the tantalizing inclination to take, for life, the mould of one or other point of view.

How *obliviously* they all talked on. She thanked them. With their talk flowing across the table, giving the central golden glow of light a feeling of permanence, her failures in life, strident about the room, were visible and audible only to herself. If she could remain silent, they would die down, and the stream of her unworthy life would merge, before he appeared, into a semblance of oneness with these other lives. She caught the dark Russian eyes of Mr Rodkin sitting opposite. He smiled through his glasses, his dry, sweet, large-eyed smile, his head turned listening to his neighbour. She beamed her response, relieved, as if they had had a long satisfactory conversation. He would have understood . . . in spite of his commercial city life. He accepted everybody. He was the central kindliness of the room. No wonder Mrs Bailey was so fond of him and leant upon his presence, in spite of his yawning hatred of Sundays. He was illuminated; she had his secret at last given her by Mr Shatov. *Russian* kindliness. Russians understand silence and are not afraid of it? Kindly silence comes out of their speech, and lies behind it, leaving things the same whatever has been said? This would be truer of him than of Mr Shatov. . . . Moy wort! Shatov at the station with his father! You never saw such a thing. Talking to the old boy as if he was a porter; snapping his head off whenever he spoke. . . . She pulled up sharply. If she thought of him, the fact that she was only passing the time would become visible. What was that just now, opening; about silence?

There is no need to go out into the world. Everything is there without anything; the world is added. And always, whatever happens, there is everything to return to. The pattern round her plate was life, alive, everything . . . what was that idea I used to have? Enough for one person in the world would be enough for everybody . . . how did it go? It was so clear, while the voice corneted out spoiling the sunshine . . . 'Oh, yes, we were *very* jolly; very jolly party, talking all the time. Miss Hood's song sounding out at intervals, *halcyon* weather.' . . . 'Do you ever feel how much there is everywhere?' 'Nachah's abundance?' 'No. I don't mean that. I mean that nearly everything is wasted. Not things, like soap; but the meanings of things. If there is enough for one person there is enough for everybody.' 'You mean that one happy man makes the whole universe glad?' 'He does.

But I don't mean that. I mean—everything is wasted all the time, while people are looking about and arranging for more things.' 'You would like to simplify life? You feel man needs but little here below?' 'He doesn't need *anything*. People go on from everything as if it were nothing and never seem to know there is anything.' 'But isn't it just the stimulus of his needs that keeps him going?' 'Why need he keep going? that is just my point.' 'Je n'en vois pas la nécessité, you would say, like Voltaire?' 'The necessity of living? Then why didn't he hang himself.' 'I suppose because he taught in song what he learned in sorrow.' . . . How many people knew that Maeterlinck had explained in words what life was like inside? Seek ye first the Kingdom . . . the test is if people want you at their death-beds. None of these people would want me at their death-beds. Yet they all ask deliberate questions, shattering the universe. Maeterlinck would call them innocent questions about the weather and the crops, behind which they gently greet each other. . . . Women always know their questions are insincere, a treachery towards their silent knowledge.

He must read the chapter on silence and then the piece about the old man by his lamp. That would make everything clear. Where was he all this time? Dinner was nearly over. Perhaps he was going out. She contemplated her blank evening. His voice sounded in the hall. How inconvenient for people with very long eyelashes to have to wear glasses, she thought, engrossing herself in a sudden vision of her neighbour's profile. He was coming through the hall from seeing somebody out of the front door. If she could be talking to someone she would feel less huge. She tried to catch Mr Rodkin's eye to ask him if he had read Tolstoi. Mr Shatov had come in, bowing his deep-voiced greeting, and begun talking to Mr Rodkin before he was in his chair, as if they were in the middle of a conversation. Mr Rodkin answered at once without looking at him, and they went on in abrupt sentences one against the other, the sentences growing longer as they talked.

Sissie did not hear the remark about the weather because she, too, was attending to the rapid Russian sentences. She was engrossed in them, her pale blue eyes speculative and serene. Miriam watched in swift glances. The brilliant colour that Mr Shatov had seemed to distribute when he sat down, had shrunk to himself. He sat there warm and rich, with easy movements and easily moving thoughts, his mind far away, his features animated under his raised carelessly singing eyebrows, by his irascible comments on Mr Rodkin's rapped-out statements. The room grew cold, every object stiff with lifeless memory, as they sat talking Mr Rodkin's business. Every one sitting round the table was clean-cut, eaten into by the raw edge of the winter night, gathered for a moment in the passing gas-lit warmth, to separate presently and face an everlastingly renewed nothingness. . . .

The charm of the Russian words, the fascination of grasping the gist of the theme, broke in vain against the prevailing chill. If the two should turn away from each other and bend their glowing faces, their strangely secure foreign independence, towards the general bleakness, its dreadful qualities would swell to a more active torment, all meanings lost in empty voices uttering words that no one would watch or explain. There was a lull. Their conversation was changing. Mr Shatov had sat back in his chair with a Russian word that hung in the air and spread music. His brows had come down and he was glancing thoughtfully about the table. She met Mr Rodkin's eyes and smiled and turned again to Sissie with her remark about the weather. Sissie's face came round, surprised. She disagreed, making a perfect comment on the change that left Miriam marvelling at her steady ease of mind. She agreed in an enthusiastic paraphrase, her mind busy on the hidden source of her random emphasis. It could rest, everything could rest for a while, for a little time to come, for some weeks perhaps. . . . But he would bring all those books; with special meanings in them that every one seemed to understand and agree about; real at the beginning and then going off into things and never coming back. Why could she not understand them? Finding things without following the story was like being interested in a lesson without mastering what you were supposed to master and not knowing anything about it afterwards that you could pass on or explain. Yet there *was* something, or why did school which had left no knowledge and no facts seem so alive? Why did everything seem alive in a way it was impossible to explain? Perhaps part of the wrong of being a lazy idiot was being happy in a way no one else seemed to be happy.

If one were an idiot, people like Mr Shatov would not. . . . He looked straight across, a swift observant glance. She turned once more towards Sissie, making herself smilingly one with the conversation that was going on between her and her further neighbour and listened eagerly across the table; '*Gracieuse*,' Mr Shatov was saying at the end of a sentence, dropping from objection to restatement. Mr Rodkin had asked him if he did not think her pretty. That would be his word. He would have no other word. Mr Shatov had looked considering the matter for the first time. '*Gracieuse*.' Surely that was the very last thing she could be. But he thought it.

Grace was a quality, not an appearance. Strong-minded and plain. That, she knew, was the secret verdict of women; or, doesn't know how to make the best of herself. She pondered, seeking in vain for any source of grace. Grace was delicacy, refinement, little willowy cattish movements of the head, the inner mind fixed always on the proprieties, making all the improprieties visible . . . streaming from the back-view of their unconscious hair . . .

A gracieuse effect means always deliberate *behaving*. Madame de Something. But people who keep it up can never let thoughts take their course. They must behave to their thoughts as they behave to people. When they are by themselves they can only go on mincing quietly, waiting for their next public appearance. When they are not talking they wait in an attitude, as if they were talking; ready to behave. Always on guard. Perhaps that was what Mr Wilson meant when he said it was the business of women to be the custodians of manners. . . . Their 'sense of good form, and their critical and selective faculties.' Then he had no right to be contemptuous of them. . . . 'Donald Braden . . . *lying* across the dinner-table . . . a drink-sodden hull, *swearing* that he would

never again go to a dinner-party where there were no ladies'
. . . 'Good *talk* and particularly good *stories* are not expected
of women, at dinner-tables. It's their business to *steer* the
conversation and head it off if it gets out of bounds.' . . . To
simper and watch, while the men were free to be themselves,
and then step in if they went beyond bounds. In other words
to head the men off if they talked 'improperly'; thus showing
knowledge of improprieties . . . 'tactfully' ignoring them and
leading on to something else with a gracious pose. Those
were the moments when the improprieties streamed from their
hair. . . . Somebody saying 'ssh,' superior people talking together, modern friends-in-council, a week-end in a beautiful
house, *subjects* on the menu, are you high church or low church,
the gleam of a woman's body through water. 'Ssh.' *Why?* . . .

But her impression to himself was good. A *French* impression; that was the extraordinary thing. Without any consideration that was the impression she had made. Perhaps
every one had a sort of style, and people who liked you could
see it. The style of one's family would show, to strangers, as
an unknown strange outside effect. Every one had an effect.
. . . She had an *effect*, a stamp, independent of anything she
thought or felt. It ought to give one confidence. Because
there would certainly be some people who would not dislike it.
But perhaps he had not observed her at all until that moment,
and had been misled by her assumption of animation.

If I tried to be gracious, I could never keep it up, because I
always forget that I am visible. She called in her eyes, which
must have been staring all the time blankly about the table,
so many impressions had she gathered of the various groups,
animated now in their unconscious relief at the approaching
end of the long sitting. Here again was one of those moments
of being conscious of the strange fact of her incurable illusion,
and realizing its effects in the past and the effects it must always
have if she did not get away from it. Nearly always she must
appear both imbecile and rude, staring, probably with her
mouth half open, lost. Well-brought-up children were *trained*
out of it. No one had dared to try and train her for long. They
had been frightened, or offended, by her scorn of their brisk

cheerful pose of polite interest in the *surface* of everything that was said. It was not worth doing. Polite society was not worth having. Every time one tried for a while, holding oneself in, thinking of oneself sitting there as others were sitting, consciousness came to an end. It meant having opinions. Taking sides. It presently narrowed life down to a restive discomfort . . .

Jan went about the streets thinking she was invisible . . . 'and then quite suddenly I saw myself in a shop mirror. My *dear*! I got straight into an omnibus and went home. I could not stand the sight of my hips.' But with people, in a room, she never forgot she was there.

The sight of Mr Shatov, waiting for her under the gas in the drawing-room, gathered all her thoughts together, struggling for simultaneous expression. She came slowly across the room, with eyes downcast to avoid the dimly lit corner where he stood, and sought rapidly amongst the competing threads of thought for some fragment that could be shaped into speech before he should make the communication she had seen waiting in his face. The sympathetic form must listen and make some understanding response. She felt herself stiffening in angry refusal to face the banishment of her tangled mass of thought by some calmly oblivious statement, beginning nowhere and leading them on into baseless discussion, impeded on her part by the pain of unstated vanishing things. They began speaking together and he halted before her formal harsh-voiced words.

'There is always a bad light on Saturday evenings because nearly every one goes out,' she said and looked her demand for his recognition of the undischarged burden of her mind impatiently about the room.

'I had not observed this,' he said gently, 'but now I see the light is indeed very bad.' She watched him as he spoke, waiting, counting each syllable. He paused, gravely consulting her face; she made no effort to withhold the wave of anger flowing out over the words that stood mocking her on the desolate air, a bridge, carrying them up over the stream of her mind and forward, leaving her communications behind for ever. She waited, watching cynically for whatever he might offer to her dumbness, wondering whether it surprised him, rebuked, as she regarded him, by his unchanged gentle lustre.

'Oh, *please*,' he said hurriedly, his downcast inturned smile suddenly irradiating his forehead, bringing down the eyebrows that must have gone singing thoughtfully up as he spoke about the light . . . a request of some kind; one of his extraordinary unashamed demands. . . . 'You must help me. I must immediately pone my watch. ˙Where is a poning shop?'

Miriam stared her consternation.

'Ah, no,' he said, his features working with embarrassment, 'it is not for myself. It is my friend, the Polish doctor, who was only now here.' Miriam gazed, plunging on through relief into a chaos of bewildered admiration.

'But you hardly know him,' she exclaimed, sitting down for more leisurely contemplation.˙

'That is not the point,' he said seriously, taking the chair on the other side of the little table. 'Poor fellow, he is not long in London, and has almost no friends. He is working in abstruse researchings, needing much spendings on materials, and is threatened by his landlady to leave his apartments.'

'Did he tell you this?' said Miriam sceptically recalling the Polish head, its smooth cold perfect beauty and indifference.

'Most certainly he told me. He must immediately have ten pounds.'

'Perhaps you would not get so much,' persisted Miriam. 'And suppose he does not pay it back?'

'You are mistaken. The watch, with the chain, is worth more than the double this sum.' His face expressed a grave simple finality.

'But it is a *shame*,' she cried, jealously eyeing the decoration that seemed now to have been an essential part of their many meetings. Without this mark of opulence, he would not be quite the same. . . .

'Why a shame?' demanded Mr Shatov, with his little abrupt snorting chuckle. 'I shall again have my watch when my father shall send me the next portion of my allowance.' He was not counting on the return of the money! Next month, with his allowance, he would have the watch and forget the incident. . . . Wealth made life safe for him. People could be people to him; even strangers; not threats or problems. But even a wealthy Englishman would not calmly give ten pounds to a disreputable stranger . . . he would suspect him, even if he were not disreputable. It *might* be true that the Pole was in honest difficulties. But it was impossible to imagine him really working at anything. Mr Shatov did not feel this at all.

'I 'm afraid I don't know any pawn-shops,' she said, shrinking even from the pronunciation of the word. She scanned her London. They had always been there . . . but she had never noticed or thought of them . . . 'I don't remember ever having seen one; but I know you are supposed to recognize them,' here was strange useful knowledge, something picturesque floating in from somewhere . . . 'by three gold balls hanging outside . . . I *have* seen one,' they were talking now, the Polish doctor was fading away. 'Yes . . . on a bus,' his wide child's eyes were set impersonally on what she saw, 'somewhere down by Ludgate Circus.'

'I will at once go there,' he said sitting leisurely back with dreaming eyes and his hands thrust into his pockets.

'Oh, no,' she cried, thrusting off the disaster, 'it would be *closed*.'

'That is bad,' he reflected. 'Ach, no matter. I will write to him that I come on Monday.'

'He would not get your letter until Monday.'

'That is true. I did not think of this.'

There must be pawn-shops quite near; in the Tottenham Court Road. Perhaps they would still be open. Not to suggest this would be to be responsible if anything happened to the Pole. . . . Thrusting down through the numbed mass of her forgotten thoughts to the quick of her nature came the realization that she was being tested and found wanting . . . another of those moments had come round. . . . She glanced into the open abyss at her own form staring up from its depths, and through her brain flew, in clear record, decisive moments of the past; herself, clearly visible, clothed as she had been clothed, her poise and bearing as she had flinched and fled. Here she was, unchanged, not caring what happened to the man, so long as her evening was not disturbed . . . she was a murderess. This was the hidden truth of her life. Above it her false face turned from thing to thing, happy and forgetful for years, until a moment came again to show her that she could face and let slip the risk of anything for any one, anywhere, rather than the pain of renouncing personal realization. Already she was moving away. A second suggestion was in her mind and she was not going to make it. She glanced enviously at the unconscious kindliness lolling in the opposite chair. It was clear to its depths; unburdened by spectres of remembered cruelty. . . . But there was also something else that was different . . . easy circumstances; the certainty, from the beginning, of self-realization. . . .

'Perhaps someone in the house could tell you.' Oh, *stupidity*; blurting out *anything* to hide behind the sound of voices.

'Possibly. But it is a delicate matter. I could not for instance mention this matter to Mrs Bailey.'

'Do you like him? Didn't you find him amongst those dreadful men looking like monkeys?'

'At this Vienna café. Ah, indeed it is dreadful there upstairs.'

'He is very handsome.'

'The Poles are perhaps the most beautiful of European peoples. They have also *immense* courage' . . . unsuspicious thoughtfully talking face, lifting her up and out again into light and air. . . . 'But the Pole is undoubtedly the most *treacherous* fellow in Europe.' Grave live eyes flashed across at her, easily, moulding the lounging form into shapeliness. 'He is at the same time of the most distinguished mentality.' Why should any one help a distinguished mentality to go on being treacherous? 'And in particular is this true of the Polish *Jew*. There are in all European universities amongst the very most distinguished professors and students very many Polish Jews.' Le Juif Polonais . . . *The Bells*. It was strange to think of Polish Jews going on in modern everyday life. . . . But if Poles were so evil . . . That was Dr Veslovsky's expression. Cold evil.

'There was an awful thing last week in Woburn Place.'

'Yes?'

'Mrs Bailey told me about it. There was a girl who owed

her landlady twenty-five shillings. She threw herself out of her bedroom window on the top floor, because her landlady spoke to her about it.'

'That is *terrible*,' whispered Mr Shatov. His eyes were dark with pain; his face shrunk as if with cold. 'That could *never* happen in Russia,' he said reproachfully.

'Why not?'

'No. In Russia such a thing is impossible. And in student circles most particularly. This young girl living in this neighbourhood without salary was probably some sort of student.'

'Why? She might have been a governess out of work or a poor clerk. Besides, I thought people were always committing suicide in Russia.'

'That is of course a gross exaggeration. There are certainly suicides in Russia, as everywhere. But in Russia suicide, which does certainly occur in abnormally high frequency amongst the young intelligentsia, arises from trouble of *spirit*. They are psychopath. There comes some spiritual crisis and —phwtt— . . . It is characteristic of the educated Slav mind to lose itself in face of abstractive insolubilities. But for need of *twenty-five shillings*. I find in this something peculiarly horrible. In midst of your English civilization it is pure-barbaric.'

'There has not been any civilization in the world yet. We are still all living in caves.' The quotation sounded less convincing than at Wimpole Street. . . .

'That is too superficial. Pardon me, but it implies a too slight knowledge of what has been in the past and what still persists in various developmental stages.' Miriam felt about among the statements which occurred to her in rapid succession, all contradicting each other. Yet somebody in the world believed each one of them. . . . Mr Shatov was gravely waiting, as if for her agreement with what he had just said. Far away below her clashing thoughts was something she wanted to express, something he did not know, and that yet she felt he might be able to shape for her if only she could present it. But between her and this reality was the embarrassment of a mind that could produce nothing but quotations. She had no mind of her own. It seemed to be there when she was alone;

only because there was no need to express anything.   In speech
she could produce only things other people had said and with
which she did not agree.   None of them expressed the underlying thing. . . . Why had she not brought down Maeterlinck ?

Mr Shatov's quiet waiting had ended in a flow of eager talk.
She turned unwillingly.   Even he could go on, leaving things
unfinished, talking about something else. . . . But his mind
was steady.   The things that were there would not drop away.
She would be able to consider them . . . watching the effect
of the light of other minds upon the things that floated in her
own mind; so dreadfully *few*, now that he was beginning to
look at them; and all ending with the images of people who
had said them, or the bindings of books where she had found
them set down. . . . Yet she felt familiar with all points of
view.   Every generalization gave her the clue to the speaker's
mind . . . wanting to hear no more, only to criticize what was
said by pointing out, whether she agreed with it or no, the
opposite point of view. . . .

She smiled encouragingly towards his talk, hurriedly summoning an appearance of attention into her absent eyes while
she contemplated his glowing pallor and the gaze of unconscious wide intelligence, shining not only towards her own, but
also with such undisturbed intentness upon what he was describing.   She could think later on, next year, when he had
gone away leaving her to confront her world with a fresh
armoury.   As long as he stayed, he would be there, without
effort or encouragement from her, filling her spare hours with
his untired beauty, drawing her along his carefully spun
English phrases, away from personal experiences, into a world
going on independently of them; unaware of the many scattered
interests waiting for her beyond this shabby room, and yet
making them shine as he talked, newly alight with rich superfluous impersonal fascination, no longer isolated, but vivid
parts of a whole, growing more and more intelligible as he
carried her further and further into a life he saw so distinctly,
that he made it hers; too quickly for her to keep account of the
inpouring wealth. . . .

She beamed in spacious self-congratulation and plunged into

the midst of his theme in holiday mood.   She was in a theatre,
without walls, her known world and all her memories spread,
fanwise about her, all intent on what she saw, changing, retreating to their original form, coming forward, changing again,
obliterated, and in some deep difficult way challenged to
renewal.   The scenes she watched opened out one behind the
other in clear perspective, the earlier ones remaining visible,
drawn aside into bright light as further backgrounds opened.
The momentary sound of her own voice in the room, encouraging his narrative, made no break; she dropped her
remarks at random into his parentheses, carefully screening
the bright centres as they turned one by one into living
memories. . . .

Suddenly she was back withering in the cold shabby room
before the shock of his breaking off to suggest, with a swift
personal smile, that she herself should go to Russia.   For a
moment she stared at him.   He waited, smiling gently.   It
did not matter that he thought her worthy.   The conviction
that she had already been to Russia, that his suggestion was
foolish in its recommendation of a vast superfluous undertaking,
hung like a veil between her and the experiences she now passed
through in imagining herself there.   The very things in the
Russian student circles that had most appealed to her, would
test and find her out.   She would be one of those who would
be mistrusted for not being sufficiently careless about her dress
and hair.   It would not suit her to catch up her hair with one
hairpin.   She would not be strong enough to study all day and
half the night on bread and tea.   She was sure she could not
associate perpetually with men students, even living and sharing
rooms with them, without the smallest flirtation.   If she were
wealthy like him, she would not so calmly accept having all
things in common; poor, she would be uneasy in dependence
on other students.   She sat judged.   There was a quality
behind all the scenes, something in the Russians that she did
not possess.   It was the thing that made him what he was.
It answered to a call that was being made all the time to every
one, everywhere.   Yet why did so many of them *drink*?

'Well?' said Mr Shatov.   The light was going down.

'*What* is this?' he asked staring up impatiently at the lessening flame. 'Ah, it is simply *stupid*.' He hurried away and Miriam heard his voice shouting down to Mrs Bailey from the staircase as he went, and presently in polite loud-toned remonstrance from the top of the basement stairs. The gas went up, higher than it had been before. It must be eleven. It was not fair to keep the gas going for two people. She must wind up the sitting and send him away.

'What a piece of English stupidity,' he bellowed gently, coming back across the room.

'I suppose she is obliged to do it,' said Miriam feeling incriminated by her failure to resent the proceeding in the past.

'How *obliged*?'

'She has had an awful time. She was left penniless in Weymouth.'

'That is bad; but it is no cause for *stupidity*.'

'I know. She doesn't understand. She managed quite well with lodgers; she will never make boarders pay. It's no use giving her hints. The house is full of people who don't pay their bills. There are people here who have paid nothing for eighteen months. She has even lent them money.'

'Is it possible?' he said gravely.

'And the Irish journalist *can't* pay. He is a Home-ruler.'

'He is a most distinguished-looking man. Ah, but she is *stupid*.'

'She can't *see*,' said Miriam—he was *interested*; even in *these* things. She dropped eagerly down amongst them. The whole evening and all their earlier interchange stood far off, shedding a relieving light over the dismal details and waiting to be resumed, enriched by this sudden excursion—'that when better people come she ought to alter things. It isn't that she would think it wrong, like the doctor who felt guilty when he bought a carriage to make people believe he had patients, though of course speculation *is* wrong'—she felt herself moving swiftly along, her best memories with her in the cheerful ring of her voice, their quality discernible by him, a kind of reply to all he had told her—'because she believes in keeping up appearances; but she doesn't know how to make people comfortable.'

She was creating a wrong impression but with the right voice. Without Miss Scott's suggestions, the discomforts would never have occurred to her.

'Ah she is *stupid*. That is the whole thing.' He sat forward, stretching and contracting his hands till the muscles cracked; his eyes, flashing their unconcerned contemptuous judgment, were all at once the brilliant misty eyes of a child about to be quenched by sudden sleep.

'*No*,' she said resentfully, 'she wants good people, and when they come she has to make all she can out of them. If they stayed, she would be able to afford to do things better. Of course they don't come back or recommend her; and the house is always half empty. Her *best* plan would be to fill it with students at a fixed low figure.' Miss Scott again. . . . His attention was wandering. . . . 'The dead *flowers*,' he was back again, 'in dirty water, in a cracked vase; Sissie rushing out, while breakfast is kept waiting, to buy just enough butter for one meal.'

'Really?' he giggled.

'She has been most awfully good to me.'

'Why not?' he chuckled.

'Do you think you will go and see your Polish friend to-morrow?' She watched anxiously.

'Yes,' he conceded blinking sleepily at the end of a long yawn. 'I shall perhaps go.'

'He might be driven to desperation,' she muttered. Her accomplished evening was trembling in the balance. Its hours had frittered away the horrible stranger's chance.

'Ah no,' said Mr Shatov with a little laugh of sincere amusement, 'Veslovski will not do foolish things.' She rose to her feet on the tide of her relief, meeting, as she garnered all the hours of her long day and turned with an outspreading sheaf of questions towards the expanses of evening leisure so safely at her disposal in the oncrowding to-morrows, the rebuke of the brilliantly burning midnight gas.

'But tell me; how has Mrs Bailey been so good?' He sat conversationally forward as if it were the beginning of the evening.

'Oh well.' She sought about distastefully amongst the phrases she had collected in descriptions given to her friends, conveying nothing. Mr Shatov, knowing the framework, would see the detail alive and enhance her own sense of it. She glanced over the picture. Any single selection would be misleading. There was enough material for days of conversation. He was waiting eagerly, *not* impatient, after all, of personal experiences. Yet nothing could be told. . . .

'You see she lets me be amphibious.' Her voice smote her. Mrs Bailey's kindliness was in the room. She was squandering Mrs Bailey's gas in an effort that was swiftly transforming itself under the influence of her desire to present an adequate picture of her own separate life. His quickening interest drove her on. She turned her eyes from the gas and stared at the carpet, her picture broken up and vanishing before the pathos of its threadbare faded patterns.

'I'm neither a lodger nor a boarder,' she recited hurriedly. 'I have all the advantages of a boarder; the use of the whole house. I've had this room and the piano to myself for years, on Sunday mornings until dinner time, and, when there are interesting people, I can go down to dinner. I do for weeks on end sometimes, and it is so convenient to be able to have meals on Sundays.'

'It is really a most *admirable* arrangement,' he said heartily.

'And last year I had a bicycle accident. I was brought back here with a very showy arm; in a cab. Poor Mrs Bailey fainted. It was not at all serious. But they gave me their best room, the one behind this, for weeks, and waited upon me most beautifully, and mind you they did not expect any compensation, they knew I could not afford it.'

'An injury that should disable for so many weeks shall not have been a light one.'

'That was the doctor. You see it was Saturday. It was more than an hour before they could find any one at all, and then they found a small surgeon in Gower Street. He stitched up my arm with a rusty darning needle taken from Mrs Bailey's work-basket just as it was. I told him I had some carbolic in my room; but he said, "Nevorr mind that. I'm not one of

yrr faddists," and bound it all up and I came down to dinner.
I had just come back from the first week of my holiday;
bicycling in Buckinghamshire, perfect, I never felt so well in
my life. I was going to Paris the next day.'

'That was indeed most unfortunate.'

'Well, I don't know. I was going with a woman I did not
really know. I meant to go, and she had been thinking of
going and knew Paris and where to stay cheaply and suggested
we should join forces. A sort of marriage of convenience. I
was not really disappointed. I was relieved; though awfully
sorry to fail her. But every one was so kind I was simply
astonished. I spent the evening on the sofa in the dining-room;
and they all sat quietly about near me. One man, a Swede,
who had only just arrived, sat on the end of the sofa and told
Swedish folk stories in a quiet motherly voice, and turned out
afterwards to be the noisiest, jolliest, most screamingly funny
man we have ever had here. About eleven o'clock I felt faint,
and we discovered that my arm must have broken out again
some time before. Two of the men rushed off to find a doctor
and brought an extraordinary little old retired surgeon with
white hair and trembling hands. He wheezed and puffed and
bound me up afresh and went away refusing a fee. I wanted
some milk, and the Swede went out at midnight and found
some somewhere. . . . "I come back with at least one cow or
I come not at all." . . . Of course a week later I had stitch
abscesses.'

'But this man was a *criminal*.'

'Yes, wasn't it abominable? Poor man. The two doctors
who saw my arm later said that many limbs have been lost for
less. He counted on my being in such good health. He told
Mrs Bailey I was in splendid health. But he sent in a big bill.'

'I sincerely trust you did not pay this.'

'I sent him a description of his operation, told him the result,
and said that my friends considered that I ought to prosecute
him.'

'Certainly it was your duty.'

'I don't know. I hate cornering people. It would not
have made him different and I am no better than he is.'

'That is a most extraordinary point of view.'

'I was sorry afterwards that I had written like that.'

'Why ?'

'Because he threw himself into Dublin Harbour a year later. He must have been in *fearful* difficulties.'

'No excuse for criminal neglect.'

'The most wonderful thing in the accident itself,' pursued Miriam firmly, grasping her midnight freedom and gazing into the pattern her determination that for another few minutes no one should come up to interrupt, 'was being so near to death.' She glanced up to gauge the effect of her improvisation. The moment she was now intent upon had not been 'wonderful.' She would not be able to substantiate it; she had never thought it through. It lay ahead now for exploration if he wished, ready to reveal its quality to her for the first time. He was sitting hunched against the wall with his hands driven into his pockets, waiting without resistance, with an intentness equal to her own. She returned gratefully to her carpet. 'It was a skid,' she said feeling the oily slither of her front tyre. 'I fell with my elbow and head between the horses' heels and the wheel of a dray. The back-thrown hoof of the near horse caught the inner side of my arm, and for a long long time I saw the grey steel rim of the huge wheel approaching my head. It was strained back with all my force, my elbow pressing the ground, but I thought it could not miss me. There was a moment of absolute calm; *indifference* almost. It came after a feeling of hatred and yet pity for the wheel. It was so awful, wet glittering grey, and relentless; and stupid, it could not help going on.'

'This was indeed a most *remarkable* psychological experience. It happens rarely to be so near death with full consciousness. But this absence of fear must be in you a personal idiosyncrasy.'

'But I *was* afraid. The thing is that you don't go *on* feeling afraid. Do you see ?'

'I hear what you say. But while there is the chance of life the instinct of self-preservation is so strong.'

'But that is the surprise; the tumult in your body, something surging up and doing things without thinking.'

'Instinctive nervous reaction.'

'But there is something else. In the moment you are *sure* you are going to be killed, death changes. You wait, for the moment after.'

'That is an illusion, the strength of life in you that cannot, midst good health, accept death. But tell me; your arm was certainly broken?' His gently breathed question took away the sting of his statement.

'No. The wheel went over it just above the bend of the elbow. I did not feel it, and got up feeling only a little dizzy just for a moment and horribly annoyed at the crowd round me. But the two men who were riding with me told me afterwards that my face was grey and my eyes quite *black*.'

'That was shock.' He rose and stood facing her, in shadow; dark and frock-coated, like a doctor.

'Yes; but I mean it shows that things look worse than they are.'

'That is most certainly a deduction that might be drawn. Nevertheless you suffered a most formidable *shock*.'

She moved towards the gas looking decisively up at it; and felt herself standing unexpressed, under the wide arch of all they had said. He must be told to remember to put out the gas before he went. That said, there was nothing in the world but a reluctant departure.

CHAPTER III

THREE months ago, Christmas had been a goal for which she could hardly wait. It had offered her, this time, more than its usual safe deep firelit seclusion beyond which no future was visible. It was to pay her in full for having missed the begin-. ning of Eve's venture, taking her down into the midst of it when everything was in order and the beginnings still near enough to be remembered. But having remained during the engrossing months, forgotten, at the same far-distant point, Christmas now suddenly reared itself up a few days off, offering nothing but the shadow of an unavoidable interruption. For the first time, she could see life going on beyond it. She would go down into its irrelevance, taking part in everything with absent-minded animation, looking towards her return to town. It would not be Christmas, and the long days of forced absence threatened the features of the year that rose, far away and uncertain, beyond the obstruction.

But the afternoon she came home with four days' holiday in her hand, past and future were swept from her path. To-morrow's journey was a far-off appointment, her London friends remote shadows, banished from the endless continuance of life. She wandered about between Wimpole Street and St Pancras, holding in imagination wordless converse with a stranger whose whole experience had melted and vanished like her own, into the flow of light down the streets; into the un-ending joy of the way the angles of buildings cut themselves out against the sky, glorious if she paused to survey them; and almost unendurably wonderful, keeping her hurrying on press-ing, through insufficient silent outcries, towards something, anything, even instant death, if only they could be expressed when they moved with her movement, a maze of shapes, flowing, tilting into each other, in endless patterns, sharp against the light; sharing her joy in the changing same same song of the London traffic; the bliss of post offices and railway stations, cabs going on and on towards unknown space; omnibuses rumbling securely from point to point, always within the magic circle of London.

Her meal was a crowded dinner-party, all the people in the restaurant its guests, plunging with her, released from experience, unhaunted by hope or regret, into the endless beginning. Into the rapt contemplation of the gathering, the thought of her visit flashed like a star, dropping towards her and, when she was gathering things together for her packing, her eagerness flamed up and lit her room.

The many Christmases with the Brooms had been part of her long run of escape from the pain-shadowed family life; their house at first a dream-house in the unbroken dream of her own life in London, a shelter where agony was unknown, and lately a forgetfulness, for the long days of the holiday, of the challenge that lived in the walls of her room. For so long the walls had ceased to be the thrilled companions of her freedom, they had seen her endless evening hours of waiting for the next day to entangle her in its odious revolution. They had watched her, in bleak daylight, listening to life going on obliviously all round her, and scornfully sped her desperate excursions into other lives, greeting her empty glad return with the reminder that relief would fade, leaving her alone again with their unanswered challenge. They knew the recurring picture of a form, drifting, grey face upwards, under a featureless grey sky, in shallows, 'unreached by the human tide,' and had seen its realization in her vain prayer that life should not pass her by; mocking the echoes of her cry, and waiting indifferent, serene with the years they knew before she came, for those that would follow her meaningless impermanence. When she lost the sense of herself in moments of gladness, or in the long intervals of thought that encircled her intermittent reading, they were all round her, waiting, ready to remind her, undeceived by her daily busy passing in and out, relentlessly noting its secret accumulating shame.

During the last three months they had not troubled her. They had become transparent, while the influence of her summer still held them at bay, to the glow shed up from the hours she had spent downstairs with Mrs Bailey, and before there was time for them to close round her once more, the figure of Michael Shatov, with Europe stretching wide behind him, had forced them into companionship with all the walls in the world. She had been conscious that they waited for his departure; but it was far away out of sight and, when she should be once more alone with them, their attack would find her surrounded; lives lived alone within the vanquished walls of single poor bare rooms in every town in Europe would come visibly to her aid, driving her own walls back into dependence.

But to-night they were radiant. On no walls in the world could there be a brighter light. Streaming from their gaslit spaces, wherever she turned, was the wide brilliance that had been on everything in the days standing behind the shadow that had driven her into their enclosure. Eve and Harriett, waiting for her together, in a new sunlit life, were the full answer to their challenge. She was going *home*. The walls were traveller's walls. That had been their first fascination; but they had known her only as a traveller; now as she dipped into the unbroken life that would flow round her with the sound of her sisters' blended voices, they knew whence she came and what had been left behind. They saw her years of travel contract to a few easily afforded moments, lit, though she had not known it, by light instreaming from the past and flowing now visibly ahead across the farther years.

The distant forgotten forms of the friends of her London life, turning away slighted, filled her, watching them, with a half-repenting solicitude. But they had their mysterious secret life, incomprehensible, but their own; they turned away towards each other and their own affairs, all of them set, at varying angles, unquestioningly towards a prospect she did not wish to share.

She went eagerly to sleep and woke in a few moments in a morning whose sounds, coming through the open window, called to her as she leapt out towards them, for responsive demonstrations. Her desire to shout, thrilling to her feet, winged them.

Sitting decorously at the breakfast-table, she felt in equal relationship to all the bright assembly, holding off Mr Shatov's efforts to engage her in direct conversation, that she might hear, thoughtless and uncomprehending, the general sound of interwoven bright inflections echoing quietly out into the vast morning. She ran out into it, sending off her needless telegram for the joy of skimming over the well-known flags with endless time to spare. The echoing London sky poured down upon them the light of all the world. Within it her share gleamed dancing, given to her by the London years, the London life, shining now, far away, in multitudinous detail, the contemplated enviable life of a stranger.

The third-class carriage was stuffy and cold, crowded with excited travellers whose separate eyes strove in vain to reach the heart of the occasion through a ceaseless exclamatory interchange about what lay just behind them and ahead at the end of the journey. . . . At some time, for some moments during the ensuing days, each one of them would be alone. Consulting the many pairs of eyes, so different yet so strangely alike in their method of contemplation, so hindered and distracted, she felt, with a stifling pang of conviction, that their days would pass and bring no solitude, no single touch of realization, and leave them going on, with eyes still quenched and glazed, striving outwards, now here now there, to reach some unapprehended goal.

Immersing herself in her corner she saw nothing more until Eve's face appeared in the crowd waiting upon the seaside platform. Eve beamed welcome and eager wordless communications and turned at once to lead the way through the throng. They hurried, separated by Miriam's hand-luggage, silenced by the din of the traffic rattling over the cobblestones, meeting and parting amongst the thronging pedestrians, down the steep slope of the narrow street until Eve turned, with a piloting backward glance, and led the way along the cobbled pavement of a side-street, still narrower, and sloping even more steeply downhill. It was deserted, and as they went single-file along the narrow pavement, Miriam caught in the distance the unwonted sound of the winter sea. She had not thought of the sea as part of her visit, and lost herself in the faint familiar roll and flump of the south-coast tide. It was enough. The holiday came and passed in the imagined sight of the waves tumbling in over the grey beach, and the breaking of the brilliant seaside light upon the varying house-fronts behind the promenade. She returned restored, the prize of far-off London renewed already, keenly, within her hands, to find Eve standing still just ahead, turned towards her; smiling too breathlessly for speech. They were in front of a tiny shop-front, slanting with the steep slant of the little road. The window was full of things set close to the panes on narrow shelves. Miriam stood back, pouring out her appreciation. It *was* perfect; just as she had imagined it; exactly the little shop she had dreamed of keeping when she was a child. She felt a pang of envy.

'*Mine*,' said Eve blissfully, 'my own.' Eve had property; fragile delicate *Eve*, the problem of the family. This was her triumph. Miriam hurried, lest her thoughts should become visible, to glance up and down the street and acclaim the perfection of the situation.

'I know,' said Eve with dreamy tenderness, 'and it's all my own; the shop and the house; all mine.' Miriam's eyes rose fearfully. Above the shop, a narrow strip of bright white plaster house shot up, two stories high; charming, in the way it was complete, a house, and yet the whole of it, with a strip of sky above, and the small neat pavement below, in your eye at once, and beside it, right and left, the irregular heights and widths of the small houses, close-built and flush with the edge of the little pavement, up and down the hill. But the thought of the number of rooms inside the little building brought, together with her longing to see them, a sense of the burden of possessions, and her envy disappeared. While she cried 'You've got a *house*,' she wondered, scanning Eve's radiant slender form, whence she drew, with all her apparent helpless-ness, the strength to face such formidable things.

'I've let the two rooms over the shop. I live at the top.'

As she exclaimed on the implied wealth, Miriam found her
envy wandering back with the thought of the two rooms under
the sky, well away from the shop in another world, the rest of
the house securely cared for by other people. She moved to
the window. 'All the right things,' she murmured, from her
shocked survey of the rows of light green bottles filled with
sweets, the boxes of soap, cigarettes, clay pipes, bootlaces,
jewellery pinned to cards, crackers and tightly packed pink
and white muslin Christmas stockings. Between the shelves
she saw the crowded interior of the little shop, a strip of
counter, a man with rolled-up shirt sleeves, busily twisting a
small screw of paper. . . . *Gerald.*

'Come inside,' said Eve from the door.

'Hullo, Mirry, what d' you think of the emporium ?' Gerald,
his old easy manner, his smooth polished gentle voice, his neat,
iron handshake across the mean little counter, gave Eve's
enterprise the approval of all the world. 'I 've done up enough
screws of tea to last you the whole blessed evening,' he went on
from the midst of Miriam's exclamations, 'and at least twenty
people have been in since you left.' A little door flew open
in the wall just behind him and Harriett, in an overall, stood
at the top of a short flight of stairs, leaping up and down in the
doorway. Miriam ran round behind the counter, freely,
Eve's shop, their shop, behind her. 'Hullo, old silly,' beamed
Harriett, kissing and shaking her, 'I just rushed down, can't
stay a minute, I 'm in the middle of nine dinners, they 're all
leaving to-morrow and you 're to come and sleep with *us.*'
She fled down the steps, out through the shop and away up
the hill, with a rousing attack on Gerald as she passed him
leaning with Eve over the till. Miriam was welcomed.
The fact of her visit was more to Harriett than her lodgers.
She collected her belongings and carried them up the steps
past a small dark flight of stairs into a dark little room. A
small fire was burning in a tiny kitchen range; a candle
guttered on the mantelpiece in the draught from the shop;
there was no window and the air of the room was close
with the combined odours of the things crowded into the
small space. She went back into the bright familiar shop.

Gerald was leaving; 'See you to-morrow,' he called from the
door with his smile.

'*Now;* I 'll light the lamp and we 'll be cosy,' said Eve
leading the way back into the little room. Miriam waited impatiently for the lamp to make a live centre in the crowded
gloom. The little black kitchen fire was intolerable as president
of Eve's leisure. But the dim lamp, standing low on a little
table, made the room gloomier and Eve was back in the shop
with a customer. Only the dingy little table, a battered tray
bearing the remains of a hasty, shabby tea, the fall below it of
a faded ugly fringed table-cloth and a patch of threadbare
carpet, were clearly visible. She could not remove her attention from them.

Lying sleepless by Eve's side late that night, she watched
the pictures that crowded the darkness. Her first moments
in the little back room were far away. The small dark bedroom
was full of the last picture of Eve, in her nightgown, quietly
relentless after explaining that she always kept the window
shut because plenty of air came in, taking a heavy string of
large blue beads out of her top drawer, to put them in readiness
with to-morrow's dress: 'No; I don't think that a bit; and if I
were a savage, I should hang myself all over with beads and
love it.' She had spoken with such *conviction.* . . . Up here,
with her things arranged round her as she had had them at
home and in her bedroom at the Greens', she kept her life as
it had always been. She was still her unchanged self, but her
freedom was giving her the strength to be sure of her opinions.
It was as if she had been saying all the evening with long accumulating preparedness, holding her poise throughout the
interruptions of customers and down into the details of the
story of her adventures, *Yes,* I know your opinions, I have
heard them all my life, and now I 'm out in the world myself
and can meet everybody as an equal, and say what I think,
without wondering whether it suits my part as the Greens'
governess. She had got her strength from the things she had
done. It was amazing to think of her summoning courage to
break again with the Greens and borrowing from them to start
in business, Mr Green 'setting his heart' on the success of the

little shop and meaning to come down and see how it was getting on. How awful it would be if it did not get on. But it was getting on. How terrifying it must have been at first not knowing the price of anything in the shop or what to buy for it . . . and then, customers telling her the prices of things and where they were kept, and travellers being *kind*; respectful and friendly and ready to go out of their way to do *anything*. That was the other side of Maupassant's 'hourra pour la petite différence' commis voyageurs . . . and well-to-do people in the neighbourhood rushing in for some little thing, taken aback to find a lady behind the counter, and coming again for all sorts of things. Eve would become like one of those middle-aged women shopkeepers in books, in the country, with a kind heart and a sarcastic tongue, seeing through everybody and having the same manner for the vicar and a ploughman, or a rather nicer manner for a ploughman. *No.* Eve was still sentimental.

Those wonderful letters were a bridge; a promise for the future. They were the letters of a boy; *that* was the struggling impression she had not been able to convey. She could start the day well by telling Eve that in the morning. They were the letters of a youth in love for the first time in his life . . . and he had *fifteen* grandchildren. 'So wonderful when you think of that old, old man,' had not expressed it at all. They were wonderful for *anybody*. Page after page, all breathing out the way things shine when the sense of someone who is not there, is there all the time. Eve knew what it had meant to him; 'age makes no difference.' Then life might suddenly shine like that at any moment, right up to the end. . . . And it made Eve so wonderful; having no idea, all those years, and thinking him just a very kind old man to come, driving, almost from his death-bed, with a little rose tree in the carriage for her. It was so perfect that he wrote only after she had gone, and he knew he was dying; a youth in love for the first time. If there were a future life he would be watching, for Eve to walk gently in crowned with song and making everything sing all round her.

But what of the wife, and of Eve's future husband? In

heaven there is neither marrying nor giving in marriage . . . but Kingsley said, 'then that has nothing to do with me and my wife.' Perhaps that was an example of the things he suddenly thought of, walking quickly up and down the garden with a friend, and introduced by saying 'I have *always* thought.' . . . But perhaps the things that occur to you suddenly for the first time in conversation *are* the things you have always thought, without knowing it . . . that was one of the charms of talking to Michael Shatov, finding out thoughts, looking at them when they were expressed and deciding to change them, or think them more decidedly than ever . . . she could explain all that to Eve in the morning as an introduction to him. Or perhaps she could again say, having Eve's attention free of the shop, 'I have two pounds to spend on chocolate. Isn't it extraordinary? I must, I am on my honour,' and then go on. It was *horrible* that Eve had hardly noticed such a startling remark. . . . She turned impatiently; the morning would never come; she would never sleep in this stagnant shut-in motionless air. To-morrow night she would be in a room by herself at Harry's; but not quite so near to the sea. How *could* Eve shut out life and the sound of the sea? She puffed her annoyance, hardly caring if Eve were disturbed, ready to ask her if she could not smell the smell of the house and the shop and the little back room. But that was not true. She was imagining it because the motionless air was getting on her nerves. If she could not forget it, she would have no sleep until she dozed with exhaustion in the morning. And to-morrow was Christmas Day. She lay still, straining her ears to catch the sound of the sea.

The next night the air poured in at an open window, silently lifting long light muslin curtains and waving them about the little narrow room filled as with moonlight by the soft blue light from the street-lamp below. The sound of the sea drowned the present in the sense of seaside summers; bringing back moments of chance wakenings on seaside holidays, when the high blaze of yesterday and to-morrow were together in the darkness. Miriam slept at once and woke refreshed and careless in the frosty sunrise. Her room was blazing with golden light. She lay motionless, contemplating it. There was no sound in the house. She could watch the sunlight till something happened. Harry would see that she got up in time for breakfast. There would be sunlight at breakfast in the room below; and Harry and Gerald and the remains of Christmas leisure. 'We only keep going because of Elspeth.' How could she have gone off to sleep last night without recalling that? If Harry and Gerald found marriage a failure, it was a failure. Perhaps it was a passing phase and they would think differently later on. But they had spoken so simply, as if it were a commonplace fact known to everybody. They had met so many people by this time. Nearly all their lodgers had been married, and unhappy. Perhaps that was because they were nearly all theatrical people? If Harry had stayed in London and not had to work for a living would she have been happier? No; she was gayer down here; even more herself. It *amused* her to have rushes, and turn out three rooms after ten o'clock at night. They both seemed to run the house as a sort of joke, and remained absolutely themselves. Perhaps that was just in talking about it, at Christmas, to her. It certainly must be horrible in the season, as Harry said, the best part of the house packed with selfish strangers for the very best part of the year; so much to do for them all day that there was never even time to run down to the sea. Visitors did not think of that. If they considered their landlady, it would spoil their one fortnight of being free. Landladies ought to be old; not minding about working all day for other people and never seeing the sea. Harry was too young to be a landlady. The gently moving curtains were flat against the window again for a moment, a veil of thin muslin screening the brilliant gold, making it an even tone all over the room; a little oblong of misty golden light. Even for Harry's sake she could not let any tinge of sadness invade it. . . . That was being exactly like the summer visitors. . . .

'Good *Gracious!*' The door was open and Harry, entering with a jug of hot water, was enveloped in the end of the out-blown curtains. 'Why on earth d' you have your window like that? It's simply *bitter*.'

'I love it,' said Miriam, watching Harriett's active little moving form battle with the flying draperies. 'I'm revelling in it.'

'Well, I won't presume to shut it; but revel *up*. Here you are. Breakfast's nearly ready. Hold the ends while I get out and shut the door.'

Harry *too*; and she used to be so fond of open windows. But it was not a snub. She would say to Gerald, 'She's got her window bang open, isn't she an old *cure*?' She got out singing into the fresh golden air, leaving the window wide. The London temptation to shirk her swift shampoo and huddle on a garment did not come. The sense of summer was so strong in the bright air that she felt sure, if only she could have always bright screened light in her room, summer warmth and summer happiness would last the whole year round.

Gerald was pouring out coffee. In the kitchen the voices of Harriett and Mrs Thimm were railing cheerfully together. Harriett came in with a rush, slamming the door. 'Is it too warm for you in here, Miss Henderson?' she asked as she drove Gerald to his own end of the table.

'It's glorious,' said Miriam subsiding into indefinite anticipation. The room was very warm with sunlight and a blazing fire. But there was no pressure anywhere. It was their youth and the way being with them made things go backwards as far as one could see and confidently forward from any room they happened to be in. A meal with them always seemed as if it might go on for ever. She glanced affectionately from one to the other, longing to convey to them in some form of words the thing they did not seem to know, the effect they made, together, through having been together from such early beginnings, how it gave and must always give a *confidence* to the very expression of their hair, making them always about to start life together. It came from Harriett, and was reflected by Gerald, a light that played about him, decking him in his most unconscious, busy, man's moments with the credit of having found Harriett. They seemed more suitably arranged, confronted here together in this bright eventful house, meeting adventures together, mutually efficient towards a common end, than with Gerald in business and Harry silken and leisurely in a suburban house.

'We'll be more glorious in a minute,' said Gerald, sweeping actively about. 'I'll just move that old fern.'

'Oh, of *course*,' mocked Harriett, '*look* at the importance . . .'

Whistling softly, Gerald placed a small square box on the table amongst the breakfast things.

'*Oh* dear me,' moaned Harriett from behind the coffee pot, smirking coyly backwards over her shoulder, 'hoh, *aren't* we grand? — It's the new *toy*,' she rapped avertedly towards Miriam, in a despairing whisper. Gerald interrupted his whistling to fix on to the box a sort of trumpet, a thing that looked like a wide-open green nasturtium.

'Is it a musical box?' asked Miriam.

'D' you mean to say you've never seen a gramophone yet?' murmured Gerald, frowning and flicking away dust with his handkerchief. They did not mean so much as they appeared to do when they said life was not worth living. They had not discovered life. Gerald did not know the meaning of his interest in things. 'People grieve and bemoan themselves, but it is not half so bad with them as they say.' : . .

'I haven't. I've heard them squeaking from inside public houses of course.'

'Now's your chance then. Woa, Jemima! That's the ticket. *Now* she's off——'

Miriam waited, breathless; eagerly prepared to accept the coming wonder. A sound like the crackling of burning twigs came out into the silence. She remembered her first attempt to use a telephone, the need for concentrating calmly through the preliminary tumult, on the certainty that intelligible sounds would presently emerge, and listened encouragingly for a voice. The crackling changed to a metallic scraping, labouring steadily round and round, as if it would go on for ever; it ceased, and an angry stentorian voice seemed to be struggling, half-smothered, in the neck of the trumpet. Miriam gazed, startled, at the yawning orifice, as the voice suddenly escaped and leapt out across the table with a shout—'Edison-BELL RECord!' Lightly struck chords tinkled far away, fairy music, sounding clear and distinct on empty space remote from the steady scraping of the machine. Then a song began. The whole machine seemed to sing it; vibrating with effort, sending forth the notes in a jerky staccato, the scarcely touched words clipped and broken to fit the jingling tune; the sustained upper notes at the end of the verse wavered chromatically, as if the machine were using its last efforts to reach the true pitch; it ceased and the far-away chords came again, fainter and further away. In the second verse the machine struggled more feebly and slackened its speed, flattened suddenly to a lower key, wavered on, flattening from key to key, and collapsed, choking, on a single downward-slurring squeak——

'Oh, but that's absolutely *perfect*,' gasped Miriam.

'You want to set it *slower*, silly; it all began too *high*.'

'*I* know, la reine, *he* knows, he'll set it slower all right.'

This time the voice marched lugubriously forth, with a threatening emphasis on each word; the sustained notes blared wide through their mufflings; yawned out by an angry lion.

'My *word*,' said Harriett, 'it's a funeral this time.'

'But it's *glorious*! Can you make it go as slowly as you like?'

'We'll get it right presently, never fear.'

Miriam felt that no correct performance could be better than what she had heard, and listened carelessly to the beginning of the third attempt. If it succeeded, the blissful light flowing from the room out over her distant world must either be shattered by her tacit repudiation of the cheaply devised ditty, or treacherously preserved at the price of simulated satisfaction. The prelude sounded nearer this time, revealing a piano and an accompanist, and the song came steadily out, a pleasant kindly baritone, beating along on a middle key; a nice unimaginative brown-haired young man, who happened to have a voice. She ceased to attend; the bright breakfast-table, the cheerfully decorated square room bathed in the brilliant morning light that was flooding the upward slope of the town from the wide sky towering above the open sea, was suddenly outside space and time, going on for ever untouched; the early days flowed up, recovered completely from the passage of time, going forward with to-day added to them, for ever. The march

of the refrain came lilting across the stream of days, joyfully
beating out the common recognition of the three listeners. She
restrained her desire to take it up, flinging out her will to hold
back the others, that they might face out the moment and
let it make its full mark. In the next refrain they could all
take the relief of shouting their acknowledgement, a hymn to
the threefold life. The last verse was coming successfully
through; in an instant the chorus refrain would be there. It
was old and familiar, woven securely into experience, beginning
its life as memory. She listened eagerly. It was partly too,
she thought, absence of singer and audience that redeemed
both the music and the words. It was a song overheard;
sounding out innocently across the morning. She saw the
sun shining on the distant hill-tops, the comrades in line, and
the lingering lover tearing himself away for the roll-call. The
refrain found her far away, watching the scene until the last
note should banish it.

The door opened and Elspeth stood in the doorway.

'*Well*, my pet?' said Harriett and Gerald gently, together.

She trotted round the open door, carefully closing it with
her body, her steady eyes taking in the disposition of affairs.
In a moment she stood near the table, the silky rounded golden
crown of her head rising just above it. Miriam thrilled at her
nearness, delighting in the firm clutch of the tiny hand on the
edge of the table, the gentle shapely bulge of the ends of her
hair inturned towards her neck, the little busy bustling expression of her bunchy motionless little muslin dress. Suddenly
she looked up in her way, Gerald's disarming gentleness, all
Eve's reined-in gaiety . . . 'I your baby?' she asked with a
small lunge of affection. Miriam blushed. Elspeth had
remembered from yesterday. . . . 'Yes,' she murmured encircling
her and pressing her lips to the warm silken top of her head.
Gerald burst into loud wailing. Elspeth moved backwards
towards Harriett and stood propped against her, contemplating
him with sunny interest. Harriett's firm ringed hand covered
the side of her head.

'Poor Poppa,' she suggested.

'Be *cri*-ut, Gerald!' Elspeth cried serenely, frowning with effort. She stood on tiptoe surveying the contents of the table and waved a peremptory hand towards the gramophone. Gerald tried to make a bargain. Lifted on to Harriett's knee she bunched her hands and sat compact. The direct rays made her head a little sunlit sphere, smoothly outlined with silky pale-gold hair bulging softly over each ear, the broken curve continued by the gentle bulge of her cheeks as she pursed her face to meet the sunlight. She peered unsmiling, but every curve smiled; a little sunny face, sunlit. Fearing that she would move, Miriam tried to centre attention by seeming engrossed in Gerald's operations, glancing sideways meanwhile in an entrancement of effort to define her small perfection. The list of single items summoned images of children who missed her charm by some accentuation of character, pointing backwards to the emphatic qualities of a relative and forward so clearly that already they seemed adult. Elspeth predicted nothing. The closest observation revealed no point of arrest. Her undivided impression, once caught, could be recovered in each separate feature.

Eve came in as the music ceased. In the lull that followed the general greetings, Miriam imagined a repetition of the song, to carry Eve back into what had gone before and forward with them in the unchanged morning. But Mrs Thimm broke in with a tray and scattered them all towards the fire. Let's hear *Molly Darling* once more, she thought in a casual tone. After yesterday, Eve would take that as a lack of interest in her presence. Supposing she did? She was so changed that she could be treated without consideration, as an equal. But she overdid it, preening herself, caring more for the idea of independence than for the fact. That would not keep her going. She would not be strong enough to sustain her independence.

The sense of triumph threw up an effulgence even while Miriam accused herself of cruelty in contemplating the droopy exhaustion which had outlived Eve's day of rest. But she was not alone in this; nice good people were secretly impatient with relatives who were always threatening to break down and become problems. And Eve had almost ceased to be a relative.

Descending to the rank of competitor she was no longer a superior. She was an inferior masquerading as an equal. That was what men meant in the newspapers. Then it couldn't be true. There was some other explanation. It was because she was using her independence as a revenge for the past. What men resented was the sudden reflection of their detachment by women who had for themselves discovered its secret, and knew what uncertainties went on behind it. She was resenting Eve's independence as a man would do. Eve was saying she now understood the things that in the past she had only admired, and that they were not so admirable, and quite easy to do. But she disgraced the discovery by flaunting it. It was so evident that it was her shop, not she, that had come into the room and spoiled the morning. Even now she was dwelling on next week. Inside her mind was nothing but her customers, travellers, the possible profits, her many plans for improvement. Nothing else could impress her. Anything she contributed would rest more than ever, now that Christmas Day was over, upon a background of absent-minded complacency. Like herself, with the Brooms? Was it she who was being judged and not Eve? No, or only by herself. Harriett shared her new impressions of Eve, saw how eagerly, in her clutch on her new interests, she had renounced her old background of inexhaustible sympathy. Gerald did not. But men have no sense of atmosphere. They only see the appearances of things, understanding nothing of their relationships. Bewilderment, pessimistic philosophies, *regretful* poetry. . . .

The song might banish Eve's self-assertion and bring back something of her old reality. Music, any music, would always make Eve real. Perhaps Elspeth would ask for it. But in the long, inactive seconds, things had rushed ahead shattering the sunlit hour. Nothing could make it settle again. Eve had missed it for ever. But she had discovered its presence. Its broken vestiges played about her retreat as she turned away to Elspeth; Gerald, who alone was unconscious of her discovery, having himself been spell-bound without recognizing his whereabouts, was inaccessibly filling his pipe. She was far off now, trying to break her way in by an attack on Elspeth. Miriam

watched anxiously, reading the quality of their daily intercourse. Elspeth was responding with little imitative movements, arch smiles and gestures. Miriam writhed. Eve
would teach her to see life as people, a few prominent over-
emphasized people in a fixed world. But Elspeth soon broke
away to trot up and down the hearth-rug, and when Gerald
caught and held her, asking, as he puffed at his pipe above her
head, a rallying question about the shop, she stood propped
looking from face to face, testing voices.

The morning had changed to daytime.

Gerald and Eve made busy needless statements, going over
in the form of question and answer the history of the shop, and
things that had been obviously already discussed to exhaustion.
Across Harriett's face, thoughts about Eve and her venture
passed in swift comment on the conversation. Now and again
she betrayed her impatience, leaping out into abrupt ironic
emendations, and presently rose with a gasp, thumping Miriam
gently, 'Come on, you 've got to try on that blouse.' The
colloquy snapped. Eve turned a flushed face and sat back,
looking uneasily into vacancy as if for something she had
forgotten to say.

'Try it on down here,' said Gerald.

'Don't be idiotic.'

'It 's all right. *We* shan't mind. We won't look till she 's
got it on.'

'If you look then, you will be dazzled by my radiance.'
Miriam stood listening in astonishment to the echoes of the
phrase, fashioned from nothing upon her lips by something
within her, unknown, wildly to be welcomed if its power of
using words that left her not merely untouched and unspent,
but taut and invigorated, should prove to be reliable. She
watched the words go forward outside her with a life of their
own, palpable, a golden thread between herself and the world,
the first strand of a bright pattern she and Gerald would weave
from their separate engrossments whenever their lives should
cross. Through Gerald's bantering acknowledgment she gazed
out before her into the future, an endless perspective of blissful
unbroken silence, shielded by the gift of speech. The figure of

Eve, sitting averted towards the fire, flung her back.   To Eve
her words were not silence; but a blow deliberately struck.
With a thrill of sadness she recognized the creative power of
anger.   If she had not been angry with Eve she would have
wondered whether Gerald were secretly amused by her continued interest in blouses, and have fallen stupidly dumb before
the need of explaining, as her mind now rapidly proceeded to
do, cancelling her sally as a base foreign achievement, that her
interest was only a passing part of holiday relaxation, to be
obliterated to-morrow by the renewal of a life that held everything he thought she was missing, in a way and with a quality
new and rich beyond anything he could dream, and contemplating these things, would have silently left him with his
judgment confirmed.   She had moved before Gerald, safely
ensphered in the life of words, and in the same movement was
departing now, on the wings of Harriett's rush, a fiend denying
her kindred.

Running upstairs, she reflected that if the finished blouse
suited her it was upon Eve that it would most powerfully cast
its spell.   The shoulders had been good.   Defects in the other
parts could not spoil them, and the squareness of her shoulders
was an odd thing for which she was not responsible.   Eve
only admired them because hers sloped.   She would come
down again as the gay buffoon Eve used to know, letting the
effect of the blouse be incidental, making to-day to-day, shaking
them all out of the contemplation of circumstances.   She would
give some of her old speeches and musical sketches, if she
could manage to begin when Gerald was not there, and Eve
would laugh till she cried.   No one would guess that she was
buoyed up by her own invisible circumstances, forgotten as she
browsed amongst new impressions, and now returning upon
her moment by moment with accumulated force.   But upstairs,
confronted by Harriett in the summerlit seaside sunshine, she
found the past half-hour between them, pressing for comment,
and they danced, silently confronting each other, dancing and
dancing till they had said their say.

The visit ended in the stillness that fell upon the empty
carriage as the train left the last red-roofed houses behind and

slid out into the open country. She hung for an instant over
the spread of the town, serene unchanging sunlit grey and
brilliant white, green-shuttered and balconied, towards the
sea, warm yellow brick, red-roofed, towards the inland green,
her visit still ahead of her. But the interiors of Eve's dark
little house and Harriett's bright one slipped in between her
and the pictured town, and the four days' succession of incidents overtook her in disorder, playing themselves out, backwards and forwards, singly, in clear succession, two or three
together, related to each other by some continuity of mood
within herself, pell-mell, swiftly interchanging, each scene in
turn claiming the foremost place; moments stood out dark and
overshadowing; the light that flooded the whole strove in vain
to reach these painful peaks. The far-away spring offered a
healing repetition of her visit; but the moments remained immovable. Eve would still be obstinately saying 'the Baws' and
really thinking she knew which side she was on. Wawkup and
Poole Carey. Those were quotations as certainly as were
Eve's newspaper ideas; Wimpole Street quotations. The thing
was that Eve had learned to want to be always in the right and
was not swift enough in gathering things, not *worldly* enough.
The train was rocking and swaying in its rush towards its first
stop. After that the journey would seem only a few minutes,
time passing more and more rapidly, filled with the pressure of
London coming nearer and nearer. But the junction was still
a good way off.

'No. It's nothing of that kind. All Russian students are
like that. They have everything in common. On the inside
of the paper he had written, "It will be unfriendly if it should
occur to you to feel any sentiment of resentment." What could
I do? Oh, yes, they would. A Russian would think nothing
of spending two pounds on chocolate if he wanted to. They
live on bread too, nothing but bread and tea, some of them, for
the sake of being able to work. What I can't make him see is
that although I am earning my living and he is not, he is preparing to earn a much more solid living than I ever shall. He
says he is ashamed to be doing nothing while I am already
independent. The next moment he is indignant that I have

not enough for clothes and food; I have to be absolutely rude to make him let me pay for myself at restaurants. When I say it is worth it and I have enough, much more than thousands of women workers, he is silent with indignation. Then when I say that what is really wrong is that I have been cheated of my student period and ought to be living on somebody as a student, he says, "Pairhaps, but you are in *life*, that is the more important."

'All right, I will ask him. Poor little man. He has spent his Christmas at Tansley Street. He would adore Elspeth; although she is not a "beef-steak." He says there are no children in Europe finer than English children, and will stop suddenly in the middle of a serious conversation to say "Look, look; but *that* is a *real* English beef-steak."'

Harry had partly understood. But she still clung to her private thoughts. Meeting him to-day would not be quite the same as before she had mentioned him to any one. Summoning his familiar form she felt that her talk had been treachery. Yet not to have mentioned him at all felt like treachery too.

'There's quite an interesting Russian at Tansley Street now.' That meant simply nothing at all. Christmas *had* been an interruption. . . . Perhaps something would have happened in his first days of London without her. Perhaps he would not appear this evening.

Back at her work at Wimpole Street, she forgot everything in a sudden glad realization of the turn of the year. The sky was bright above the grey wall opposite her window. Soon there would be bright light on it at five o'clock, daylight remaining to walk home in, then at six, and she would see once more for another year the light of the sun on the green of the park. The alley of crocuses would come again, then daffodils in the grass and the green of the oncoming blue-bells. Her table was littered with newly paid accounts, enough to occupy her pen for the short afternoon with pleasant writing, the reward of the late evenings spent before Christmas in hurrying out overdue statements, and the easy prelude to next week's crowded work on the yearly balance sheets. She sat stamping and signing, and writing picturesque addresses, her eyes dwelling all the while in contemplation of the gift of the outspread year. The patients were few and no calls came from the surgeries. Tea came up while she still felt newly arrived from the outside world, and the outspread scenes in her mind were gleaming still with fresh high colour in bright light, but the last receipt was signed, and a pile of envelopes lay ready for the post.

She welcomed the sound of Mrs Orly's voice, tired and animated at the front door, and rose gladly as she came into the room with little bright broken incoherent phrases, and the bright deep unwearied dauntless look of welcome in her little tired face. She was swept into the den and kept there for a prolonged tea-time, being questioned in detail about her Christmas in Eve's shop, seeing Mrs Orly's Christmas presents and presently moving in and out of groups of people she knew only by name. An extraordinary number of disasters had happened amongst them. She listened without surprise. Always all the year round these people seemed to live under the shadow of impending troubles. But Mrs Orly's dolorous list made Christmas seem to be, for them, a time devoted to the happening of things that crashed down in their midst, dealing out lifelong results. Mrs Orly talked rapidly, satisfied with gestures of sympathy, but Miriam was conscious that her sympathy was not falling where it was demanded. She watched the family centres unmoved, her mind hovering over their imagined houses, looking regretfully at the shattered whole, the views from their windows that belonged to the past and were suddenly strange, as when they had first seen them; passing on to their servants and friends and outwards into their social life, following results as far as she could, the principal sufferers impressing her all the time in the likeness of people who suddenly make avoidable disturbances in the midst of a conversation. Driven back, from the vast questioning silence at the end of her outward journey, to the centres of Mrs Orly's pictures, she tried to dwell sympathetically with the stricken people and fled aghast before their inexorable circumstances. They were all so hemmed in, so closely grouped that they had no free edges, and were completely,

III—* D

publicly, at the mercy of the things that happened. Every one in social life was aware of this. Experienced people said 'there is always *something*,' 'a skeleton in every cupboard.' . . . But why did people get into cupboards? Something or someone was to blame. In some way that pressed through the picture now in one form and now in another, just eluding expression in any single statement she could frame, these bright-looking lives, free of all that civilization had to offer, were all to blame; all facing the same way, unaware of anything but the life they lived among themselves, they *made* the shadow that hung over them all; they invited its sudden descents. . . . She felt that her thoughts were cruel; like an unprovoked blow, worthy of instant revenge by some invisible observant third party; but even while in the presence of Mrs Orly's sympathy she accused herself of heartlessness and strove to retreat into a kindlier outlook, she was aware, moving within her conviction, of some dim shape of truth that no sympathy could veil.

At six o'clock the front door closed behind her, shutting her out into the multitudinous pattering of heavy rain. With the sight of the familiar street shortened by darkness to a span lit faintly by dull rain-shrouded lamps, her years of daily setting forth into London came about her more clearly than ever before as a single unbroken achievement. Jubilantly she reasserted, facing the invitation flowing towards her from single neighbourhoods standing complete and independent, in inexhaustibly various loveliness through the procession of night and day, linked by streets and by-ways living in her as mood and reverie, that to have the freedom of London was a life in itself. Incidents from Mrs Orly's conversation, pressing forward through her outcry, heightened her sense of freedom. If the sufferers were her own kindred, if disaster threatened herself, walking in London, she would pass into that strange familiar state, where all clamourings seemed unreal, and on in the end into complete forgetfulness.

Two scenes flashed forth from the panorama beyond the darkness, and while she glanced at the vagrants stretched asleep on the grass in the Hyde Park summer, carefully to be skirted and yet most dreadfully claiming her companionship, she saw, narrow and gaslit, the little unlocated street that had haunted her first London years, herself flitting into it, always unknowingly, from a maze of surrounding streets, feeling uneasy, recognizing it, hurrying to pass its awful centre where she must read the name of a shop, and, dropped helplessly into the deepest pit of her memory, struggle on through thronging images threatening, each time more powerfully, to draw her willingly back and back through the intervening spaces of her life to some deserved destruction of mind and body, until presently she emerged faint and quivering, in a wide careless thoroughfare. She had forgotten it; perhaps somehow learned to avoid it. Her imagined figure passed from the haunted scene, and from the vast spread of London the tide flowed through it, leaving it a daylit part of the whole, its spell broken and gone.

She struggled with her stiffly opening umbrella, listening joyfully to the sound of the London rain. She asked nothing of life but to stay where she was, to go on. . . . London was her pillar of cloud and fire, undeserved, but unsolicited, life's free gift. In still exultation she heard her footsteps go down into the street and along the streaming pavement. The light from a lamp just ahead fell upon a figure, plunging in a swift diagonal across the muddy roadway towards her. He had come to meet her . . . invading her street. She fled exasperated, as she slackened her pace, before this postponement of her meeting with London, and silently drove him off, as he swept round to walk at her side, asking him how he dared unpermitted to bring himself, and the evening, and the evening mood, across her inviolable hour. His overcoat was grey with rain and, as she glanced, he was scanning her silence with that slight quivering of his features. Poor brave little lonely man. He had spent his Christmas at Tansley Street.

'Well? How was it?' he said. He was a jailer, shutting her in.

'Oh, it was all right.'

'Your sisters are well? Ah I *must* tell you,' his voice boomed confidently ahead into the darkness; 'while I waited, I have seen two of your doctors.'

'They are not doctors.'

'I had an immensely good impression. I find them both most fine English types.'

'H'm; they're absolutely English.' She saw them coming out, singly, preoccupied, into their street. English. He, standing under his lamp, a ramshackle foreigner whom they might have regarded with suspicion, taking them in with a flash of his prepared experienced brown eye.

'Abso-lutully. This unmistakable expression of humanity and fine sympathetic intelligence. Ah, it is fine.'

'I *know*. But they have very simple minds, they quote their opinions.'

'I do not say that you will find in the best English types a striking originality of *mentality*,' he exclaimed reproachfully. Her attention pounced unwillingly upon the promised explanation of her own impressions, tired in advance at the prospect of travelling through his carefully pronounced sentences while the world she had come out to meet lay disregarded all about her. 'But you will find what is perhaps more important, the characteristic features of your English civilization.'

'I know. I can *see* that; because I am neither English nor civilized.'

'That is a nonsense. You are most English. No, but it is really most wonderful,' his voice dropped again to reverence and she listened eagerly, 'how in your best aristocracy and in the best types of professional men, your lawyers and clerics and men of science, is to be read so strikingly this history of your nation. There is a something common to them all that shines out, durchleuchtend, showing, sometimes, understand me, with almost a naïvety, the centuries of your freedom. Ah, it is not for nothing that the word gentleman comes from England.'

'I know, I know what you mean,' said Miriam in contemplation. They *were* naïve; showing their thoughts, in sets, readable, with shapes and edges, but it was the Tories and clerics who had the roomiest, most sympathetic expressions, liberals and nonconformists had no thoughts at all, only ideas. Lawyers had no ideas even. . . .

'You would like my father; he hasn't a scrap of originality, only that funny old-fashioned English quality from somewhere or other heaven knows' . . . and they could play chess together! . . . 'But lawyers are not gentlemen. They are perfectly awful.'

'That is a prejudice. Your English law is the very basis of your English freedom.'

'They are awful. The others look Christians. They *don't*.' Fancy defending Christianity. . . . 'The thing you are seeing is Christianity. I don't mean that there is anything in it; but Christian ideas have made English civilization: that's what it is. But how can you say all these things when you believe we are grabbing diamond mines?' Haw, *what?* Champagne and grand pianos. Nice, jolly prejudiced *simpletons*; not even able to imagine that England ought not to have everything there was to be had, everywhere. Quite right, better for everybody . . . but . . . wir reiten, Pieter, reiten . . . oh Lord . . . *who* was right?

'Stop a bit, stop a bit. Christianity will not explain. There are other Christian countries where there is no sign of this thing that is in England. No. The explanation is very simple. It is that you have had in England through a variety of causes, not the least of which is your Protestant Reformation, a relatively very rapid and unrestricted *secular* development.'

'What about Germany and Holland?'

'Both quite different stories. There was in England a specially favourable gathering of circumstances for rapid secularistic development.'

'Then if we have been made by our circumstances it is no credit to us.'

'I have not said anything about *credit*.'

'But there are people now who think we are dying of the Reformation; not the break with Rome; but with Catholic history and tradition. No, wait a minute, it's interesting. They have discovered, *proved*, that there was Christianity in Britain, and British Christian Churches, long before the Romans came. That means that we are as old, and as direct as Rome. The Pope is nothing but a Roman bishop. I feel it is an immense relief, to know we go right back, *ourselves*; when I think of it.'

'All these clericalisms are immaterial to *life*.'

'Then there were two Popes at one time, and there is the Greek Church. I wonder Newman didn't think of that. Now *he* is one of your fine English types, although he looks scared, as if he had seen a ghost. If he had known about the early British Church perhaps he would not have gone over to Rome.'

'I cannot follow all this. But what is indisputable is, that in every case of religious authority, secular development has been held back. Your Buckle has completely demonstrated this in a most masterly exhaustive consideration of the civilizations of Europe. Ah, it is *marvellous*, this book, one of your finest decorations; and without any smallest touch of fanaticism; he is *indeed* perhaps one of your greatest minds of the best English type, full of sensibility and fine gentleness.'

Miriam was back, as she listened, in the Chiswick villa, in bed in the yellow lamp-light with a cold, the pages of the *Apologia* reading themselves without effort into her molten mind, as untroubled beauty and happiness, making what Newman sought seem to be at home in herself, revealing deep inside life a whole new strange place of existence that was yet familiar, so that the gradual awful gathering of his trouble was a personal experience, and the moment of conviction that schism was a deliberate death, a personal conviction. She wondered why she always forgot that the problem had been solved. Glancing beyond the curve of her umbrella she caught, with his last words, the sudden confident grateful shining of Mr Shatov's lifted face and listened eagerly.

'It is this one thing——' She lifted the umbrella his way in sudden contrition, shifting it so that it sheltered neither of them. 'Thank you, I am quite well. It is hardly now raining,' he muttered at his utmost distance of foreign intonation and bearing. She peered out into the air, shutting her umbrella. They had come out of their way, away from the streets into a quietness. It must be the Inner Circle. They would have to walk right round it.

'It is this one thing'—again it was as if her own voice were speaking—'this thesis of the *conditions* of the development of peoples'—Anglican priests *married*; but not the highest high Anglican. But they were always going over to Rome — 'that has made your Buckle so precious to the Russian intelligentsia. In England he is scarcely now read, though I have seen by the way his works in this splendid little edition of World Classics, the same as your Emerson; why did you take only Emerson? There is a whole row, the most fascinating things.'

'My Emerson was given to me. I didn't know it came from anywhere in particular.'

'This Richards must be a most enlightened publisher. I should wish to possess all those volumes. The Buckle I will certainly take at once and you shall see. He is of course out of date in the matter of exact science and this is no doubt part reason why in England he is no more read. It is a great pity. His mind is perhaps greater than even your Darwin, certainly with a far wider philosophical range, and of *far* greater originality. What is wonderful is his actual anticipation, in idea, without researches, of a large part of what Darwin discovered more accidentally, as a result of his immense naturalistic researches.'

'Someone will discover some day that Darwin's conclusions were wrong, that he left out some little near obvious thing with big results, and his theory, which has worried thousands of people nearly to death, will turn out to be one of those everlasting mannish explanations of everything which explain nothing. I know what you are going to say; a subsequent reversal of a doctrine does not invalidate scientific method. I know. But these everlasting theories, and men are so "eminent" and important about them, are appalling; in medicine, it is simply *appalling*, and people are just as ill as ever; and when they know Darwin was mistaken, there will be an end of Herbert Spencer. There's my father, really an intelligent man, he has done scientific research himself and knew Faraday, and he thinks *First Principles* the greatest book that was ever written. I have argued and argued but he says he is too old to change his cosmos. It makes me simply ill to think of him living in a cosmos made by Herbert Spencer.'

'*Wait*. Excuse me, but that is all too easy. In matter of science the conclusions of Darwin will *never* be displaced. It is the alphabet of biology, as Galilei is of astronomy. More. These researches even need not be made again. They are for all time verified. Herbert Spencer, I agree, has carried too far in too wholesale a manner conclusions based on Darwin's discoveries; conclusions may lead to many inapplicable theories. That is immaterial. But Darwin himself made no such theories. There is no question of *opinion* as to his discoveries; he supplies simply unanswerable *facts*.

'I think it's Huxley who makes me angry with Darwinism. He didn't find it out, and he went swaggering about using it as a weapon; *frightfully* conceited about it. That Thomas Henry Huxley should come off best in an argument was quite as important to him as spreading the Darwinian theory. I *never* read anything like his accounts of his victories in his letters.'

'That is most certainly not the spirit of Darwin, who was a most gentle creature. But you really surprise me in your attitude towards the profession of law.'

'I don't know anything whatever about laws; but I have met lawyers, barristers and solicitors, and I think they are the most ignorant, pig-headed people in the world. They have no minds at all. They don't affect *me*. But if I were ever before a judge, I should shoot him. They use cases to show off their silly wit, sitting thinking of puns; and people are put to death.'

'You are in this matter both prejudiced and unjust, believe me. You cannot in any case make individuals responsible in this matter of capital punishment. That is for all humanity. I see you are like myself, a dreamer. But it is bad to let what might be, blind you to *actuality*. To the great actuality, in this case, that in matters of justice between man and man *England* has certainly led the civilized world. In France, it is true, there is a certain special generosity towards certain types of provoked crime; but France has not the large responsibilities of England. The idea of abstract justice is stronger in England than anywhere. But what you do not see is that in confessing ignorance of your law you pay it the highest possible tribute.

You do not know what individual liberty is because you know nothing of any other condition. Ah you cannot conceive what strangeness and wonder there is for a Russian in this spectacle of a people so free that they hold their freedom as a matter of course.'

Decked. Distinguished. Marked among the nations, for unconscious qualities. What *is* England? What do the qualities mean?

'I 'm not interested in laws. If I knew what they were I should like to break them. "Trespassers will be prosecuted" always makes me furious.'

'That is merely a technical by-law. That is just one of your funny English high-churchishnesses, this trespassers . . . ah, I must tell you I was just now in the Hyde Park. There was a meeting, ah, it was indeed wonderful to me all these people freely gathered together! There was some man addressing them, I could not hear, but suddenly a man near me on the outskirt of the crowd shouted in full voice, 'Chamberlain is a damned *liar*!' Yes, but wait for your English laughter. That is not the whole. There was also quite near me, a very big John Bull *bobby*. He turned to pass on, with a *smile*. Ah that indeed for a Russian was a most *wonderful* spectacle.'

'We ought to be hurrying,' said Miriam, burning with helpless pity and indignation, 'you will be late for dinner.'

'That is true. Shall you not also take dinner? Or if you prefer we can dine elsewhere. The air is most pure and lovely. We are in some park?'

'Regent's Park,' she said hastily, breathing in its whole circumference, her eyes passing, through the misty gloom, amongst daylit pictures of every part. He had not known even where he was; completely foreign, a mind from an unknown world, obliviously at her side. A headlong urgency possessed her; the coming back to London had not yet been; perhaps this time she would miss it; already she was tired with thought and speech. Incoherently improvising an appointment, she hurried along, her mind set excitedly towards Tansley Street. There was always some new thing waiting there when she returned from an absence; she could hear about it and get over her greetings and out for an hour by herself. She increased her pace until Mr Shatov panted for breath as he plunged along by her side. The random remarks she made to cover her thoughts hurtled about in the darkness, stabbing her with vindictive unhelpful comments on her English stiffness, embarrassing her gait and increasing her angry fatigue. He responded in breathless shouts, as if they were already in the crowded streets. They reached pavement, big houses loomed up out of the mist, the gates were just ahead. 'We had better rather at once take an omnibus,' he shouted as they emerged into the Euston Road and a blue umbrella bus passed heavily by. She hurried forward to catch it at the corner. 'That goes only to *Gower* Street,' thundered his following voice. She was in amongst the crowd at the corner and as again the bus lumbered off, inside it in the one remaining seat.

In the dimly lit little interior, moving along through the backward flowing mist-screened street lights, she dropped away from the circling worlds of sound, and sat thoughtless, gazing inward along the bright kaleidoscopic vistas that came unfailing and unchanged whenever she was moving, alone and still, against the moving tide of London. When the bus pulled up for a moment in a block, she searched the gloom-girt forms within her view. The blue light of the omnibus lamp lit up faces entangled in visible thoughts, unwillingly suffering the temporary suspension of activity, but in the far corner there was one, alive and aware, gazing untrammelled at visions like her own, making them true, the common possession of all who would be still. Why were these people only to be met in omnibuses and now and again walking sightless along crowded streets? Perhaps in life they were always surrounded by people with whom they did not dare to be still. In speech that man would be a little defensive and cynical. He had a study, where he went to get away from everything, to work; sometimes he only pretended to work. He did not guess that any one outside books, certainly not any *women* anywhere . . . the bus rumbled on again; by the time it reached Gower Street she had passed through thoughtless ages. The brown house, and her room in it, called to her recreated. Once through the greetings awaiting her, she would be free upstairs amongst its populous lights and shadows; perhaps get in unseen and keep her visions untouched through the evening. She would have an evening's washing and ironing. Mr Shatov would not expect her to-night.

Mrs Bailey, hurrying through the hall to dinner, came forward dropping bright quiet cries of welcome from the edge of her fullest mood of excited serenity, gently chiding Miriam's inbreaking expectant unpreparedness with her mysterious gradual way of imparting bit by bit, so that it was impossible to remember how and when she had begun, the new thing; lingering silently at the end of her story to disarm objections before she turned and flitted, with a reassuring pleading backward smile, into her newly crowded dining-room. A moment later Miriam was in the drawing-room, swiftly consulting the profile of a tweed-clad form bent busily writing at the little table under the gas. The man leapt up and faced her with a swift ironic bow, strode to the hearth-rug and began to speak. She remained rooted in the middle of the room, amplifying her impression as his sentence went on, addressed not to her, though he occasionally flung a cold piercing glance her way, but to the whole room, in a high, narrowly rounded, fluting tone as if he were speaking into a cornet. His head had gone up above the level of the brighter light but it looked even more greyish yellow than before, the sparse hair, the eyes, the abruptly branching moustache moving most remarkably with his fluting voice, the pale tweed suit, all one even yellowish grey, and his whole reared-up, half soldierly form, at bay, as if the room were full of jeering voices. His long declamation contained all that Mrs Bailey had said and told her also that the lecture was about Spanish literature. London was extraordinary. A Frenchman, suddenly giving a lecture in English on Spanish literature; at the end of next week. He wound up his tremendous sentence by telling her that she was a secretary, and must excuse his urgency, that he required the services of an English secretary and would now, with her permission, read the first part of the lecture, that she might tell him whenever his intonation was at fault. That would be *immensely* interesting and easy she thought, and sat down on the music stool while he gathered up his sheaf of papers and explained that intonation was the always neglected corner-stone of the mastery of a foreign tongue.

In a moment he was back again on the hearth-rug, beginning his lecture in a tone that was such an exaggeration of his conversational voice, so high-pitched and whistlingly rounded, so extremely careful in enunciation that Miriam could hear nothing but a loud thin hooting, full of the echoes of the careful beginnings and endings of English words.

The first sentence was much longer than his address to her and, when it ended, she did not know how or where to begin. But he had taken a step forward on the hearth-rug and begun another sentence, on a higher pitch, with a touch of anger in his voice. She checked a spasm of laughter and sat tense, trying to ignore the caricature of his style that gambolled in her mind. The sentence, even longer than the first, ended interrogatively with a fling of the head. It was *tragic*. She was quick, quicker than any one she knew, in catching words or meanings through strange disguises. An audience would be either furious or hysterical.

'You don't want to *threaten* your audience,' she said very quietly in a low tone, hoping by contrast to throw up his clamour.

'I dew not threaten,' he said with suave patience, 'doubtless hew are misled. It is a great occasion; and a great subject; of hwich I am master; in these circumstances a certain bravura is imperative. Hew du not propose that I should *plead* for Cervantes for example? I will continue.'

The sentences grew in length, each one climbing, through a host of dependent clauses, small sharp hammer blows of angry assertion, and increasing in tone to a climax of defiance flung down from a height that left no further possibility but a descent to a level quiet deduction . . . and *now*, dear brethren. . . . But the succeeding sentence came fresh to the attack, crouching, gathering up the fury of its forerunner, leaping forward, dipping through still longer dependent loops, accumulating,. swelling and expanding to even greater emphasis and volume.

She gave up all hope of gathering even the gist of the meaning; he seemed to be saying one thing over and over again. You protest too much. Don't *protest*; don't *gesticulate*. The English don't gesticulate. But he used no gesticulations; he was aware; that was a deliberate attempt to be English. But his whole person was a gesture, expanding, vibrating.

'You mean, by intonation, only the intonation of single words, not of the whole?'

'Precisely. Correctness of accent and emphasis is my aim. But you imply a criticism,' he fluted, unshaken by his storm.

'Yes. First you must not pronounce each word quite so carefully. It makes them *echo* into each other. Then of course if you want to be quite English you must be less emphatic.'

'I must assume an air of indifference?'

'An English audience will be more likely to understand if you are slower and more quiet. You ought to have gaps now and then.'

'Intervals for yawning. Yew shall indicate suitable moments. I see that I am fortunate to have met-hew. I will take lessons, for this lecture, in the true frigid English dignity.'

The door opened, admitting Mr Shatov.

'Mr—a—Shatov; will be so good; as to grant five minutes; for the conclusion of this interview.' He walked forward bowing with each phrase, hiding the intruder and bowing him out of the room. The little dark figure reappeared punctually, and he rose with a snap of the fingers. 'The English,' he declaimed at large, 'have an excellent phrase; hwich says, time is money. This phrase, good though it is, might be improved. Time is let out on usury. So, for the present, I shall leave hew.' He turned on the sweeping bow that accompanied his last word and stepped quickly with a curious stiff marching elegance down the room towards Mr Shatov as though he did not see him, avoiding him at the last moment by a sharp curve. Outside the closed door he rattled the handle as if to make sure it was quite shut.

Miriam sought intently for a definition of what had been in the room . . . a strange echoing shadow of some real thing . . . there was something real . . . just behind the empty sound of him . . . somewhere in the rolled-up manuscript so remarkably in her hands, making a difference in the evening brought in by Mr Shatov. Hunger and fatigue were assailing her; but the long rich day mounting up to an increasing sense of incessant life crowding upon her unsought, at her disposal, could not be snapped by retirement for a solitary meal. He walked quickly to the hearth-rug, bent forward and spat into the empty grate.

'*What* is this fellow?'

She broke through her frozen astonishment. 'I have just undertaken a perfectly frightful thing,' she said, quivering with disgust.

'I find him insufferable.'

'The French sing their language. It is like a recitative, the tone goes up and down and along and up and down again with its own expression; the words have to fit the tune. They have no single abrupt words and phrases, the whole thing is a *shape* of *tones*. It's extraordinary. All somehow arranged; in a pattern; different patterns for the expression of the different emotions. In their English it makes the expression swallow up the words, a wind driving through them continuously . . . liaison.'

'It is a musical tongue certainly.'

'That's it; music. But the individual is not there; because the tunes are all arranged for him and he sings them, according to rule. The Academy. The purity of the French language. I'm getting so interested.'

'I find this Lahitte a most *pretentious* fellow.'

'He is not in the least what I expected a Frenchman to be like. I can't understand his being so fair.'

'What is it you have undertaken?'

He was suddenly grave and impressed by the idea of the lecture . . . why would it be such good practice for her to read and correct it?

Her answer plunged him into thought from which he branched forth with sudden eagerness . . . a French translation of a Russian book revealing marvellously the interior, the self-life, of a doctor, through his training and experience in

practice. It would be a revelation to English readers and she
should translate it; in collaboration with him; if she would
excuse the intimate subjects it necessarily dealt with. He was
off and back again with the book and reading rapidly while
she still pondered his grave enthusiasm over her recent undertaking. In comparison with this idea of translating a book, it
seemed nothing. But that was only one of his wild notions.
It would take years of evenings of hard work. Meanwhile
someone else would do it. They would work at it together.
With Saturdays and Sundays it would not take so long. It
would set her standing within the foreign world she had
touched at so many points during the last few years, and that
had become, since the coming of Mr Shatov, more and more
clearly a continuation of the first beginnings at school. . . .
Alors un faible chuchotement se fit entendre au premier . . .
à l'entrée de ce bassin, des arbres . . . se fit entendre . . .
alors un faible chuchotement se fit entendre . . . all one word
on one tone . . . it must have been an extract from some dull
mysterious story with an explanation, or deliberately without
an explanation; then a faint whispering was audible on the
first floor; that was utterly different. It was the shape and
sound of the sentences, without the meaning, that was so
wonderful—alors une faible parapluie se fit entendre au
premier—Jan would scream, but it was just as wonderful.
There must be some meaning in having so passionately loved
the little book without having known that it was selections
from French prose; in getting to Germany and finding there
another world of beautiful shape and sound, apart from
people and thoughts and things that happened . . . Durch
die ganze lange Nacht, bis tief in den Morgen hinein . . . it
was opening again, drawing her in away from the tuneless,
shapeless——

'Are you listening?'

'Yes, but it hasn't begun.'

'That is true. We can really omit all this introduction and
at once begin.'

As the pages succeeded each other, her hunger and fatigue
changed to a fever of anxious attention.

'Well? Is not that a masterly analysis? You see. That should be translated for your Wimpole Street.'

'I don't know. We are not like that. It would never occur to an English doctor to write for the general public anything that could shake its confidence in doctors. Foreigners are different. They think nothing of revealing and discussing the most awful things. It's pessimism. They *like* pessimism.'

'It is a serious mistake to regard enlightenment as pessimism.'

'I don't believe in continental luminaries.'

'Your prejudices are at least frank.'

'I had forgotten the author was Russian. That idea of the rush of mixed subjects coming to the medical student too quickly one after the other for anything to be taken in, is awful, and perfectly true. Hosts of subjects, hosts of different theories about all of them; no general ideas. Doctors have to specialize when they are boys and they remain ignorant all their lives.'

'This is not only for doctors. You have touched the great problem of modern life. No man can, to-day, see over the whole field of knowledge. The great Leibniz was the last to whom this was possible.'

To be ignorant always, knowing one must die in ignorance. What was the use of going on? Life looked endless. Suddenly it would seem short. 'Wait till you're fifty and the years pass like weeks.' You would begin to see clearly all round you the things you could never do. Never go to Japan. Already it was beginning. No college. No wanderjahre. Translating books might lead to wanderjahre.

'It's certainly a book that ought to be translated.' At least there could be no more 'eminent men.' There might always be someone at work somewhere who would suddenly knock him down like a ninepin.

'Well, you shall see. I will read you a passage from later, that you may judge whether you will care. I must tell you it deals of intimate matters. You must excuse.'

It was not only that he thought she might object. He also realized that the English reserves between them were being swept away. It was strange that a free Russian should have these sensibilities. He read his extract through, bringing it to a close in shaken tones, his features sensitively working.

Every one ought to know. It ought to be shouted from the house-tops that a perfectly ordinary case leaves the patient sans connaissance et nageant dans le sang.

'It 's very interesting,' she said hurriedly, 'but in English it would be condemned as unsuitable for general reading.'

'I thought that possible.'

'The papers would solemnly say that it deals with subjects that are better veiled.'

'Indeed it is remarkable. John Bull is indeed the perfect ostrich.'

'Oh, those men who write like that don't want them veiled from *themselves*.'

'I will tell you more than that. The Paris pornographia *lives* on its English patrons.'

'Oh, no; I 'm sure it doesn't.'

'On the contrary I assure you this is a fact. Any French bookseller will tell you. I see that this distresses you. It is not perhaps in every case so base as would appear. There is always even in quite deliberate French obscenity a certain *esprit*. These subjects lend themselves.'

'Oh, they don't care about the esprit. It 's because they think they are being improper. They like to be what they call men of the world, in possession of a fund of things they think can't be talked about; you can see their silly thoughts by the way they glance at each other; it 's all about nothing. What *is* obscenity? And the other half of them is *ladies*, who shout things by always carefully avoiding them; or, if they are 'racy,' flatter men's topics by laughing in a pretended hilarious embarrassment, hitting them as it were, and rushing on to something else, very animated by a becoming blush. I never realized that before. But that 's the secret. What *is* obscenity?'

'You have touched a most interesting problem of psychology.'

'Besides, Paris is full of Americans.'

'It is the same proposition. They are the cousins of the English.'

'I think the American "man of the world" is much more

objectionable. He is so horribly raw that he can't help boasting openly, and the American woman flatters him, openly. It's extraordinary. I mean the kind of heavy-featured fat middle-aged American woman who doesn't smoke and thinks that voting would be unseemly for women. It used to make me simply ill with fury. Dr Bunyan Hopkinson's brother came over for July and August two years ago. He was appalling. With a bright fair beard, and a most frightful twang; the worst I've ever heard. He used to talk incessantly, as if the whole table were waiting for his ideas. And knew everything, in the most awful superficial newspaper way. They have absolutely no souls at all. I never saw an American soul. The Canadians have. The Americans, at least the women, have reproachful ideals that they all agree about. So that they are all like one person; all the same effect. But wasn't it *screaming*? Bunyan Hopkinson's brother was called *Bacchus*. Yes. Did you ever hear anything so screaming? Isn't that enough? Doesn't it explain everything? He was a doctor too. He sat next to an elderly woman who was always scolding and preaching. She had an enormous American figure, and Guelph eyelids and Guelph cheeks coming down below her chin making great lengthways furrows on either side of it. But when Dr Bacchus began to talk about Paris she would listen respectfully. He used always to be offering to show other men round Paris. "There's no one alive," he would say, "can show me anything in Parrus night-life I've not seen." "*Ah*," she would say, "any one can see you're a man of the *world*, doctor." It spoils the very idea of those little cabarets and whatever awful haunts there may be in Paris to think of Americans there, seeing *nothing*.'

'They have certainly a most remarkable naïvety.'

'"I've to-day seen your queen. She's just a vurry *hoamely* little old lady."'

'What? What is that?'

'Then they *were* funny.' She searched her memory to make him go on giggling. It was extraordinary, too, to discover what impressions she had gathered without knowing it, never considering or stating them to herself. He was getting them. If she ever stated them again they would be stale; practised clever talk; *that* was how talk was done . . . saying things over and over again to numbers of people, each time a little more brilliantly and the speaker a little more dead behind it. Nothing could be repeated.

'That was the same year. Mrs Bailey had a splendid August. Eighteen Americans. I used to go down to meals just to be in the midst of the noise. You never heard anything like it in your life. If you listened without trying to distinguish anything it was *marvellous*, in the bright sunshine at breakfast. It sent you up and up, into the sky, the morning stars singing together. *No.* I mean there was something *really* wonderful about it. It reminded me of the effect that almost comes when people decide to have a Dutch concert. You know. All singing different songs at the same time. It's *always* spoilt. People begin it prepared not to hear the whole effect. I did. I did not realize there would be a wonderful whole. And always just as the effect is beginning, two or three people break down because they cannot hold their songs, and some laugh because they are prepared only to laugh, and the unmusical people put their fingers to their ears, because they can never hear *sound*, never anything but a tune. Oh, it would be so wonderful, if only it could be really *held*, every one singing for all they were worth.'

'Have you heard that the Shah preferred of a whole concert, only the tuning of the orchestra?'

'I know. That's always supposed to be a joke. But the tuning of an orchestra, if there is enough of it at once, *is* wonderful. Why not *both*? It's the appalling way people have of liking only one thing. Liking "good" music and disapproving of waltzes. The Germans don't.

'But when I thought of one of my sisters, I used to want to die. If she had been there we should both have yelled, without moving a muscle of our faces. Harriett is perfect for that. We learnt it in church. But when she used to twist all the fingers of her gloves into points, under the seat, and then show them to me suddenly, in the Litany . . .'

'What? What is this? No. Tell me. You were very happy with your sisters.'

'That's all.   She waggled them, suddenly.'

'A happy childhood is perhaps the *most*-fortunate gift in life.'

'You don't know you 're happy.'

'That is not the point.   This early surrounding lingers and affects all the life.'

'It 's not quite true that you don't know.   Because you know when you are quite young how desperately you love a place. The day we left our first home I remember putting marbles in my pocket in the nursery, not minding, only thinking I should take them out again by the *sea*, and downstairs in the garden I suddenly realized, the sun was shining on to the porch and bees swinging about amongst the roses, and I ran back and kissed the warm yellow stone of the house, sobbing most bitterly and knowing my life was at an end.'

'But you were six years old.   That is what is important. You do not perhaps realize the extent of the remaining of this free life of garden and woods with you.'

'I know it is there.   I often dream I am there and wake there, and for a few minutes I could draw the house, the peaked shapes of it, and the porches and french windows and the way the lawns went off into the mysterious parts of the garden; and I feel then as if going away were still to come, an awful thing that had never happened.   Of course after the years in the small house by the sea, I don't remember the house, only the sea and the rocks, the house at Barnes grew in a way to be the same, but I never got over the suddenness of the end of the garden and always expected it to branch out into distances, every time I ran down it.   I used to run up and down to make it more.'   He was no longer following with such an intentness of interest.   There ought to have been more about those first years.   Now, no one would ever know what they had been.

'But you know, although nothing the Americans say is worth hearing, there is something wonderful about the way they go on.   The way they all talk at once, nobody listening. It 's because they all know what they are going to say and every one wants to say it first.   They used to talk in parties; a set of people at one part of the table all screaming together towards a set at another part, and other people screaming across them at another set. The others began screaming back at once, endless questions, and if two sets had seen the same thing they all screamed together as soon as it was mentioned. I never heard one person talking alone; not in that August set. And there was one woman, a clergyman's wife, with a little pretty oval face and the most perfect muslin dresses which she did not appreciate, who used to begin as soon as she came in and go on right through the meal, filling up the gaps in her talk with gasps and exclamations. Whenever any place was mentioned she used to turn and put her hand over her husband's mouth till she had begun what she wanted to say, jumping up and down in her chair.'

'Is it *possible*?'

'I know now why they all have such high piercing voices. It comes from talking in sets. But I always used to wonder what went on behind; in their own minds.'

'Do not wonder. There is no arrière-boutique in these types. They are most simple.'

'They don't like us. They think we are frigid; not cordial, is one of their phrases.'

'That is a most superficial judgment. Stay! I have a splendid idea. We will leave for the present this large book. But why should you not immediately translate a story of Andreyeff? They are quite short and most beautiful. You will find them unlike anything you have read. I have them here. We will at once read one.'

'I must go out; it will soon be too late.'

'You have had no dinner? Ach, that is *monstrous*. Why did you not tell me? It is half eleven. There is yet time. We will go to my dumme August in the East End.'

In her room, Miriam glanced at the magic pages, hungrily gathering German phrases, and all the way to Aldgate, sitting back exhausted in her corner she clung to them, resting in a 'Stube' with 'Gebirge' all round it in morning and evening light. When they reached their destination she had forgotten she was in London. But the station was so remote and unknown to her that it scarcely disturbed her detachment. The wide thoroughfare into which they emerged was still and serene within its darkness behind the spread veil of street sounds, filled with the pure sweet air of adventure. The restaurant across the road was a little square of approaching golden light. It was completely strange. There was a tang of coarse tobacco in the air, but not the usual restaurant smell. There were no marble-topped tables; little square wooden-legged tables, with table-covers of red and blue chequered cotton; pewter flagons, foreigners, Germans, sturdy confident Germans sitting about. It was Germany.

'Well? Is it not perfectly dumme August?' whispered Mr Shatov as they took an empty corner table, commanding the whole room. There was a *wooden* partition behind them, giving out life. Her fatigue left her.

'Für mich ist es absolut als wär ich in Hannover.'

'At least here you shall have an honest meal. Kellner!'

She did not want to eat; only to sit and hear the deep German voices all round her and take in, without observation, kindly German forms.

'Simply you are too tired. We will have at least some strong soup and lager.'

The familiar smooth savoury broth abolished the years since she had left Germany. Once more she was finding the genuine honest German quality reflected in the completeness of their food; all of it, even the bread, savoury and good through and through, satisfying in a way no English food was satisfying, making English food seem poor, ill-combined, either heavy and dull, or too exciting. She saw German kitchens, alles rein und sauber, blank poliert, large bony low-browed angry-voiced German servants in check dresses and blue aprons, everlastingly responsibly at work.

And here was lager, the lager of the booming musical German cafés. She was sure she would not like it. He was taking for granted that she was accustomed to beer, and would not know that she was having a tremendous adventure. To him it did not seem either shocking or vulgar. Protected by his unconsciousness, she would get perhaps further than ever before into the secret of Germany. She took a small sip and shuddered. The foamy surface was pleasant; but the strange biting bitterness behind it was like some sudden formidable personal attack.

'That is the first time I 've tasted beer,' she gasped, 'I don't like it.'

'You have not yet tasted it. You must swallow, not sip.'

'It makes your throat sore. It 's so bitter. I always imagined beer was sweet.'

'There is perhaps something a little acid in this imported lager; but the bitterness is most good. It is this biting quality that is a most excellent apéritif. We will have also honey cakes.'

The light, not too sweet, porous crisp mealiness of the little cakes was German altogether. Mr Shatov was whispering busily. She feared he would be heard. There was not much conversation in the room; large deep solid sentences reverberated through it with a sound of thoughtfulness, as though the speakers were preoccupied, like travellers, talking with their eyes turned inward upon their destination. All of them appeared serious and sober.

'Just as we crossed the frontier, one big fat German roused up and said in an *immense* rolling voice, "Hier kann man wenigstens vernünftiges *Bier* haben!"'

'Ssh! They will hear.'

'What then? They are here nearly all Jews.'

'Jews? But they are nearly all *fair*!'

'There may be a few Germans. But many Jews are fair. But you have not told me what you think of this story.'

'Oh, I can *see* the man and hear his voice.' . . . Nearly all the people in the room were dark. It was the man sitting near, with the large fresh fair German face, who had made her imagine the room was full of Germans. But there were no hooked noses; no one in the least like Shylock. What *were* Jews? How did he know the room was full of them? Why did the idea cast a chill on the things she had brought in with her? She drew the little book from her pocket and took a long draught of lager. It was still bitter, but the bitterness was only an astringent tang in the strange cool lively frothy tide; a tingling warmth ran through her nerves, expanding to a golden glow that flowed through the room and held her alight within itself, an elastic impalpable bodiless mind. Mr Shatov was sitting far away at her side, in his eyes a serene communion with his surroundings. It was not his usual restaurant manner; it was strange. Pewter was right; lager was a bright tumult, frothing and flowing easily over the smooth dull metal.

Translating the phrases made them fall to pieces. She tried several renderings of a single phrase; none of them would do; the original phrase faded and, together with it just beyond her reach, the right English words. Scraps of conversation reached her from all over the room; eloquent words, fashioned easily, without thought, a perfect flowing of understanding, to and fro, without obstruction. No heaven could be more marvellous. People talked incessantly because in silence they were ghosts. A single word sounded the secret of the universe. There is a dead level of intelligence throughout humanity. She listened in wonder whilst she explained aloud that she had learned most of her French by reading again and again for the sake of the long, even rhythm of its sentences, one book; that this was the only honest way to acquire a language. It was like a sea, each sentence a wave rolling in, rising till the light shone through its glistening crest, dropping to give way to the next oncoming wave, the meaning gathering, accumulating, coming nearer with each rising falling rhythm; each chapter a renewed tide, monotonously repeating throughout the book in every tone of light and shade the same burden, the secret of everything in the world.

'I cannot appreciate these literary preciosities; but I am quite sure that you are wrong in confining yourself to this one French book. This mystical philosophy is énervant. There are many French books you should read before this man. Balzac for instance.'

She wanted to explain that she used to read novels but could not get interested in them after Emerson. They showed only one side of people, the outside; if they showed them alone, it was only to explain what they felt about other people. Then he would say Levin, Levin. But she could not attend to all this. What she had meant to say in the beginning, she now explained, was that her German, neglected so long, grew smaller and smaller, whilst, most inconveniently, her reputation for knowing German grew larger and larger. Mr Wilson might have said that. . . .

'The lager is doing you immensely much good.'

Speech did something to things; set them in a mould that was apt to come up again; repeated, it would be dead; but perhaps one need never repeat oneself? To say the same things to different people would give them a sort of fresh life; but there would be death in oneself as one spoke. Perhaps the same thing could be said over and over again, with other things with it, so that it had a different shape, sang a different song and laughed all round itself in amongst different things.

Intoxication. A permanent intoxication in and out amongst life, all the time with an increasing store of good ideas about things; in time, about everything. A slight intoxication began it, making it possible to look at things from a distance, in separate wholes and make discoveries about them. It was being somewhere else, and suddenly looking up, out of completion, at distant things, that brought their meanings and the right words.

'But you must at once finish. They are closing. It is now midnight.'

It did not matter. Nothing was at an end. Nothing would ever come to an end again. She passed, talking emphatically out into the wide dimly-lit sky-filled East End street, and walked unconscious of fatigue, carrying Mr Shatov along at his swiftest plunge, mile after mile, in a straight line westward along the opening avenue of her new permanent freedom from occasions. From detail to detail, snatched swiftly by the slenderest thread of coherence, she passed in easy emphatic talk, covering the bright endless prospect of her contemplation, her voice alive, thrilling with joyful gratitude, quivering now and again as it moved, possessed and controlled by the first faint dawning apprehension of some universal password, from one bright tumultuously branching thing to another, with a gratitude that poured itself out within her in a rain of tears. Mr Shatov followed her swift migrations with solid responsive animation; he seemed for the first time to find no single thing to object to or correct; even restatement was absent, and presently he began to sing.

'It is a Russian song with words of Pushkin and music of Rubinstein. Ah, but it requires Chaliapin. A most profound bass. There is nothing in singing so profoundly moving as pure basso; you should hear him. He stands *alone* in Europe.'

The thronging golden multitudes moved to the tones of this great Russian voice, the deepest in the world, singing out across Europe from beyond Germany. With faltering steps, just begun, whilst now and for ever she passionately brooded on distant things, she was one of this elect shining army 'wandering amongst the mountains, the highest notes if they leap up pure and free, soprano, touch the sky.'

'That is true. But in concerts, the strength and most profound moving quality come from the bass. Ah, you should hear a Russian male choir. There is not in Europe such strength and flexibility and most particularly such marvel of unanimity, making one single movement of phrase in all these many voices together. There is singing in the great Russian churches, all colourful and with a splendour of ornate decoration, singing that the most infidel could not hear unmoved.'

The Russian *voice* was melancholy poetry in itself; somewhere within the shapely rough strength of the words, was a pleading tender melancholy.

The Bloomsbury squares were changed. It was like seeing them for the first time; before they had taken hold; and for the last time, for their spell was turning into memory. Already they were clearly seen backgrounds of which in the cold winter moonlight she could, as her feet, set in a pathway that spread throughout the world, swiftly measured them, coolly observe the varying proportions and character. Offence was removed from the tones of visitors who had in the past, in her dumb outraged presence, taken lightly upon their lips the sacred names. Within them the echo of her song mingled with the silent echoes of the footfalls and voices of these enchanted busy passengers.

CHAPTER IV

It was not only that it was her own perhaps altogether ignorant and lazy and selfish way of reading *everything* so that she grasped only the sound and the character of the words and the arrangement of the sentences, and only sometimes a long time afterwards, and with once-read books never, anything, except in books on philosophy, of the author's meaning . . . but always the author; in the first few lines; and after that, wanting to change him and break up his shape or going about for days thinking everything in his shape.

It was that there was nothing there. If there had been anything, reading so attentively, such an odd subject as Spanish literature, she would have gathered some sort of vague impression. But in all the close pages of cramped cruel pointed handwriting she had gleaned nothing at all. Not a single fact or idea; only Mr Lahitte; a voice like an empty balloon. The lecture was a fraud. *He* was. How far did he know this? Thinking of the audience, those few who could learn quickly enough to follow his voice, waiting and waiting for something but strings of superlatives, the same ones again and again, until the large hall became a prison and the defiant yellow-grey form a tormentor, and their impatience and restlessness turned to hatred and despair, she pitied him. Perhaps he had not read Spanish literature. But he must have consulted numbers of books about it, and that was much more than most people did. But what could she do? She glanced at her little page of notes. Break up sentences. Use participles instead of which. Vary adjectives. Have gaps and pauses here and there. Sometimes begin further off. What is picaresque? They had been written enthusiastically, seeming like inspirations, in the first pages, before she had discovered the whole of the nothingness. Now they were only alterations that were not worth making; helping an imposition and being paid for it.

Stopford Brooke . . . lecturing on Browning . . . blissful moonface with fringe of white hair, talking and talking, like song and prayer and politics, the past and the present showing together, Browning at the centre of life and outside it all over the world, and seeing forward to the future. Perfect quotations, short and long, and the end with the long description of Pompilia . . . rising and spreading and ceasing, not ending . . . standing out alive in the midst of a world still shaped by the same truths going on and on. 'A marvellous piece of analysis.' That young man had been waiting to say that to the other young man.

Introduce their philosophies of life, if any, she wrote; introduce quotations. But there was no time; quotations would have to be translated. Nothing could be done. The disaster was completely arranged. There was no responsibility. She gathered the accepted pages neatly together and began pencilling in improvements.

The pencilled sentences made a pleasant wandering decoration. The earlier ones were forgotten and unfamiliar. Re-read now, they surprised her. How had she thought of them? She had not thought of them. She had been closely following something, and they had come, quietly, in the midst of engrossment; but they were like a photograph, funny in their absurd likeness, set there side by side with the photograph of Mr Lahitte. They were alive, gravely, after the manner of her graver self. It was a curious marvel, a revelation irrevocably put down, reflecting a certain sort of character . . . more oneself than anything that could be done socially, together with others, and yet not oneself at all, but something mysterious, drawn uncalculatingly from some fund of common consent, part of a separate impersonal life she had now unconsciously confessed herself as sharing. She remained bent motionless in the attitude of writing, to discover the quality of her strange state. The morning was raw with dense fog; at her Wimpole Street ledgers she would by this time have been cramped with cold; but she felt warm and tingling with life as if she had been dancing, or for a long while in happy social contact; yet so differently; deeply and serenely alive and without the blank

anxious looking for the continuance of social excitement. This
something would continue, it was in herself, independently.
It was as if there were someone with her in the room, peopling
her solitude and bringing close around her all her past solitudes,
as if it were their secret. They greeted her; justified. Never
again, so long as she could sit at work and lose herself to awake
with the season forgotten and all the circumstances of her life
coming back, as if narrated from the fascinating life of someone
else, would they puzzle or reproach her.

She drew forth her first page of general suggestions, written
so long ago that they already seemed to belong to some younger
self, and copied them in ink. The sound of the pen shattered
the silence like sudden speech. She listened entranced. The
little strange sound was the living voice of the brooding
presence. She copied the phrases in a shape that set them like
a poem in the middle of the page, with even spaces between a
wide uniform margin; not quite in the middle; the lower margin
was wider than the upper; the poem wanted another line. She
turned to the manuscript listening intently to the voice of Mr
Lahitte pouring forth his sentences, and with a joyous rush
penetrated the secret of its style. It was *artificial*. There
was the last line of the poem summing up all the rest. Avoid,
she wrote, searching; some word was coming; it was in her
mind, muffled, almost clear; avoid—it flashed through and
away, just missed. She recalled sentences that had filled her
with hopeless fury, examining them curiously, without anger.
Avoid ornate alias. So *that* was it! Just those few minutes
glancing through the pages, standing by the table while the
patient talked about her jolly, noisy, healthy, thoroughly *wicked*
little kid, and now remembering every point he had made . . .
extraordinary. But this was life! These strange unconsciously noticed things, living on in one, coming together at the
right moment, part of a *reality*.

Rising from the table she found her room strange, the new
room she had entered on the day of her arrival. She remembered drawing the cover from the table by the window and
finding the ink-stains. There they were in the warm bright
circle of midmorning lamplight, showing between the scattered

papers. The years that had passed were a single short interval leading to the restoration of that first moment. Everything they contained centred there; her passage through them, the desperate graspings and droppings, had been a coming back. Nothing would matter now that the paper-scattered lamplit circle was established as the centre of life. Everything would be an everlastingly various joyful coming back. Held up by this secret place, drawing her energy from it, any sort of life would do that left this room and its little table free and untouched.

CHAPTER V

THE spell of the ink-stained table had survived the night. Moving about, preparing for to-day, she turned continually towards the window-space, as to an actual presence, and was answered by the rising within her of a tide of serenity, driving her forward in a stupor of confidence, impervious to strain and pain. It was as if she had entered a companionship that now spread like a shield between her and the life she had so far dealt with unaided.

The week of working days, standing between her and next Sunday's opportunity, was a small space that would pass in a dream; the scattered variously-developing interests of life outside Wimpole Street changed, under her eyes, from separate bewildering competitively attractive scraps of life, to pleasantly related resources, permitted distractions from an engrossment so secure that she could, without fear of loss, move away and forget it.

She felt eager to jest. Ranged with her friends she saw their view of her own perpetually halting scrupulousness and marvelled at their patient loyalty. She shared the exasperated intolerance of people who disliked her. . . . It could be disarmed . . . by fresh, surprising handling. . . . Because, she asked herself scornfully as she opened the door to go downstairs, she had corrected Mr Lahitte's unspeakable lecture? No. Sitting over there, forgetting, she had let go . . . and found something. And waking again had seen distant things in their right proportions. But leaving go, not going through life clenched, would mean losing oneself, passing through, not driving in, ceasing to affect and be affected. But the forgetfulness was itself a more real life, if it made life disappear and then show only as a manageable space and at last only as an indifferent distance. A game to be played, or even not played.

It meant putting life and people second; only entering life to come back again, *always*. This new joy of going into life, the new beauty, on everything, was the certainty of coming back.

She was forgetting something important to the day; the little volume of stories for her coat pocket. Anxiety at her probable lateness tried to invade her as she made her hurried search. She beat it back and departed indifferently, shutting the door of a seedy room in a cheap boarding-house, neither hers nor another's, a lodger's passing abode, but holding a little table that was herself, alive with her life, and whose image sprang, set for the day, centrally into the background of her thoughts as she ran wondering if there were time for breakfast, down to the dining-room. St Pancras clock struck nine as she poured out her tea. Mr Shatov followed up his greeting with an immediate plunge into unfamiliar speech which she realized, in the midst of her wonderment over Mr Lahitte's presence at early breakfast, was addressed to herself. She responded absently, standing at the tea-tray with her toast.

'You do not take your fish? Ah, it is a pity. It is true it has stood since half-nine.'

'Asseyez-vous, mademoiselle. I find; the breakfast hour; *charming*. At this hour one always is, or should be; gay.'

'Mps; if there is time; yes, Sunday breakfast.'

'Still you are gay. That is good. We will not allow philosophy; to darken; these most happy few moments.'

'There are certain *limits* to cheerfulness,' bellowed Mr Shatov. They had had some mighty collision. She glanced round.

'None; within the purview of my modest intelligence; none. Always would I rather be; a cheerful coal-heaver; than a philosopher who is learned, dull, and more depressing than the bise du nord.'

That was meant for Mr Shatov! The pale sensitive features were quivering in control. Her fury changed to joy as she leapt between them, murmuring reflectively but across the table that she agreed, but had met many depressing coal-heavers and knew nothing about philosophers dull or otherwise. In the ensuing comfortable dead silence, she wandered away marvelling at her eloquence. *Cats* said that sort of thing, with disarming smiles. Was that what was called sarcasm? How fearfully funny. She had been sarcastic. To a Frenchman. Perhaps she had learned it from him. Mr Shatov overtook her as she was getting on to a bus at the corner.

'You do not go walkingly?' he bellowed from the pavement. Poor little man; left there with his day and his loneliness till six o'clock.

'All right,' she said, jumping off, 'we'll walk. I'll be late. I don't mind.'

They swept quickly along, looking ahead in silence. Presently he began to sing. Miriam dropped her eyes to the pavement, listening. How unconsciously wise he was. How awful it would have been if she had gone on the omnibus. Here he was safe, healing and forgetting. There *was* some truth in the Frenchman's judgment. It wasn't that he was a dull philosopher. Lahitte was utterly incapable of measuring his big sunlit mind; but there was something, in his manner, or bearing, something that many people would not like, an absence of gaiety; it was true, the Frenchman's quick eye had fastened on it. Who wanted gaiety? There was a deep joyfulness in his booming song that was more than gaiety. His rich dark vitality challenged the English air as he plunged along, beard first, without thoughts, his eyebrows raised in the effort of his eager singing. He was quite unaware that there was no room for singing more than below one's breath, however quickly one walked, in the Euston Road in the morning.

She composed herself to walk unconcernedly past the row of lounging overalled figures. Sullen hostile staring would not satisfy them this morning. The song would rouse them to some open demonstration. They were endless; muttering motionlessly to each other in their immovable lounging. Surely he must feel them. 'Go 'ome,' she heard, away behind. . . 'Blooming foreigner'; close by, the tall lean swarthy fellow, with the handsome grubby face. That he *must* have heard. She fancied his song recoiled, and wheeled sharply back, confronting the speaker, who has just spat into the middle of the pavement.

'Yes,' she said, 'he is a foreigner, and he is my friend. What do you *mean*?' The man's gazing face was broken up into embarrassed awkward youth. Mr Shatov was safely ahead. She waited, her eyes on the black-rimmed expressionless blue of the eyes staring from above a rising flush. In a moment she would say, 'It is abominable and simply *disgraceful*,' and sweep away and never come up this side of the road again. A little man was speaking at her side, his cap in his hand. They were all moving and staring. 'Excuse me, miss,' he began again in a quiet, thick, hurrying voice, as she turned to him. 'Miss, we know the sight of you going up and down. Miss, he ain't good enough forya.'

'Oh,' said Miriam, the sky falling about her. She lingered a moment speechless, looking at no one, sweeping over them a general disclaiming smile, hoping she told them how mistaken they all were and how nice she thought them, she hurried away to meet Mr Shatov waiting a few yards off. The *darlings*. In all these years of invisible going up and down . . .

'Well?' he laughed, 'what is this?'

'British workmen. I've been lecturing them.'

'On what?'

'In general. Telling them what I think.'

'Excellent. You will yet be a socialist.' They walked on, to the sound of his resumed singing. Presently the turning into Wimpole Street was in sight. His singing must end. Dipping at a venture she stumbled upon material for his arrest.

'It it nay-cessary; *deere* bruthren;' she intoned dismally in a clear interval, 'to obtain; the m*Ahstery*; o-ver-the-*Vile*; bhuddy.'

'What? What?' he gurgled delightedly, slackening his pace. 'Please say this once more.'

Summoning the forgotten figure straining out over the edge of the pulpit, she saw that there was more than the shape and sound of his abruptly ending whine. She saw the incident from Mr Shatov's point of view and stood still to laugh his laugh; but it was not her kind of joke.

'It was in a university church, presided over by a man they all say has a European reputation; it was in Lent; this other man

was a visitor, for Lent. That was the beginning of his sermon.
He began at once, with a yell, flinging half out of the pulpit,
the ugliest person I have ever seen.'
'Hoh,' shouted Mr Shatov from the midst of immense
gusts of laughter, 'that is a most supreme instance of unconscious ironic commentary. But really, please you shall
say this to me once more.'
If she said, 'You know he was quite sincere,' the story would
be spoiled. This was the kind of story popular people told.
To be amusing must mean always to be not quite truthful.
But the sound. She was longing to hear it again. Turning
to face the way they had come she gave herself up to howling
the exhortation down the empty park-flanked vista.
'It is a chef-d'œuvre,' he sighed.
He ought not to be here, she irritably told herself, emerging
as they turned and took the few steps to her street, tired and
scattered and hopelessly late, into the forgotten chill of her day.
It was all very well for him, with his freedom and leisure to
begin the first thing in the morning with things that belonged
to the end of the day. She took swift distracted leave of him
at the corner and hurried along the length of the few houses
to her destination. Turning remorsefully at the doorstep to
smile her farewell, she saw the hurrying form of Mr Hancock
crossing the road with grave appraising glance upon the strange
figure bowing towards her bareheaded in the wind from the
top of the street. He had seen her loitering, standing still,
had heard her howls. Mercifully the door opened behind her,
and she fled within . . . the corner of the very street that
made him, more than any other street, look foreign, and, in
the distance, disgraceful.
For days she read the first two stories in the little book,
carrying it about with her, uneasy amongst her letters and
ledgers unless it were in sight. The project of translation
vanished in an entranced consideration at close quarters of
some strange quality coming each time from the printed page.
She could not seize or name it. Both stories were sad, with
an unmitigated relentless sadness, casting a shadow over the
spectacle of life. But some spell in their weaving, something

abrupt and strangely alive, remaining alive, in the text, made a beauty that outlived the sadness. They were *beautiful*. English people would not think so. They would only see tragedy of a kind that did not occur in the society they knew. They would consider Andreyeff a morbid foreigner, and a liking for the stories an unhealthy pose. Very well. It was an unhealthy pose. The strange beauty in the well-known sentences that yet were every time fresh and surprising, was an unshareable secret. Meanwhile the presence of the little book exorcized the everyday sense of the winding off of days in an elaborate unchanging circle of toil.

To Michael Shatov she poured out incoherent enthusiasm. 'Translate, translate,' he cried; and when she assured him that no one would want to read, he said, each time, 'No matter; this work will be good for you.' But when at last suddenly in the middle of a busy morning, she began turning into rounded English words the thorny German text, she eluded his inquiries and hid the book and all signs of her work even from herself. Writing she forgot, and did not see the pages. The moment she saw them, there was a sort of half-shame in their exposure, even to the light of day. And always in transcribing them a sense of guilt. Not, she was sure, a conviction of misspending her employers' time. Had not they agreed in response to her graceless demands in the course of that first realization of the undeveloping nature of her employments, that she should use chance intervals of leisure on work of her own? But even abusing this privilege, writing sudden long absorbing letters in the best part of the morning with urgent business waiting all round her, had brought no feeling of guilt; only a bright enclosing sense of dissipation; a sort of spreading, to be justified by the shortness of her leisure, of its wild free quality over a part of the too-long day. It was in some way from the work itself that this strange gnawing accusation came, and as strangely, each time she had fairly begun, there came, driving out the sense of guilt, an overwhelming urgency; as if she were running a race.

Presently everything in her life existed only for the sake of the increasing bunch of pencilled half-sheets distributed between the leaves of her roomy blotter. She thanked her circumstances, into whose shape this secret adventure had stolen unobserved and sunk, leaving the surface unchanged, and finding, ready for its sustaining, an energy her daily work had never tapped, from the depth of her heart. In the evenings she put away the thought of her pages lest she should find herself speaking of them to Mr Shatov.

But they would arrive suddenly in her mind, thrilling her into animation, lighting up some remote part of her consciousness from which would come pell-mell, emphatic and incoherently eloquent, statements to which she listened eagerly, Mr. Shatov, too, reduced to a strangely silenced listener, and dropping presently off along some single side issue, she would be driven back by the sheer pain of the effort of contraction, and would impatiently bring the sitting to an end and seek solitude. It was as if she were confronted by some deeper convinced self who did, unknown to her, take sides on things, both sides, with equal emphasis, impartially, but with a passion that left her in an entrancement of longing to discover the secret of its nature. For the rest of the evening this strange self seemed to hover about her, holding her in a serenity undisturbed by reflection.

Sometimes the memory of her work would leap out when a conversation was flagging, and lift her as she sat inert, to a distance whence the dulled expiring thread showed suddenly glowing, looping forward into an endless bright pattern interminably animated by the changing lights of fresh inflowing thoughts. During the engrossing incidents of her day's work she forgot them completely, but in every interval they were there; or not there; she had dreamed them.

With each fresh attack on the text, the sense of guilt grew stronger; falling upon her the moment, having read the page of German, she set to work to apply the discoveries she had made. It was as if these discoveries were the winning, through some inborn trick of intelligence not her own by right of any process of application or of discipline, of an unfair advantage. She sought within her for a memory that might explain the acquisition of the right of escape into this life, within, outside,

securely away from, the life of every day. The school memories
that revived in her dealings with her sentences were the best,
the most secret and the happiest, the strands where the struggle
to acquire had been all a painless interested adventuring. The
use of this strange faculty, so swift in discovery, so relentless
in criticism, giving birth, as one by one the motley of truths
urging its blind movements came recognizably into view, to
such a fascinating game of acceptance and fresh trial, produced
in the long run, when the full balance was struck, an overweight
of joy bought without price.

There was no longer unalleviated pain in the first attack on
a fresh stretch of the text. The knowledge that it could, by
three stages, laborious but unchanging and certain in their
operation, reach a life of its own, the same in its whole effect,
and yet in each detail so different from the original, radiated
joy through the whole slow process. It was such a glad
adventure, to get down on the page with a blunt stump of
pencil in quivering swift thrilled fingers the whole unwieldy
literal presentation, to contemplate, plunging thus roughshod
from language to language, the strange lights shed in turn upon
each, the revelation of mutually enclosed unexpandable meanings, insoluble antagonisms of thought and experience, flowing
upon the surface of a stream where both were one; to see,
through the shapeless mass the approaching miracle of shape
and meaning.

The vast entertainment of this first headlong ramble down
the page left an enlivenment with which to face the dark length
of the second journey, its separate single efforts of concentration, the recurring conviction of the insuperability of barriers,
the increasing list of discarded attempts, the intervals of hours
of interruption, teased by problems that dissolved into meaninglessness, and emerged more than ever densely obstructive,
the sudden almost ironically cheerful simultaneous arrival of
several passable solutions; the temptation to use them, driven
off by the wretchedness accompanying the experiment of
placing them even in imagination upon the page, and at last
the snap of relinquishment, the plunge down into oblivion of
everything but the object of contemplation, perhaps ill-sus-

tained and fruitful only of a fury of irritated exhaustion, postponing further effort, or through the entertaining distraction of a sudden irrelevant play of light, turned to an outbranching series of mental escapades, leading, on emergence, to a hurried scribbling, on fresh pages, of statements which proved when read later, with clues and links forgotten, unintelligible; but leading always, whether directly in one swift movement of seizure or only at the end of protracted divings, to the return, with the shining fragment, whose safe placing within the text made the pages, gathered up in an energy flowing forward transformingly through the interval, towards the next opportunity of attack, electric within her hands.

The serene third passage, the original banished in the comforting certainty that the whole of it was represented, the freedom to handle until the jagged parts were wrought into a pliable whole, relieved the pressure of the haunting sense of trespass, and when all was complete it vanished into peace and a strange unimpatient curiosity and interest. She read from an immense distance. The story was turned away from her towards people who were waiting to read and share what she felt as she read. It was no longer even partly hers; yet the thing that held it together in its English dress was herself, it had her expression, as a portrait would have, so that by no one in her sight or within range of any chance meeting with herself might it ever be contemplated. And for herself it was changed. Coming between her and the immediate grasp of the text were stirring memories; the history of her labour was written between the lines; and strangely, moving within the whole, was the record of the months since Christmas. On every page a day or group of days. It was a diary. . . . Within it were incidents that for a while had dimmed the whole fabric to indifference. And passages stood out, recalling, together with the memory of overcoming their difficulty, the dissolution of annoyances, the surprised arrival on the far side of overwhelming angers.

The second story lay untouched, wrapped in its magic. Contemplating the way, with its difference, it enhanced the first and was enhanced by it, she longed to see the two side by side and found, while she hesitated before the slow scattering process of translation, a third that set her headlong at work towards the perfect finished group. There was no weariness in this second stretch of labour. Behind her lay the first story, a rampart, of achievement and promise, and ahead, calling her on, the one that was yet to be attempted, difficult and strange, a little thread of story upon a background of dark thoughts, like a voice heard through a storm. Even the heaviest parts of the afternoon could be used, in an engrossed forgetfulness of time and place. Time pressed. The year was widening and lifting too rapidly towards the heights of June when everything but the green world, fresh gleaming in parks and squares through the London swelter, sweeping with the tones of spring and summer mingled amongst the changing trees, towards September, would fade from her grasp and disappear.

CHAPTER VI

'WELL. What did he say?'

'Oh, nothing; he made a great opportunity. He didn't like the stories.'

'Remarkable!'

'I did it all the wrong way. When I accepted their invitation I wrote that I was bringing down some translations of the loveliest short stories I had ever read.' I was suddenly proud, in Lyons, of remembering 'short stories' and excited about having something written to show him at last. The sentence felt like an entry into their set.

'If he did not agree with this, I pity him.'

'I don't know how it would have been if I had said nothing at all.' He might have said, 'Look here, this is good stuff. You must do something with this.'

'I tell you again this man is superficial.'

'He said the sentiment was gross and that they were feeble in construction.' Waiting, in the window seat, with the large fresh light from the sea pouring in from behind across the soft clear buffs and greens of the room; weaving for Alma, with the wonder of keeping him arrested, alone in his study, with his eyes on her written sentences, a view of the London life as eventful, enviable leisure; the door opening at last, the swift compact entry of the little figure with the sheaf of manuscript, the sudden lifting jubilance of the light; the eager yielding to the temptation to enhance the achievement by a disclaiming explanation of the difficult circumstances, the silencing minatory finger—wait, wait, you're taking it the wrong way—and at last the high-pitched, colourless, thinking voice in brief comprehensive judgment; the shattering of the bright scene, the end of the triumphant visit, with a day still to pass, going about branded as an admirer of poor stuff.

'That is no *opinion*. It is simply a literary finessing. I will tell you *more*. This judgment indicates an *immense* blindness. There is in Andreyeff a directness and simplicity of feeling towards life that is entirely lacking in this man.'

'M'm. Perhaps the Russians are more simple; less' . . . civilized.

'Simplicity and directness of feeling does not necessarily indicate a less highly organized psychological temperament.'

'I know what he meant. Andreyeff does try deliberately to work on your feelings. I felt that when I was writing. But the pathos of those little boys and the man with the Chinese mask is his *subject*. What he does is artistic exaggeration. That is Art. Light and shade' . . . a "masterly study" of a little boy . . .?

'Very well then. What is the matter?'

'No, but I'm just thinking the whole trouble is that life is not pathetic. People don't feel pathetic; or never *altogether* pathetic. There is something else; that 's the worst of novels, something that has to be left out. Tragedy; curtain. But there never *is* a curtain and, even if there were, the astounding thing is that there is *anything* to let down a curtain on; so *astounding* that you can't feel really, completely, things like "happiness" or "tragedy"; they are both the same, a half-statement. Everybody is the same really, inside, under all circumstances. There 's a dead level of astounding . . . *something*.'

'I cannot follow you in all this. But you may not thus lightly deny tragedy.'

'He also said that the translation was as good as it could be.' . . . You 've brought it off. That 's the way a translation ought to be done. It 's slick and clean and extraordinarily well Englished.

'Well? Well? Are you not satisfied?'

'Then he said in a contemptuous sort of way, "You could make from two to three hundred a year at this sort of thing."'

'But that is most excellent. You should most certainly try this.'

'I don't believe it. He *says* that kind of thing.'

'He ought to know.'

'I don't know. He said in a large easy way, You'd get seven or eight guineas apiece for these things, and then do 'em in a book.'''

'Well?'

'Everybody would be doing it if it were so easy.'

'You are really remarkable. A good translation is most rare; and particularly a good English translation. You have seen these Tolstois. I have not met in German or French anything so vile. It is a whole base trade.'

'The public does not know. And if these things sell why should publishers pay for good translations? It's like machine- and hand-made embroidery. It does not pay to do good work. I've often heard translations are badly paid and I can quite understand it. It could be done in a factory at an immense pace.'

'You are right. I have known a group of poor Russian students translate a whole book in a single night. But you will not find cynical vulgarization of literature anywhere but in England and America. It is indeed remarkable to the foreigner the way in this country the profession of letters has become a speculation. Never before I came here did I meet this idea of writing for a living, in this naïve widespread form. There is something very bad in it.' Miriam surveyed the green vista, thinking guiltily of her envy and admiration of the many young men she had met at the Wilsons' who were mysteriously 'writing' or 'going to write,' of her surprise and disappoint- ment in meeting here and there things they had written . . . don't, Miss Henderson . . . *don't* take up . . . a journalistic *career* on the strength of being able to write; as badly as Jenkins. Editors—poor dears—are *beleaguered*, by aspiring relatives. She thought out now, untrammelled by the distraction of listening to the way he formed his sentences, the meaning of these last words. It spread a chill over the wide stretch of sunlit grass; in the very moments that were passing, the writing world was going actively on, the clever people who had ideas and style and those others, determined, besieging, gradually making themselves into writers, indistinguishable by most

readers, from the others, sharing, even during their dreadful
beginnings, in the social distinctions and privileges of 'writers,'
and all of them, the clever ones and the others, quite untroubled by any sense of guilt, and making, when they were
all together, a social atmosphere that was, in spite of its
scepticism, and its scorn of everyday life, easier to breathe
than any other.   But being burdened with a hesitating sense
of guilt, unable to be really interested in the things clever
people wrote about, being beguiled by gross sentimentality
because of its foreign dress and the fascination of transforming
it, meant belonging outside the world of clever writers, tried
in their balance and found wanting; and cut off from the world
of innocent unconscious determined aspirants by a mysterious
fear.

It was mean to sit waiting for life to throw up things that
would distract one for a while from the sense of emptiness.
Sitting, moving about from place to place, in the dress of the
period.   Being nowhere, one had no right even to the dress
of the period.   In the bottom of the lake . . . hidden, and
forgotten.   Round the far-off lake were feathery green trees,
not minding.   She sat imagining their trunks, filmed over
with the murk of London winters, but all the more beautiful
now, standing out black amongst the clouds of green.   There
were trees in the distance ahead, trees, forgotten.   She was
here to look at them.   It was urgent, important.   All this
long time, and she had never once looked.   She lifted her eyes
cautiously, without moving, to take in the wide belt beyond
the stretch of grass.   It was perfect.   Full spring complete,
prepared and set there, ungrudgingly, demanding nothing but
love; embanked between the sky and the grass, a dense perfect shape of various pure colour, an effect, that would pass;
but she had seen it.   The sharp angle of its edge stood out
against a farther, far-off belt of misty green, with here and there
a dark maroon blot of copper beech.

'Whatever happens, as long as one lives, there is the spring.'
'Do not be too sure of this.'
'Of course, if the world suddenly came to an end.'
'This appreciation of spring is merely a question of youth.'

'You can't be sure.'

'On the contrary. Do you imagine for instance that this old woman on the next seat feels the spring as you do?'

Miriam rose, unable to look; wishing she had come alone; or had not spoken. The green vistas moved all about her, dazzling under the height of sky. 'I'm perfectly sure I shall always feel the spring; perhaps more and more.' She escaped into irrelevant speech, hurrying along so that he should hear incompletely until she had firm hold of some far-off topic; dreading the sound of his voice.

The flower-beds were in sight, gleaming in the gaps between the tree trunks along the broad walk. Ragged children were shouting and chasing each other round the fountain. 'I must always here think,' he said, as they passed through the wicket gate, 'of this man who preaches for the conversion of infidels, Jews, Christians, and other unbelievers.'

She hurried on preparing to face the rows of Saturday afternoon people on the chairs and seats along the avenue, their suspicious English eyes on her scrappy, dowdy, out-of-date English self and her extraordinary looking foreigner. Her spirits lifted. But they must be walking quickly and talking. The staring self-revealing faces must see that it was a privilege to have converse with any one so utterly strange and far away from their English life.

'I'm not interested in him,' she said as they got into their stride.

'Why not?'

'I don't know why. I can't fix my thoughts on him; or any of these people who yell at crowds.' Not quite that; but it made a sentence and fitted with their walk.

'It is perhaps that you are too individualistic,' panted Mr. Shatov. There was no opening in this for an appearance of easy conversation; the words were leaping and barking round her like dogs.

But she turned swiftly, leading the way down a winding side path and demanding angrily as soon as they were alone how it was possible to be too individualistic.

'I agree to a certain extent that it is impossible. A man is first himself. But the peril is of being cut off from his fellow creatures.'

'Why *peril*? Men descend to meet. Are you a socialist? Do you believe in the opinions of mediocre majorities?'

'Why this adjective? Why mediocre? No, I would call myself rather one who believes in the *race*.'

'*What* race? The race is nothing without individuals.'

'What is an individual without the race?'

'An individual, with a consciousness; or a soul, whatever you like to call it. The race, apart from individuals, is nothing at all.'

'You have introduced here several immense questions. There is the question as to whether a human being isolated from his fellows would retain any human characteristics. Your great Buckle considered this in relation to the problem of heredity. But aside of this, has the race not a soul and an individuality? Greater than that of its single parts?'

'Certainly not. The biggest thing a race does is to produce a few big individualities.'

'The biggest thing that the race does is that it *goes on*. Individuals perish.'

'You don't know that they do.'

'That is speculation; without evidence. I have the most complete evidence that the race survives.'

'It may die, according to science.'

'That also is a speculation. But what is certain is—that the greatest individual is great only as he gives much to the race; to his fellow creatures. Without this, individuality is pure-negative.'

'Indviduality *cannot* be negative.'

'There speaks the Englishwoman. It is certainly England's highest attainment that the rights of the individual are sacred here. But even this is not complete. It is still impeded by class prejudice.'

'*I* haven't any class prejudice.'

'You are wrong; believe me you have immensely these

prejudices. I could quite easily prove this to you. You are in many ways most exceptionally, for an Englishwoman, emancipated. But you are still pure-Tory.'

'That is only my stamp. I can't help that. But I myself have no prejudices.'

'They are so far in you unconscious.' He spoke with extreme gentleness, and Miriam looked uneasily ahead, wondering whether with this strange knowledge at her side she might be passing forward to some fresh sense of things that would change the English world for her. English prejudices. He saw them as clearly as he saw that she was not beautiful. And gently, as if they were charming as well as funny to him. Their removal would come; through a painless association. For a while she would remain as she was. But even seeing England from his point of view, was being changed; a little. The past, up to the last few moments, was a life she had lived without knowing that it was a life lived in special circumstances and from certain points of view. Now, perhaps moving away from it, these circumstances and points of view suddenly became a possession, full of fascinating interest. But she had lived blissfully. Something here and there in his talk *threatened* happiness.

He seemed to see people only as members of nations, grouped together with all their circumstances. Perhaps everything could be explained in this way. . . . All her meaning for him was her English heredity, a thing she seemed to think the finest luck in the world, and her free English environment, the result of it; things she had known nothing about till he came, smiling at her ignorance of them, and declaring the ignorance to be the best testimony. That was it; he gave her her nationality and surroundings, the fact of being England to him made everything easy. There was no need to do or be anything, individual. It was too easy. It must be demoralizing . . . just sitting there basking in being English . . . Everything she did, everything that came to her in the outside world turned out to be demoralizing . . . too easy . . . some *fraud* in it. . . . But the pity she found herself suddenly feeling for all English people who had not intelligent foreign friends gave her courage to go on. Meanwhile there was an unsettled troublesome point. Something that could not be left.

'Perhaps,' she said, 'I dare say. But at any rate, I have an open mind. Do you think that the race is *sacred*, and has purposes, superman, you know what I mean, Nietzsche, and that individuals are fitted up with the instincts that keep them going, just to blind them to the fact that they don't matter?'

'If one must use these terms, the race is *certainly* more sacred than the individual.'

'Very well then; I know what I think. If the sacred race plays tricks on conscious human beings, using them for its own sacred purposes and giving them an unreal sense of mattering, I don't care a button for the race, and I'd rather kill myself than serve its purposes. Besides, the instincts of self-preservation and reproduction are *not* the only human motives. They are not human at all.'

CHAPTER VII

THE picturesque building had been there, just round the corner, all these years, without once attracting her interested notice. The question she directed towards it, crossing the road for a nearer view, went forth, not from herself, but from the presence, close at her side, of Michael Shatov. During the hour spent in her room, facing the empty evening, she had been aware of nothing, outside the startling disturbance of her own movements, but the immense silence he had left. Driven forth to walk away its hours out of doors, she found, accompanying her through the green-lit evening squares, the tones and gestures of his voice, the certainty, that so long as she should frequent the neighbourhood, she would retain the sense of his companionship. The regions within her, of un-expressed thought and feeling, to which he had not reached, were at once all about her as she made her old, familiar, un-impeded escape through the front door, towards the blur of feathery green standing in the bright twilight at the end of the grey street; but beyond these inner zones, restored in a tumult of triumphant assertion of their indestructibility, the outer difficult life of expression and association was changed. If, as she feared, he should finally disappear into the new world towards which, with such urgent irritated determination, she had driven him, she would, for life, have reaped a small fund of his Russian courage and indifference. It was with his impulse and interest, almost it seemed, actually in his person, that she drew up in front of the placard at the side of the strange low ecclesiastical-looking porch. But as she read its contents, he left her, sped into forgetfulness by the swift course of her amazement. She had come, leaving her room at exactly the right moment, directly, by appointment, to this spot. Glancing once more for perfect assurance, at the liberal invitation printed in large letters at the foot of the heavenly announcement, she went boldly into the porch.

At the top of the shallow flight of grey stone steps up which she passed almost directly from the ecclesiastical doorway, a large black-draped figure, surmounted by the sweeping curves of an immense black hat voluminously swathed in a gauze veil of pale grey, stood bent towards a small woman standing on the step below her in dingy indoor black. The large outline, standing generously out below the broad low stone archway curving above the steps, against the further grey stone of what appeared to be part of a low-ceiled corridor, was in extraordinary contrast to the graciously bending, surrendered attitude of the figure. Passing close to the group, Miriam caught a glimpse of large plump features, bold eyebrows, and firm dark eyes. The whole face, imagined as unscreened, was rounded, simple, and undistinguished; blurred by the veil, it swam, without edges, a misty full moon. Through the veil came a voice that thrilled her as she moved on, led by a card bearing an arrowed instruction, down the grey stone corridor, with the desire for immediate audible mimicry. The behaviour of the voice was a perfect confirmation of deliberate intentional blurring of the large face. The little, scanty, frugally upstanding woman, who had appeared to be of the artisan class, was either a humorous brick, or a toady, or of the old-fashioned respectful servant type, to stand it. The superfluous statement might, at least, even if the voice had become second nature—she might be thirty—have been delivered at an ordinary conversational pace. But to make the unimportant comment in the deliberately refined distressed ladylike voice, with pauses, as if every word were a precious gift . . . She was waiting for some occasion, keeping her manner going, and the little woman had to stand out the performance.

On her way down the corridor she met a young man with a long neck above a low collar, walking like an undergraduate, with a rapid lope and a forward hen-like jerk of the head, but with kind religious-looking eyes. Underneath his conforming manner and his English book-and-talk-found thoughts, he was acutely miserable, but never alone long enough to find it out;

never even long enough to feel his own impulses. Two girls came swiftly by, bare-headed, in reform dresses, talking eagerly in high-pitched, out-turned, cultured voices, their uncommunicating selves watchfully entrenched behind the polite Norman idiom. She carried on their manner of speech at lightning speed in her mind, watching its effect upon everything it handled, of damming up, shaping, excluding all but ready-made thought and opinion. Just ahead was an arched doorway and a young man with a sheaf of pamphlets standing within it. 'It may,' she announced, in character, to an imaginary companion, 'prove necessary to have some sort of conversational interchange with this individual.' Certainly it left one better prepared for the interview than saying Good Lord, shall we have to *say* something to this creature? She got safely through the doorway, exchanging a slight bow with the young man as he provided her with a syllabus, and entered a large lofty quietly-lit room, where a considerable audience sat facing a raised platform more brightly illuminated, and from which they were confronted by a row of seated forms. She went down the central gangway, bold in her desire for a perfect hearing, and slipped into a seat in the second row of chairs. The chairman was taking his place and, in the dying down of conversation, she heard a quiet flurry of draperies approaching with delicate apologetic rhythm up the gangway. It was the tall young woman. She passed, a veiled figure with bent head and floating scarf, along the little passage between the front row of the audience and the fern-edged platform, upon which she presently emerged, taking her place next to a lady who now rose and came forward, tall and black-robed, and whose face, sharply pointing beneath the shadow of a plumy hat, had the expression of an eagle searching the distance with calm piercing eyes. In rousing ringing grievous tones she begged to be allowed to precede the chairman with an important announcement. Miriam inwardly groaned as the voice chid tragically on, demanding a realization on the part of all, of the meaning for London of the promised arrival in its midst of a world-famed authority in Greek letters. She felt the audience behind her quelled into absolute stillness, and took angry refuge in the cover of her syllabus. 'The Furthermore Settlement' she read, printed boldly at the head of the page. It was one of those missions; to bring culture amongst the London poor . . . 'devoted young men from the universities.' Those girls in the corridor, wrapped in their code, were doing 'settlement work.' They did not look philanthropic. What they loved most was the building, the grey stone corridors and archways, and being away from home on a prolonged adventure, free to weave bright colours along the invisible edges of life. She could not imagine them ever becoming in the least like the elderly philanthropists on the platform. But they were not free. The place was a sort of monastery of culture. If they wore habits they would be free and deeply inspiring. But they went about dressed longingly in the colours of sunlit landscapes, and lived their social life with ideas. There was something monastic about the lofty hall, with its neutral-tinted walls and high-placed windows. But the place was modern and well ventilated, even sternly chilly. Turning on her shoulder to examine the dutiful audience, she was startled by its effect of massed intellectuality. These people were certainly not the poor of the neighbourhood. By far the larger number were men and, wherever she looked, she met faces from which she turned quickly away lest she should smile her pleasure. Even those that were heavy with stoutness and beards had the same lit moving look of kindly adventurous thought. They were a picked gathering; like the Royal Institution; but more glowing. She turned back to the platform in high hope, amidst the outburst of applause greeting the retirement of the distressful lady and deepening to enthusiasm as there emerged timidly from behind one of the large platform screens a tall figure in evening dress, a great grown-up boy, with a large fresh face and helpless straight-hanging arms and hands. He sat big and fixed, like an idol, whilst the chairman, standing bowing over his table, hurriedly remarked that an introduction was superfluous, and gazed at the audience with large moist blue eyes that seemed permanently open and expressionless and yet to pray for protection, or permission to retreat once more behind his screen.

Miriam pitied him from the bottom of her heart and saw
with relief when he rose that he produced a roll of papers
for which a little one-legged ecclesiastical reading-desk was
conveniently waiting. He was going to read. But he placed
his papers with large incapable fingers and she feared they
would flutter to the ground, till he turned and took one fumbling expressionless step clear of the little desk and, standing
just as he was, his arms hanging once more heavy and helpless
at his side, his eyes motionlessly fixed neither on the distance
nor on any part of the audience, as if sightlessly focusing
everything before him, began, without movement, or warning
gesture, to speak. With the first sound of his voice, Miriam
surrendered herself to breathless listening. It sounded out,
at conversational pitch, with a colourless serenity that instantly
explained his bearing, revealing him beyond the region either
of diffidence or of temerity. It was a voice speaking to no
one, in a world emptied of everything that had gone before.

'The progress of philosophy,' went the words, in letters of
gold across the dark void, 'is by a series of systems; that of
science by the constant addition of small facts to accumulated
knowledge.' In the slight pause, Miriam held back from the
thoughts flying out in all directions round the glowing words.
They would come again, if she could memorize the words
from which they were born, coolly, registering the shape and
length of the phrases and the leading terms. Before the voice
began again she had read and re-read many times; driving
back an exciting intruder trying, from the depths of her mind
to engage her on the subject of the time-expanding swiftness
of thought.

'A system,' pursued the voice, 'very generally corrects the
fallacy of the preceding system, and leans perhaps in the
opposite direction.' She flushed warm beneath the pressure
of her longing to remain cool. . . . 'Thus the movements of
philosophic thought may be compared to the efforts of a
drunken man to reach his home.' The blue eyes remained
unaltered, while the large fresh face expanded with a smiling
radiance. He was a darling. 'He reels against the wall to his
right and gains an impetus which sends him staggering to the

left, and so on; his progress being a series of zigzags. But in the end he gets home. And we may hope that philosophy will do the same, though the road seems at times unnecessarily broad.'

He turned back to his papers, leaving his sentence on the air in an intense silence through which Miriam felt the eager expectancy of the audience flow and hang waiting, gathered towards the fresh centre whence, unless he suddenly vanished, would come, through the perfect medium of the unobstructive voice, his utmost presentation of reasons for the tantalizing hope.

At the end of the lecture she sat hurriedly sorting and re-sorting what she had gleaned; aware that her attention had again and again wandered off with single statements that had appealed to her, longing to communicate with other members of the audience in the hope of filling up the gaps. Perhaps the questions would bring back some of the things she had missed. But no one seemed to have anything to ask. The relaxation of the hearty and prolonged applause had given way to the sort of silence that falls in a room after vociferous greet-ings, when the anticipated occasion vanishes and the gathered friends become suddenly unrecognizably small and dense. She looked at the woman at her side and caught a swift respon-sive glance that shocked her, clear blue and white and remote in limpid freshness though it was, with its chill understanding familiarity. Something had gone irrevocably from the evening and from herself. The strange woman was exactly like some-body . . . a disguise of somebody. Shattering the silence, came a voice from the back of the hall. 'If the lecturer *thinks* and seems to deprecate the fact, that theology deals with meta-physical problems in an *unmetaphysical* way, that is, from the point of view of metaphysic, in an *unscientific* way . . .' com-pared with Dr M'Taggart's, his voice was like the voice of an intoxicated man arguing to himself in a railway carriage . . . 'may we not *say* that when metaphysic takes upon itself to criticize the validity of *scientific* conceptions, it does so, from the point of view of *science*, in an unscientific way ?'

This, Miriam felt, was terribly unanswerable. But the

hushed platform was alive with the standing figure almost before the muffling of the last emphatic word told that the assailant had reassumed his seat.

'I think I have said'—his face beaming with the repressed radiance of an invading smile, was lifted towards the audience, but the blue eyes modestly addressed the frill of green along the platform edge—'that metaphysic, with respect to some of the conceptions of science, while admitting that they have their uses for practical purposes, denies that they are exactly true. Theology does not deny the problems of metaphysic, but answers them in a way metaphysic cannot accept.'

'In that case *theology*,' began a rich, reverberating clerical voice . . .

'This is veggy boring,' said the woman.

He was going to claim, thought Miriam, noting the evidence of foreign intelligence in her neighbour's pronunciation, that religion, like metaphysic and science, had a right to its premises and denied that metaphysic was adequate for the study of the ultimate nature of reality, exactly as metaphysic denied that science was adequate.

'Yes, isn't it?' she murmured, a little late, through the deep caressing thunder of the clerical voice, wondering how far she had admitted her willingness to be at the disposal of any one who found, in these tremendous onslaughts, nothing but irrelevance.

'If one could peacefully fall asleep until the summing up.'

She spoke out quite clearly, moving so that she was half turned towards Miriam, and completely exposed to her, as she sat with an elbow on the back of her chair and her knees comfortably crossed, in all her slender grey-clad length, still set towards the centre of the platform. Miriam unwillingly searched her curious effect of making in the atmosphere about her, a cold, delicate, blue and white glare. She had seemed, all the evening, a well-dressed presence. But her little oval toque, entirely covered with a much washed piece of cream-coloured lace and set back from her forehead at the angle of an old-fashioned flat lace cap, had not been bought at a shop, and the light grey garment so delicate in tone and expression, open at the neck, where creamy lace continued the effect of the hat, was nothing but a cheap rain-cloak. Either she was poor, and triumphing over her poverty with a laborious depressing ingenuity, or she was one of those people who deliberately do everything cheaply. There was something faintly horrible, Miriam felt, about the narrowness of her escape from dowdiness to distinction. . . . Washable lace was the simplest possible solution of the London hat problem. No untravelled English-woman would have thought of it. . . . Behind the serenity of her smooth white brow, behind her cold wide clearly-ringed sea-blue eyes, was the dominant intelligence of it all, the secret of the strange atmosphere that enveloped her whole effect; so strong and secure that it infected her words and movements with a faint robust delicate levity. In most women the sum of the tangible items would have produced the eye-wearying, eye-estranging pathos of the spectacle of patience fighting a lost battle, supplied so numerously all over London by women who were no longer young; or at least a consciously resigned cheer-fulness. But she sat there with the enviable cool clear radiant eyes of a child that is held still and unsmiling by the deep entrancement of its mirth.

The chairman had risen and suddenly quelled the vast voice in the midst of its rising tide of tone, with the reminder that there would be opportunity for discussion a little later. A question rang out, short and sharp, exploding, as if released automatically by the renewal of stillness, so abruptly that Miriam missed its significance. The woman laughed instantly, a little clear tinkling gleeful sound, hesitatingly supported here and there amongst the forward rows of chairs by stirrings and small sounds of amusement. Miriam glowed with shame. It had been a common voice; perhaps some lonely uninstructed man, struggling with problems that were as terrible to him as to any one; in the end desperately getting round them, by logical somersaults, so funny, that these habitually cultured minds could see only the absurdity. Her heart beat with gratitude as the lecturer, with gentle respectful gravity, para-phrased at some length an extract from the earlier part of his address. She was once more recalled by the voice at her side.

Turning, she found the unchanged face still set towards the platform. She answered the question in a low toneless voice that yet sounded more disturbing than the easy smooth conversational tone of her neighbour. She talked on, questioning and commenting, in neat inclusive phrases, and Miriam, turned towards her, reading the history of the duel of audience and lecturer in the flickerings across her face, of amusement or of scorn, responded freely, delighting in a converse that was more wonderful, with its background of cosmic discussion, than even the untrammelled exchange of confidences with a stranger on a bus. Presently there was a complete stillness.

'If there are no more questions,' said the chairman, rising.

'I should just *like*,' broke in a ringing cheerful voice quite near at hand, 'to ask Dr M'Taggart *why*, if he considers that metaphysic is of no use in a man's life, he finds it worth *while*, to *pursue* such a fruitless study?'

'*Don't answer*,' said the woman in clear penetrating tones.

'Don't answer; don't answer,' repeated in the immediate neighbourhood two or three masculine voices. The lecturer, sitting bent forward, his friendly open brow yielded up to the invading audience, his big hands clasped capaciously between his knees, sent a blue glance swiftly in her direction, hesitated a moment, and then sat silent, smiling broadly down at his clasped hands.

'Isn't he a perfect *darling*?' murmured Miriam while the chairman declared the lecture open for discussion and she gathered herself together for close attention.

'There will be nothing worth heahghing till he sums up,' said her companion and went on to ask her if she meant to attend the next lecture. Miriam perceived that unless she chose to escape forcibly, her companion had her in a close net of conversation. She glanced and saw that her face was already that of a familiar associate, no longer spurring her to trace to its source the strange impression that at first it had given her of being a forgotten face, whose sudden return, unrecognizably disguised, and yet so recognizable, filled her with a remembered sentiment of dislike.

'Rather,' she said and then, watching the opening prospect

III—F

of the long series of speeches, and protected by the monotonous booming of a pessimistic male voice, 'I'm so awfully relieved to find that science is only half true. But I *can't* see why he says that metaphysic is no practical use. It would make *all* the difference every moment, to know for certain that mind is more real than matter.'

'Pahghfaitement.'

Dr M'Taggart's voice interrupted her, damming up the urgent flow of communications. She watched him, listening without attention.

'He's like a marvellously intelligent bolster,' she said tonelessly, 'but with a heart and a soul. He certainly has a soul.'

Flattered by a soft chuckle of amusement, she added in a low murmuring man's voice, 'The objectors are like candle-lit turnip ghosts,' and was rewarded by the first direct glance from the blue eyes, smiling, assuring her that she was acceptable. The ghost of the remembered face was laid. Whoever it was, if in reality it were to reappear in her life, she would be able to overcome her aversion by bold flirtation.

When the lecturer at last rose to reply, the guiding phrases of his discourse were the worn familiar keys to a past experience. Used for the second time in the doors of the chambers they had opened within the background of life, they grated, hesitating, and the heavy sound threw the bright spaces into shadow and spread a film of doubt over Miriam's eagerness to escape and share her illumination with people waiting outside in the surrounding gloom. The light would return and remain for her. But it was something accomplished unaccountably. The mere reproduction of the magic phrases, even when, after solitary peaceful contemplation, she should have reassembled them in their right relations and their marvellously advancing sequence, would not carry her hearers along the road she had travelled. The something that held them together, lively and enlivening, was incommunicable.

'Don't huggy away. The audience will take a considerable time to disperse.'

Miriam desired only to escape into the night. Just outside,

in the darkness, was the balm that would disperse her dis-
quietude. The grey-clad woman held it suspended in the
hot room, piling mountainously up. But they sat enclosed, a
closely-locked party of two. Conversation was going on all
over the room. This woman with her little deprecating frown
at the idea of immediate departure, had the secret of the con-
gregational aspect of audiences. Miriam sat still, passively
surrendering to the forcible initiation into the new role of
lingerer, to the extent of floundering through absent-minded
responses.

'What?' she said suddenly, turning full round. Something
had thrilled the air about her, bringing the whole evening to a
head.

'Haldane's *Pathway to Reality,*' repeated the woman as their
eyes met. Miriam was held by the intense radiance of the blue
eyes. Light, strangely cool and pure, flowed from the still
face. She was beautiful, with a curious impersonal glowless
beauty. The light that came from her was the light of something she saw, habitually.

'But I ought not to recommend you to read. You ought to
spend all your free time in the open air. Moreover, it's very
stiff reading.'

Miriam rose, beleaguered and flinching. How did people
find out about books? Where did they get them from? This
woman could not afford to buy big expensive volumes. . . .
Why did her quick mind assume that the difficulty of the book
would be a barrier, and not see that it was the one book she was
waiting for, even if it were the stiffest and dryest in the world?
. . . But the title was unforgettable; one day she would come
across the book somewhere and get at its meaning in her own
way.

'Well; we may meet next week, if we are both early; I shall
be early.' She rose, enlivening her grey cloak with the swift
grace of her movements, and together they proceeded down the
rapidly emptying room.

'My name is Lucie Duclaux.'

The shock of this unexpected advance arrested Miriam's
rapid flight towards the harbour of solitude. She smiled a

formal acknowledgment, unable and entirely unwilling to identify herself with a name. Her companion, remaining close in her neighbourhood as they threaded their way amongst talking groups along the corridor, said nothing more and, when they reached the doorway, Miriam's determination to be free kept her blind and dumb. She was aware of an exclamation about the rain. That was enough. She would not risk a parting intimate enough to suggest another meeting, with any one who, at the sight of rain, belaboured the air and the people about her, with an exclamation that was, however gracious and elegant, a deliberate assault, condemning her moreover of the possession of two voices. . . . Gathering up her Marie Duclaux cloak, the woman bowed swiftly and disappeared into the night.

The girls had understood that the evening had been a vital experience. But they had sat far away, seeming to be more than ever enclosed in their attitude of tolerant amusement at her doings; more than ever supporting each other in a manner that told, with regard to herself, of some final unanimous conclusion reached and decision taken, after much discussion, once for all. In the old days they would have thought nothing of her dropping in at eleven o'clock at night, with no reason but that of just dropping in. But now, their armoury of detached expectancy demanded always that she should supply some pretext. To-night, feeling that the pretext was theirs, every one's, news too pressing to wait, she had rushed in unprepared, with something of her old certainty of welcome. It was so simple. It *must* be important to Jan that what Hegel meant was only just beginning to be understood. If Jan's acceptance of Haeckel made her sad, here was what she wanted; even though M'Taggart said that we have no right to believe a theory because we could not be happy unless it were true. All the same a theory that makes you miserable can't be altogether true. *Miserable;* not sorry. Everything depends upon the kind of man who sets up the theory. Pessimists can find as good reasons as optimists. But if the optimist is cheerful because he is healthy and the pessimist gloomy because . . . everything is a matter of temperament. Neither of them sees that the fact of there being anything anywhere is more wonderful than any theory about the fact. Making optimists and pessimists look exactly alike. Then why is philosophy so fascinating?

'You will lose your colour, my child, and get protuberances on your brow.'

'What then?'

St Pancras clock struck midnight as she reached home. The house was in darkness. She went noiselessly up the first two flights and forward, welcomed, towards the blue glimmer of street lamps showing through the open drawing-room door. It was long since she had seen the room empty. Mr Shatov's absence had restored it to her in its old shadowy character; deep black shadows, and spaces of faint blue light that came in through the lace curtains, painting their patterned mesh on the sheen of the opposite walls. The old familiar presence was there in the hush of the night, dissolving the echoes of the day and promising, if she stayed long enough within it, the emergence of to-morrow, a picture, with long perspectives, seen suddenly in the distance, alone upon a bare wall. She stood still, moving rapidly into the neutral zone between the two days, further and further into the spaces of the darkness, until everything disappeared, and all days were far-off strident irrelevances, for ever unable to come between her and the sound of the stillness and its touch, a cool breath, passing through her unimpeded.

She could not remember whether she had first seen him rise or heard the deep tones coming out of the velvety darkness.

'No, you did not startle me. I've been to a lecture,' she said sinking in a sleep-like stupor into a chair drawn up beyond the light of the window, opposite his own, across which there struck a shaft of light falling, now that he was again seated, only on his face. Miriam gazed at him from within the sheltering darkness, fumbling sleepily for the way back to some lucid recovery of the event of her evening.

'Ah. It is a pity I could not be there.' His words broke into the stillness, an immensity of communication, thrown forward through their unrestricted sitting, in the darkness, where, to bridge, before to-morrow, the gap made by his evening's absence, he had waited for her. She sat silent, her days once more wound closely about her, an endless hospitable chain.

'Tell me of this lecture.'

'Philosophy.'

'Tsa. It is *indeed* a pity.'

'It is a series' . . . are you sitting there already involved in engagements . . . cut off; changed ? . . .

'Excellent. I shall most certainly come.' He was looking freely ahead. His evening had not interested him . . . he had gone and come back, his horizons unenlarged . . . but not seeing the impression he had made on those people; the steps they would take.

'It would be splendid for you. The lecturer's English, *wonderful*. The way the close thought made his sentences, fascinated me so much, that I often missed the meaning in listening to the rhythm; like a fugue.' Aren't you *glad* you 've enlarged your horizons ? Don't you know what people are . . . what you, a person, are, to people ? Are you a person ? In a blankness, life streamed up in spirals, vanishing, leaving nothing.

'That is not bad. Ah, I should not have paid this visit. It was also in some respects most painful to me.' Poor little man, poor little lonely man, white-faced and sensitive, in a world without individuals; grown and formed and wise without realizing an individual; never to realize. Audible within the darkness was a singing, hovering on spaces of warm rosy light.

'You must not regret your visit.'

'Regret, no; it was much as I anticipated. But it is disheartening, this actual witnessing.' They were disposed of in some way; in one piece; he would have a formula.

'What are they like ? '

'Quite as I expected; good simple people, kind and hospitable. I have been the whole evening there. Ah, but it is sad for me, this first meeting with English Jews.'

'Perhaps you can make Zionists of them.'

'That is absolutely impossible.'

'Did you talk to them about Zionism?'

'It is useless to talk to these people whose first pride is that they are *British*.'

'But they 're *not*.'

'You should tell them so. They will tell you they are British of the Jewish persuasion. Ah, it has revolted me to hear them talk of this war, the British Empire, and the subject races.'

'I know; disgusting; but very British. But the British Empire has done a good deal for the Jews and I suppose the Jews feel loyal.'

'That is true. But what they do not see is that they are not, and never can be, British; that the British do not accept them as such.'

'That 's true, I know; the general attitude; but there are no disabilities. The Jews are free in England.'

'They are free; to the honour of England in all history. But they are nevertheless Jews and not Englishmen. Those Jews who deny, or try to ignore, this have ceased to be Jews without becoming Englishmen. The toleration for Jews, moreover, will last only so long as the English remain in ignorance of the immense and increasing power and influence of the Jew in this country. Once that is generally recognized, even England will have its anti-Semitic movement.'

'*Never*. England can assimilate anything. Look at the races that have been built into us in the past.'

'No nation can assimilate the Jew.'

'What about intermarriages?'

'That is the minority.'

'If it was right to make a refuge for the Jews here, it is still right and England will never regret it.'

'Believe me it is not so simple. Remember that British Jewry is perpetually and increasingly reinforced by immigration from those countries where Jews are segregated and ever more terribly persecuted. At present there is England, both for the Jewish speculator and the refugee pauper. But for those who look at *facts*, the end of this possibility is in sight. The time for the closing of this last door is approaching.'

'I don't believe England will ever do it. How can they? Where will the Jews go? It's impossible to think of. It will be the end of England if we begin that sort of thing.'

'It may be the beginning of Jewish nationality. Ah, at least this visit has reawakened all the Zionist in me.'

'It is a glorious idea.' His evening *had* been eventful; sending him back to the freshness of the days at Basel. It was then, she thought, at the moment he was bathed in the unceasing beauty of the surroundings, and immersed within it, in inextinguishable association with the students of the photographs, poised blissfully irresponsible in a permanent boundless beguilement, himself the most untouched of all, the most smoothly rounded, and elastically surrendered with his deep-singing, childlike confident face, that he had been touched and shaped and sent forth; his future set towards a single separate thing, the narrowest, strangest, most unknown of movements, far away from the wide European life that had flowed through his mind.

'It is a dream, far off. In England, hardly even that.' There was a blankness before him. Unconscious of his youth, and his radiating charm, distilled from the modern world; Frenchman, Russian, philosophical German-brained, he sat there white-faced, an old old Jew, immeasurably old, cut off, alone with his conviction, facing the blank spaces of the future. Why could he not be content to be a European? She swayed, dragging at the knot. In his deeply saturated intelligence there still was a balance on the side from which he had declared to his father, that he was first a man; then a Jew. By the accidents of living, this might be cherished. The voices of the night cried out against the treachery. She glanced remorsefully across at him and recognized with a sharp pang of pity, in his own eyes, the well-known eyes wide open towards the darkness where she sat invisible, the look he had described . . . *wehmütig*; in spite of his sheltered happy prosperous youth it was there; he *belonged* to those millions whose sufferings he had revealed to her, a shadow lying for ever across the bright unseeing confidence of Europe, hopeless. And now, at this moment, standing out from their midst, the strange

beautiful Old Testament figure in modern clothes; the fine,
beautifully moulded Hebrew head, so like his own.

'But it *is* extraordinary; that just when everything is at its
worst, this idea should have arisen. It's all very well for
people to laugh at Micawber.'

'Who is this man?'

'The man who is always waiting for something to turn up.
Things *do* turn up, exactly at the right moment. It doesn't
mean fatalism. I don't believe in laisser-aller as a principle;
but there is something *in* things, something the people who
make plans and think they are thinking out everything in
advance, don't know; their oblivion of it, while they go busily
on knowing exactly what they are going to do and why, even
at picnics, is a terrible thing. And somehow they always fail.'

'They do not by any means always fail. In all concerted
action there must be a plan. Herzl is certainly a man with
a plan.'

'Yes but it's different; his idea *is* his plan. It isn't *clever*.
And now that it is here it seems so simple. Why was it never
put forward before?'

'The greatest ideas are always simple; though not in their
resultants. This dream, however, has always been present
with Jews.'

'Of course. The Zionist Movement, coming now, when it
is most wanted, is not altogether Herzl. It's that strange
thing, the thing that makes you stare, in history. A sort of
shape . . .'

'It is the collective pressure of life; an unseen movement.
But, if you feel this, what now becomes of your individualism?
Eh?' He chuckled his delight. Passing so easily and
leisurely to personal things.

'Oh, the shape doesn't affect the *individual*, in himself.
There's something behind all those outside things that goes
on independently of them, something much more wonderful.'

'You are wrong. What you call the shape, affects most
profoundly every individual in spite of himself.'

'But he must be an individual to be affected at all, and no
two people are affected in the same way. After this evening

III—* F

I'm more of an individualist than before. It is *relief* to know
that science is a smaller kind of truth than philosophy. The
real difficulty is not between science and religion at all, but
between religion and *philosophy*. Philosophy seems to think
science assumes too much to begin with, and can never get
any further than usefulness.'

'Science can afford to smile at this.'

'And that religion is philosophically unsound, though
modern religious controversy is metaphysical.'

'*All* controversy depends from differences in estimation of
term significations.'

'That's why arguments are so maddening; even small
discussions; people go rushing on, getting angrier and angrier,
talking about quite different things, especially men, because
they never want to get at the truth, only to score a point.'

'You are unjust; many men put truth before any other consideration whatsoever. It is not only unjust, it is most bad
for you to hold this cynical estimation.'

'Well, men arguing always look like that, to women. That's
why women always go off at a tangent; because they reply not
to what men *say* but to what they *mean*, which is to *score a
point*, which *anybody* can do, with practice, and while they
hold on to the point they mean to score, they are revealed,
under all sorts of circumstances, all sorts of things about them
are as plain as a pike-staff, to a woman, and the results of these
things; so that she suddenly finds herself saying something
that sounds quite irrelevant, but isn't.'

'Nevertheless there is honourable controversy, and most
fruitful.'

'There are people here and there with open minds. Very few.'

'The point is not the few, but that they *are*.'

'The few just men, who save the city.'

'Exactly.'

'But even existence is not quite certain.'

'*What* is this?'

'Descartes *said*, my existence is certain; that is a fallacy.'

'If this is a fallacy for metaphysic, so much the worse for
metaphysic.'

'That is argumentum ad hominem.'

'I am not afraid of it.'

'But what can you put in place of metaphysic?'

'Life is larger.'

'I know. I know. I know. Something exists. Meta-physic admits that. I nearly shouted when Dr M'Taggart said that. It's enough. It answers everything. Even to have seen it for a moment is enough. The first time I thought of it I nearly died of joy. Descartes should have said, 'I am aware that there *is* something, therefore I am.' If I am, other people are; but that does not seem to matter. That is their own affair.'

'Beware of solipsism.'

'I don't care what it is called. It is certainty. You *must* begin with the individual. There we are again.' There was an end to the conversation that could not be shared. The words of it already formed, intangibly, waited, ready to dis-appear, until she should be alone and could read them on a clear background. If she stayed they would disappear irrevo-cably. She rose, bidding him a hurried good night, suddenly aware of the busily sleeping household, friendly guardian of this wide leisurely night-life. He too was aware and grateful, picking his way cautiously through the shadows of the large room, sheltered from his loneliness, invisibly enclosed by the waiting incommunicable statement that yet left him, accusing him of wilful blindness, so cruelly outside.

'Materialism,' scribbled Miriam eagerly, 'has the recom-mendation of being a monism, and therefore a more perfect explanation of the universe than a dualism can be. . . . And matter forms one great whole, persisting through many ages. Mind appears in the form of separate individuals, isolated from each other by matter, and each ceasing, so far as observation goes, after a very few years. Also the changes which we can observe mind to make in matter are comparatively insignifi-cant, while a very slight change in matter will either destroy mind, or, at least, remove it from the only circumstances in which we can observe its existence. All these characteristics make matter appear much more powerful and important than mind.'

'I consider this a very strong reasoning,' muttered Mr Shatov.

'Ssh. Wait.' He was sitting intent, with an awakened youthful student's face, meeting, through her agency, in England, a first-class intelligence. He would hear the beautiful building up, strophe and antistrophe, of the apparently unassailable argument, the pause, and then, in the same shapely cadences, its complete destruction, for ever, the pleasant face smiling at the audience above the ruins, like a child who has just shattered a castle of bricks.

'Idealism was weakened by being supposed to be bound up with certain theological doctrines which became discredited. All these things account for the great strength of materialism some years ago. There has been a reaction against this, but the extent of the reaction has been exaggerated.'

'Quite so.'

'Wait, wait.'

'It still remains the belief to which most people tend on first leaving an unreflecting position. And many remain there. Science is a large element in our lives now, and if we try to make science serve as metaphysic, we get materialism. Nor is it to be wished—even by idealists—that materialism should become too weak. For idealism is seldom really vigorous except in those who have had a serious struggle with materialism. . . . It would be very difficult to disprove materialism, if we once accepted the reality of matter as a thing in itself. But, as we saw when considering dualism, such a reality of matter is untenable. And this conclusion is obviously more fatal to materialism than it was to dualism. And again, if materialism is true, all our thoughts are produced by purely material antecedents. These are quite blind, and are just as likely to produce falsehood as truth. We have thus no reason for believing any of our conclusions—including the truth of materialism, which is therefore a self-contradictory hypothesis.'

'I find this too easily stated.'

Then God is *proved* . . .

'You weren't here *before*. Philosophy is not difficult. It is common sense systematized and clarified.' . . . Wayfaring men, though fools, shall not err therein. It is not what people think but what they know. Thought is words. Philosophy will never find words to express life; the philosopher is the same as the criminal?

'He seems to say spirit when he means *life*.'

'What *is* life?'

'Moreover presentationism is incompatible with the truth of general propositions — and therefore with itself, since it can only be expressed by a general proposition. And closer analysis shows that it is incompatible even with particular propositions, since these involve both the union of two terms and the use of general ideas.' People know this faintly when they say things; not *why*; but faintly every one knows that nothing can be said. Then why listen any more? Because if you know, exactly, that nothing can be said and the expert reasons for it, you know for certain in times of weakness, how much there is that might be expressed if there were any way of expressing it. . . . But there was no need to listen any more since God was proved by the impossibility of his absence, like an invisible star. No one seemed at all disturbed; the lecturer least of all. Perhaps he felt that the effects of real realization would be so tremendous that he could not face them. The thought of no God made life simply silly. The thought of God made it embarrassing. If a hand suddenly appeared writing on the wall, what would he do? He would blush; standing there as a competitor, fighting for his theories, amongst the theories of other men. Yet if there were no philosophers, if the world were imagined without philosophy, there would be nothing but theology, getting more and more superstitious.

Everybody was so *calm*. The calmness of insanity. Nobody quite all there. Yet intelligent. *What* were they all thinking about, wreathed in films of intelligent insanity; watching the performance in the intervals of lives filled with words that meant nothing? Breath is more than words; the fact of breathing . . . but every one is in such a hurry.

'I would ask' . . . one horrified glance revealed Mr

Shatov's profile quivering as he hesitated. A louder, confident, dictatorial English voice had rung out simultaneously from the other side of the hall. He would have to sit down, shaken by his brave attempt. But to the whole evening, the deep gentle tones had been added, welling through and beyond the Englishman's strident, neat proclamation, and containing, surely every one must hear it, so much of the answer to the essential question. The chairman hesitated, turned decisively, and the other man sat down.

'What the lectchooroor makes of the psycho-physical paralellism ?'

He drove home his question on a note of reproachful expostulation and sat down drawn together, with bent head and eye downcast, but listening intently with his serene child's brow. Miriam was instantly sorry that his words had got through, their naked definiteness changing the eloquent tone, sharpening it to a weapon, a borrowed weapon.

'That's it,' she breathed, hoping the lecturer's answer would throw some light on the meaning of the fascinating phrase, floating before her, fresh from far-off philosophical battle-fields, bright from centuries of contemplation, flashing out now, to-day, in Europe triumphantly, in desperate encounters. The lecturer was on his feet, gleaming towards their centre of the audience his recognition of the clean thrust.

'The correlation between physical and mental gives an empirical support to materialism.' That *couldn't* be spirited away. The scientists *swore* there was no break; so convincingly; perhaps they would yet win and prove it. 'But it is necessary to distinguish between metaphysic and psychology. Psychology, like physical science, is to be put to the score of our knowledge of matter.'

'In which he doesn't believe,' scoffed Miriam, distractedly poised between Mr Shatov's drama and the prospect opening within her mind.

'I find this a most arbitrary statement.'

'Yes, *rather*,' murmured Miriam emphatically, and waited for a moment as if travelling with him along his line of thought. But he was recovering, had recovered, did not seem to be dwelling or moving in any relation to what he had said, appeared to be disinterestedly listening to the next question.

'Besides,' she said, 'the empirical method is a most important method, and jolly.'

'Poor chap; what a stupidity is this question.' Miriam smiled solicitously, but she had travelled back enraptured across nine years to the day, now only yesterday, of her first meeting with her newly recovered word. Jevons. From the first the sienna-brown volume had been wonderful, the only one of the English books that had any connection with life; and that day, Sunday afternoon prep in the dining-room, with the laburnum and pink may outside the window changing as she read from a tantalizing reproach to a vivid encirclement of her being by all the spring scenes she had lived through, coming and going, the sight and scent and shimmering movement of them, as if she moved, bodiless and expanded, about in their midst. Something about the singing, lifting word appearing suddenly on the page, even before she had grasped its meaning, intensified the relation to life of the little hard motionless book, leaving it, when she had read on, centred round the one statement; the rest remaining in shadow, interesting but in some strange way ill-gotten.

The recovery of the forgotten word at the centre of 'the philosophical problems of the present day,' cast a fresh glow of reality across her schooldays. The efforts she had so blindly made, so indolently and prodigally sacrificing her chances of success in the last examination, to the few things that had made the world shine about her, had been in some way right, with a shapeliness and fruitfulness of their own. Her struggles with Jevons had been bread cast upon the waters. How differently the word now fell into her mind, with 'intuition' happily at home there to keep it company. If materialism could be supported empirically, there was something in it, something in matter that had not yet been found out. Meantime philosophy proved God. And Hegel had not brushed away the landscape. There was God *and* the landscape.

'Materialism isn't dead *yet*,' she heard herself say recklessly.

'*More*. Chemistry will yet carry us further than this kind of metaphysical surmising.'

Taking part, even being with someone who took part in the proceedings, altered them. Some hidden chain of evidence was broken. Things no longer stood quietly in the air for acceptance or rejection. The memory of the evening would be a memory of social life, isolated revelations of personality.

CHAPTER VIII

WHEN they emerged from the dusty shabbiness of the Euston
Road it was suddenly a perfect June morning. Now was the
moment. She opened the letter unnoticed, with her eyes on
the sunlit park-lined vista. 'London owes much to the fact
that its main thoroughfares run east and west; walk westward
in the morning down any one of them, or in the afternoon
towards the east and whenever the sun shines you will see'
. . . and without arousing his attention hurriedly read the
few lines. Was that man still in London, trying to explain it
to himself, or had he been obliged to go away, or perhaps to
die? London is heaven and can't be explained. To be
sent away is to be sent out of heaven.

'I've been telling'... useless words, coming thin and helpless
out of darkness and pressing against darkness . . . a desperate clutching at a borrowed performance to keep alive and keep
on . . . 'my employers what I think of them just lately.'

'Excellent. What have you told?'

His unconscious voice steadied her, as the darkness drove
nearer, bringing thoughts that must not arrive. The morning
changed to a painted scene, from which she turned away,
catching the glance of the leaves near by, trickily painted, as
she turned to steer the eloquence flowing up in her mind.

'Well, it was a whole point of view I saw suddenly in the
train coming back after Easter. I read an essay, about a
superannuated clerk, an extraordinary thing, very simple and
well written, not in the least like an essay. But there was
something in it that was horrible. The employers gave
the old man a pension, with humorous benevolence. He is so
surprised and so blissfully happy in having nothing to do
but look at the green world for the rest of the time, that he feels
nothing but gratitude. That's all right, from his point of

view, being that sort of old man. But how dare the firm be humorously benevolent? It is no case for *humour*. It is *not* funny that prosperous people can use up lives on small fixed salaries that never increase beyond a certain point, no matter how well the employers get on, even if for the last few years they give pensions. And they don't give pensions. If they do, they are thought most benevolent. The author, who is evidently in a way a thoughtful man, ought to have known this. He just wrote a thing that looks charming on the surface and is beautifully written and is really perfectly horrible and disgusting. Well, I suddenly thought employers ought to know. I don't know what can be done. *I* don't want a pension. I hate working for a salary, as it is. But employers ought to *know* how fearfully unfair everything is. They ought to have their complacency smashed up.' He was engrossed. His foreign intelligence sympathized. Then she was right.

'Anyhow. The worst of it is that my employers are so frightfully nice. But the principle's the same, the frightful unfairness. And it happened that just before I went away, just as Mr Hancock was going off for his holiday, he had been annoyed by one of his Mudie books going back before he had read it, and no others coming that were on his list, and he suddenly said to me in a grumbling tone, "You might keep an eye on my Mudie books." I was simply furious. Because before I began looking after the books—which he had never asked me to do, and was quite my own idea—it was simply a muddle. They all kept lists in a way, at least put down books when they hit upon one they thought they would like, and then sent the whole list *in*, and never kept a copy, and of course forgot what they'd put down. Well, I privately took to copying those lists and crossing off the books as they came and keeping on sending in the rest of the list again and again till they had *all* come. Well, I know a wise person would not have been in a rage and would meekly have rushed about keeping more of an eye than ever. But I can't stand unfairness. It was the principle of the thing. What made it worse was that for some time I have had the use of one of his books myself, his idea, and of course most kind. But it doesn't alter the principle. In the train I saw the whole unfairness of the life of employees. However hard they work, their lives don't alter or get any easier. They live cheap poor lives, in anxiety, all their best years and then are expected to be grateful for a pension, and generally get no pension. I 've left off living in anxiety; perhaps because I 've forgotten how to have an imagination. But that is the principle, and I came to the conclusion that no employers, however generous and nice, are entitled to the slightest special consideration. And I came back and practically said so. I told him that in future I would have nothing to do with his Mudie books. It was outside my sphere. I also said all sorts of things that came into my head in the train, a whole long speech. About unfairness. And to prove my point to him individually I told him of things that were unfair to me and their other employees in the practice; about the awfulness of having to be there first thing in the morning from the country after a week-end. *They* don't. They sail off to their expensive week-ends without even saying good-bye, and without even thinking whether we can manage to have any sort of recreation at all on our salaries. I said that, and also that I objected to spend a large part of a busy Monday morning arranging the huge bunches of flowers he brought back from the country. That was not true. I loved those flowers and could always have some for my room; but it *was* a frightful nuisance sometimes, and it came into the principle, and I wound up by saying that in future I would do only the work for the practice and no odd jobs of any kind.'

'What was his reply?'

'Oh, well, I 've got the sack.'

'Are you serious?' he asked in a low frightened tone. The heavens were clear, ringing with morning joy; from far away in the undisturbed future she looked back smiling upon the episode that lay before her growing and pressing.

'I 'm not serious. But they are. This is a solemn, awfully nice little note from Mr Orly; he had to write, because he 's the senior partner, to inform me that he has come to the conclusion that I must seek a more congenial post. They have absolutely made up their minds. Because they know quite well I have no training for any other work, and no resources, and they would not have done this unless they were absolutely obliged.'

'Then you will be obliged to leave these gentlemen?'

'Of course long before I had finished talking, I was thinking about all sorts of other things; and seeing all kinds of points of view that seemed to be stated all round us by people who were looking on. I always do when I talk to Mr Hancock. His point of view is so clear-cut and so reasonable that it reveals all the things that hold social life together, and brings the ghosts of people who have believed and suffered for these things into the room, but also all kinds of other points of view. . . . But I'm not going to leave. I can't. What else could I do? Perhaps I will, a little later on, when this is all over. But I'm not going to be dismissed in solemn dignity. It's too silly. That shows you how nice they are. I know that really I must leave. Any one would say so. But that's the extraordinary thing; I don't believe in those things; solemn endings; being led by the nose by the necessities of the situation. That may be undignified. But dignity is silly; the back view. Already I can't believe all this solemnity has happened. It's simply a most fearful bother. They've managed it splendidly, waiting till Saturday morning, so that I shan't see any of them again. The Orlys will be gone away for a month when I get there to-day, and Mr Hancock is away for the week-end and I am offered a month's salary in lieu of notice, if I prefer it. I had forgotten all this machinery. They're perfectly in the right, but I'd forgotten the machinery. I knew yesterday. They were all three shut up together in the den, talking in low tones, and presently came busily out, each so anxious to pass the dismissed secretary in hurried preoccupation, that they collided in the doorway, and gave everything away to me by the affable excited way they apologized to each other. If I had turned and faced them then, I should have said worse things than I had said to Mr Hancock. I *hated* them, with their resources and their serenity, complacently pleased with each other because they had decided to smash an employee who had spoken out to them.'

'This was indeed a scene of remarkable significance.'

'I don't know. I once told Mr Hancock that I would give notice every year, because I think it must be so horrible to dismiss anybody. But I'm not going to be sent away by machinery. In a way, it is like a family suddenly going to law.'

But with the passing of the park and the coming of the tall houses on either side of the road, the open June morning was quenched. It retreated to balconies, flower-filled by shocked condemning people, prosperously turned away towards the world from which she was banished. Wimpole Street, Harley Street, Cavendish Square. The names sounded in her ears the appeal they had made when she was helplessly looking for work. It was as if she were still waiting to come. . . .

Within the Saturday morning peace of the deserted house, lingered the relief that had followed their definite decision. . . . They were all drawn together to begin again, renewed, freshly conscious of the stabilities of the practice; their enclosed co-operating relationship.

She concentrated her mental gaze on their grouped personalities, sharing their long consultations, acting out in her mind, with characteristic gesture and speech, the part each one had taken, confronting them one by one, in solitude, with a different version, holding on, breaking into their common-sense finalities. . . . It was all nothing; meaningless . . . like things in history that led on to events that did not belong to them because nobody went below the surface of the way things appear to be joined together but are not. . . . But the words belonging to the underlying things were far away, only to be found in long silences, and sounding, when they came out into conversations, irrelevant, often illogical and self-contradictory, impossible to prove, driving absurdly across life towards things that seemed impossible, but were true. . . . There are two layers of truth. The truths laid bare by common sense in swift decisive conversations, founded on apparent facts, are incomplete. They shape the surface, and make things go kaleidoscoping on, recognizable, in a sort of general busy prosperous agreement; but at every turn, with every application of the common-sense civilized decisions, enormous things are left behind, unsuspected, forced underground, but never dying, slow things with slow, slow fruit. . . . The surface shape is powerful, every one is in it, that is where free will breaks down, in the moving on and being spirited away for another spell from the underlying things, but in every one, alone, often unconsciously, is something, a real inside personality that is turned away from the surface. In front of every one, away from the bridges and catchwords, is an invisible plank, that will bear. Always. Forgotten. Nearly all smiles are smiled from the bridges. . . . Nearly all deaths are murders or suicides. . . .

It would be such an awful labour. . . . In the long interval, the strength for it would disappear. Thoughts must be kept away. Activities. The week-end would be a vacuum of tense determination. That was the payment for headlong speech. Speech, thought-out speech, does nothing but destroy. There had been a moment of hesitation in the train, swamped by the illumination coming from the essay.

The morning's letters lay unopened on her table. Dreadful. Dealing with them would bring unconsciousness, acceptance of the situation would leap upon her unawares. She gathered them up conversationally, summoning presences and the usual atmosphere of the working day, but was disarmed by the trembling of her hands. The letters were the last link. Merely touching them had opened the door to a withering pain. When the appointments were kept, she would no longer be in the house. The patients crowded through her mind; individuals, groups, families, the whole fabric of social life richly unrolled day by day, for her contemplation; spirited away. Each letter brought the sting of careless indifferent farewell.

At the hall door, James was whistling for a hansom; it was a dream picture, part of the week that was past. A hansom drew up, the abruptly reined-in horse slipping and scrabbling. Perhaps there *was* a patient hidden in Mr Leyton's quiet-sounding surgery. Once more she could watch a patient's departure; the bright oblong of street. There was no patient. It was a dream picture. Dream figures were coming downstairs. . . . Mrs Orly, Mr Orly, not yet gone; coming hurriedly straight towards her. She rose without thought, calmly unoccupied, watching them come, one person, swiftly and gently. They stood about her, quite near; silently radiating their kindliness.

'I suppose we must say good-bye,' said Mrs Orly. In her sweet little sallow face not a shadow of reproach; but lively bright sorrow, *tears* in her eyes.

'I say, we 're awfully sorry about this,' said Mr Orly gustily, shifting his poised bulk from one foot to the other.

'So am I,' said Miriam seeking for the things they were inviting her to say. She could only smile at them.

'It *is* a pity,' whispered Mrs Orly. *This* was the Orlys; the reality of them; an English reality; utterly unbusinesslike; with no codes but themselves; showing themselves; without disguises of voice or manner, to a dismissed employee; the quality of England; old-fashioned.

'I know.' They both spoke together and then Mrs Orly was saying, 'No, Ro can't bear strangers.'

'If *you* don't want me to go I shall stay,' she murmured. But the sense of being already half reinstated was driven away by Mrs Orly's unaltered distress.

'Ungrateful?' The gustily panting tones were the remainder of the real anger he had felt, listening to Mr Hancock's discourse. They had no grievance and they had misunderstood his.

'No,' she said coldly, 'I don't think so.'

'Hang it all, excuse my language, but y' know he 's done a good deal for ye.' 'All expectation of gratitude is meanness and is continually punished by the total insensibility of the obliged person' . . . 'we are lucky; we ought to be grateful'; meaning, to God. Then unlucky people ought to be ungrateful. . . .

'Besides,' the same gusty tone, 'it 's as good as telling us we 're not gentlemen; y' see?' The blue eyes flashed furiously.

Then all her generalizations had been taken *personally*. . . . 'Oh, well,' she said helplessly.

'We shall be late, laddie.'

'Surely that can be put right. I must talk to Mr Hancock.'

'Well, to tell y' honestly I don't think y'll be able to do anything with Hancock.' Mrs Orly's distressed little face supported his opinion and her surprising sudden little embrace and Mr Orly's wringing handshake meant not only the enduring depths of their kindliness but their pained dismay in seeing her desolate and resourceless, their certainty that there was no hope. It threw a strong light. It would be difficult for him to withdraw; perhaps impossible; perhaps he had already engaged another secretary. But she found that she had not watched them go away and was dealing steadily with the letters, with a blank mind upon which presently emerged the features of the coming week-end.

'Well, as I *say*——' Miriam followed the lingering held-in cold vexation of the voice, privately prompting it with informal phrases fitting the picture she held, half-smiling, in her mind, of a moody, uncertain, door-slamming secretary, using the whole practice as material for personal musings, liable suddenly to break into long speeches of accusation. But if they were spoken, they would destroy the thing that was being given back to her, the thing that had made the atmosphere of the room. 'It will be the most unbusinesslike thing I've ever done; and I doubt very much whether it will answer.'

'Oh, well. There's not any reason why it shouldn't.' She smiled provisionally. It was not yet quite time to rise and feel life flowing about her in the familiar room, purged to a fresh austerity by the coming and passing of the storm. There was still a rankling and, glorious as it was to sit talking at leisure, the passing of time piled up the sense of ultimate things missing their opportunity of getting said. She could not, with half her mind set towards the terms, promising a laborious future of her resolution that he should never regret his unorthodoxy find her way to them. And the moments as they passed gleamed too brightly with confirmation of the strange blind faith she had brought as sole preparation for the encounter, hovered with too quiet a benediction to be seized and used deliberately, without the pressure of the sudden inspiration for which they seemed to wait.

'Well, as I say, that depends entirely on yourself. You must clearly understand that I expect you to fulfil all reasonable requests whether referring to the practice or no, and moreover to fulfil them *cheerfully*.'

'Well, of course I have no choice. But I can't promise to be *cheerful*; that's impossible.' An obstinate tightening of the grave face.

'I think perhaps I might manage to be *serene*; generally. I can't *pretend* to be cheerful.' 'Assume an air of cheerfulness, and presently you will be cheerful, in spite of yourself.' Awful. To live like that would be to miss suddenly finding the hidden something that would make you cheerful for ever.

'Well, as I say——'

'You see there's always the awful question of right and wrong mixed up with everything; all sorts of rights and wrongs, in the simplest things. I can't think how people can go on so calmly. It sometimes seems to me as if every one ought to stop and do quite other things. It's a nightmare, the way things go on. I want to stay here, and yet I often wonder whether I ought; whether I ought to go on doing this kind of work.'

'Well, as I say, I know quite well the work here leaves many of your capabilities unoccupied.'

'It's not that. I mean everything, in general.'

'Well—if it is a question of right and wrong, I suppose the life here like any other, offers opportunities for the exercise of the Christian virtues.'

Resignation; virtues deliberately set forth every day like the wares in a little shop; and the world going on outside just the same. A sort of sale of mean little virtues for respectability and a living; the living coming by amiable co-operation with a world where everything was wrong, turning the little virtues into absurdity; respectable absurdity. He did not think the practice of the Christian virtues in a vacuum was enough. But he had made a joke, and smiled his smile. . . . There was no answer anywhere in the world to the question he had raised.

Did he remember saying 'Why shouldn't you take up dentistry?'
Soon it would be too late to make any change; there was
nothing to do, now, but to stay and justify things . . . it
would be impossible to be running about in a surgery with
grey hair; it would make the practice seem dowdy. All dental
secretaries were young. . . . The work . . . nothing but the
life all round it; the existence of a shadow amidst shadows
unaware of their shadowiness, keeping going a world where
there were things, more than people. The people moved sunlit and prosperous, but not enviable, their secrets revealed at
every turn; unaware themselves, they made and left a space in
which to be aware. . . .

'I want to say that I think it is kind of you to let me air my
grievances so thoroughly.'

'Well, as I *say*, I feel extremely uncertain as to the advisability
of this step.'

'You needn't,' she said rising as he rose, and going buoyantly
to move about in the neighbourhood of the scattered results
of his last operation, the symbols of her narrowly rescued continuity. She was not yet free to touch them. He was still
wandering about the other part of the room, lingering with
thoughtful bent head in the mazes of her outrageous halting
statements. But a good deal of his resentment had gone. It
was something outside herself, something in the world at large,
that had forced him to act against his 'better judgment.' He
was still angry and feeling a little shorn, faced, in the very
presence of the offender, with the necessity of disposing of the
fact that he had been driven into inconsistency.

Miriam drew a deep sigh, clearing her personal air of the
burden of conflict. Was it an affront? It had sounded to her
like a song. His thoughts must be saying, Well, there you are,
it's all very well to throw it all off like that. His pose stiffened
into a suggested animation with regard to work delayed. If
only now there could be an opportunity for one of his humorous
remarks so that she could laugh herself back into their indestructible impersonal relationship. It was, she thought,
prophetically watching his gloriously inevitable recovery,
partly his unconscious resentment of the blow she had struck

at their good understanding that had made him so repeatedly declare that if they started again it must be on a new footing; that all possibility of spontaneity between them had been destroyed.

How could it be, with the events of daily life perpetually building it afresh?

CHAPTER IX

THE power of London to obliterate personal affairs depended upon unlimited freedom to be still. The worst suffering in the days of uncertainty had been the thought of movements that would make time move. Now that the stillness had returned, life was going on, dancing, flowing, looping out in all directions, able to bear its periods of torment in the strength of its certainty of recovery, so long as time stayed still. Life *ceased* when time moved on. Out in the world life was ceasing all the time. All the time people were helplessly doing things that made time move; growing up, old people growing onwards, with death suddenly in sight, rushing here and there with words that had lost their meaning, dodging and crouching no matter how ridiculously, to avoid facing it. Young men died in advance; it was visible in their faces, when they took degrees and sat down to tasks that made time begin to move; never again free from its movement, always listening and looking for the stillness they had lost. . . . But why is the world which produces them so fresh and real and free, and then seizes and makes them dead old leaves whirled along by time, so different from people alone in themselves when time is not moving? People in themselves want nothing but reality. Why can't reality exist in the world? All the things that happen produce friction because they distract people from the reality they are unconsciously looking for. That is why there are everywhere torrents of speech. If she had not read all those old words in the train, and had been silent. Silence is reality. Life ought to be lived on a basis of silence, where truth blossoms. Why isn't such an urgent thing known? Life would become like the individual; alive . . . it would show, inside and out, and people would leave off talking so much. Life does show, seen from far off, pouring down into stillness. But the contemplation of it, not caring for pain or suffering except as part of a picture, which no one who is in the picture can see, seems mean. Old women sitting in corners, suddenly making irrelevant remarks and chuckling, see; they make a stillness of reality, a mind picture that does not care, out of the rush of life. Perhaps they do not fear death. Perhaps people who don't take part don't fear death? The outsider sees most of the game; but that means a cynical man who does not care for anything; body and mind without soul. Lying dead at last, with reality left unnoticed on his dressing-table, along the window sill, along the edge of things outside the window. . . .

But one day in the future time would move, by itself, not through anything one did, and there would be no more life. She looked up hurriedly towards the changing voice. He was no longer reading with a face that showed his thoughts wandering far away.

'The thought of death is, throughout life, entirely absent from the mind of the healthy man.' His brilliant, thought-filled eyes shone towards her at the end of the sentence.

'There is *indeed* a vulgarity in perfect health,' he exclaimed.

'Yes,' she said hurriedly, carrying off the statement for examination, as peacefully he went on reading. What did vulgarity mean, or perfect health? Nobody knew. Dante ennobled the vulgar tongue. . . . People went on for ever writing books using the same words with different meanings. Her eyes returned to the relaxed unconscious form. He thought too much of books. Yet it did not appal him to think of giving up his free intellectual life and taking to work. 'I shall still be an interested amateur.' . . . He would go on reading, all his life, sitting as he was sitting now, grave and beautiful; with a mind outspread in a mental experience so wide that he was indifferent to the usual ideas of freedom and advantage. Yet he did not seem to be aware how much the sitting like this, linked to the world by its deep echo in the book, was a realization of life as he saw it. It did not occur to him that this serenity, in which were accumulated all the hours they had passed together, *was* realization, the life of the world in miniature, making a space where everything in human experience could emerge like a reflection in deep water, with its proportions held true and right by the tranquil opposition of their separate minds. She summoned onlookers, who instantly recognized themselves in this picture of leisure. It was in every life that was not astray in ceaseless movement. It was the place where everything was atoned. He fitted, placed thus, happy, without problems or envies, in possession of himself and his memories in the room where he had voiced them, into the centre of English life where all turned to good, in the last fastness of the private English mind where condemnation could not live. He reinforced it with a consciousness that was not in the English, making it show as an idea, revealing in plain terms their failure to act it out. Thus would his leisure always be. But it was no part of her life. In this tranquillity there was no security . . . we will always sit like this; we must, she said within herself impatiently towards his unconsciousness. Why did he not *perceive* the life there was, the mode of life, in this sitting tranquilly together? Was he thinking of nothing but his reading? She listened for a moment half carried into the quality of the text. There was reality there, Spinoza, by himself, sounding as if the words were being traced out now, for the first time. One day in a moment of blankness, she would read it and agree and disagree and carry away some idea and lose and recover it and go on, losing and recovering, agreeing and disagreeing. . . .

When he went away, her life would be swept clear of intelligently selected books and the sting of conflict with them. That would not matter; perhaps; books would come, somehow, in the unexpected way they always did. But it was impossible to face the ending of these settled tranquil elderly evenings of peaceful unity, the quiet dark-bearded form, sitting near, happily engrossed. . . .

'Well, what do you think of this?'

'I haven't been attending. But I will read it . . . some time.'

'Ah, it is a pity. But tell me your thoughts at least.'

'Oh, I was thinking of my sisters.'

'Ah. You must tell me,' and again with unrelaxed interest he was listening to story after story, finding strange significances, matter for envy and deep chuckles of appreciative laughter.

CHAPTER X

WITH a parting glance at Mr Shatov's talked-out indolent vacuity, she plunged, still waiting in the attitude of conversation, into a breathless silence. She would make no more talk. There should be silence between them. If he broke it, well and good; in future she would take measures to curtail the hours of conversation leading, now that she was at home in possession of the Russian life and point of view, only to one or other of his set of quoted opinions, beyond which he refused to move. If not, the quality of their silence would reveal to her what lay behind their unrelaxed capacity for association. The silence grew, making more and more space about her, and still he did not speak. It was dismantling; unendurable. With every moment they both grew smaller and smaller, moving quickly towards the quenching of all their interchange. But there was no doubt now. The question was there between them, for equal contemplation. His easy indolence had fled; his usual pallor heightened, and he sat regarding her with an unhesitating personal gaze. Her determination closed about him, blocking his way, filling the room. He *must* emerge, admit. He must at least *see*, as she saw, if it were only the extent of their dependence on each other. He knew his need. Perhaps she fulfilled it less than she thought? Perhaps it was hers alone. . . . His multiplied resources made hers humiliatingly greater. The shrine of her current consciousness stood before her; the roots of her only visible future planted for ever within it. Losing it, she would be left with her burden of being once more scattered and unhoused.

He rose, bringing her to her feet, and stood before her ready to go or stay as she should choose, heaping up before her, with an air of gently ironic challenge, the burden of responsibility, silently offering her one of his borrowed summaries, some

irrelevant and philosophic worldly wisdom.   But it was what
he felt.   There was something he feared.   Alone, he would
not have initiated this scene.   She faltered, driven back and
disarmed by the shock of an overwhelming pity . . . an unexpected terrible challenge from within, known to no one, to
be accepted or flouted on her sole eternal responsibility. . . .
In a torment of acceptance she pressed through it and returned
remorseless to her place, flooded as she moved by a sudden
knowing of wealth within herself now being strangely quarried.

The long moment was ending; into its void she saw the
seemings of her grown life pass and disappear.   His solid
motionless form, near and equal in the twilight, grew faint,
towered above her, immense and invisible in a swift gathering
swirling darkness bringing him nearer than sight or touch.
The edges of things along the margin of her sight stood for an
instant sharply clear and disappeared leaving her faced only
with the swirling darkness shot now with darting flame.   She
ceased to care what thoughts might be occupying him, and
exulted in the marvel.   Here, already, rewarding her insistence,
was payment in royal coin.   She was at last, in person, on a
known highway, as others, knowing truth alive.   She stared
expostulation as she recognized the celebrated nature of her
experience, hearing her own familiar voice as on a journey, in
amazed expostulation at the absence everywhere of simple
expression of the quality of the state. . . . A voyage, swift and
transforming, a sense of passing in the midst of this marvel of
flame-lit darkness, out of the world in glad solitary confidence
with wildly, calmly beating morning heart.

The encircling darkness grew still, spread wide about her;
the moving flames drew together to a single glowing core.
The sense of his presence returned in might.   The rosy-
hearted core of flame was within him, within the invisible
substance of his breast.   Tenderly transforming his intangible
expansion to the familiar image of the man who knew her
thoughts she moved to find him and marvel with him.

His voice budded gently, but with the same quality that had
flung her back solid and alone into the cold gloom.

'We must consider' . . . what did he think had happened?

He had kissed a foreign woman. Who did he think was hearing him? . . . 'what you would do under certain circumstances.' The last words came trembling, and he sat down clearly visible in the restored blue twilight; waiting with willing permanence for her words.

'I should do nothing at all, under any circumstances.'

'Do not forget that I am Jew.'

Looking at him with the eyes of her friends Miriam saw the Russian, standing free, beyond Europe, from the stigma of 'foreigner.' Many people would think, as she had in the beginning, that he was an intellectual Frenchman, different from the usual 'Frenchman'; a big-minded cosmopolitan at any rate; a proud possession. The mysterious fact of Jewishness could remain in the background . . . the hidden flaw . . . as there was always a hidden flaw in all her possessions. To her, and to her adventure, its first step now so far away, an accepted misery powerless to arrest the swift rush of the transforming moments, it need make no difference.

'Perhaps it shall be better I should go away.'

Where? Into the world of people, who would seem to him not different from herself, see his marvellous surrendered charm, catch him, without knowing who or what he was. Who else could know 'Mr Shatov'?

'Do you want to go away?'

'I do not. But it must be with you to decide.'

'I don't see why you should go *away*.'

'Then I shall stay. And we shall see.'

The summer lay ahead, unaltered; the threat of change gone from their intercourse. To-morrow they would take up life again with a stability; years at their disposal. The need for the moment was to have him out of sight, kill the past hour and return to the idea of him, already keeping her standing, with relaxed power of attention to his little actual pitiful obstructive form, in an independent glow, an easy wealth of assurance towards life whose thronging images, mysteries of cities and crowds, single fixed groups of known places and inexorable people were alight and welcoming with the sense of him. She bade him a gentle good night and reached her room, unpursued

III—G

by thought, getting to bed in a trance of suspension, her own life left behind, façades of life set all about her, claiming in vain for troubled attention, and sank at once into a deep sleep.

Putting on her outdoor things next morning, left in the drawing-room while she snatched her breakfast, she was immensely embarrassed to find him standing silently near. The woman facing her in the mirror as she put on her hat was the lonely Miriam Henderson, unendurably asked to behave in a special way. For he was standing eloquently silent and the hands arranging her hat trembled reassuringly. But what was she to do? How turn and face him and get back through the room and away to examine alone the surprises of being in love? Her image was disconcerting, her clothes and the act of rushing off to tiresomely engrossing work inappropriate. It was paralysing to be *seen* by him struggling with a tie. The vivid colour that rushed to her cheeks turned her from the betraying mirror to the worse betrayal of his gaze. But it was enough for the moment, which she faced out, downcast, yet joyful in giving what belonged to his grave eyes.

'We cannot be as boy and girl,' he said gently, 'but we may be very happy.'

Overwhelmed with the sense of inadequate youth Miriam stared at his thought. A fragment of conversation flashed into her mind. Jewish girls married at eighteen, or never. At twenty-one they were old maids. . . . He was waiting for some sign. Her limbs were powerless. With an immense effort she stretched forth an enormous arm and, with a hand frightful in its size and clumsiness, tapped him on the shoulder. It was as if she had knocked him down, the blow she had given resounding through the world. He bent to catch at her retreating hand with the attitude of carrying it to his lips, but she was away down the room, her breath caught by a little gurgle of unknown laughter.

He was at the end of the street in the evening, standing bright in the golden light with a rose in his hand. For a swift moment, coming down the shaded street towards the open light, she denied him, and the rose. He had bought a rose from some flower-woman's basket, an appropriate act suggested by his thoughts. But his silent, most surrendered, most childlike gesture of offering, his man's eyes grave upon the rose for her, beneath uplifted childlike plaintive brows, went to her heart, and with the passing of the flower into her hand, the gold of the sunlight, the magic shifting gleam that had lain always day and night, year-long in tranquil moments upon every visible and imagined thing, came at last into her very hold. It *had* been love then, all along. Love *was* the secret of things.

They wandered silently, apart, along the golden-gleaming street. She listened, amidst the far-off sounds about them, to the hush of the great space in which they walked, where voices, breaking silently in from the talk of the world, spoke for her, bringing out, to grow and expand in the sunlight, the thoughts that lay in her heart. They had passed the park, forgetting it, and were enclosed in the dust-strewn narrowness of the Euston Road. But the dust-grains were golden, and her downcast eyes saw everywhere, if she should raise them, the gleam of roses flowering on the air, and when, their way coming too soon towards its familiar end, they turned, with slow feet, down a little alley, dark with voices, the dingy house-fronts gleamed golden about her, the narrow strip of sky opened to an immensity of smiling spacious blue, and she still saw, just ahead, the gleam of flowers and heard, on a breath purer than the air of the open country, the bright sound of distant water.

CHAPTER XI

For many days they spent their leisure wandering in the green spaces of London, restored to Miriam with the frail dream-like wonder they had held in her years of solitude, deepened to a perpetual morning brightness. She recalled, in the hushed reconciliation of the present, while they saw and thought in unison, breaking their long silences with anecdotes, reliving together all they could remember of childhood, their long exhausting, thought-transforming controversies. And as her thoughts had been, so now, in these same green places, were her memories transformed.

She watched, wondering, while elderly relatives, hated and banished, standing, forgotten like past nightmares, far away from her independent London life, but still powerful in memory to strike horror into her world, came forth anew, food, as she breathlessly spoke their names and described them, for endless speculation. With her efforts to make him see and know them, they grew alive in her hands, significant and attractive as the present, irrecoverable, gone, lonely and pitiful, conquered by her own triumphant existence in a different world, free from obstructions, accompanied, understood. Between the movements of conversation from figure to figure, a thread of reflection wove itself in continuous repetition. Perhaps to all these people, life had once looked free and developing. Perhaps, if she went their way, she might yet share their fate. Never. She was mistress of her fate; there was endless time. The world was changed. They had never known freedom or the endlessness of the passing moment. Time for them had been nothing but the continuous pressure of fixed circumstances.

Distant parts of London, whither they wandered far through unseen streets, became richly familiar, opening, when suddenly they would realize that they were lost, on some scene, stamped as unforgettably as the magic scenes of holiday excursions. They lingered in long contemplation of all kinds of shop windows, his patient unmoved good humour while she realized his comparative lack of tastes and preferences, and held forth at length on the difference between style and quality, and the products of the markets, his serene effrontery in taking refuge at last behind the quaintest little tales, satirical, but dreadfully true and illuminating, disarmed her impatience and sent her forward in laughter. He seemed to have an endless supply of these little tales, and told them well, without emphasis, but each one a little drama, perfectly shaped and staged. She collected and remembered and pondered them, the light they shed on unfamiliar aspects of life, playing comfortingly over the future. If judges and generals and emperors and all sorts of people fixed and labelled in social life were really absurd, then social life, with him, might be not merely unaffrighting, but also amusing. At the same time she was affronted by his inclusion of English society in his satirical references. There were, she was sure, hidden and active, in all ranks in England, a greater proportion of people than in any country of his acquaintance, who stood outside his criticism.

She avoided the house, returning only when the hour justified a swift retreat from the hall to her room; escape from the dimly lit privacy of the deserted drawing-room. Not again could she suffer his nearness, until the foreigner in him, dipped every day more deeply into the well of English feeling, should be changed. When she was alone, she moved, thoughtless, along a pathway that led backwards towards a single memory. Far away in the distance, coming always nearer, was the summer morning of her infancy, a permanent standing arrested, level with the brilliance of flower-heads motionless in the sunlit air; no movement but the hovering of bees. Beyond this memory towards which she passed every day more surely, a marvellous scene unfolded. And always with the unfolding of its wide prospects, there came a beautifying breath. The surprise of her growing comeliness was tempered by a sudden curious indifference. These new looks of hers were not her own. They brought a strange publicity. She felt,

turned upon her, the welcoming, approving eyes of women she
had contemptuously neglected, and upon her own face the
dawning reflection of their wise, so irritating smile. She
recognized them, half fearfully, for they alone were the company gathered about her as she watched the opening marvel.
She recognized them for lonely wanderers upon the earth.
They, these women, then were the only people who *knew*.
Their smile was the smile of these wide vistas, wrought and
shaped, held back by the pity they turned towards the blind
life of men; but it was *alone* in its vision of the spaces opening
beyond the world of daily life.

The open scene, that seemed at once without her and within,
beckoned and claimed her, extending for ever, without horizons, bringing to her contemplating eye a moving expansion
of sight ahead and ahead, earth and sky left behind, across
flower-spread plains whose light was purer and brighter than
the light of day. Here was the path of advance. But, pur-
suing it, she must be always alone; supported in the turmoil of
life that drove the haunting scene away, hidden beyond the
hard visible horizon, by the remembered signs and smiles of
these far-off lonely women.

Between them and their second week stood a promised
visit to the Brooms; offering itself each time she surveyed it,
under a different guise. But when, for their last evening together, he surprised her, so little did he ever seem to plan or
reflect, with stall tickets for the opera, she was overwhelmed
by the swift regardless pressure of events. Opera, for ever
outside her means and forgotten, descending thus suddenly
upon her without space for preparation of mind, would seem
to be wasted. Not in such unseemly haste could she approach
this crowning ornament of social life. She was speechless,
too, before the revelation of his private ponderings. She knew
he was indifferent, even to the theatre, and that he could not
afford this tremendous outlay. His recklessness was selfless;
a great planning for her utmost recreation. In her satisfaction

he was to be content. Touched to the heart, she tried to express her sense of all these things, much hampered by the dismayed anticipation of failure, on the great evening, to produce any satisfying response. She knew she would dislike opera; fat people, with huge voices, screaming against an orchestra, in the pretence of expressing emotions they had never felt. But he assured her that opera was very beautiful, *Faust* perhaps the most beautiful and charming of all, and drew her attention to the massed voices. To this idea she clung, in the interval, for enlightenment.

But after spending all her available funds on an evening blouse and borrowing a cloak from Jan, she found herself at the large theatre impressed only by the collected mass of the audience. The sense of being small and alone, accentuated by the presence of little Mr. Shatov, neatly in evening dress at her side, persisted, growing, until the curtain rose. So long as they had wandered about London and sat together in small restaurants, the world had seemed grouped about them, the vast ignored spectator of a strange romance. But in this huge enclosure, their small, unnoticed, unquestioned presences seemed challenged to account for themselves. All these unmoved people, making the shut-in air cold with their unconcern, even when they were hushed with the strange appealing music of the overture, were moving with purpose and direction because of their immense unconsciousness. Where were they going? What was it all about? What, she asked herself, with a crowning pang of desolation, as the curtain went relentlessly up, were he and she to be or do in their world? What would they become, committed, identified, two small desolate, helpless figures, with the crowding mass of unconscious life?

'I find something of grandeur in the sober dignity of this apartment. It is medieval Germany at its best.'

'It is very dark.'

'Wait, wait. You shall see life and sunshine, all in the most beautiful music.'

The sombre scene offered the consolation, suddenly insufficient, that she had found in the past in sliding idly into

novels, the restful sense of vicarious life. She had heard of
a wonderful philosophy in *Faust*, and wondered at Mr Shatov's
claim for its charm. But there was, she felt, no space, on the
stage, for philosophy. The scene would change, there was
'charm' and sunshine and music ahead. This scene itself
was changing as she watched. The old man talking to himself
was less full of meaning than the wonderful German interior,
the pointed stonework and high, stained windows, the carved
chairs and rich old manuscripts. Even as he talked, the light
from the night sky, pouring down outside on a beautiful old
German town, was coming in. And presently there would be
daylight scenes. The real meaning of it all was scenes, each
with their separate, rich, silent significance. The scenes were
the story, the translation of the people, the actual picture of
them as they were by themselves behind all the pother. . . .
She set herself, drifting in solitude away from the complications of the present, to watch Germany. The arrival of
Mephistopheles was an annoying distraction suggesting pantomime. His part in the drama was obscured by Mr Shatov's
whispered eulogies of Chaliapin, 'the only true Mephistopheles
in Europe.' It certainly seemed right that the devil should
have 'a most profound bass voice.' The chanting of angels in
paradise, she suggested, could only be imagined in high clear
soprano, whereat he maintained that women's voices un-
supported by the voices of men were not worth imagining
at all.

'Pippa passes. It is a matter of opinion.'

'It is a matter of fact. These voices are without depth of
foundation. What is this Pippa?'

'And yet you think that women can rise higher, and fall
lower, than men.'

She walked home amidst the procession of scenes, grouped
and blending all about her, free of their bondage to any thread
of story, bathed in music, beginning their life in her as memory
set up for ever amongst her store of realities. It *had* been a
wonderful evening, opera *was* wonderful. But the whole
effect was threatened, as it stood so lovely all about her in the
night air, by his insistence upon a personal interpretation,

surprising her in the midst of the garden scene and renewed now as they walked, by little attempts to accentuate the relationship of their linked arms. Once more she held off the threatened obliteration. But the scenes had retreated, far away beyond the darkness and light of the visible street. With sudden compunction she felt that it was she who had driven them away, driven away the wonders that were after all his gift. If she had softened towards him, they would have gone, just the same. . . . It was too soon to let them work, as an influence.

Absurd, too, to try to invent life which did not come of itself. He had desisted and was away, fallen into his thoughtful forgetful singing, brumming out shreds of melody that brought single scenes vividly penetrating the darkness. She called him back with a busy repentance, carelessly selecting from her thronging impressions a remark that instantly seemed meaningless.

'Yes,' he said heartily, 'there is, absolutely, something echt, kern-gesund about these old German things.'

That was it. It had all meant, really, the same for him; and he knew what it was that made the charm; admitting it, in spite of his strange deep dislike of the Germans. Kern-gesundheit was not a sufficient explanation. But the certainty of his having been within the charm made him real, a related part of the pageant of life, his personal engaging small attribute her own undivided share. On the doorstep, side by side with his renewed silent appeal, she turned and met, standing free, his gentle tremulous salutation.

For a moment the dark silent house blazed into light before her. She moved forward, as he opened the door, as into a brightness of light where she should stand visible to them both, in a simplicity of golden womanhood, no longer herself, but his Marguerite, yet so differently fated, so differently identified with him in his new simplicity, going forward together, his thoughts and visions as simple as her own in the life now just begun, from which their past dropped away grey and cold, the irrelevant experience of strangers.

But the hall was dark and the open dining-room door showed

III—* G

blank darkness. She led the way in; she could not yet part from him and lose the strange radiance surrounding herself. They ought to go forward now, together, from this moment, shedding a radiance. To part was to break and mar, for ever, some essential irrecoverable glory. They sat side by side on the sofa by the window. The radiance in which she sat crowned, a figure visible to herself, recognizable, humble and proud and simple, back in its Christian origin, a single weak small figure, transfixed with light, dreadfully trusted with the searing, brightly gleaming dower of Christian womanhood, was surrounded by a darkness unpenetrated by the faint radiance the high street lamps must be sending through the thick lace curtains. This, she thought, is what people mean by the golden dream; but it is not a dream. No one who has been inside it can ever be the same again or quite get out. The world it shows is the biggest world there is. It is *outer* space where God is and Christ waits. 'I am very happy, do you feel happy?' The small far-off man's voice sounded out, lost the impenetrable darkness. Yet it was through him, through some essential quality in him, that she had reached this haven and starting-place, he who had brought this smiting descent of certainties which were to carry her on her voyage into the unknown darkness and, since he could not see her smile, she must speak.

'I think so,' she said gently. She must, she suddenly realized, never tell him more than that. His happiness was, she now recognized, hearing his voice, different from hers. To admit and acclaim her own would be the betrayal of a secret trust. If she could dare to lay her hand upon him, he might know. But they were too separate. And if he were to touch her now, they would again be separated for longer than before, for always. 'Good night,' she said, brushing his sleeve with the tips of her fingers, 'dear, funny little man.'

He followed her closely but she was soon away up the familiar stairs in the darkness, in her small close room, and trying to chide herself for her inadequate response, while within the stifling air the breath of sunlit open spaces moved about her.

But in the morning when the way to King's Cross station was an avenue of sunlight, under a blue sky triumphant with the pealing of church bells, his sole conversation was an attempt to induce her to reproduce the epithet. The small scrap of friendliness had made him happy! No one, it seemed, had ever so addressed him. His delight was all her own. She was overcome by the revelation of her power to bless without effort. The afternoon's visit now seemed a welcome interval in the too swift succession of discoveries. In the cool noisy shelter of the station, Sunday holiday-makers were all about them. He was still charmingly preening himself, set off by the small busy crowd, his eye wandering with its familiar look, a childlike contemplation of the English spectacle. To Miriam's unwilling glance it seemed for observation a fruitless field; nothing exhibited there could challenge speculation.

On each face, so naïvely engrossed with immediate arranged circumstance, character, opinion, social conditions, all that might be expected under the small tests of small circumstances, was plainly written in monotonous reiteration. Moving and going, they could go, with all their busy eagerness, no further than themselves. At their destinations other similar selves awaited them, to meet and send them back, unchanged; an endless circling. Over their unchanging, unquestioned world, no mystery brooded with black or golden wings. They would circle unsurprised, until, for each one, came the surprise of death. It was all they had. They were dreadful to contemplate, because they suggested only death, unpondered death. Her eye rested for relief upon a barefooted newspaper boy running freely about with his cry, darting head down towards a shouted challenge.

'Before you go,' Mr Shatov was saying. She turned towards his suddenly changed voice, saw his pale face, grave, and working with the determination to difficult speech; saw him, while she stood listening to the few tense phrases in painful admiration of his courage, horribly transformed, by the images he evoked far away, immovable in the sunshine of his earlier days. The very trembling of his voice had attested the agonizing power of his communication. Yet behind it all, with what a calmness of his inner mind, had he told her, now, only now, when they were set in the bright amber of so many days, that he had been lost to her, for ever, long ago in his independent past. The train was drawing in. She turned away speechless.

'Miriam, Miriam,' he pleaded in hurried shaken tones close at her side, 'remember, I *did not know* that you would come.'

'Well, I must go,' she said briskly, the words sounding out to her like ghostly hammer-blows upon empty space. Never again should her voice sound. The movement of getting into the train brought a nerve-crisping relief. She had taken the first step into the featureless darkness where, alone, she was to wait, in a merciful silence, for ever.

'I shall meet you this evening,' said his raised voice from the platform. He stood with bowed head, his eyes gravely on her unconsidering gaze, until the train moved out. She set her teeth against the slow movement of the wheels, grinding it seemed, smoke-befouled, deliberate, with awful circling relentlessness over her prostrate body, clenched together for the pang, too numb to feel it if only it would come, but left untouched.

The crushing of full realization, piling up behind her numbness, must pass over her. There was not much time. The train was carrying her steadily onward, and towards conversation with the unconscious Brooms. She tried to relax to its movement, to hold back from the entanglements of thought and regard the day as an interval outside the hurrying procession of her life. A way opened narrowly ahead, attainable by one rending effort, into a silence, within which the grey light filtering through the dingy windows on to the grime-greyed floor offered itself with a promise of reassurance. It was known to her; by its unvexed communion with her old self. One free breath of escape from the visions she was holding clutched for inspection, and herself would be given back to her. This awful journey would change to an eternity following serenely on a forgotten masquerade. She would not lose her knowledge that all solitary journeys go on for ever, waiting, through intervals, to renew themselves. But the effort, even if she

could endure the pain of it, would be treachery until she had
known and seen without reservations the whole meaning of
the immovable fact. The agony within her must mean that
somewhere behind the mere statements, if she could but get
through and discover it, there must be a revelation that would
set the world going again; bring back the vanquished sunlight.
Meanwhile life must pause, humanity must stay hushed and
waiting while she thought.

A grey-shod foot appeared on her small empty patch of
floor. With the fever of pain that flooded her she realized
that she could go neither forward nor back. Life pinned her
motionless, in pain. Her eye ran up and found the dreaming
face of a girl; the soft fresh lineaments of childhood, shaped
to a partial awareness by some fixed daily toil, but still, on all
she saw, the gleam she did not know could disappear, did not
recognize for what it was, priceless and enough. She would
never recognize it. She was one of those women men wrap
in lies, persisting unchanged through life, revered and yet
odious in the kindly stupidity of thoughts fixed immovably on
reality, the gleam gone, she knew not why, and yet avenged
by her awful unconscious production of the kind of social
life to which men were tied, compelled to stimulate life in her
obstinate, smiling fool's . . . hell. The rest of the people
in the carriage were aware, in the thick of conscious deceits;
playing parts. The women, strained and defaced, all masked
watchfulness, cut off from themselves, weaving romances in
their efforts to get back, the men betraying their delight in
their hidden opportunities of escape by the animation behind
the voices and manners they assumed for the fixed calculable
periods of forced association; ready to distract attention from
themselves and their hidden treasures by public argument, if
accident should bring it about, over anything and everything.

At least she saw. But what was the *use* of not being deceived?
How in the vast spread of humanity expose the sham? How
escape, without surrendering life itself, treacherous countenan-
cing of the fiendish spectacle? What good would death do?
What did 'Eine für Viele' do? Brought home the truth to one

man, who probably, after the first shock, soon came to the conclusion that she had been mad.

She talked through lunch to the Brooms with such an intensity of animation that when at last the confrontation was at an end and the afternoon begun in the shelter of the dim little drawing-room, she found Grace and Florrie grouped closely about her, wrapped and eager for more. She turned, at bay, explaining in shaken unmeditated words that the afternoon must be spent by her in thinking out a frightful problem, and relapsed, averted swiftly from their sensitive faces, suddenly pale about eyes that reflected her distress, towards the open door of the little greenhouse leading miserably into the stricken garden. They remained motionless in the chairs they had drawn close to the little settee where she sat enthroned, clearly prepared so to sit in silent sympathy while she gazed at her problem in the garden. She sat tense, but with their eyes upon her she could not summon directly the items of her theme. They appeared transformed in words, a statement of the case that might be made to them, 'any one's' statement of the case, beginning with 'after all'; and leaving everything unstated. Applied to her own experience they seemed to have no meaning at all. Summaries were no good. Actual experience must be brought home to make anything worth communicating. ' When he first kissed me,' started her mind, 'those women were all about him. They have come between us for ever.' She flushed towards the garden. The mere presence in her mind of such vileness was an outrage on the Broom atmosphere. She could not again face the girls. For some time she sat, driving from point to point in the garden the inexorable fact that she had reached a barrier she could not break down. She could, if she were alone, face the possibility of dashing her life out against it. If she were to turn back from it, she would be rent in twain, and how, then, base and deformed, could she find spirit to face any one at all? At last, still with her eyes on the garden, she told them, she must go and think in the open air. They cherished and indulged her in their unaltered way and she escaped, exempted from coming back to tea.

Suppose, said the innumerable voices of the road, as she wandered down it relieved and eager in the first moments of freedom, he had not told you? It was sincere and kind of him to tell. Not at all. He wanted to have an easy mind. He has only explained what it was that came between us at the first, and has been waiting ever since to be there again. . . .

'Remember; I *did not know* you would come.'

Why did men not know? That was the strange thing. Why did they make their first impressions of women such as would sully everything that came after? That was the extraordinary thing about the average man and many men who were not average at all. Why?

The answer must be there if she could only get through to it. Some immovable answer. The wrong one perhaps, but sufficient to frame an irreversible judgment. There was an irreversible judgment at the heart of it all that would remain, even if further, fuller, truer reasons were reached later on. Anything that could take the life out of the sunlight was wrong. Every twist and turn of the many little side roads along which she made her way told her that. It was useless to try to run away from it. It remained, the only point of return from the wilderness of anger into which, with every fresh attempt at thought, she was immediately flung. The more angry she grew the further she seemed to move from the possibility of finding and somehow expressing, in words that had not sounded in her mind before, the clue to her misery.

She reached the park at tea-time. Its vistas were mercifully empty. She breathed more freely within its greenery. Hidden somewhere here, was relief for the increasing numbness of her brain and the drag of her aching heart. The widening sky understood and would presently, when she had reached the statement that lay now, just ahead, offer itself in the old way, for companionship.

Wandering along a little path that wound in and out of a thicket of shrubs, she heard a subdued rumble of voices and came in a moment upon two men, bent-headed in conversation side by side on a secluded seat. They looked up at her and upon their shiny German faces, and in the cold rheumy blue eyes beneath their unconscious intelligent German foreheads, was the horrible leer of their talk. Looking up from it, scanning her in the spirit of the images of life they had evoked in their sequestered confidential interchange, they identified her with their vision. She turned back towards the wide empty avenues. But there was no refuge in them. Their bleak emptiness reflected the thoughtless lives of English men. Behind her the two Germans were immovably there, hemming her in. They were the answer. Sitting hidden there, in the English park, they were the whole unconscious male mind of Europe surprised unmasked. Thought out and systematized by them, openly discussed, without the cloudy reservations of Englishmen, was the whole masculine sense of womanhood. One image; perceived only with the body, separated and apart from everything else in life. Men were *mind* and *body*, separated mind and body, looking out at women, below their unconscious men's brows, variously moulded and sanctified by thought, with one unvarying eye. There was no escape from its horrible blindness, no other life in the world to live. . . . The leer of a prostitute was . . . reserved . . . beautiful, suggesting a daily life lived independently amongst the impersonal marvels of existence, compared with the headlong desirous look of a man. The greed of men was something much more awful than the greed of a prostitute. She used her last strength to wrench herself away from the hopeless spectacle and wandered impatient and thoughtless in a feverish void. Far away from this barren north London, the chosen perfect stage for the last completion of a misery as wide at the world, was her own dreamworld at home in her room, her strange unfailing self, the lovely world of lovely things seen in silence and tranquillity, the coming and going of the light, the myriad indescribable things of which day and night, in solitude, were full, at every moment; the marvellous forgetfulness of sleep, followed by the smiling renewal of inexhaustible *sameness*. . . . Thought flashed in, stabbing her weakness with the reminder that solitude had failed and from its failure she had been saved by the companionship of a man; of whom until to-day she had been proud in a world lit by the glory and pride of achieved companionships. But it was an illusion, fading and failing more swiftly than the real things of solitude.

There is no release save in madness; a suddenly descending merciful madness, blotting everything out. She imagined herself raging and raving through the park, through the world, attacking the indifferent sky at last with some final outbreaking statement, something, somewhere within her she *must* say, or die. She gazed defiance upwards at the cloudless blue. The distant trees flattened themselves into dark clumps against the horizon. Swiftly she brought her eyes back to the diminishing earth. Something must be said; not to the sky, but in the world. She grew impatient for Mr Shatov's arrival. If only she could convey to him all that was in her mind, going back again and again endlessly to some central unanswerable assertion, the truth would be out. Stated. At least one man brought to book, arrested and illuminated. But what was it? That men are not worthy of women? He would agree, and remain pleading. That men never have, never can, understand the least thing about even the worst woman in the world? He would find things to say. She plunged back groping for weapons of statement, amongst the fixities of the world, there from the beginning, and pressing at last with their mocking accomplishment, against her small thread of existence. Long grappling in darkness against the inexorable images, she fell back at last upon wordless repudiation, and again the gulf of isolation opened before her. The struggle was not to be borne. It was monstrous, unforgivable, that it should be demanded of her. Yet it could not be given up. The smallest glance in the direction of even the simulation of acceptance, brought a panic sense of treachery that flung her back to cling once more to the vanishing securities of her own untouched imagination.

When at last he appeared, the sight of the familiar distinctive little figure plunging energetically along, beard first, through the north London Sunday evening crowd drifting about the park gates, their sounds quenched by the blare of the Salvation Army's band marching townwards along the battered road, for one strange moment while a moving light came across the

gravel pathway at her feet, decking its shabby fringe of grass
with the dewy freshness of some remembered world far away
and unknown to this trampling blind north London, she asked
herself what all the trouble was about.   What, after all, had
changed?   Not herself, that was clear.   Walking in fevered
darkness had not destroyed the light.   But he had joined her,
pulling up before her with white ravaged face and hands
stretched silently towards her.

'For pity's sake don't touch me,' she cried involuntarily
and walked on, accompanied, examining her outcry.   It was
right.   It had a secret *knowledge*.   They rode in silence on
tram and bus.   Below them on the dimly-lit pavements people
moved, shadows broken loose and scattered in the grey of
night.   Gaslit, talking faces succeeded each other under the
street lamps; not one speaking its thoughts; no feeling expressed that went even as deep as the screening chatter of
words in the mind.   But presently all about her, as she sat
poised for the length of the journey between the dead stillness
within her and the noise of the silence without, a world most
wonderful was dawning with strange irrelevance, forcing her
attention to lift itself from the abyss of her fatigue.   Look at
us, the buildings seemed to say, sweeping by massed and various
and whole, spangled with light.   We are here.   We, are the
accomplished marvel.   Buildings had always seemed marvellous; and in their moving, changing aspects an endless fascination, except in north London, where they huddled without
distinction, defaced in feature and outline by a featureless
blind occupancy.   But to-night, it was north London that
was revealing the marvel of the mere existence of a building.
North Londoners were not under the spell; but it was there.
Their buildings rising out of the earth where once there had
been nothing, proclaimed it as they swept dreaming by,
making roadways that were like long thoughts, meeting and
crossing and going on and on, deep alleyways and little courts
where always was a pool of light òr darkness, pouring down
from their secret communion with the sky a strange single
reality upon the clothed and trooping multitude below.   And
all the strange unnoticed marvel of buildings and clothes, the

even more marvellously strange unnoticed clothing of speech, all existing alone and independent outside the small existence of single lives and yet proclaiming them. . . . An exclamation of wonder rose to her lips, and fell back checked, by the remembered occasion, to which for an instant she returned as a stranger seeing the two figures side by side chained in suspended explanations that would not set them free, and left her gazing again, surrendered, addressing herself with a deepening ease of heart to the endless friendly strength flowing from things unconsciously brought about. It brought a balm that lulled her almost to sleep, so that when at last their journey was at an end she found herself wordless and adrift in a tiresome pain, that must be removed only because it blotted out marvels.

He began at once, standing before her, relating in simple unbroken speech the story of his student days, without pleading or extenuation; waiting at the end for her judgment.

'And that first photograph that I liked, was before; and the other, after.'

'That is so.'

'In the first there is someone looking out through the eyes; in the other that someone has moved away.'

'That is so. I agree.'

'Well, can't you see? Never to come back. Never to come back.'

'Miriam. Remember I am no more that man. I was in suffering and in ignorance. It would have been better otherwise. I agree with you. But that is all past. I am no more that man.'

'Can't you see that there is no past?'

'I confess I do not understand this.'

'It is crowding all round you. I felt it. Don't you remember? Before I knew. It comes between us all the time. I know now. It's not an idea; or prudishness. It's more solid than the space of air between us. I can't get through it.'

'Remember I was suffering and *alone*.' Somewhere within the vibrating tones was the careless shouting of his boyhood; that past was there too; and the eager lifting voice of his earlier student days, still sometimes alive in the reverie of his lifted brows. The voice had been quelled. In his memory, as he stood there before her, was pain, young lonely pain. Within the life thrown open without reservation to her gaze, she saw, confronting her determination to make him suffer, the image of unhealed suffering, still there, half stifled by his blind obedience to worldly ignorant advice, but waiting for the moment to step forward and lay its burden upon her own unwilling heart, leaving him healed and free. Tears sprang to her eyes, blotting him out, and with them she sprang forth into a pathless darkness, conscious far away behind her, soon to be obliterated on the unknown shores opening ahead, but there gladly in hand, of a debt, signed and to be honoured even against her will, by life, surprised once more at this darkest moment, smiling at her secretly, behind all she could gather of opposing reason and clamourous protests of unworthiness. 'Poor boy,' she murmured, gathering him as he sank to his knees, with swift enveloping hands against her breast. The unknown woman sat alone, with eyes wide open towards the empty air above his hidden face. This was man; leaning upon her with his burden of loneliness, at home and comforted. This was the truth behind the image of woman supported by man. The strong companion was a child seeking shelter; the woman's share an awful loneliness. It was not fair.

She moved to raise and restore him, at least to the semblance of a supporting presence. But with a sudden movement he bent and caught a fold of her dress to his lips. She rose with a cry of protest, urging him to his feet.

'I know now,' he said simply, 'why men kneel to women.' While in her heart she thanked heaven for preserving her to that hour, the dreadful words invested her in yet another loneliness. She seemed to stand tall and alone, isolated for a moment from her solid surroundings, within a spiral of unconsuming radiance.

'No one ought to kneel to any one,' she lied in pity, and moved out restlessly into the room. We are real. As others have been real. There is a sacred bond between us now, ratified by all human experience. But oh, the cost and the demand.

It was as if she were carrying in her hands something that
could be kept safe only by a lifelong silence. Everything she
did and said in future must hide the sacred trust. It gave a
freedom; but not of speech or thought. It left the careless
dreaming self behind. Only in ceaseless occupation could it
hold its way. Its only confidant would be God. Holding to
it, everything in life, even difficulties, would be transparent.
But seen from the outside, by the world, an awful mysteriously
persistent commonplace. It was not fair that men did not
know the whole of this secret place and its compact. Why was
God in league only with women?

CHAPTER XII

IT 's not altogether personal. . . . Until it is understood and admitted, there is a darkness everywhere. The life of every man in existence, who does not understand and admit it, is perfectly senseless. Until they know, they are all living in vain.

'What on earth did you mean?' she said as soon as the omnibus had started.

He turned a startled musing face. He had *forgotten*.

'What have I said?'

'Kindly think.'

'Really I am at a loss.'

'When that woman collided with me, crossing the road.'

'Ah, ah, I remember. Well?'

'You pronounced an opinion.'

'It is not my opinion. It is a matter of ascertained fact.'

'Facts are invented by people who start with their conclusions arranged beforehand.'

'Perhaps so.'

'Ah, well; that is an admission.'

'The conclusion is amply verified.'

'Where?'

'I speak only of women in the mass. There are of course exceptions.'

'Go on, go on.'

'I see you are annoyed. Let us leave this matter.'

'Kindly go on.'

'There is nothing more to say.' He *laughed*. He was not even being aware that it was a matter of life and death. He could go on serenely living in an idea, that turned life into a nightmare.

'Oh, if it amuses you.' He was silent. The moments went beating on. She turned from him and sat averted. She would

go now onward and onward till she could get away over the
edge of the world. There was nothing else to do. There
were no thoughts or words in which her conviction could take
shape. Even looking for them was a degradation. Besides,
argument, if she could steady herself to face the pain of it,
would not, whatever he might say, even dislodge his satisfied
unconcern. He was uneasy; but only about herself, and would
accept reassurance from her, without a single backward glance.
But what did their personal fate matter beside a question so all-
embracing? What future could they have in unacknowledged
disagreement over central truth? And if it were acknowledged,
what peace?

The long corridor of London imprisoned her. Far away
beneath her tumult it was making its appeal, renewing the
immortal compact. The irregular façades, dull greys absorbing
the light, bright buffs throwing it brilliantly out, dadoed below
with a patchwork of shops, and overhead the criss-cross of
telephone wires, shut her away from the low-hung soft grey
sky. But far away, unfailing, retreating as the long corridor
telescoped towards them, an obliterating saffron haze filled
the vista, holding her in her place.

The end of the journey brought them to grey streets and
winding alleys where the masts and rigging that had loomed
suddenly in the distance, robbing the expedition of its promise
of ending in some strange remoteness with their suggestion of
blind busy worlds beyond London, were lost to sight.

'This must be the docks,' she said politely.

With the curt permission of a sentinel policeman they went
through a gateway appearing suddenly before them in a high
grey wall. Miriam hurried forward to meet the open scene
for one moment alone and found herself on a little quay surrounding a square basin of motionless grey water shut in by
wooden galleries, stacked with mouldering casks. But the air
was the air that moves softly on still days over wide waters and,
in the shadowed light of the enclosure, the fringe of green
where the water touched the grey stone of the quay gleamed
brilliantly in the stillness. She breathed in, in spite of herself,
the charm of the scene; an ordered completeness, left to itself

in beauty; its lonely beauty to be gathered only by the chance passer-by.

'This is a strange romantic place,' said Mr Shatov conversationally by her side.

'There is nothing,' said Miriam unwillingly, feeling her theme weaken as she looked away from it to voice well-known words, '*nothing* that reveals more completely the spiritual'— her voice gave over the word which broke into meaninglessness upon the air—'the status of a man, as his estimate of women.'

'I entirely agree. I was a feminist in my college days. I am still a feminist.'

Miriam pondered. The word was new to her. But how could any one be a feminist and still think women most certainly inferior beings?

'Ah,' she cried, 'you are one of the Huxleys.'

'I don't follow you.'

'Oh well. *He*, impertinent schoolboy, graciously suggested that women should be given every possible kind of advantage, educational and otherwise; saying almost in the same breath that they could never reach the highest places in civilization; that Nature's Salic Law would never be repealed.'

'Well, how is it to be repealed?'

'I don't know, I'm sure. I'm not wise enough to give instruction in repealing a law that has never existed. But who is Huxley, that he should take upon himself to say what are the highest places in civilization?'

'Miriam,' he said, coming round to stand before her. 'We are not going to quarrel over this matter.' She refused to meet his eyes.

'It is not a question of quarrelling, or even discussion. You have told me all I want to know. I see exactly where you stand; and for my part it *decides*, many things. I don't say this to amuse myself or because I want to, but because it is the only thing I can possibly do.'

'Miriam. In this spirit nothing can be said at all. Let us rather go have tea.'

Poor little man, perhaps he was weary; troubled in this strange grey corner of a country not his own, isolated with an unexpected anger. They had tea in a small dark room behind a little shop. It was close packed with an odorous dampness. Miriam sat frozen, appalled by the presence of a negro. He sat near by, huge, bent, snorting and devouring, with a huge black bottle at his side. Mr Shatov's presence was shorn of its alien quality. He was an Englishman in the fact that he and she could *not* sit eating in the neighbourhood of this marshy jungle. But they were, they had. They would have. Once away from this awful place she would never think of it again. Yet the man had hands and needs and feelings. Perhaps he could sing. He was at a disadvantage an outcast. There was something that ought to be said to him. She could not think what it was. In his oppressive presence it was impossible to think at all. Every time she sipped her bitter tea, it seemed that before she should have replaced her cup, vengeance would have sprung from the dark corner. Everything hurried so. There was no *time* to shake off the sense of contamination. It *was* contamination. The man's presence was an outrage on something of which he was not aware. It would be possible to make him aware. When his fearful face, which she sadly knew she could not bring herself to regard a second time, was out of sight, the outline of his head was desolate, like the contemplated head of any man alive. Men ought not to have faces. Their real selves abode in the expressions of their heads and brows. Below, their faces were moulded by deceit. . . .

While she had pursued her thoughts, advantage had fallen to the black form in the corner. It was as if the black face grinned, crushing her thread of thought.

'You see, Miriam, if instead of beating me, you will tell me your *thoughts*, it is quite possible that mine may be modified. There is at least nothing of the bigot in me.'

'It is not what people may be made to see for a few minutes in conversations that counts. It is the conclusions they come to, instinctively, by themselves.' ·He wanted to try and think as she did . . . 'chose attendrissante; ils se rassemblaient.' . . . *Life* . . . *was* different, to everybody, even to intellectual male vain-boasters, from everybody's descriptions; there was nothing to point to anywhere that exactly corresponded to spoken opinions. But the relieving truth of this was only realized privately. The things went on being said. Men did not admit their private discoveries in public. It was not enough to see and force the admittance of the holes in a theory privately, and leave the form of words going on and on in the world perpetually parroted, infecting the sky. 'Wise women know better and go their way without listening,' is not enough. It is not only the insult to women; a contempt for men is a bulwark against that, but introduces sourness into one's own life. It is the impossibility of witnessing the pouring on of a vast, repeating public life that is missing the significance of everything.

Yet what a support, she thought with a sideways glance, was his own gentleness . . . gentillesse . . . and humanity, to his own theory. He was serene and open in the presence of this central bitterness. If she could summon, in words, convincing evidence of the inferiority of man, he would cheerfully accept it and go on unmaimed. But a private reconstruction of standards in agreement with one person would not bring healing. It was history, literature, the way of stating records, reports, stories, the whole method of statement of things from the beginning that was on a false foundation.

If only one could speak as quickly as one's thoughts flashed, and several thoughts together, all with a separate life of their own and yet belonging, everybody would be understood. As it was, even in the most favourable circumstances, people could hardly communicate with each other at all.

'I have nothing to say. It is not a thing that can be argued out. Those women's rights people are the worst of all. Because they think women have been "subject" in the past. Women never have been subject. Never can be. The proof of this is the way men have always been puzzled and everlastingly trying fresh theories; founded *on* the very small experience of women any man is capable of having. Disabilities, imposed by law, are a stupid insult to women, but have never touched them as individuals. In the long run they injure only men. For they keep back the civilization of the outside

world, which is the only thing men can make. It is not everything. It is a sort of result, poor and shaky because the real
inside civilization of women, the one thing that has been in
them from the first and is not in the natural man, not made by
"things," is kept out of it. Women do not need civilization.
It is apt to bore them. *But* it can never rise above their level.
They keep it back. That does not matter, to themselves. But
it matters to men. And if they want their old civilization to
be anything but a dreary-weary puzzle, they must leave off
imagining themselves a race of gods fighting against chaos, and
thinking of women as part of the chaos they have to civilize.
There isn't any "chaos." Never has been. It's the principal
masculine illusion. It is not a truth to say that women must
be civilized. Feminists are not only an insult to womanhood.
They are a libel on the universe.' In the awful presence she
had spoken herself out, found and recited her best, most
liberating words. The little unseen room shone, its shining
speaking up to her from small things immediately under her
eyes. Light, pouring from her speech, sent a radiance about
the thick black head and its monstrous bronze face. He might
have his thoughts, might even look them, from the utmost
abyss of crude male life, but he had helped her, and his blind
unconscious outlines shared the unknown glory. But she
doubted if she would remember that thoughts flowed more
easily, with surprising ease, as if given, waiting, ready to be
scanned and stated, when one's eyes ceased to look outwards.
If she could remember it, it might prove to be the solution of
social life.

'These things are all matters of opinion. Whereas it is a
matter of indisputable *fact* that in the past women have been
subject.'

'If you believe that it is impossible for us to associate.
Because we are living in two utterly different worlds.'

'On the contrary. This difference is a most excellent basis
for association.'

'You think I can cheerfully regard myself as an emancipated
slave, with traditions of slavery for memory and the form of a
slave as an everlasting heritage?'

'Remember that heredity is cross-wise. You are probably more the daughter of your father . . .'

'*That* won't help you, thank you. If anything I am my mother's son.'

'Ah—ah, what is this, you are a *son*? Do you see?'

'That's a piece of English feudalism.'

'The demands of feudalism do not explain a woman's desire for sons.'

'That is another question. She hopes *they* will give her the understanding she never had from their father. In that I *am* my mother's son for ever. If there's a future life, all I care for is to meet *her*. If I could have her back for ten minutes I would gladly give up the rest of my life. . . . Is heredity really criss-cross? Is it proved?'

'Substantially.'

'Oh, yes. Of course. I know. To prevent civilization going ahead too fast! I've seen that somewhere. Very flattering to men. But it proves there's no separate race of men and women.'

'Exactly.'

'Then how have men the face to go on with their generalizations about women?'

'You yourself have a generalization about women.'

'That's different. It's not about brains and attainments. I can't make you see. I suppose it's Christianity.'

'What is Christianity? You think Christianity is favourable to women? On the contrary. It is the Christian countries that have produced the prostitute and the most vile estimations of women in the world. It is only in Christian countries that I find the detestable spectacle of men who will go straight from association with loose women into the society of innocent girls. That I find unthinkable. . . . With Jews, womanhood has always been sacred. And there can be no doubt that we owe our persistence as a race largely to our laws of protection for women; *all* women. Moreover in the older Hebrew civilization women stood very high. You may read this. To-day there is a very significant Jewish wit which says that women make the best wives and mothers in the world.'

'There you are. No Englishman would make a joke like that.'

'Because he is a hypocrite.'

'No. He may, as you say, think one thing and say another; but long, long ago he had a jog. It *was* Christianity. Something happened. Christ was the first man to see women as individuals.'

'You speak easily of Christianity. There is no Christianity in the world. It has never been imagined, save in the brain of a Tolstoi. And he has shown that if the principles of Christianity were applied, civilization as we know it would at once come to an end.'

'There may not be much Christianity. But Christianity has made a difference. It has not given things to women that were not there before. Nothing can do that. But it has shed a light on them *which* the best women run away from. Never imagine I am speaking of myself. I'm as much a man as a woman. That's why I can't help seeing things. But I'm not really interested. Not inside myself. Now look here. You prefer Englishwomen to Jewesses. I can't bear Jewesses, not because they are not really like other women, but because they reflect the limitations of the Jewish male. They talk and think the Jewish man's idea of them. It has nothing to do with them as individuals. But they are waiting for the light to go up.'

'I speak always of these assimilated and half-assimilated English Jewesses. Certainly to me they are most inimical.'

'More so than the Germans?'

'In a different way. They have here less social disabilities. But they are most absolutely terre à terre.'

'Why are Russian Jewesses different?'

'Many of them are idealist. Many live altogether by one or two ideas of Tolstoi.'

'Why do you smile condescendingly?'

'These ideas can lead only to revolution. I am not a revolutionary. While I admire everywhere those who suffer for their ideals.'

'You admit that Tolstoi has influenced Russian Jewesses.

He got his ideas from Christ. So you say. I did not know he was religious.'

'It is a later development. But you remember Levin. But tell me, do you not consider that wife and mother is the highest position of woman?'

'It is neither high nor low. It may be anything. If you define life for women, as husbands and children, it means that you have no consciousness at all where women are concerned.'

'There is the evidence of women themselves. The majority find their whole life in these things.'

'That is a description, from outside, by men. When women use it they do not know what they say.'

CHAPTER XIII

IT was strange that it should be the house that had always caught her eye, as she crossed the square; one of the spots that always made the years of her London life show as a continuous communion with the rich brightness of the West End. The houses round about it were part of the darker colour of London, creating even in sunlight the beloved familiar London atmosphere of dun-coloured mist and grime. But this house was a brilliant white, its windows fringed, during the season, with the gentle deep velvet pink of ivy-leaf geraniums and having, across the lower half of its façade, a fine close trellis of green painted wood, up which a green creeper clambered, neat and sturdy, with small bright polished leaves making a woodland blur across the diamond-patterned mesh of white and green. There were other creepers in the square, but they hung in festoons, easily shabby, spoiled at their brightest by the thought of their stringy bare tendrils hung with shrivelled leaves. These small green leaves faded and dried and fell crisply, leaving a network of clean twigs to gleam in the rain, and the trellis bright green against the white house-front, suggesting summer all the year around.

She went eagerly towards this permanent summer created by wealth, warmed by the imagined voice of a power that could transform all difficulties, setting them in a beauty that lived by itself.

The little leaves, seen from the doorstep, shone like bright enamel in the misty twilight; but their beautiful wild clean-cut shapes, so near, suddenly seemed helpless, unable to escape, forced to drape the walls, life-fevered within, to which their stems were pinned. Yet these was a coming in and out. All people in houses had a coming in and out, those moments of coming, anew out into endless space. And everywhere at moments, in houses, was the sense of the life of the whole world flowing in. Even Jewish houses were porous to the life of the world, and to have a house, however strangely shaped one's life, would be to have a vantage point for breathing in the life of the world.

She stood in a lull, reprieved, her endlessly revolving problem left behind, the future in abeyance, perhaps to be shown her by the woman waiting within, set in surroundings that now called to her jubilantly, proclaiming themselves to be the only object of her visit. For a moment she found herself back in her old sense of the marvel of existence, gazing at the miraculous spectacle of people and things, existing; herself, however, perplexed and resourceless, within it, everything sinking into insignificance beside the fact of being alive, having lived on to another moment of unexplainable happiness. Light-heartedly she rang the bell. The small movement of her lifted hand was supported, a permitted part of the whole tremendous panorama; and in that whole she was *England*, a link in the world-wide being of England and English life. The bell, grinding out its summon within the house, brought her back within the limits of the occasion, but she could not drive away the desire to go forward without return, claiming welcome and acceptance in a life permanently set in beauty.

The door flew open, revealing a tall resentfully handsome butler past whom she went confidently announcing her appointment, into an immense hall, its distances leading in every direction to doors, suggesting a variety of interiors beyond her experience. She was left standing. Someone who had come up the steps as the door opened, was being swiftly conveyed, a short squat polished wealthy old English Jew with curly grey hair and an eager busy plunging gait, across the hall to the centremost door. It opened on a murmur of voices and the light from within fell upon a table just outside, its surface crowded with gleaming top-hats. Some kind of men's meeting was in progress. The woman was not in it. Had she anticipated, before she married, what it would be, however she might fortify herself with scorn, to breathe always the atmosphere of the Jewish religious and social oblivion of women? Had she had any experience of Jewesses, their sultry conscious femineity, their dreadful acceptance of being admitted to a synagogue on sufferance, crowded away upstairs in a stuffy gallery, while the men downstairs, bathed in light, draped in the symbolic shawl, thanked God aloud for making them men and not women? Had she thought what it must be to have always at her side a Jewish consciousness, unconscious of her actuality, believing in its own positive existence, seeing her as human only in her consecration to relationships?

The returning butler ushered her unannounced through a doorway near at hand into a room that spread dimly about her in a twilight deepened by a single core of rosy light at the centre of the expanse. Through a high, curtain-draped archway she caught a glimpse, as she came forward, of a further vastness, shadowy in undisturbed twilight.

Mrs Bergstein had risen to meet her, her head obscured in the gloom above the lamplight, so that only her gown met Miriam's first sally of investigation; a refined middle-class gown of thin dull black whose elbow sleeves and little vee neck were softened at the edge with a ruche of tulle; the party dress of a middle-aged spinster schoolmistress. Miriam braced herself in vain against its seductions; it called her so powerfully to come forth and rejoice. She revelled off, licensed and permitted, the free deputy of this chained presence, amongst the enchantments of the great house; the joy of her escapade leaping bright against the dark certainty that there was no help awaiting her. It was no longer to be feared that an unscrupulous, successful, brightly cajoling woman would persuade her that her problem did not exist; but neither from this woman to whom the fact of life as a thing in itself never had time to appear, could she hope for support in her own belief in the unsoundness of compromise.

Mrs Bergstein bowed, murmured a greeting, and indicated a little settee near the low chair into which she immediately subsided, her face still in shadow, the shape of her coiffure so much in keeping with the dress that Miriam could hardly refrain from departing then and there. She sat down, a schoolgirl waiting for judgment against which she was armed

III—H

in advance, and yet helpless through her unenvious, scornful admiration.

'I was much interested by your letter,' said Mrs Bergstein. The interview was at an end. There was no opening in the smooth close surface represented by the voice, through which questions could be driven home. She was smitten into silence where the sound of the voice echoed and re-echoed, whilst she fumbled for a suitable phrase, clinging to the memory of the statement, still somewhere, which she had come, so desperately, to hear and carry away and set down, a ray of light in the darkness of her revolving thoughts. A numb forgetfulness assailed her, threatening the disaster of irrelevance of speech or behaviour coming from the tides of expression she felt beating below it. She forced a murmured response from her lips, and the tumult was stilled to an echo that flung itself to and fro within, answering the echo of the woman's voice on the air. She had caught hold and contributed. It was now the turn of the other to go on and confirm what she had revealed. . . .

'Music is so *beautiful*—so *elevating*.' 'That depends upon the music.' Never said. Kept treacherously back for the sake of things that might be lost in a clashing of opinions . . . the things they never thought of in exercising their benevolence, and demanding in return acceptance of their views . . . the light of a whole world condensed in the bright old town, the sweet chiming sound of it, coming in at the windows, restoring childhood, the expanses of leisure made by their small hard circle, a world of thoughtless ideas, turning a short week-end into a life, lived before, familiar, building out in the nerves a glorious vitality.

It was the same voice, the English lady's voice, bringing all Christendom about her, all the traditions within which, so lately, she had felt herself committed steadfastly to tread. But there was something left out of it, a warmth was missing, it had not in it the glow that was in those other women's voices, of kindliness towards the generous things they had secretly, willingly renounced. It had, instead, something that was like a cold clean blade thrusting into an intelligible future, something inexorable, founded not upon fixed ideas, but upon ideas, single and cold. This woman would not make concessions; she would always stand, uncompromisingly, in face of every one, men and women, for the same things, clear cut, delicate and narrowly determining as her voice.

'You are considering the possibility of embracing the Jewish faith?'

'Well, *no*,' said Miriam startled into briskness by the too quickly developing accumulation of speech. 'I heard that you had done so; and wondered, how it was possible, for an Englishwoman.'

'You are a Christian?'

'I don't know. I was brought up in the Anglican Church.'

'Much depends upon the standpoint from which one approaches the very definite and simple creed of Judaism. I myself was a Unitarian, and therefore able to take the step without making a break with my earlier convictions.'

'I see,' said Miriam coldly. Fate had deceived her, holding in reserve the trick of this simple explanation. She gazed at the seated figure. The glow of her surroundings was quenched by the chill of a perpetually active *reason*. . . . Science, ethics, withering common sense playing over everything in life, making a harsh bareness everywhere, seeing nothing alive but the cold processes of the human mind; having Tennyson read at services because poetry was one of the superior things produced by humanity. She wondered whether this woman, so exactly prepared to meet a Jewish reform movement, had been helplessly born into Unitarianism, or had taken it up as she herself had nearly done.

'Much of course depends upon the synagogue through which one is admitted.' Ah; she *had* felt the impossibilities. She had compromised and was excusing her compromise.

'Of course I have heard of the reform movement.' . . . The silence quivered with the assertion that the reformers were as much cut off from Judaism as Unitarianism from Anglican Christianity. To enter a synagogue that made special arrangements for the recognition of women was to admit that women were dependent on recognition. The silence admitted the dilemma. Mrs Bergstein had passed through these thoughts, suffering? Though she had found a way through, following her cold clear reason, she still suffered?

'I think I should find it impossible to associate with Jewish *women*.'

'*That* is a point you must consider very carefully indeed.' The room leapt into glowing reality. They *were* at one; Englishwomen with a common incommunicable sense. Outcasts. Far away, within the warm magic circle of English life, sounded the careless easy slipshod voices of Englishmen, she saw their averted talking forms, aware in every line, and protective, of something that Englishwomen held in their hands.

'Don't you find,' she began breathlessly, but calm even tones drove across her eagerness: 'What is your fiancé's attitude towards religion?'

'He is not exactly religious and not fully in sympathy with the reform movement because he is a Zionist and thinks that the old ritual is the only link between the persecuted Jews and those who are better placed; that it would be treachery to break with it as long as any are persecuted. Nevertheless, he is willing to renounce his Judaism.'

The queen, who is religious, puts love before religion, for woman. Her Protestantism. He for God only, she for God in him and able to change her creed when she marries. A Catholic *couldn't*. And she would call Catholics idolaters. *She* is an idolater; of men.

Mrs Bergstein was amazed at his willingness. Envious. . . . *I am a Jew, a 'head' man incapable of 'love.'* . . . *It is your eyes. I must see them always. I know now what is meant by love. I am even willing to renounce my Judaism. Michael,* to think and say that. I am crowned, for life; by a sacrifice I cannot accept. He must keep his Judaism. You *must* marry me. The discovery, flowing through the grey noisy street, of the secret of the 'mastery' idea; that women can only be sure that a man is sure when——

'There is then *no* common religious feeling between you?'

She had moved. The light fell upon her. She was about *forty*. She had come forth, so late, from the secret numbness of her successful independent life, and had not found what she came to seek. She was still alone in her circling day. At the period of evening dress she put on a heavy gold bracelet, ugly, a heavy ugly shape. Her face was pinched and drawn; before her lay the ordeal of belated motherhood. Vulgarly violating her refined endurance had come this incident. Dignified condemnation spoke from her averted eyes. She had said her say and was desiring that there should be no further waste of time.

Miriam made no sound. In the stillness that followed the blow she faced the horrible summary, stricken to her feet, her strength ebbing with her thoughts into the gathering swirling darkness. She waited for a moment. But Mrs Bergstein made no sign. Imponderable, conscious only of the weight of her body about her holding her to the ground beneath her feet, she went away from the room and the house. In the lamplit darkness her feet carried her joyously forward into the freshness of the tree-filled air. The large square lying between her and the street where he was waiting seemed an immensity. She recovered within it the strange unfailing freedom of solitude in the sounding spaces of London and hurried on to be by his side generally expressive of her rejoicing. The world's condemnation was out of sight behind her. But he would ask, and whatever she said, the whole problem would be there afresh, insoluble. He would never see that it had been confirmed, never admit anything contemptible in their association. It was because there was no contempt in him that she was hurrying. But alone again with him, the troubled darkness behind her would return with its maddening influence. She was fleeing from it only towards its darkest centre.

REVOLVING LIGHTS

TO

F. E. W.

CHAPTER I

THE building of the large hall had been brought about by people who gave no thought to the wonder of moving from one space to another and up and down stairs. Yet this wonder was more to them than all the things on which their thoughts were fixed. If they would take time to realize it. No one takes time. No one seems to know it. But I know it. These seconds of knowing, of being told, afresh, by things speaking silently, make up for the pain of failing to find out what I ought to be doing.

Away behind, in the flatly echoing hall, was the busy planning world of socialism, intent on the poor. Far away in tomorrow, stood the established, unchanging world of Wimpole Street, linked helpfully to the lives of the prosperous classes. Just ahead, at the end of the walk home, the small isolated Tansley Street world, full of secretive people drifting about on the edge of catastrophe, that would leave, when it engulfed them, no ripple on the surface of the tide of London life. In the space between these surrounding worlds was the everlasting solitude; ringing as she moved to cross the landing, with voices demanding an explanation of her presence in any one of them.

'Now *that*,' she quoted, to counter the foremost attack, 'is a man who can be trusted to say what he thinks.'

That cloaked her before the clamorous silence. She was an observant intelligent woman; approved. *He* would never imagine that the hurriedly borrowed words meant, to her, nothing but a shadow of doubt cast across the earnest little socialist. But they carried her across the landing. And here, at the head of the stairs, was the showcase of cold Unitarian literature. Yet another world. Bright, when she had first become aware of it, with freedom from the problem of Christ, offering, until she had met its inhabitants face to face, a congenial home. Sending her away, at a run, from cold, humorous intellectuality. She paused in front of the case, avoiding the sight of the well-known, chilly titles of the books, to read what had gathered in her mind during the evening.

A group of people who had come out just behind her were going down the stairs arguing in high-pitched, public platform voices from the surfaces of their associated minds. Not saying what they thought. Not thinking. Strong and controlled enough to keep within pattern of clever words. Most of them had been born to it. Born on the stage of clever words, which yet meant nothing to them. But to one or two people in the society these words *did* mean something. . . .

Nothing came after these people had gone but the refrain that had been the mental accompaniment of her listening throughout the evening, stepping forth now as part of a high-pitched argumentative to and fro. Her part, if she could join in and shout them all down. Sounding irrelevant and yet coming right down to earth, one small part of a picture puzzle set in place . . . a clue.

'Any number of barristers,' she vociferated in her mind, going on down the shallow stair, 'take up JOURNALISM. Get into Parliament. On the strength of being both *educated* and *articulate*. Weapons, giving an unfair advantage. The easy touch of prominence. Only a good nervous system wanted. They are psychologists. Up to a point. Enough to convince nice busy people, rushing through life without time to bethink themselves. Enough to alarm and threaten and cajole. They can raise storms; in newspapers. And brandish about by *name*, at their centres, like windmills, kept going by the wind of their psychological cheap-jackery. Yes, sir. Psychological cheap - jackery. . . . Purple - faced John Bull paterfamilias. Paterfamiliarity. Avenging his state by hitting out. . . . With an eye for a pretty face. . . .

The little man had no *axe* to grind. That was the only test. An Englishman, and a barrister, and yet awake to foreign art. His opaque English temperament not weakened by it; but worn a little transparent. He would be silent in an instant before a superior testimony.

He did not count on anything. When socialism came, he would be placed in an administrative post, and would fill it quietly, working harder than ever.

He brought the future nearer because he already moved within it; by being aware of things most men did not consider; aware of *relationships*: possibly believing in God, certainly in the soul.

Modern man, individually, is in many respects less capable than primitive man. Evolution is related development. Progress towards social efficiency. Benjamin Kidd.

'These large speculations are most-fatiguing.'

'No. When you see truth in them they are refreshing. They are all there is. All I live for now, is the arrival in my mind, of fresh generalizations.'

'That is good. But remember also that these things cost life.'

'What does it matter what they cost? A shape of truth makes you at the moment want to die, full of gratitude and happiness. It fills everything with a music to which you *could* die. The next piece of life comes as a superfluity.'

'Le superflu; chose nécessaire.'

At the foot of the stairs stood the yellow street light, framed in the oblong of the doorway. She went out into its shelter. The large grey legal buildings that stood by day a solid, dignified pile against the sky, a whole remaining region of the pride of London, showed only their lower façades, near, gentle frontages of mellow golden light and soft rectangular shadow, just above the brightly gilded surface of the deserted roadway. For a moment she stood listening to the reflection of the fostering light and breathing in the dry warm freshness of the London night air.

The illuminated future faded. The street lights of that coming time might throw their rays more liberally, over more beautiful streets. But something would be lost. In a world consciously arranged for the good of everybody there would be something personal . . . without foundation . . . like a nonconformist preacher's smile. The pavements of these streets that had grown of themselves, flooded by the light of lamps rooted like trees in the soil of London, were more surely pavements of gold than those pavements of the future?

They offered themselves freely; the unfailing magic that would give its life to the swing of her long walk home, letting her leave without regret the earlier hidden magic of the evening, the thoughts that had gathered in her mind whilst she listened, and that had now slipped away unpondered, leaving uppermost the outlines of the lecture to compete with the homeward walk. The surrounding golden glow through which she could always escape into the recovery of certainty, warned her not to return upon the lecture. But she could not let all she had heard disappear unnoted, and postponed her onward rush, apologizing for the moments about to be spent in conning over the store of ideas. In an instant the glow had gone, miscarried like her private impressions of the evening. The objects about her grew clear; full of current associations; and she wondered as her mind moved back across the linked statements of the lecture, whether these were her proper concern, or yet another step upon a long pathway of transgression. She was grasping at incompatible things, sacrificing the bliss of her own uninfluenced life to the temptation of gathering things that had been offered by another mind. Things to which she had no right?

But all the things of the mind that had come her way had come unsought; yet finding her prepared; so that they seemed not only her rightful property, but also in some way, herself. The proof was that they had passed her sisters by, finding no response; but herself they had drawn, often reluctant, perpetually escaping and forgetting; out on to a path that it sometimes seemed she must explore to the exclusion of everything else in life, exhaustively, the long way round, the masculine way. It was clearly not her fault that she had a masculine mind. If she must pay the penalties, why should she not also reap the entertainments?

Still, it was *strange*, she reflected, with a consulting glance at the returning brilliance, that without any effort of her own, so very many different kinds of people and thoughts should have come, one after the other, as if in an ordered sequence, into the little backwater of her life. What for? To what end was her life working by some sort of inner arrangement? To turn, into a beautiful distance outspread behind her as she moved on? What then?

For instance, the sudden appearance of the revolutionaries, just at this moment, seemed so apt. She had always wanted to meet revolutionaries, yet had never gone forth to seek them. Since her contact with socialists, she had been more curious about them than ever. And here they were, on their way to her, just as the meaning and some of the limitations of socialism were growing distinct. Yet it was absurd to suppose that their visit to England, in the midst of their exciting career, should have been timed to meet her need. Nor would they convince her. The light that shone about them was the anticipation of a momentary intense interest that would leave her a step farther on the lonely wandering that so distracted her from the day's work, and kept her family and the old known life at such an immeasurable distance. It was her ruling devil who had just handed her, punctually on the eve of their arrival, material for conversation with revolutionaries.

But it also seemed to be the mysterious friend, her star, the queer strange *luck* that dogged her path, always reviving happiness, bringing a sudden joy when there was nothing to account for it, plunging her into some new unexpected thing at the very moment of perfect helplessness. It was like a game . . . something was having a game of hide-and-seek with her. She winked, smiling, at the returned surrounding glow, and turned back to run up and down the steps of the neglected argument.

It was clear in her mind. Freed from the fascinating distraction of the little man's mannerisms, it spread fresh light, in all directions, tempering the golden light of the street; showing, beyond the outer darkness of the night, the white radiance of the distant future. Within the radiance, troops of people marched ahead, with springing footsteps; the sound of song in their ceaselessly talking voices; the forward march of a unanimous, light-hearted humanity along a pathway of white morning light. . . . The land of promise that she would never see; not through being born too soon, but by being incapable of unanimity. All these people had one mind. They approved of each other and were gay in unity.

The spectacle of their escape from the shadows lessened the pain of being left behind. Perhaps even a moment's contemplation of the future helped to bring it about? Every thought vibrates through the universe. Then there was absolution in thought, even from the anger of everlastingly talking people, contemptuous of silence and aloofness. And there was unity with the future.

The surrounding light glowed with a richer intensity. Flooded through her, thrilling her feet to swiftness.

If the revolutionaries could be with her now, they would find in her something of the state towards which they were violently straining? They would pause and hover for a moment, with half envious indulgence. But sooner or later they would say things about robust English health; its unconsciousness of its surroundings.

The *mystery* of being English. Mocked at for stupidity and envied for having something that concerned the mocking people of the two continents and challenged them to discover its secret.

But by to-morrow night she would have nothing but the little set of remembered facts, dulled by the fatigue of her day's work. These would save her, for the one evening, from appearing as the unintelligent Englishwoman of foreigners' experience. But they would also keep out the possibility of expressing anything.

Even the bare outlines of socialism, presented suddenly to unprepared English people, were unfailing as a contribution to social occasions. They forced every one to look at the things they had taken for granted in a new light, and to remember, together with the startling picture, the person who first drew it for them. But to appear before these Russians talking English socialism was to be nothing more than a useful person in uniform.

What *was* the immediate truth that shone, independent of speculation, all about her in the English light; the only thing worth telling to inquiring foreigners?

It was there at once when she was alone, or watching other people as an audience, or as an uncommitted guest, expressing in a great variety of places different sets of opinions. It was there radiant, obliterating her sense of existence, whenever she was in the midst of things kept going by other people. It could be given her by a beggar, purposefully crossing a street . . . not 'pitiful,' as he was so carelessly called—but something that shook her with gratitude to the roots of her being. But the instant she was called upon there came the startled realization of being in the world, and the sense of nothingness, preceding and accompanying every remark she might make.

One opinion self-consciously stated made the light go down. Immediate substitution of the contrary produced a chill followed by darkness. . . . *Men* called out these contradictory statements, each one with its way of having only one set of opinions.

How powerful these Russians were, in advance, making her count herself up. If she saw much of them she would fail and fade into nothing under the Russian test. If there were only one short interview she might escape unknown, and knowing all the things about Russian revolutionaries that Michael Shatov had left incomplete.

Their scornful revolutionary eyes watched her glance about amongst her hoard of contradictory ideas. Statements about different ways of looking at things were irrelevancies that perhaps with Russians might be abandoned altogether. Yet to appear before them empty-handed, hidden in her earlier uninfluenced personality, would be not to meet them at all. Personal life to them was nothing, could be summed up in a few words, the same for everybody. They lived for an idea.

She offered them a comprehensive glimpse of the many pools of thought in which she had plunged, rising from each in turn, to recover the bank and repudiate; unless a channel could be driven, that would make all their waters meet. They laughed when she cried out at the hopelessness of uniting them. 'All these things are nothing.'

But a revolutionary is a man who throws himself into space. In Russia there is nowhere else to throw himself? That would do as an answer to their criticisms of English socialism. She could say also that conservatives are the best socialists; being liberal-*minded*. Most socialists were narrow and illiberal, holding on to liberal ideas. The aim of the Lycurgans, alone amongst the world's socialists, was to show the English aristocracy and middle classes that they were, still, socialists.

There *were* things in England. But they struggled at cross purposes, refusing to get into a shape that would draw one, *whole*, along with it. But there were things in England with truth shining behind them. English people did not shine. But something shone behind them. Russians shone. But there was nothing behind them. There were things in England. She offered them the contents of books. They were as real as the pools of experience. Yet they, too, were irreconcilable.

A little blue-lit street; lamps with large round globes, shedding moonlight; shadows, grey and black. She had somehow got into the West End—a little West End street, giving out its character. She went softly along the middle of the blue-lit glimmering roadway, narrow between the narrow pavements skirting the high façades, flat and grey, broken by shadowy pillared porticoes; permanent exits and entrances on the stage of the London scene; solid lines and arches of pure grey shaping the flow of the pageant, and emerging, when it ebbed away, to stand in their own beauty, conjuring back the vivid tumult to flow in silence, a continuous ghostly garland of moving shapes and colours, haunting their self-sufficient calm.

Within the stillness she heard the jingling of hansoms, swinging in morning sunlight along the wide thoroughfares of the West End; saw the wide leisurely shop-fronts displaying in a restrained profusion, comfortably within reach of the experienced eye half turned to glance from a passing vehicle, all the belongings of West End life; on the pavements, the trooping succession of masked life-moulded forms, their unobservant eyes, aware of the resources all about them, at gaze upon their continuous adventure, yesterday still with them as they came out, in high morning light, into the adventure of to-day. Campaigners, sure of their weapons in the gaily decked mêlée, and sure every day of the blissful solitude of the interim times.

For as long as she could remember she had known something of their secret. During the years of her London life she had savoured between whiles the quality of their world, divined its tests and passwords, known what kept their eyes unseeing and their speech clipped to a jargon.

Best of all was the illumination that had come with her penetration of the mystery of their attitude towards direct *questions*. There was something here that had offered her again and again a solution of the problem of social life, a safe-guard of individuality. Here it was once more, a still small voice urging that every moment of association would be trans-formed if she would only remember the practice the technique revealed by her contemplation of this one quality. Always to be solid and resistent; unmoved. Having no opinions and only one enthusiasm—to be unmoved. Momentary experi-ments had proved that the things that were about her in solitude could be there all the time. But forgetfulness always came. Because most people brought their worlds with them, their opinions, and the set of things they believed in; forcing in the end direct questions and disagreements. And most people were ready to answer questions, showing by their angry defence of their opinions that they were aware, and afraid, of other ways of looking at things. But these society people did not seem to be aware of anything but their one world. Perhaps that was why their social method was not able to hold her for long together.

'Is this the way to Chippenham?' But *every one* delights in telling the way. It brings the teller out into adventure; with his best self and his best moments all about him. The sur-roundings are suddenly new with life, and beautiful like things seen in passing, on a journey. English people delight because they are adventurous. They prolong the moment, beaming and expanding, and go on their way refreshed. Foreigners, except perhaps Germans, answer differently. Obsequiously; or with a studied politeness that turns the occasion into an opportunity for the display of manners; or indifferently, with a cynical suggestion that they know what you are like, and that you will be the same when you reach your destination. They are themselves, without any fullness or wonder. English people are always waiting to be different, to be fully themselves. Strangers, to them, are gods and angels.

But it is another kind of question that is meant, the question that is a direct attack on the unseeing gaze; a speech to the man at the wheel. That is where, without knowing it, these people are philosophers. What Socrates saw, answered all his questions; and his counterings of the young men's questions were invitations to them to look for themselves. The single world these people see is, to them, so unquestionable that there is no room for question. Nothing can be communicated except the latest news; and scandal; information about people who have gone outside the shape. But, to each other, even their statements are put in the form of questions. 'Fine day, what?' So that every one may be not questioned, but questioner. It is also a sort of apology for falling into speech at all.

It was Michael Shatov's amused delight in her stories of their method that had made her begin to cherish them as a possession. Gradually she had learned that irritation with their apparent insolence was jealousy. Within her early interested unenvious sallies of investigation amongst the social élite of the Wimpole Street patients, or as a fellow guest amongst the Orlys' society friends, there had been moments of longing to sweep away the defences and discountenance the individual. But gradually the conviction had dawned that with the genuine members of the clan this could not be done. Their quality went right through, shedding its central light, a brightness that could not be encircled, over the whole of humanity. They disarmed attack, because in their singleness of nature they were not aware of anything to defend. They had no contempts, not being specially intellectual; and, crediting every one with their own condition, they reached to the sources of nobility in all with whom they came in contact. It was refreshment and joy merely to be in the room with them. But also it was an arduous exercise. They brought such a wide picture and so

long a history. They were England. The world-wide spread
of Christian England was in their minds; and to this they
kindled, more than to any personal thing.

The existence of these scattered few, explained those who
were only conventional approximations.

To-night, immersed in the vision of a future that threatened
their world, she found them one and all bright figures of
romance. She sped, as her footsteps measured off the length
of the little street, into the recesses, the fair and the evil, of
aristocratic English life, and affectionately followed the small
bright freely moving troupe as it spread in the past and was at
this moment spreading, abroad over the world, the unchangeable English quality and its attendant conventions.

The books about these people are not satisfactory. Those
that show them as a moral force, suggest that they are the fair
flower of a Christian civilization. But a Christian civilization
would be abolishing factories. Lord Shaftesbury . . . Arnold's
barbarian idea made a convincing picture, but it suggested in
the end, behind his back, that there was something lacking in
the Greeks. Most of the modern books seemed to ridicule
the English conventions, and to choose the worst types of
people for their characters.

But in *all* the books about these people, even in novelettes,
the chief thing they all left out, was there. They even described it, sometimes so gloriously that it became *more* than
the people; making humanity look like ants, crowding and
perishing on a vast scene. Generally the surroundings were
described separately, the background on which presently the
characters began to fuss. But they were never sufficiently
shown as they were to the people when there was no fussing;
what the floods of sunshine and beauty indoors and out meant
to these people as single individuals, whether they were aware
of it or not. The 'fine' characters in the books, acting on
principle, having thoughts, and sometimes, the less likeable
of them, even ideas, were not shown as being made strong
partly by endless floods of sunshine and beauty. The feeble
characters were too much condemned for clutching, to keep,
at any price, within the charmed circle.

The antics of imitators, all down the social scale, were wrongly condemned.

But *here*, in this separate existence, *was* a shape that could draw her, whole, along with it . . . and here suddenly, warmly about her in its evening quiet, was the narrow winding lane of Bond Street. Was this bright shape, that drew her, the secret of her nature . . . the clue she had carried in her hand through the maze?

It would explain my love for kingly old Hanover, the stately ancient house in Waldstrasse; the way the charm of the old-fashioned well-born Pernes held me so long in the misery of north London; the relief of getting away to Newlands, my determination to remain from that time forth, at any cost, amidst beautiful surroundings. Though life has drawn me away these things have stayed with me. They were with me through the awful months. . . . If *she* had been able to escape into the beauty of outside things, it would not have happened.

It was not the fear of being alone with the echoes of the tragedy that made me ill in suburban lodgings, but the small ugliness and the empty crude suburban air; the knowledge that if I stayed and forgot its ugliness in happiness, it would mould me unawares. My drifting to the large old house in grey wide Bloomsbury was a movement of return.

Then I am attached for ever to the spacious gentle surroundings in which I was born? Always watching and listening and feeling for them to emerge? My social happiness dependent upon the presence of some suggestion of its remembered features, my secret social ambition its perfected form in circumstances beyond my reach?

No. There was something within her that could not tolerate either the people or the thoughts existing within that exclusive world. In the silences that flowed about its manifold unvarying expressions, she would always find herself ranging off into lively consciousness of other ways of living, whose smiling mystery defied its complacent patronage. It drew only her nature, the ease-and-beauty-loving soul of her physical being, and that only in critical contemplation. She would never desire to bestir herself to achieve stateliness.

So that that far-away moment of being driven forth seemed to bear two meanings. It was life's stupid error, a cruel blind destruction of her helpless youth. At this moment, if it were possible, she would reverse it and return. During all these years she had been standing motionless, fixed tearfully in the attitude of return. The joy she had found in her invisible life amongst the servants was the joy of remaining girt and ready for the flight of return, her original nature stored up and hidden behind the adopted manner of her bondage.

Or it was life's wisdom, the swift movement of her lucky star, providence pouncing. And providence, having seized her indolent blissful protesting form and flung it forth with a laugh, had continued to pamper her with a sense of happiness that bubbled unexpectedly out in the midst of her utmost attempts to achieve misery by a process of reason.

It is my strange bungling in misery that makes every one seem far off. A perpetual oblivion not only of my own circumstances, but, at the wrong moments, of those of other people, makes me disappoint and shock them, suddenly disappearing before their eyes in the midst of a sympathy that they had eagerly seemed to find satisfying and rare. . . . A light frivolous elastic temperament? A helpless going to and fro between two temperaments. A solid charwomanly commonplace kindliness, spread like a doormat at the disposal of everybody, and an intermittent perfect dilettantism that would disgust even the devil?

That was *his* temperament? The quality that had made him gravitate, unaided, towards exclusive things, was also in her. But weaker, because it was less narrow? He had thrown up everything for leisure to wander in the fields of art and science and philosophy; shutting his eyes to the fact of his diminishing resources. She, with no resources at all, had dropped to easy irresponsible labour to avoid being shaped and branded, to keep her untouched strength free for a wider contemplation than he would have approved, a delight in everything in turn, a *plebeian* dilettantism, aware and defensive of the exclusive things, but unable to restrict herself to them, unconsciously from the beginning resisting the drawing of lines and setting up of oppositions? More and more consciously ranged on all sides simultaneously. More *catholic*. That was the other side of the family. But if, with his temperament and his sceptical intuitive mind, she had also the nature of the other side of the family, what a hopeless problem. . . . If she belonged to both, she was the sport of opposing forces that would never allow her to alight and settle. The movement of her life would be like a pendulum. No wonder people found her unaccountable. But being her own solitary companion would not go on for ever. It would bring in the end, somewhere about middle age, the state that people called madness. Perhaps the lunatic asylums were full of people who had refused to join up? There were happy people in them? 'Wandering' in their minds. But remembering and knowing happiness all the time? In dropping to nothingness they escaped for ever into that state of amazed happiness that goes on all the time underneath the strange forced quotations of deeds and words.

Oxford Street opened ahead, right and left, a wide empty yellow-lit corridor of large shuttered shop-fronts. It stared indifferently at her outlined fate.

Even at night it seemed to echo with the harsh sounds of its oblivious conglomerate traffic. Since the high light-spangled front of the Princess's Theatre had changed, there was nothing to obliterate the permanent sense of the two monstrous streams flowing all day, fierce and shattering, east and west. Oxford Street, unless she were sailing through it perched in sunlight on the top of an omnibus lumbering steadily towards the graven stone of the City, always wrought destruction, pitting its helpless harshness against her alternating states of talkative concentration and silent happy expansion. Going west it *was* destruction; for ever approaching the West End, reaching its gates and passing them by.

Stay here, suggested Bond Street. Walking here you can keep alive, out in the world, until the end, an aged crone, still a citizen of my kingdom, hobbling in the sun, along my sacred pavements. She turned gladly, encompassing the gift of the whole length of the winding lane with a plan of working round through Soho, to cross Oxford Street painlessly where it blended with St Giles's, and would let her through northwards into the squares. The strange new thoughts were about her the moment she turned back. They belonged to these old, central finely-etched streets where they had begun, a fresh proof of her love for them; a new enrichment of their charm.

Whatever might be the truth about heredity, it was immensely disturbing to be pressed upon by two families, to discover, in their so different qualities, the explanation of oneself. The sense of existing merely as a link, without individuality, was not at all compensated by the lifting, and distribution backwards, of responsibility. To be set in a mould, powerless to alter its shape . . . to discover, too late for association and inquiry, the people she helplessly belonged to. Yet the very fact that young people fled their relatives, was an argument on the side of individuality. But not all fled their relatives. Perhaps only those of St Paul's evil generation, 'lacking in natural affection.'

She glanced narrowly, with a curiosity that embarrassment could no longer hold back, at her father's side of the family, and while she waited for them to fall upon her and wrathfully consume her, she met the shock of a surprise that caught her breath. They did not *object*. Boldly faced, in the light of her new interest, the vividly remembered forms, and paintings and photographs almost as vividly real, came forward and grouped themselves about her as if mournfully glad at last of the long-deferred opportunity. They offered, not themselves, but what they saw and knew, holding themselves withdrawn, rigorously in place about the centre of their preoccupation. Yet they *were* personal. The terrible gentleness with which they asked her why for so long she had kept aloof from consultation with them, held a personal appeal that made her glow. Deeply desiring it, she held herself away from the solicited familiarity in a stillness of fascinated observation.

They were *Puritans*. More wonderful than she had known in thinking of them as nonconformists, a disgrace her father had escaped together with the trade he had abandoned in youth. They were the Puritans she had read of; but not

Cromwellian, certainly not Roundheads. Though they were tall and gaunt with strongly moulded features, their thought-less, generous English ancestry showed in them, moulded by their sternness to a startling *beauty*. They had well-shaped hands, alive and speaking amongst their rich silks and fine old laces. They wore with a dignified austerity, but still they wore, and must therefore have thought about, silk and lace and broadcloth and fine frilled linen, as well as the sin in themselves and in the world. But principally they were aware of sin, gazing with stern meditative eyes, through the pages of their gloomily bound books, into the abyss yawning at their feet. She held herself in her place, growing bolder, longing now for parley with their silent resistance, disguising nothing, offering them, pell-mell, the least suitable of her thoughts. But the eyes they turned on her, still dreadfully begging her to remember now, in the days of her youth, were kind, lit by a special smiling indulgence. . . . Their strong stern lives, full of the knowledge of experience, that had led down to her, had made them *kind*. However far she might stray, she was still their favourite, their different stubby round-faced darling, never to be condemned to the abyss. Listening as they called to their part in her, she shared the salvation they had wrought . . . salvage . . . of hard fine lives, reared narrowly, in beauty, above the gulf.

Yet it was also from their incompleteness that they called to her; the *darkness* in them, visible in the air about them as they moved, that she had always feared and run away from. The thought of the stern gaunt chairs in which they sat and died of old age was horrible even at this moment, and now that she no longer feared them, she knew, though she felt a homesick longing for their stern righteousness, that it was incomplete. The pressing darkness kept them firm, fighting the devil every inch of the way.

But the devil was not dark, he was bright. Brightest and best of the sons of the morning. What shocking profanity. Something has made me drunk. I am always drunk in the West End. Satan was proud. God revenged himself. Re-vengeful, omnipotent, jealous, 'the first of the autocrats.'

There was a glory hidden in that old darkness, but they did not know it; though they followed it,   Accepting them, plunging into their darkness she would never be able to keep from finding the bright devil and wandering wrapped in gloom, but forgetful, perpetually in the bright spaces within the darkness. And perhaps it was God. Impossible to say. Religious people shunned the bright places believing them haunted by the devil. Other religious people believed they were the gift of God and would presently be everywhere, for everybody, the kingdom of God upon earth. But even if factories were abolished and the unpleasant kinds of work shared out so that they pressed upon nobody, how could the kingdom of heaven come upon earth as long as there were childbirth and cancer ?

Light makes *shadows*. The devil is God's shadow ? The Persians believed that in the end the light would absorb the darkness. That was credible. But it could never happen on earth. That was where the Puritans were right with their vale of tears, and why they were more deeply attractive than the other side of the family. Their roots in life were deeper and harder and the light from the Heavenly City fell upon their foreheads *because* they struggled in the gloom. If only they knew what the gloom was, the marvel of its being there. They were solemn and reproachful because they could not get at their own gaiety.

The others were *too* jolly, too much turned out towards life, deliberately cheerful and roistering, not aware of the wonder and beauty of gloom, yet more dreadfully haunted and afraid of it, showing its uncomprehended presence by always deliberately driving it away. They spread gloom about them, by their perpetual impatient cheerfulness, afraid to listen and look. Their wild spirits were tragic, bright tragedy, making their country life sound in the distance like one long maddening unbroken noise, afraid to stop, rushing on, taking everything for granted, and troubling about nothing. People who lived in the country *were* different. Fresh. All converted by their surroundings into perpetual noise ? The large spaces gave them large rich voices . . . rounded sturdy west country yeomen, blunt-featured and jolly, with big voices. Jesting with women. The women all dark and animated . . . arch . . . minxes. Any amount of flirting. All the scandals of the family were on that side. Girls, careering, with flying hair, round paddocks, on unbroken bare-backed ponies. Huge families. Hunting. Great Christmas and harvest parties. Maypoles in the spring. They always saw the spring, every year without fail. Perhaps that was their secret? Wherever they were they saw nothing but dawn and spring, the light coming from the darkness. They shouted against the darkness because they knew the light was hidden in it. If you're waking, call me early, call me early . . .

> So ear-ly in, the mor-ning,
> My Belov-ed,
> *My* Belov-ed.

Those women's voices pealed out into the wakening air of pure silver dawns. The chill pure dawn and dark over the fields where L'Allegro walked in her picture, the dewy dawn-lit grass under her white feet, her hair blown softly back by the morning breeze flowing over her dawn-lit face, shaping her garments to her happy limbs as she wàlked dancing, towards the increasing light. Little pools and clumps of wet primroses over the surface of the grey-green grass, flushed with rose, like her glowing dancing face as she skimmed, her whole bright form pealing with song towards the *increasing light*. Was that sort of life still going on somewhere?

Yet Il Penseroso *knew* and L'Allegro did not.

Long-featured Sarah was on the Puritan side, with a strain of the artist, drawn from the other half, tormenting her. Eve, delicately and unscrupulously adventurous, was the west-country side altogether.

Within me . . . the *third* child, the longed-for son, the two natures, equally matched, mingle and fight? It is their struggle that keeps me adrift, so variously interested and strongly attracted, now here, now there? Which will win? . . . Feeling so identified with both, she could not imagine either of them set aside. Then her life *would* be the battlefield of her two natures. Which of them had been thrilled through and through, so that she had seemed to enter, lightly waving

her hand to all that had gone before, for good, into a firelit
glow, the door closing behind her, and leaving her launched,
without her belongings, but richly accompanied, on a journey
to the heart of an unquenchable joy? It was not socialism
that had drawn her, though the moment before, she had been,
spontaneously, a socialist, for the first time. The glow that
had come with his words was still there, drawing her, an un-
fulfilled promise. She was still waiting to be, consciously, in
league and everlasting company with others, a socialist. Yet
the earlier lonely moment had been so far her only experience
of the state; everything that had followed had been a slow
gradual undoing of it.

What was the secret of the immense relief, the sense of being
and doing in an unbounded immensity that had come with her
dreamy sudden words? One moment sitting on the hearth-
rug living in the magic of the woven text, feeling its message
rise from the quiet firelit room, drive through the sound of the
winter sea and out and away over the world, to every one who
had ears to hear; giving the power of hearing to those who had
not, until they equally possessed it. And then hearing her
own voice, like a whisper in the immensity, thrilled with the
sense of a presented truth, coming *given*, suddenly, from nowhere, the glad sense of a shape whose denial would be death,
and bringing, as she dreamily followed its prompting, a willingness to suffer in its service.

'You ought to cut out the pathos in that passage.'

'*Which* passage, Miriametta?' The effort of throwing off
the many distractions of the interested, mocking, critical voice.

'You weaken the whole argument by coming forward in
those three words to tell your readers what they ought to feel.
An *enormous* amount of time is lost, while attention is turned
from the spectacle to yourself.'

'Yes. *Which* passage?'

'In the moment that the reader turns away, everything goes,
and they come back distracted and different, having been
racing all over their own world, perhaps *indifferent*.'

'Passage, passage——'

'The *real* truth is that you don't feel that pathos to yourself,

or not in that way and in those words . . . there are one or
two earlier passages that stopped me, the same sort of thing.'

'Right. We 'll have 'm all out.'

'Without them the book will convince everybody.'

'No sane person can read it and keep out of socialism.'

'No.' But how fearful that sounds, said by the author.
As if he knew something else as well.

'Y' know *you* ought to be a Lycurgan, Miriam.' And then
had come the sense of the door closing on all past loneliness,
the rich sense of being carried forward to some new accompanied moulding change; but without any desire to go. Even
with him, a moment of expression, seeming, while it lasted,
enough in itself; the whole of life, when it happened not alone,
but in an understanding presence; led to *results*, the destructive
demand for the pinning of it down to some small shape of
specialized action. Could he not see that the thing so surprising her and coming to him also as a surprise, was enough
in itself . . . would disappear if she rushed forward into
activities, masquerading, with empty hands, as one who had
something to give. Yet *he* was going forward into activities.
. . . She ought, having learned from him a clear theory of
the working of the whole of human life, to be willing to follow,
only too glad of the opportunity of any sort of share, even as
an onlooker, in the making of the new world.

But if she responded, she would be supporting his wrong
estimate of her, his way of endowing every one with his own
gifts, seeing people only as capability, waiting for opportunities
for action. She wanted only further opportunities with him, of
forgetfulness, and the strange following moments of expression.

'Every one will be socialist soon; there 's no need to join
societies.'

'There 's mountains, my dear Miriam, *mountains* of work
ahead, that only an organized society can compass. And you 'd
like the Lycurgans. We 'll make you a Lycurgan.'

'What could I do ?'

'You can talk. You might write. Edit. You 've got a deadly
critical eye. Yes, you are a Lycurgan. That 's settled.'

'How *can* you say I can talk ?'

'You 've got a *tenacity*. I 'd back you against any one in argument, when you 're roused.'

'Argument is no good to anybody, world without end, amen.'

'Don't be frivolous, Miriam. Real argument 's a fine clean weapon.'

'Cutting both ways; proving *anything*.'

'Quarrelsome Miriam.'

'And you know what you think about my writing. That I, or *anybody*, could *learn* to write passably.'

'If you *have* written anything, I 've not seen it. You shall learn to write, passably, in the interests of socialism.'

What an awful fate. To sit in a dusty corner, loyally doing odd jobs, considered by him 'quite a useful intelligent creature,' among other much more clever, and to him, more attractive creatures, all working submissively in the interests of a theory that he understood so well that he must already be believing in something else. But she was already a useful fiercely loyal creature, that was how he described her, at Wimpole Street —— But that was for the sake of freedom. Working with him there would be no freedom at all. Only a series of loyal posings.

Standing upon the footstool to get out, back, away from the wrong turning into the sense of essential expression. The return into the room of the sound of the sea, empty and harsh, in a void.

'That 's admirable. You could carry off any number of inches, Miriam. You only want the helmet and the trident. You 're Britannia, you know. The British Constitution. You 're infinitely more British than I am.'

'Foreigners always tell me I am the only English person who understands them.'

'*Flattery*. You 've no *idea* how British you are. A mass of British prejudice and intelligent obstinacy. I shall put you in a book.'

'Then how can you want me to be a socialist? I am a Tory and an anarchist by turns.'

'You 're certainly an anarchist. You 're an individualist, you know, that 's what 's wrong with you.'

'And what's wrong with *you*?'

'And now you shall experiment in being a socialist.'

'Tories are the best socialists.'

'You shall be a Tory socialist. My dear Miriam, there will be socialists in the House of *Lords*.'

The same group of days had contained the relief of the beginning of generalizations; the end, on her part, of stories about people, told with an eye upon his own way of observing and stating. These stories had, during the earlier time, kept him so amused and, with his profane comments and paraphrases, so perpetually entertaining, that a large part of her private councils during the visits were spent in reviewing the long procession of Tansley Street boarders, the patients at Wimpole Street, and people ranged far away in her earlier lives, as material for anecdote. But throughout the delight of his interest and his surprising reiterated envy of the variety of her contacts, there had been a haunting sense of misrepresentation, and even of treachery to him, in contributing to his puzzling, almost unvarying vision of people as pitifully absurd, from the small store of experiences she had dropped and forgotten, until he drew them forth and called them wealth.

His refusal to believe in a Russian's individuality because no one had heard of him had set a term to these communications, leaving an abrupt pain. It was so strange that he should fail to recognize the distinction of the Russian *being*, the quality of the Russian attitude towards life. He had followed with interest, gentle and patient at first before her overwhelming conviction, allowing her to add stroke after stroke to her picture, seeming for a moment to see what she saw and then——
What has he *done*? Either it was that his pre-arranged picture of European life had no place for these so different, inactive Russians, or her attempts to represent people in themselves, without borrowed methods of portrayal, were useless because they fell between the caricature which was so uncongenial to her and the methods of description current in everyday life, which equally refused to serve by reason of their tacit reference to ideas she could not accept.

But the beginnings of abstract discussion had brought a

most joyful relief, and a confirming intensification of the beauty of the interiors and of the surrounding landscape, in which their talks were set. Discussing people, save when he elaborated legend and profanity until privately she called upon the hosts of heaven to share this brightest terrestrial mirth, cast a spell of sadness all about her. With every finished vignette there came a sense of ending. Sacrificed to its sharp expressiveness were the real moments of these people's lives; and the moments of the present, counting themselves off, ignored and irrecoverable, offering, as their extension, time that was unendurably narrow and confined, a narrow featureless darkness, its walls grinning with the transfixed features of consciousness that had always been, and must, if the pictures were accepted as true, for ever be, a motionless absurdity.

Launched into wide opposition, no longer trying to see with his eyes, while still hoarding, as a contrasting amplification of her own visions, much that he had given her, she found people still there; rallying round her in might, ranging forward through time, each one standing clear of everything that offered material for ironic commentary, in a radiant individuality.

Wide generalization was, she had immediately vowed, the way to illuminating contemplation of humanity. Its exercise made the present moment a life in itself, going on for ever; the thought of the speakers and the surroundings blended in an unforgettable whole; her past life gleaming about her in a chain of moments; leaping glad acceptances or ardent refusals, of large general views.

The joy of making statements not drawn from things heard or read but plumbed directly from the unconscious accumulations of her own experience was fermented by the surprise of his interested attention, and the pride of getting him occasionally to accept an idea or to modify a point of view. It beamed compensation for what she was losing in sacrificing, whenever expression was urgent in her, his unmatchable monologue to her own shapeless outpourings. But she laboured, now and then successfully, to hold this emotion in subjection to the urgency of the things she longed to express.

'*Women*, everybody knows nowadays, have made civilization,

the thing civilization is so proud of—social life. It's one of the things I dislike in them. There you are, by the way, women were the first socialists.' Havelock Ellis; and Emerson quoting Firdausi's description of his Persian Lilla . . . but the impression, remaining more sharp and deep than the event, became one's own by revealing an inborn sharing of the view expressed. And waiting behind it now, was the proof, in life, as she had seen it.

'I don't mean that idea of public opinion, "the great moulding and civilizing force steered by women," that even the most pessimistic men admit, in horror.'

'What *do* you mean, Miriam?' Patient scepticism.

'Something quite different. It's amazing, the blindness in men, even in you, about women. There must be a reason for it. Because it's universal. It's no good looking, with no matter *what* eyes, if you look in the wrong place. All that men have done, since the beginning of the world, is to find out and give names to and do, the things that were in women from the beginning, and that the best of them have been doing all the time. Not me.'

'*You*, Miriam, are an incorrigible *loafer*. I've a sneaking sympathy with *that*.'

'Well, the thing is, that whereas a few men here and there are creators, originators, *artists*, women are this all the time.'

'My dear Miriam, I don't know *what* women are. I'm enormously interested in sex; but I don't know *anything* about it. Nobody does. That's just where we are.'

'Because you're a man and have no personality.'

'Don't talk nonsense, Miriam.'

'How can a man have personality?'

'All right. *Men*—have no personality.'

'You see women simply as a sex. That's one of the proofs.'

'Right. Women have no sex.'

'You are doubtful about "emancipating" women, because you think it will upset their sex-life.'

'I don't know *anything*, Miriam. No personality. No knowledge. But there's Miss Waugh, with a thoroughly able career behind her; been *everywhere*, done *everything*, my dear Miriam; come out of it all, shouting you back into the nursery.'

'I don't know her. Perhaps she 's jealous, like a man, of her freedom. But the point is, there 's no emancipation to be done. Women are emancipated.'

'Prove it, Miriam.'

'I can. Through their pre-eminence in an art. The art of making atmospheres. It 's as big an art as any other. Most women can exercise it, for reasons, by fits and starts. The best women work at it the whole of the time. Not one man in a million is aware of it. It 's like air within the air. It may be deadly. Cramping and awful, or simply destructive, so that no life is possible within it. So is the bad art of men. At its best it is absolutely life-giving. And not soft. Very hard and stern and austere in its beauty. And like mountain air. And you can't get behind it, or in any way divide it up. Just as with "Art." Men live in it and from it all their lives without knowing. Even recluses.'

'Don't drive it too far, Miriam.'

'Well; I 'm so staggered by it. All women, of course, know about it, and *there* 's the explanation of why women clash. Over what men call "trifles." Because the thing I mean goes through everything. A woman's way of "being" can be discovered in the way she pours out tea. *Men* can't get on together. If they 're boxed up. Do you know there 's hardly a partnership in Wimpole Street that 's not a permanent feud. Yes. Would you believe it? And for scandal and gossip and jealousy there 's *nothing* to beat the professors in a university town. Several of them don't speak. They communicate by letter. . . . But it 's the women who are not grouped who can see all this most clearly. By moving, amongst the grouped women, from atmosphere to atmosphere. It 's one of my principal social entertainments. I feel the atmosphere created by the lady of the house as soon as I get on to the door-step.'

'Perceptive Miriam. . . . You *have* a flair, Miriam. I grant you that. I believe in your flair.'

'Well, it 's *true*, what I 'm trying to tell you. It 's one of the answers to the question about women and art. It 's all there. It doesn't show, like men's art. There 's no drama or publicity. *There;* d' you see? It 's hard and exacting; needing "the maximum of detachment and control." And people have to learn, or be taught, to see it.'

'Y . . . es. Is it conscious?'

'Absolutely. And there you are again. Artists, well, and *literary* people, say they have to get away from everything at intervals. They associate with queer people, and some of them are dissipated. They can only rest, stop being artists, by getting *away.* That is why so many women get nervy and break down. The only way they can rest, is by being nothing to nobody, leaving off for a while giving out any atmosphere.'

'Stop breathing.'

'Yes. But if you laugh at that, you must laugh at artists, *and* literary people.'

'I will. I *do.*'

'Yes; but in general. You must see the identity of the two things for good or for bad. If people reverence men's art and feel their sacrifices are worth while, to *themselves,* as well as to other people, they must not just *pity* the art of women. It doesn't matter to women. But it 's so jolly bad for men, to go about feeling lonely and superior. Men, and the women who imitate them, bleat about women "finding their truest fulfilment in *self-sacrifice.*" In speaking of male art it is called *self-realization.* That 's men all over. They get an illuminating theory — man must die, to live — and apply it only to themselves. If a theory is true, you may be sure it applies in a most thorough-going way to women. They don't stop dead at self-sacrifice. They reap . . . freedom. Self-realization. Emancipation. Lots of women hold back. Just as men do —from exacting careers. *I* do. *I* don't want to exercise the feminine art.'

'It 's true you don't compete or exploit yourself, Miriam.'

'Some women want to be men. And the contrary, men wanting to be women, is almost unknown. This is supposed to be evidence of the superiority of the masculine state. It isn't. Women only want to be men before they begin their careers. It 's a longing for exemptions. Young women envy men, as young men, faced with the hard work of life, envy dogs.'

'Harsh Miriam.'

'It's true. At any rate it's deserved, after all men have said. And I believe it's *true*.'

'Pugilistic Miriam. . . . Your atmospheric idea is quite illuminating. I think there's some truth in it; and I'd be with you altogether but for one . . . damning . . . yes, I think absolutely damning, *fact*.'

'Well?'

'The men women will marry. The men quite fine, intelligent women marry; and *idolize*, my dear Miriam.'

'Many artists have to use any material that comes to hand. The treatment is the thing.'

'Treatment that mistakes putty for marble, my dear Miriam——'

'And you don't see that you are proving my point. Women *see* things when they are not there. That's creativeness. What is meant by women "making" men.'

'They don't. They'll make idols of nothing at all; and go on burning incense—all their lives.'

'I don't believe women are *ever* deceived about their husbands. But they don't give up hope. And there's something in everybody. That's what women see.'

'Nonsense, Miriam. Girls with quite good brains and abilities will marry anything; accept its views and quote them.'

'Yes; just as they will show off a child's tricks. Views and opinions are masculine things. Women are indifferent to them, really. Any set will do. I know the way a woman's opinions and interests change with her different husbands, if she marries more than once, is supposed to prove the vacuity of her mind. Half the satirists of women have made their reputation on that idea. It isn't so. It is that women can hold all opinions at once, or any, or none. It's because they see the relations of things which don't change, more than things which are always changing, and mostly the importance to men of the things men believe. But behind it all their own lives are untouched.'

'Behind. . . . What *is* there behind, Miriam?'

'Life.'

'What do they do with it?'

'Live.'

'Mysterious Miriam. The business of women; the career; that makes you all rivals, is to find fathers. Your material is children.'

'Then look here, if you think *that*, there's a perfect instance. If women's material is people, their famous "curiosity" is the curiosity of the artist. Men call it "incurable" in women. Men's curiosity, about things, science and so forth, is called divine. There you are. My *word*.'

'*I* don't, Miriam.'

'Shaw knows how wildly interested women are in psychology. That's funny. . . . But about children. If only you could realize how incidental all that is.'

'Incidental to what?'

'To the *life* of the individual.'

'Try it, Miriam. Marry your Jew. You know Jew and English makes a good mix.'

'You see I never knew he was a Jew. It did not come up until a possible future came in view. I *couldn't* have Jewish children.'

'Incidents. Mere incidents.'

'No; the wrong material. I, being myself, couldn't do anything with it; couldn't be anything in relationship to it.'

'You'd *be*, through seeing its possibilities and making an atmosphere.'

'I've told you I'm *not* one of those stupendous women.'

'What *are* you?'

'Well, now here's something you will like. If I were to marry a Jew, I should feel that all my male relatives would have the right to *beat* me.'

'That's strange. . . . And, I think, great nonsense, Miriam.'

'And I'm not anti-Semite. I think Jews are better Christians than we are. We have things to learn from them. But not by marrying them, until they've learnt things from us. Women, particularly, can't marry Jews. Men can marry Jewesses, if they like.'

'Marriage is a more important affair for women than for men. Just so.'

'I didn't say so.'

'You *did*, Miriam, and it's quite true.'

'It appears to be so because, as I've been trying to show you, men don't know where they are.'

'Your man'll know, Miriam. You ought to marry and have children. You'd have good children. Good shapes and good brains.'

'The mere sight of a child, moving unconsciously, its little shoulders and busy intentions, makes me catch my breath.'

'Marry your Jew, Miriam. Well—perhaps no; don't marry your Jew.'

'The other day we were walking somewhere. I was dead tired. He knew it and kept on suggesting a hansom. Suddenly there was a woman, lugging a heavy perambulator up some steps. He stood still, shouting to *me* to help her.'

'What did you do?'

'I blazed his own words back at him. I dare say I stamped my foot. Meanwhile the woman, who was very burly, had got the perambulator up. We walked on and presently he said in a quiet, intensely interested voice, "*Why* did you not help this woman?"'

'What did you say?'

'I began to talk about something else.'

'Diplomatic Miriam.'

'Not at all. It's *useless* to talk to *instincts*. I know; because I have tried. Poor little man. I am afraid, now that I am not going to marry him, of hurting and tiring him. I talked one night. We had been agreeing about things, and I went on and on, it was in the drawing-room in the dark, after a theatre, talking almost to myself, very interested, forgetting that he was there. Presently a voice said, trembling with fatigue, "Believe me, Miriam, I am profoundly interested. Will you perhaps put all this down for me on paper?" Yes. Wasn't it funny and *appalling*? It was three o'clock. Since then I have been afraid. Besides, he will marry a Jewess. If I were not sure of that I could not contemplate his loneliness. It's heartbreaking. When I go to see friends in the evening, he waits outside.'

'I *say*. Poor *chap*. That's quite touching. You'll marry him yet, Miriam.'

'There are ways in which I like him and am in touch with him as I never could be with an Englishman. Things he understands. And his absolute sweetness. Absence of malice and enmity. It's so strange, too, with all his ideas about women, the things he will do. Little things like cleaning my shoes. But look here; an important thing. Having children is just shelving the problem, leaving it for the next generation to solve.'

That stood out as the end of the conversation; bringing a sudden bright light. The idea that there was something essential, for everybody, that could not be shelved. Something had interrupted. It could never be repeated. But surely he must have agreed, if there had been time to bring it home to him. Then it might have been possible to get him to admit uniqueness . . . individuality. He would. But would say it was negligible. Then the big world he thinks of, since it consists of individuals, is also negligible. . . .

Something had been at work in the conversation, making it all so easy to recover. Vanity? The relief of tackling the big man? Not altogether. Because there had been moments of thinking of death. Glad death if the truth could *once* be stated. Disinterested rejoicing in the fact that a man who talked to so many people was hearing *something* about the world of women. And if any one had been there to express it better, the relief would have been there, just the same, without jealousy. But what an unconscious compliment to men, to feel that it mattered whether or no they understood anything about the world of women. . . .

The remaining days of the visit had glowed with the sense of the beginning of a new relationship with the Wilsons. The enchantment that surrounded her each time she went to see them and always as the last hours went by, grew oppressive with the reminder of its impermanence, shone, at last, wide over the future. The end of a visit would never again bring the certainty of being finally committed to an overwhelming combination of poverties, cut off, by an all-round ineligibility, from the sun-bathed seaward garden, the joyful brilliant seaside light pouring through the various bright interiors of the perfect little house; the inexpressible *charm*, always renewed, and remaining, however deeply she felt at variance with the Wilson reading of life, the topmost radiance of her social year; ignored and forgotten nearly all the time, but shining out whenever she chanced to look round at the resources of her outside life, a bright enduring pinnacle, whose removal would level the landscape to a rolling plain, its modest hillocks, easy to climb, robbed of their light, the bright reflection that came, she half-angrily admitted, from this central height.

But there had been a difference in the return to London after that visit, that had filled her with misgiving. Usually upon the afterpain of the wrench of departure, the touch of her own returning life had come like a balm. That time, she had seemed, as the train steamed off, to be going for the first time, not away from, but towards all she had left behind. There had been a strange exciting sense of travelling, as every one seemed to travel, preoccupied, missing the adventure of the journey, merely suffering it as an unavoidable time-consuming movement from one place to another. She, like all these others, had a place and a meaning in the outside world. She could have talked, if opportunity had offered, effortlessly, from the surface of her mind, borrowing emphasis and an appearance of availability and interest, from a secure unshared possession. She had suddenly known that it was from this basis of preoccupation with secure unshared possessions that the easy shapely conversations of the world were made. But also that those who made them were committed, by their preoccupations, to a surrounding deadness. Liveliness of mind checked the expressiveness of surroundings. The gritty interior of the carriage had remained intolerable throughout the journey. The passing landscape had never come to life.

But the menace of a future invested in unpredictable activities in a cause that seemed, now that she understood it, to have been won invisibly since the beginning of the world,

was lost almost at once in the currents of her London life.
Things had happened that had sharply restored her normal
feeling of irreconcilableness; of being altogether differently fated,
and to return, if ever the Wilsons should wish it, only at the
bidding of the inexpressible charm. There had been things
moving all about her with an utterly reassuring independent
reality. Mr Leyton's engagement . . . bringing to light as
she lived it through, chapter by chapter, sitting at work in
the busy highway of the Wimpole Street house, a world she
had forgotten, and that rose now before her in serene difficult
perfection; a full denial of Mr Wilson's belief in the death of
family life. In the midst of her effort to launch herself into
a definite point of view, it had made her swerve away again
towards the beliefs of the old world. Meeting them afresh
after years of oblivion, she had found them unassailably new.
The new lives inheriting them brought in the fresh tones, the
thoughts and movement of modern life, and left the old symphony recreated and unchanged.

The Tansley Street world had been full and bright all that
summer with the return of whole parties of Canadians as old
friends. With their untiring sociability, their easy inclusion of
the abruptly appearing unintroduced foreigners and provincials,
they had made the world look like one great family party.

They had influenced even Michael . . . steeping him in
sunlit gaiety. By breaking up the strain of unrelieved association, they had made him seem charming again. Their immense respect for him turned him, in their presence, once more
into a proud uncriticized possession.

Rambles round the squares with him, snatched late at night,
had been easy to fill with hilarious discussions of the many
incidents; serious exhausting talk held in check by the near
presence of unquestioning people, and the promise of the
lively morrow. Yet every evening, when they had her set
down and surrounded her at the piano, there came the sense
of division. They cared only for music that interpreted their
point of view.

Captain Gradoff . . . large flat lonely face, pock-marked,
eyes looking at nothing, with an expression of fear. Improper,

naked old grizzly head, suggesting other displayed helpless heads, above his stout neat sociable Russian skipper's jacket . . . praying in his room at the top of his voice, with howls and groans. Suddenly teaching us all to make a long loud siren-shriek with half a Spanish nutshell. He had an invention for the Admiralty . . . lonely and frightened, in a ghostly world; with an invention to save the lives of ships.

Engström and Sigerson!

Engström's huge frame and bulky hard red face, shining with simplicity below his great serene intellectual brow and up-shooting hair. His first evening at Mrs Bailey's right hand, saying gravely out into the silence of the crowded dinner-table, 'There is in Pareece very much automobiles, and good wash. In London not. I send much manchettes, and all the bords are cassed.' Devout reproachfulness in his voice; and his brow pure, motherly serenity. Sweden in the room amongst all the others. Teased, like every one else, with petty annoyances. But with immense strength to throw everything off. Every one waiting in the peaceful silence that surrounded the immense gently booming voice; electing him president as he sat burying his jests with downcast eyes that left the mask of his bluntly carven face yielded up to friendship. Waves of strength and kindliness coming from him, bringing exhilaration. Making even the Canadians seem pale and small and powerless. At the mercy of life. And then the harsh kind blaze of his brown eyes again. More unhesitating phrases. He had brought strength and happiness into the house. A rough, clump-worded Swedish song, rawly affronting the English air, words of his separate country, the only words for his deepest meanings, making barriers . . . till he leapt, he was so *light* in his strength, on to a chair to bring out the top note, and the barriers fell . . . He pealed his notes in farcical agony towards the ceiling. In that moment he was kneeling, bowed before the coldest, looking through to the hidden sunlight in everybody. . . . Conducting an imaginary orchestra from behind the piano. Sind the Trommels in Ordna? Everybody had understood, and loved each word he spoke.

'Wo ist die Veoleena Sigerson? I shall bring.' Springing

from his place near the door, lightly in and out amongst the seated forms, leaping obstacles all over the room on his way back to the open door, struggling noiselessly with all his strength, strong legs sliding under him as he pulled at the handle to open the open door. He and Sigerson had stayed on after the spring visitors. Evenings, voyaging alone with the two of them into strange new music. He had forgotten that he had said, 'I play nor sing not payshionate musics in bystanding of Miss—little—Hendershon.' And the German theatre . . . a shamed moving forward into suspicion, even of Irving, in the way they all played, working equally, together . . . all taking care of the play . . . play and acting, rich with life.

Sigerson was jealous. He wanted all the bright sunlight to himself and tried to hold it with his cold scornful brains. Waspy Schopenhauerism. They went to *Peckham*. The little weepy dabby assistant of the Peckham landlady, her speech ready-made quotations in the worst London English. Impure vowels, slobbery consonants. She reflected his sunlight like a dead moon. There was a large old garden. His first English garden in summer. He had loved it with all the power of the Swedish landscape in him turned on to its romantic strangeness, and identified the dabby girl with it. She fainted when he went away. A despair like death. He had come faithfully back and married her. *What* could she, for ever Peckham, seeing nothing, distorting everything by her speech, make of Stockholm?

And all the time the Wimpole Street days had glowed more and more with the forgotten story. Thanks to the scraps of detail in Mr Leyton's confidences, she had lived in the family of girls, centred round their widowed mother in the large old suburban house, garden-girt, and bordering on countrified open spaces. She imagined it always sunlit, and knew that it rang all the morning with the echoes of work and laughter, and the sharp-tongued ironic commentary of a family of Harrietts freed from the shadows that had surrounded Harriett's young gaiety, by the presence of an income, small but secure. The bustle of shared work, all exquisitely done in the

exacting, rewarding old-fashioned way, nothing bought that
could be home-made, filled each morning with an engrossing
life of its own, lit by a surrounding endless glory, and left the
house a prepared gleaming orderliness, and the girls free to
retreat to a little room where a sewing machine was enthroned
amidst a licensed disorder of fashion papers, with coloured
plates, and things in process of making according to the newest
mode, from oddments carefully selected at the West End sales.
When they were there, during the times of busy work following
on consultations and decisions, gossip broke forth; and thrilling
the tones of their gossiping voices, and shining all about them,
obliterating the walls of the room and the sense of the day and
the hour, was a bright eternity of recurring occasions, when
the sum of their household labours blossomed into fulfilment
. . . at-home days; calls; winter dances; huge picnic parties
in the summer, to which they went, riding capably, in their
clever home-made cycling costumes, on brilliantly gleaming
bicycles. And all the year round, shed over each revolving
week, the glamour of Sunday . . . the perpetual rising up,
amongst the varying seasons and days, of a single unvarying
shape, standing, in the morning quiet, chill and accusing
between them and the warm, far-off everyday life. The relief
of the descent into the distractions of dressing for church and
bustling off in good time; the momentary return of the challenging shape with the sight of the old grey ivy-grown church;
escape from it again into the refuge of the porch amongst the
instreaming neighbours, and the final fading of its outlines
into the colour and sound of the morning service, church shapes
in stone and wood and metal, secure round about their weakness, holding them safe. The sermon, though they suffered
it uncritically, could not, preached by an intelligent or stupid
man, but secure, soft-living and married, revive the morning
strength of the challenging shape, and as it sounded on towards
its end, the grey of another Sunday morning had brought in
sight the rest of the day, when, at the worst, if nobody came,
there was the evening service, the escape in its midst into a state
of bliss that stilled everything, and went on for ever, making the
coming week, even if the most glorious things were going to

happen, wonderful only because it was so amazing to be alive
at all . . . that was too much. These girls did not consciously
feel like that; perhaps partly because they had a brother, were
the kind of girls who would have at least one brother, choking
things back by obliviousness, but breezy and useful in many
ways. It's good to have brothers; but there is something
they kill, if they are in the majority, absolutely, so that one
girl with many brothers rarely becomes a woman, but can
sometimes be a nice understanding jolly sort of man. Brothers
without sisters are worse off than sisters without brothers;
unless they are very gifted . . . in which case they are really,
as people say of the poets, more than three parts women. But
Sundays, for all girls, were in a way the same. And though
these girls did not reason and were densely unconscious of the
challenge embodied in their religion, and enjoyed being snob-
bish without knowing it, or knowing the meaning and good
of snobbishness, their unconsciousness was harmless, and the
huge Sunday things they lived in, held and steered their lives,
making, in England, in them and in all of their kind, a world
that the clever people who laughed at them had never been
inside. *They* did not laugh, except the busy enviable blissful
laughter permitted by God, from the midst of their lives, about
nothing at all. They thought liberals vulgar—mostly chapel
people; and socialists mad. But in the midst of their con-
servatism was something that could never die, and that these
other people did not seem to possess.

And the best, most Charlotte Yonge part of the story, was
the arrival of Mr Leyton and his cousin, whilst these girls
were still at home amongst their Sundays; and the opening out,
for two of them at once, of a future; with the past behind it
undivided.

And they had suddenly asked her to their picnic. And she
had been back, for the whole of that summer's afternoon, in
the world of women; and the forgotten things, that had first
driven her away from it, had emerged again, no longer mysterious, and with more of meaning in them, so that she had
been able to achieve an appearance of conformity, and had
felt that they regarded her not with the adoration or half-

pitying dislike she had had from women in the past, but as a woman, though only as a weird sort of female who needed teaching. They had no kind of fear of her; not because they were massed there in strength. Any one of them, singly, would, she had felt, have been equal to her in any sort of circumstances; her superior; a rather impatient but absolutely loyal and chivalrous guide in the lonely exclusive feminine life.

Surprised by the unanticipated joy of a summer holiday in miniature, their gift, wrested by their energies from the midst of the sweltering London July, and with their world and its ways pulling at her memory, and the door of their good fellowship wide open before her, for an hour she had let go and gone in and joined them, holding herself teachable, keeping in check, while she contemplated the transformation of Mr Leyton under the fire of their chaff, her impulse to break into the ceaseless jesting with some shape of conversation. And she had felt that they regarded her as a postulant, a soul to be snatched from outer darkness, a candidate as ready to graduate as they were to grant a degree. And the breaking of the group had left her free to watch the way, without any gap of silence or difficulty of transition, they had set the men to work on the clearing up and stowing away of the paraphernalia of the feast; training them all the while according to the Englishwoman's pattern, an excellent pattern, she could not fail to see, imagining these young males as they would be, undisciplined by this influence, and comparing them with the many unshaped young men she had observed on their passage through the Tansley Street house.

But all the time she had been half aware that she was only watching a picture, a charmed familiar scene, as significant and as unreal as the set figure of a dance. Giving herself to its discipline she would reap experience and knowledge, confirming truths; but only truths with which she was already familiar, leading down to a lonely silence, where everything still remained unanswered, and the dancers their unchanged, unexpressed selves. Individual converse with these young men on the terms these women had trained them to accept, was impossible to contemplate. Every word would be spoken in a dark void.

Breaking in, as the little feast ended in a storm of flying buns and eggshells, a little scene that she had forgotten completely at the moment of its occurrence had risen sharply clear in her mind. . . . A family party of quiet, soberly dressed Scotch Canadians from the far west, seated together at the end of the Tansley Street dinner-table, coming out, on the eve of their departure, from the enclosure of their small, subduedly conversing group, to respond, in level friendly tones, to some bold person's inquiries as to the success of their visit. The sudden belated intimacy, ripened in silence, had seemed very good, compressed into a single occasion that would leave the impression of these homely people single and strong, so well worth losing that their loss would be a permanent acquisition. Suddenly from their midst, the voice of the youngest daughter, a pale, bitter-faced girl with a long thin pigtail of sandy hair, had rung out down the table.

'London's *fine*. But the folks don't all match it. The girls don't. They're just queer. I reckon there's two things they don't know. How to wear their waists, and how to go around with the boys. When I hear an English girl talking to boys, I just have to think she's funny in the head. If Canadian girls were stiff like that, they'd have the dullest time on earth.' Her expressionless pale blue eyes had fixed no one, and she had concluded her speech with a little fling that had settled her back in her chair, unconcerned.

And in the interval before the ride home, when the men had been driven off, and she was alone with the sisters and saw them relax and yawn, speak in easy casual tones and apostrophize small things, with great gusto, in well-chosen forcible terms, while the men were no doubt also enjoying the same blessed relief, she had felt that the Canadian girl was more right than she knew. Between men and girls, throughout English life, there was no exchange, save in the ways of love. Except for those moments when they stood, to each other, for all the world, they never met. And the sense of these sacred moments embarrassed, even while it shaped and beautified, every occasion. Women were its guardians and hostesses. Their guardianship made them hostesses for life. Upon the faces of these girls as they sat about unmasked and pathetically individual, it shed its radiance and, already, its heavy shadows.

Yet American girls with their easy regardlessness seemed lacking in depth of feminine consciousness, too much turned towards the surfaces of life, and the men, with their awakened understanding and quick serviceableness, by so much the less men. In any case there was not the recognizable difference in personality that was so striking in England, and that seemed in some way, even at one's moments of greatest irritation with the women, to bring all the men under a reproach. Many young American men had faces moulded on the lines of responsible middle-aged German housewives; while some of the quite young girls looked out at life with the sharp shrewd repudiation of cynical elderly bachelors. If it were the building up of a civilization that had brought the sexes together, for generations, in relations that came in English society only momentarily, at a house-warming or a picnic, would the results remain? Or would there be, in America, later on, a beginning of the English differences, the women moving, more and more heavily veiled and burdened, towards the heart of life and the men getting further and further away from the living centre? Ought men and women to modify each other, each standing, as it were, half-way between the centre and the surface, each with a view across the other's territory? Or should they accentuate their natural differences? *Were* the differences natural?

As they rode home through the twilit lanes, the insoluble problem, sounding for her in every shouted remark, had been continually soothed away by the dewy, sweet-scented, softly streaming air. The slurring of their tyres in unison along the smooth roadway, the little chorus of bells as they approached a turning, made them all one, entered for good into the heritage of the accomplished day. Nothing could touch the vision that rose and the confessions that were made within its silence. Within each one of the indistinguishable forms the sense of the day was clearing with each moment; its incidents blending and shaping, an irrevocable piece of decisive life; but behind and around and through it all was summer, smiling. Before each pair of eyes, cleared of heat and dust by the balm of the evening air, the picture of the English summer, in blue and gold and green, stood clear within the outspread invisible distances. *That* was the harvest, the thing that drew people to the labour of organizing picnics, that remained afterwards for ever; that would remain for the lovers after their love was forgotten; that linked all the members of the party in a fellowship stronger than their differences.

But when they reached the suburbs, the problem was there again in might, incessant as the houses looming by on either side, driven tyrannously home by the easy flight ahead, as Highgate sloped to London, of the two whose machines were fitted with 'free' wheels. Only a mind turned altogether towards outside things could invent.

And then *London* came, opening suddenly before me as I rode out alone from under a dark archway into the noise and glare of a gaslit Saturday night.

Trouble fell away like a cast garment as I swung forward, steering with thoughtless ease, into the southernmost of the four converging streets.

This was the true harvest of the summer's day; the transfiguration of these northern streets. They were not London proper; but to-night the spirit of London came to meet her on the verge. Nothing in life could be sweeter than this welcoming—a cup held brimming to her lips, and inexhaustible. What lover did she want? No one in the world would oust this mighty lover, always receiving her back without words, engulfing and leaving her untouched, liberated and expanding to the whole range of her being. In the mile or so ahead, there was endless time. She would travel further than the longest journey, swifter than the most rapid flight, down and down into an oblivion deeper than sleep; and drop off at the centre, on to the deserted grey pavements, with the high quiet houses standing all about her in air sweetened by the evening breath of the trees, stealing down the street from either end; the sound of her footsteps awakening her again to the single fact of her incredible presence within the vast surrounding presence. Then, for another unforgettable night of return, she would break into the shuttered house and gain her room and lie, till she suddenly

slept, tingling to the spread of London all about her, herself
one with it, feeling her life flow outwards, north, south, east,
and west, to all its margins.

And it had been so. Nothing had intervened, but, for a
moment, the question, coming as the wild flowers fell from her
unclasped belt, bringing back the long-forgotten day—what
of those others, lost, for life, in perpetual association?

The long lane of Bond Street had come to an end, bringing
her out into the grey-brown spaciousness of Piccadilly, lit
sparsely by infrequent globes of gold. The darkness cast by
the massive brown buildings thrilled heavily about the shrouded
oblivion of West End life. She passed elderly men, black-
coated and mufflered over their evening dress, wrapped in
their world, stamped with its stamp, still circulating, like the
well preserved coins of a past reign—thinking their sets of
thoughts, going home to the small encirclement of clubs and
chambers, a little aware of the wide night and the time of year
told on the air as they had passed along where the Green Park
slept on the far side of the road. This was their moment,
between to-day and to-morrow, of freedom to move amongst
the crowding presences gathered through so many years within
themselves; slowly, mannishly; old - mannishly, perpetually
pulled up, daunted, taking refuge in their sets of thoughts; not
going far, never returning to renew a sally, for the way home
was short, and their gait showed them going, almost marching,
to the summons of their various destinations. Some of their
faces betrayed as they went by, unconscious of observation, the
preoccupation that closed in on all their solitude; a look of
counting, but with liberal evening hand, the days that remained
for them to go their rounds. One came prowling with slow,
gentlemanly stroll, half-halting to stare at her, dim-eyed, from
his mufflings. Here and there a woman, strayed away from
the searching light and the rivalry of the circus, hovered in
the shadows. Presently, across the way, the park moved by,
brimming through its railings a midnight freshness into the dry
sophisticated air. Through this strange mingling, hansoms
from the theatres beyond the circus, swinging, gold-lamped,
one by one, along the centre of the deserted roadway, drew

bright threads of younger West End life, meshed and tangled, men and women from social throngs, for whom no solitude waited.

Piccadilly Circus was almost upon her, the need for thoughtless hurrying across its open spaces; the awakening on the far side with the West End dropping away behind; and the tide of her own neighbourhood setting towards her down Shaftesbury Avenue; bringing with it the present movement of her London life? Why hadn't she a club down here; a neutral territory where she could finish her thoughts undisturbed?

Defying the surrounding influences, she glanced back at the months following the picnic . . . the shifting of the love-story into the midst of the Wimpole Street household, making her room like a little theatre where at any moment the curtain might go up on a fresh scene. Knowing them all so well, being behind the scenes as well as before them, she had watched with a really cruel indifference, and let the light of the new theories play on all she saw. For unconscious, unquestioning people were certainly ruled by *something*. The acting of the play had been all carefully according to the love-stories of the sentimental books, would always be, for good kind people brought up on the old traditions. And a predictable future was there, another home-life carrying the traditions forward. All the old family sayings applied. Many of them were quoted with a rueful recognition. But they were all proud of playing these recognizable parts. All of their faces had confessed, as they had come, one by one, between whiles, to talk freely to her alone, their belief in the story that had lain, hidden and forgotten, in the depths of her heart; making her affection for them blaze up afresh from the roots of her being. She had *seen* the new theories disproved. Not that there was not some faint large outline of truth in them, but that it was so large and loose that it did not fit individuals. It did not correspond to any individual experience because it was obliged to ignore the underlying things of individuality. . . . Blair Leighton . . . Marcus Stone . . . Watts; Mendelssohn, corresponded to an actual individual truth. The new people did not know it because they were odd, isolated people without upbringing and circumstances? They did not know because they were without backgrounds? Quick and clever, like Jews without a country? They would fasten in this story on the critical dismay of the parents, make comedy or tragedy out of the lack of sympathy between the two families, the persistence of unchanged character in each one, that would tell later on. But comedy and tragedy equally left everything unstated. No blind victimizing force could account for the part of the story they left untold, something that justified the sentimental books they all jeered at; a light that had come suddenly, holding them all gentle and hushed behind even their busiest talk; bringing wide thoughts and sympathies; centring in the girl; breaking down barriers so completely that for a while they all seemed to exchange personalities. Blind force could not soften and illuminate. There was something more than an allurement of 'nature,' a veil of beauty disguising the 'brutal physical facts.' Why brutal? Brutal is deliberate, a thing of the will. They meant brutish. But what was wrong with the brutes except an absence of free will? Their famous 'brutal frankness' was brutish frankness, showing them pitifully proud of their knowledge of facts that looked so large, and ignorant of the tiny enormous undying fact of free will. Perhaps women have more free will than men?

It is because these men *write* so well that it is a relief, from looking and enduring the clamour of the way things state themselves from several points of view simultaneously, to read their large superficial statements. Light seems to come, a large comfortable stretching of the mind, things falling into an orderly scheme, the flattering fascination of grasping and elaborating the scheme. But the after reflection is gloom, a poisoning gloom over everything. 'Good writing' leaves gloom. Dickens doesn't. . . . But people say he 's not a good writer. . . . *Youth* . . . and *Typhoon*. . . . Oh, '*Stalked about gigantically in the darkness*.' . . . Fancy forgetting that. And he is modern and a good writer. New. They all raved quietly about him. But it was not like reading a book at all. . . . Expecting good difficult 'writing,' some mannish way of looking at things, and then . . . complete forgetfulness of the

worst time of the day on the most grilling day of the year in a
crowded Lyons's at lunch-time and, afterwards, joyful strength
to face the disgrace of being an hour or more late for afternoon
work. . . . They leave life so small that it seems worthless.
He leaves everything big; and all he tells added to experience
for ever. It's dreadful to think of people missing him; the
forgetfulness and the new birth into life. Even God would
enjoy reading *Typhoon*. Then *that* is 'great fiction'? 'Creation'? Why these falsifying words, making writers look cut
off and mysterious? *Imagination*. What is imagination? It
always seems insulting, belittling, both to the writer and to life.
He looked and listened with his whole self—perhaps he is a
small pale invalid—and then came 'stalked about gigantically'
. . . not made, nor created, nor begotten, but *proceeding* . . .
and working his salvation. That is what matters to him. In
the day of judgment, though he is a writer, he will be absolved.
Those he has redeemed will be there to shout for him. But
he will still have to go to purgatory; or be born again as a
woman. *Why* come forward suddenly, in the midst of a story,
to say they live far from reality? A sudden smooth complacent male voice, making your attention rock between the
live text and the picture of a supercilious lounging form,
slippers, a pipe, other men sitting round, and then the phrase
so smooth and good that it almost compels belief. Why cannot
men exist without thinking themselves all there is?

She was in the open roadway, passing into the deeps of the
central freedom of Piccadilly Circus, the crowded corner unknowingly left behind. Just ahead was the island, the dark
outline of the fountain, the small surmounting figure almost
invisible against the shadowy upper mass of a bright-porched
building over the way. The grey trottoir, empty of the shawled
flower-women and their great baskets, was a quiet haven. The
surrounding high brilliancies beneath which people moved along
the pavements from space to space of alternating harsh gold and
shadowy grey, met softly upon its emptiness, drawing a circle
of light round the shadow cast by the wide basin of the fountain.
There. was a solitary man's figure standing near the kerb, mid-
way on her route across the island to take to the roadway

opposite Shaftesbury Avenue; standing arrested; there was no traffic to prevent his crossing; a watchful habitué; she would pass him in a moment, the last fragment of the West End . . . good-bye, and her thoughts towards gaining the wide home-ward-going lane. A little stoutish dapper grey-suited . . . *Tommy Babington!* Standing at ease, turned quite away from the direction that would take him home; still and expression-less, unrecognizable save for the tilt of his profile and the set of his pince-nez. She had never before seen him in uncon-scious repose, never with this look of a motionless unvoyaged soul encased in flesh; yet had always known even when she had been most attracted, that thus he was. He had glanced. Had he recognized her? It was too late to wheel round and save his solitude. Going on, she must sweep right across his path. Fellow-feeling was struggling against her longing to touch, through the medium of his voice, the old home-life so suddenly embodied. He had seen her, and his unawakened face told her that she would neither pause nor speak. Years ago they would have greeted each other vociferously. She was now so shrouded that he was not sure she had recognized him. Through his stupefaction smouldered a suspicion that she wished to avoid recognition. He was obviously embarrassed by the sense of having placed her amidst the images of his preoccupation. She rushed on, passing him with a swift salute, saw him raise his hat with mechanical promptitude as she stepped from the kerb and forward, pausing an instant for a passing hansom, in the direction of home. It was done. It had always been done from the very beginning. They had met equally at last. This was the reality of their early association. Her spirits rose, clamorous. It was epical, she felt. One of those things arranged above one's head and perfectly staged. Tommy of all people wakened thus out of his absorption in the separated man's life that so decorated him with mystery in the feminine suburbs; shocked into helpless inactivity; glum with an ir-revocable recognizing hostility. It had been arranged. Silent acceptance had been forced upon him, by a woman of his own class. She almost danced to the opposite pavement in this keenest, witnessed moment of her years-long revel of escape.

He would presently be returning to that other enclosed life to which, being a man, and dependent on comforts, he was fettered. Already in his mind was one of those formulas that echoed about in the enclosed life. . . . 'Oui, ma chère, little Mirry *Henderson*, strolling, at midnight, across Piccadilly Circus.'

Suddenly it struck her that the life of men was pitiful. They hovered about the doors of freedom, returning sooner or later to the hearth, where even if they were autocrats they were not free; but passing guests, never fully initiated into the house-life, where the real active freedom of the women resided behind the noise and tumult of meetings. Man's life was bandied to and fro . . . from *word* to *word*. Hemmed in by women, fearing their silence, unable to enter its freedom—being himself made of words—cursing the torrents of careless speech with which its portals were defended.

And all the time unself-conscious thoughtless little men, with neat or shabby sets of unconsidered words for everything, busily bleating through cornets, blaring through trombones and euphoniums, thrumming undertones on double-basses. She summoned Harriett and shrieked with laughter at the cheerful din. It was cheerful, even in a funeral march. There would certainly be music in heaven; but no books.

The shock of meeting Tommy had brought the grey of to-morrow morning into the gold-lit streets. There was a fresh breeze setting down Shaftesbury Avenue. Here, still on the Circus, was the little coffee-place. Tommy was going home. *She* was rescuing the last scrap of a London evening here at the very centre and then going home, on foot, still well within the charmed circle.

The spell of the meeting with Tommy broke as she went down the little flight of steps. Here was eternity, the backward vista indivisible, attended by throngs of irreconcilable interpretations. Years ago, a crisis of loneliness, this little doorway, a glimpse, from the top of the steps, of a counter and a Lockhart urn, a swift descent, unseen people about her, companions; misery left behind, another little sanctuary added to her list. The next time, coming coldly with Michael

Shatov, in a unison of escape from everlasting conflict; people clearly visible, indifferent and hard; the moment of catching, as they sat down, the flicker of his mobile eyelid, the lively unveiled recognizing glance he had flung at the opposite table, describing its occupants before she saw them; the rush of angry sympathy; a longing to *blind* him; in some way to screen them from the intelligent unseeing glance of all the men in the world.

'You don't *see* them; they are not *there* in what you see.'

'These types are generally quite rudimentary; there is no question of a soul there.'

'If you could only have seen your look; the most horrible look I have ever seen; *alive* with interest.'

'There is always a certain interest.'

The strange agony of knowing that in that moment he had been alone and utterly spontaneous; simple and whole; that it had been, for him, a moment of release from the evening's misery; a sudden plunge into his own eternity, his unthreatened and indivisible backward vista. The horrible return, again and again, in her own counsels, to the fact that she had seen, that night, for herself, more than he had ever told her; that the pity he had appealed to was unneeded; his appeal a bold bid on the strength of his borrowed conviction that women do not, in the end, really care. How absolutely men are deceived by a little cheerfulness.

And now she herself was interested; had attained unawares a sort of connoisseurship, taking in, at a glance, nationality, type, status, the difference between inclination and misfortune. Was it he who had aroused her interest? Was this contamination or illumination?

And Michael's past was a matter of indifference. . . . Only because it no longer concerned her? Then it *had* been jealousy? Her new calm interest in these women was jealousy. Jealousy of the appeal, for men, of their divine simplicity?

   . . . which women don't understand.
  And them as sez they does is not the marryin' brand.

Oh, the hopeless eternal inventions and ignorance of men; their utter cleverness and ignorance. *Why* had they been made so clever and yet so fundamentally stupid?

She ordered her coffee at the counter and stood facing upstairs towards the oblong of street. The skirts of women,
men's trousered legs, framed for an instant in the doorway,
passed by, moving slowly, with a lifeless intentness. Is the
absence of personality original in men? Or only the result of
their occupations? Original. Otherwise environment is
more than the human soul. It is original. Belonging to
maleness; to Adam with his spade; lonely in a universe of
things. It causes them to be moulded by their occupations,
taking shape, and status, from what they do. A barrister, a
waiter, recognizable. Men have no natural rank. A woman
can become a waitress and remain herself. Yet men pity
women, and think them hard because they do not pity each
other.

It is man, puzzled, astray, always playing with breakable
toys, lonely and terrified in his universe of chaotic forces, who
is pitiful. The chaos that torments him is his own rootless
self. The key, unsuspected, at his side.

In women like Eleanor Dear? Calm and unquestioning.
Perfectly at home in life. With a charm beyond the passing
charm of a man. She was central. All heaven and earth
about her as she spoke. Illiterate, hampered, feeling her way
all the time. And yet with a perfect knowledge. *Perfect*
comprehension in her smile. All the maddening moments
spent with her, the endless detail and fussing, all afterwards
showing upon a background of gold.

Men weave golden things; thought, science, art, religion,
upon a black background. They never *are*. They only make
or do; unconscious of the quality of life as it passes. So
are many women. But there is a moment in meeting a woman,
any woman, the first moment, before speech, when everything
becomes new; the utter astonishment of life is there, speech
seems superfluous, even with women who have not consciously
realized that life is astonishing. It persists through all the
quotations and conformities, and is there again, the one underlying thing that women have to express to each other, at parting. So that between women, all the practical facts, the
tragedies and comedies and events, are but ripples on a stream.

It is not possible to share this sense of life with a man; least
of all with those who are most alive to 'the wonders of the
universe.' Men have no present; except sensuously. That
would explain their *ambition* . . . and their doubting speculations about the future.

Yet it would be easier to make all this clear to a man than to
a woman. The very words expressing it have been made by
men.

It was just after coming back from the Wilsons, in the midst
of the time round about Leyton's wedding, that Eleanor had
suddenly appeared on the Tansley Street doorstep. . . . I
was just getting to know the houseful of Orly relations . . .
Mrs Sloan-Paget, whisking me encouragingly into everything.
. . . 'my dear, you've got style, and taste; stunning hair and
a good complexion. Look at my girls. Darlings, I know.
But what's the good of putting clothes on figures like that?'
Daughterless Mrs Orly looked pleased like a mother when Mrs
Paget said, 'S'Henderson's got to come down to Chumleigh.'
I almost gave in to her reading of me; feeling, whilst I was with
her, back in the conservative, church point of view. I could
have kept it up, with good coats and skirts and pretty evening
gowns. Playing games. Living hilariously in roomy country
houses, snubbing 'outsiders,' circling in a perpetual round of
family events, visits to town, everything fixed by family happenings, hosts of relations always about, everything, even sorrow,
shared and distributed by large rejoicing groups; the warm
wide middle circle of English life . . . secure. And just as
the sense of belonging was at its height, punctually, Eleanor
had come, sweeping everything away. As if she had been
watching. Coming out of the past with her claim. Skimpier
and more beset than ever. Yet steely with determination.
Deepening her wild-rose flush and her smile. It was all over
in a moment. Wreckage. Committal to her and her new set
of circumstances.

She would not understand that a sudden greeting is always
wonderful; even if the person greeted is not welcome. But
Andrew Lang did not know what he was admitting. Men
greet only themselves, their own being, past, present or future.

I am a man. The more people put you at your ease, the more eagerly you greet them. That is why we men like 'ordinary women.' And always disappoint them. They mistake the comfort of relaxation for delight in their society.

Eleanor swept everything away. By seeming to know in advance everything I had to tell, and ignore it as not worth consideration. But she also left her own circumstances unexplained; sitting about with peaceful face, talking in hints, telling long stories about undescribed people, creating a vast leisurely present, pitting it against the whole world, with graceful condescending gestures.

It was part of her mystery that she should have come back just that very afternoon. Then she was in the right. If you are in the right everything works for you. The original thing in her nature that made her so beautiful, such a perpetually beautiful spectacle, was *right*. The moment that had come whilst she must have been walking, brow modestly bent, with her refined, conversational little swagger of the shoulders, aware of all the balconies, down the street, had worked for her.

The impulses of expansive moments always make things happen. Or the moments come when something is about to happen? How can people talk about coincidence? How not be struck by the inside pattern of life? It is so obvious that everything is arranged. Whether by God or some deep wisdom in oneself does not matter. There is something that does not alter. Coming up again and again, at long intervals, with the same face, generally arresting you in mid career, offering the same choice, ease or difficulty. Sometimes even a lure, to draw you back into difficulty. Determinists say that you choose according to your temperament, even if you go against your inclinations. But what is temperament? Uniqueness. Something that has not existed before. A free edge. Contemplation is freedom. The *way* you contemplate is your temperament. Then action is slavery?

There is something always plucking you back into your own life. After the first pain there is relief, a sense of being once more in a truth. Then why is it so difficult to remember that things deliberately done, with a direct movement of the will, always have a falseness? Never meet the desire that prompted the action. The will is really meant to prevent deliberate action? That is the hard work of life? The Catholics know that desire can never be satisfied. You must not *desire* God. You must love. I can't do that. I can't get clear enough about what he wants. Yet even without God I am not lonely; or ever completely miserable. Always in being thrown back from outside happiness, there seem to be two. A waiting self to welcome me.

It can't be wrong to exist. In those moments before disaster, existence is perfect. Being quite still. Sounds come presently from the outside world. Your mind, moving about in it without envy or desire, realizes the whole world. The future and the past are all one same stuff, changing and unreal. The sense of your own unchanging reality comes with an amazement and sweetness too great to be borne alone; bringing you to your feet. There *must* be someone there, because there is a shyness. You rush forward, to share the wonder. And find somebody engrossed with a cold in the head. And are so emphatic and sympathetic that they think you are a new friend and begin to expand. And it is wonderful until you discover that they do not think life at all wonderful.

That afternoon it had been a stray knock at the front door and a sudden impulse to save Mrs Bailey coming upstairs. And Mrs Bailey, after all she had said, also surprised into a welcome, greeting Eleanor as an old friend, taking her in at once. And then the old story of detained luggage, and plans prevented from taking shape. The dreadful slide back, everything disappearing but Eleanor and her difficulties, and presently everything forgotten but the fact of her back in the house. Afterwards when the truth came out, it made no difference but the relief of ceasing to be responsible for her. But this time there had been no responsibility. She had made no confidences, asked for no help. Was it blindness, or flattered vanity, not to have found out what she was going through?

Yet if the facts had been stated, Eleanor would not have been able to forget them. In those evenings and week-ends she had forgotten, and been happy. The time had been full of reality; memorable. It stood out now, all the going about together, drawn into a series of moments when they had both seen with the same eyes. Experiencing identity as they laughed together. Her recalling of their readings in the little Marylebone room, before the curate came, had not been a pretence. Mr Taunton was the pretence. There had been no space even for curiosity as to the end of his part of the story. Eleanor, too, had not wished to break the charm by letting things in. She had been taking a holiday, between the desperate past and the uncertain future. In the midst of overwhelming things she had stood firm, her power of creating an endless present at its height. A great artist.

To Michael, a poor pitiful thing; Rodkin's victim. *She*, of course, had given Michael that version. Little Michael, stealing to her room night by night, towards the end, to sleep at her side and say consoling things; never guessing that her threat of madness was an appeal to his Jewish kindness, a way of securing his company. What a story for proper English people . . . the best revelation in the whole of her adventure. And Mrs Bailey too; true as steel. Serenely warding off the women boarders . . . gastric distension.

Rodkin . . . poor little Rodkin with his weak, dreadful little life. Weekdays; the unceasing charm of Anglo-Russian speculation, Sundays; boredom and newspapers. Then the week again, business and a City man's cheap adventures. He *had* behaved well, in spite of Michael's scoldings. It was wonderful, the way the original Jewish spirit came out in him, at every step. His loose life was not Jewish. And it was *really* comic that he should have been trapped by a girl pretending to be an adventuress. Poor Eleanor, with all her English dreams; just *Rodkin*. But he was a Jew when he hesitated to marry a consumptive, and perfectly a Jew when he decided not to see the child lest he should love it; and also when he hurried down into Sussex the moment it came, to see it, with a huge armful of flowers, for her. What a scene for the Bible-women's Hostel. All Eleanor. Her triumph. What other woman would have

dared to engage a cubicle and go calmly down without telling
them? And a week later she was in the superintendent's room
and all those prim women sewing for her and hiding her and
telling everybody she had rheumatic fever. And crying when
she came away.

She was right. She justified her actions and came through.
And now she's a young married woman in a pretty villa, *near*
the church, and the vicar calls and she won't walk on Southend
pier because 'one meets one's butcher and baker and candle-
stick maker.' But only because Rodkin is a child-worshipper.
And she tolerates him and the child and he is a brow-beaten
cowed little slave. It is tempting to tell the story. A perfect
recognizable story of a scheming unscrupulous woman; making
one feel virtuous and superior; but only if one simply outlined
the facts, leaving out all the inside things. Knowing a story
like that from the inside, knowing Eleanor, changed all 'scandalous' stories. They were scandalous only when told? Never
when thought of by individuals alone? Speech is technical.
Every word. In telling things, technical terms must be used;
which never quite apply. To call Eleanor an adventuress does
not describe her. You can only describe her by the original
contents of her mind. Her own images; what she sees and
thinks. She was an adventuress by the force of her ideals.
Like Louise going on the street without telling her young man
so that he would not have to pay for her trousseau.

Exeter was another. Keeping the shapes of civilization.
Charming at tea parties. . . . Knowing all the worldly things,
made of good style from her perfect brow and nose to the tip
of her slender foot; made to shine at Ascot. It was only because
she knew so much about Mrs Drake's secret drinking, that Mrs
Drake said suddenly in that midnight moment when Exeter
had swept off to bed after a tiff, '*I* don't go to hotels, with
strange men.' I was reading that book of Dan Leno's and
thinking that if they would let me read it aloud their voices
would be different; that behind their angry voices were real
selves waiting for the unreal sounds to stop. Up and down the
tones of their voices were individual inflexions, feminine, innocent of harm, incapable of harm, horrified since their girlhood

by what the world had turned out to be. It was an awful
shock. But Exeter paid her young man's betting debts and
kept him on his feet. And *he* was divorced. And so *nice*.
But weak. Still he had the courage to shoot himself. And
then *she* took to backing horses. And now married, in a cathe-
dral, to a vicar; looking angelic in the newspaper photograph.
He has only one regret . . . their childlessness. 'Er? Have
children?' Yet Mrs Drake would be staunch and kind to her
if she were in need. Women are Jesuits.

From the first, in Eleanor's mind, had shone, unquestioned,
the shape of English life. Church and State and Family. God
above. Her belief was perfect; impressive. In all her dealings she saw the working of a higher power, leading her to her
goal. When her health failed and her vision receded, she
clutched at the nearest material for making her picture. In
all she had waded through, her courage had never failed. Nor
her charm; the charm of her strength and her singleness of
vision. Her God, an English-speaking gentleman, with English traditions, tactfully ignored all her contrivances and waited
elsewhere, giving her time, ready to preside with full approval
over the accomplished result. Women are Jesuits. The
counterpart of all those Tansley Street women was little Mrs
Orly, innocently unscrupulous to save people from difficulty
and pain.

It was when Eleanor went away that autumn that I found I
had been made a Lycurgan; and began going to the meetings
in that small room in Anselm's Inn. Ashamed of pride in
belonging to a small exclusive group containing so many brilliant men. Making a new world. Concentrated intelligence
and goodwill. Unanimous even in their differences. Able
to joke together. Seeking, selflessly, only one thing. And
because they selflessly sought it, all the things of fellowship
added to them. . . . From the first I knew I was not a real
Lycurgan. Not wanting their kind of selfless seeking, yet
liking to be within the stronghold of people who were keeping
watch, understanding how social injustice came about, explaining the working of things, revealing the rest of the world as

naturally unconsciously blind, urgently requiring the enlightenment that only the Lycurgans could bring, that could only be
found by endless dry work on facts and figures. . . . At first
it was like going to school. Eagerly drinking in facts; a new
history. The history of the world as a social group. Realizing
the immensity of the problems crying aloud all over the world,
not insoluble, but unsolved because people did not realize
themselves as members of one group. The convincing little
Lycurgan tracts, blossoming out of all their intense labour, were
the foundation of a new social order; gradually spreading social
consciousness. But the hope they brought, the power of answering all the criticisms and objections of ordinary people,
always seemed ill-gained. Always unless one took an active
share, like listening at a door. . . . She was always catching
herself dropping away from the first eager gleaning of material
to speculations about the known circumstances of the lecturer,
from them into a trance of oblivion, hearing nothing, remembering afterwards nothing of what had been said, only the
quality of the atmosphere—the interest or boredom of the
audience, the secret preoccupations of unknown people sitting
near.

Every one was going. The restaurant was beginning to
close. The West End was driving her off. She rose to go
through the business of paying her bill, the moment of being
told that money, someone's need of profits, was her only pass-
port into these central caverns of oblivion. For ever driven
out. Passing on. To keep herself in countenance she paid
briskly, with the air of one going purposefully. The sound of
her footsteps on the little stairway brought her vividly before
her own eyes, playing truant. She hurried to get out and
away, to be walking along, by right, in the open, freed, for the
remaining time, by the necessity of getting home, to lose
herself once more.
The treelit golden glow of Shaftesbury Avenue flowed
through her; the smile of an old friend. The *wealth* of swinging along up the bright ebb-way of the West End, conscious
of being, of the absence of desire to be elsewhere or other than

herself. A future without prospects, the many doors she had tried, closed willingly by her own hand, the growing suspicion that nowhere in the world was a door that would open wide to receive her, the menace of an increasing fatigue, crises of withering mental pain, and then suddenly this incomparable sense of being plumb at the centre of rejoicing. Something always left within her that contradicted all the evidence. It compensated the failure of her efforts at conformity. Yet to live outside the world of happenings, always to forget and escape, to be impatient, even scornful, of the calamities that moved in and out of it like a well-worn jest, was certainly wrong. But it could not be helped. It was forgetfulness, suddenly overtaking her in the midst of her busiest efforts . . . memory . . . a perpetual sudden blank . . . and upon it broke forth this inexhaustible joy. The tappings of her feet on the beloved pavement were blows struck hilariously on the shoulder of a friend. To keep her voice from breaking forth, she sang aloud in her mind, a soaring song unlimited by sound.

The visit to the revolutionaries seemed already in the past, added to the long procession of events that broke up and scattered the moment she was awake at this lonely centre.

Speech came towards her from within the echoes of the night; statements in unfamiliar shape. Years falling into words, dropping like fruit. She was full of strength for the end of the long walk; armed against the rush of associations waiting in her room; going swift and straight to dreamless sleep and the joy of another day.

The long wide street was now all even light, a fused misty gold, broken close at hand by the opening of a dark byway. Within it was the figure of an old woman bent over the gutter. Lamplight fell upon the sheeny slopes of her shawl and tattered skirt. Familiar. Forgotten. The last, hidden truth of London, spoiling the night. She quickened her steps, gazing. Underneath the forward-falling crushed old bonnet shone the lower half of a bare scalp . . . reddish . . . studded with dull, wartlike knobs. . . . Unimaginable horror quietly there. Revealed. Welcome. The head turned stealthily as she passed and she met the expected sidelong glance; naked

recognition, leering from the awful face above the outstretched
bare arm. It was herself, set in her path and waiting through
all the years. Her beloved hated secret self, known to this
old woman. The street was opening out to a circus. Across
its broken lights moved the forms of people, confidently, in
the approved open pattern of life, and she must go on, uselessly,
unrevealed; bearing a semblance that was nothing but a screen
set up, hiding what she was in the depths of her being.

CHAPTER II

AT the beginning of the journey to the East End, the Lintoffs were as far away as people in another town. When the East End was reached they were too near. Their brilliance lit up the dingy neighbourhood and sent out a pathway of light across London. Their eyes were set on the far distance. It seemed an impertinence to rise suddenly in their path and claim attention.

But Michael lost his way and the Lintoffs were hidden, erupting just out of sight. The excitement of going to meet them filtered away in the din and swelter of the East End streets.

They came upon the hotel at last, suddenly. A stately building with a wide pillared porch. As they went up its steps and into the carpeted hall, cool and clean and pillared, giving on to arched doorways and the distances of large rooms, she wished the Russians could be spirited away, that there were nothing but the strange escape from the midst of squalor into this cool hushed interior.

But they appeared at once, dim figures blocking the path, closing up all the distances but the one towards which they were immediately obliged to move and that quickly ended in a bleak, harshly-lit room. And now here they were, set down, meekly herded at the table with other hotel people.

No strange new force radiated from them across the chilly expanse of coarse white tablecloth. They were able to be obliterated by their surroundings; lost in the onward-driving tide of hotel life; responding murmuringly to Michael's Russian phrases, like people trying to throw off sleep.

Her private converse with them the day before, made it impossible even to observe them now that they were exposed before her. And a faint hope, refusing to be quenched, prevented her casting even one glance across at them. If the

hope remained unwitnessed there might yet be, before they
separated, something that would satisfy her anticipations. If
she could just see what he was like. There was, even now, an
unfamiliar force keeping her eyes averted from all but the
vague sense of the two figures. Perhaps it came from him.
Or it was the harvest growing from the moment in the hotel
entrance.

A dispiriting conviction was gathering behind her blind
attention. If she looked across, she would see a man self-
conscious, drearily living out the occasion, with an assumed
manner. After all, he was now just a married man, sitting
there with his wife, a man tamed and small and the prey of
known circumstances, meeting an old college friend. This
drop on to London was the end of their wonderful adventure.
A few weeks ago she had still been his fellow student, his
remembered companion, in a Russian prison for her daring
work, ill with the beginnings of her pregnancy. Now, he was
with her for good, inseparably married, no longer able to be
himself in relation to any one else. She felt herself lapsing
further and further into isolation. Something outside herself
was drowning her in isolation.

Something in Michael. That, at least, she could escape now
that she was aware of it. She leaned upon his voice. At
present there was no sign of his swift weariness. He was
radiant, sitting host-like at the head of the table between her
and his friends, untroubled by his surroundings, his glowing
Hebrew beauty, his kind, reverberating voice expressing him,
untrammelled, in the poetry of his native speech. But he was
aware of her through his eager talk. All the time he was
tacitly referring to her as a proud English possession. It was
something more than his way of forgetting, in the presence of
fresh people, and falling again into his determined hope. Her
heart ached for him as she saw that away in himself, behind
the brave play he made, in his glance of the deliberately
naughty child relying on its charm to obtain forgiveness, he
held the hope of her changing under the influence of seeing
him thus, at his fullest expansion amongst his friends. He
was purposely excluding her, so that she might watch

undisturbed; so that he might use the spaces of her silence to persuade her that she shared his belief. She was helplessly supporting his illusion. It would be too cruel to freeze him in mid career, with a definite message. She sat conforming; expanding, in spite of herself, in the role he had planned. He must make his way back through his pain, later on, as best he could. No one was to blame; neither he for being Jew, nor she for her inexorable Englishness.

Across the table, supporting him, were living examples of his belief in the possibility of marriage between Christians and Jews. Lintoff was probably as much and as little Greek Orthodox as she was Anglican, and as pure Russian as she was English, and he had married his little Jewess.

Michael would eagerly have brought any of his friends to see her. But she understood now why he had been so cautiously, carelessly determined to bring about this meeting. They would accept his reading, and had noted her, super-ficially, in the intervals of their talk, in the light of her relation-ship to him. She was wasting her evening in a hopeless masquerade. She felt her face setting in lines of weariness as she retreated to the blank truth at the centre of her being. Narrowly there confined, cold and separate, she could glance easily across at their irrelevant forms. They could be made to understand her remote singleness; in one glance. What-ever they thought. They were nothing to her, with their alien lives and memories. She was English; an English spectacle for them, quite willing, an interested far-off spectator of foreign ways and antics. No, she would not look, until she were forced; and then some play of truth, springing in unexpectedly, would come to her aid. Reduced by him to a mere symbol she would not even risk encountering their un-founded conclusions.

She heard their voices, animated now in an eager to and fro, hers contralto, softly modulated, level and indifferent in an easy swiftness of speech; his higher, dry and chippy and staccato; the two together a broken tide of musical Russian words, rich under the cheerless hotel gaslight. It would flow on for a while and presently break and die down. Michael's social concentration would not be equal to a public drawing-room, a prolonged sitting on sofas. Coffee would come. They would linger a little over it, eagerness would drop from their voices, the business of reflecting over their first headlong communications would be setting in for each one of them, separating them into individualities, and suddenly Michael would make a break. For she could hear they were not talking of abstract things. Revolutionary ideas would be, between him and Lintoff, an old battlefield they had learned to ignore. They were just listening, in excited entrancement, to the sound of each other's voices, their eyes on old scenes, explaining, repeating themselves, in the turmoil of their attentiveness . . . each ready to stop half-way through a sentence to catch at an outbreaking voice. Michael's voice was still richer and eager. His years had fallen away from him; only now and again the memory of his settled surroundings and relentless daily work caught at his tone, levelling it out.

Coffee had come. Someone asked an abrupt question and waited in a silence. She glanced across. A tall narrow man, narrow slender height, in black, bearded, a narrow straw-gold beard below bright red lips. Unsympathetic; vaguely familiar. Him she must have observed in the dim group in the hall during Michael's phrases of introduction.

'Nu; da,' Michael was saying cordially; 'Lintoff suggests we go upstairs,' he continued, to her, politely. He looked pleased and easy; unfatigued.

She rose murmuring her agreement, and they were all on their feet, gathering up their coffee-cups. Michael made some further remark in English. She responded in the vague way he knew and he watched her eyes, standing near, taking her coffee-cup with an easy quiet pretence of answering speech, leaving her free to absorb the vision of Madame Lintoff, a small dark form risen sturdily against the cheap dingy background, all black and pure dense whiteness; a curve of gleaming black hair shaped against her meal-white cheek; a small pure profile firmly beautiful, emerging from the high close-fitting neck-shaped collar of her black dress; the sweep of a falling

fringed black shawl across the short closely sleeved arm, the
fingers of the hand stretched out to carry off her coffee, half
covered by the cap-like extension of the long black sleeve.
She might be a revolutionary, but her sense of effect was
perfect. Every line flowed, from the curve of her skull, left
free by the beautiful shaping of her thick close hair, to the
tips of her fingers. There was no division into parts, no
English destruction of lines at neck and shoulders, no ugly
break where the dull stuff sleeve joined the wrist. In the
grace of her small sturdy beauty there seemed only scornful
womanish triumph, weary; a suggestion of unspeakable ennui.
She was utterly different from English Jewesses.

Without breaking the rhythm of her smooth graceful movement, she turned her head and glanced across at Miriam; a
faint slight radiance, answering Miriam's too-ready irrecoverable beaming smile, and fading again at once as she moved
towards the door. Too late—already they were moving,
separated, in a single file up the long staircase, Madame
Lintoff now a little squarish dumpy Jewish body, stumping
up the stairs ahead of her—Miriam responded to the gleam
she had caught in the deep wehmütig Hebrew eyes, of something
in her that had escaped from the confines of her tribe and sex.
She was not one of those Jewesses, delighting in instant
smiling familiarity with women, immediate understanding,
banding them together. She had not a trace of the half
affectionate, half obsequious envy, that survived the discovery
of their being more intelligent or better informed than English
women. She had looked impersonally, and finding a blankness would not again inquire. She had gone back to the
European world of ideas into which somehow since her childhood she had emerged. But she was weary of it; of her idea-
haunted life; of everything that had so far come into her mind
and her experience. Did the man leading the way upstairs
know this? Perhaps Russian men could read these signs?
In any case a Russian would not have Michael's physiological
explanations of everything; even if they proved to be true.

'I forgot to tell you, Miriam, that of course Lintoffs both
speak French. Lintoff has also a little English.'

It was his bright *beginning* voice. They were to spend the *evening* . . . shut in a small cold bedroom . . . resourceless, shut in with this slain romance . . . and the way already closed for communication between herself and the Russians before she had known that they could exchange words that would at least cast their own brief spell. Between herself and Madame Lintoff nothing could pass that would throw even the thinnest veil over their first revealing encounter. To the unknown man anything she might say would be an announcement of her knowledge of his reduced state.

The coming upstairs had stayed the tide of reminiscences. There was nothing ahead but obstructive conversation, perhaps in French; but steered all the time by Michael's immovable European generalizations; his clear, swiftly manœuvring encyclopaedic Jewish mind.

With her eyes on the fatiguing vista she agreed that of course Monsieur and Madame Lintoff would know French; letting her English voice sound at last. The instant before she spoke she heard her words sound in the dim street-lit room, an open acknowledgment of the death of her anticipations. And when the lame words came forth, with the tone of the helplessly insulting, polite, superfluous English smile, she knew that it was patent to every one that the evening was dimmed, now, for them all. It was not her fault that she had been brought in amongst these clever foreigners. Let them think what they liked, and go. If even anarchists had their world linked to them by strands of clever easy speech, had she not also her world, away from speech and behaviour?

Lintoff was lighting a candle on the chest of drawers. The soft reflected glare, coming in at the small square windows, was quenched by its gleam. He was standing quite near, in profile, his white face and bright beard lit red from below. The bent head full of expression, yet innocent, was curious, neither English nor foreign. He was a doctor of philosophy. But not in the way any other European man would have been. His figure had no bearing of any kind. Yet he did not look foolish. A secret. There was some secret power in him . . . Russia. She was seeing Russia; far-away Michael blessedly there in the room; keeping her there.   He had sat down in his way, in a small bedroom chair, his head thrust forward on his chest, his hands in his pockets, his legs stretched out across the thread-bare carpet, his coffee on the floor at his side.   He was at home in Russia after his English years.   Madame Lintoff in the small corner beside the bed was ferreting leisurely in a cupboard with her back to the room.   Lintoff was holding a match to the waxy wick of the second candle.   No one was speaking. But the cold dingy room, with its mean black draperies and bare furniture, was glowing with life.

There was no pressure in the room; no need to buy peace by excluding all but certain points of view.   She felt a joyful expansion.   But there was a void all about her.   She was expanded in an unknown element; a void, filled by these people in some way peculiar to themselves.   It was not filled by themselves or their opinions or ideas.   All these things they seemed to have possessed and moved away from.   For they were certainly animals; perhaps intensely animal, and cultured.   But principally they seemed to be movement, free movement.   The animalism and culture, so repellent in most people, showed, in them, rich jewels of which they were not aware.   They were moving all the time in an intense joyous dreamy repose.   It centred in him and was reflected, for all her weariness, upon Madame Lintoff.   It was into this moving state that she had escaped from a Jewish family life.

If the right question could be found and addressed to him, the secret might be plumbed.   It might rest on some single inacceptable thing that would drop her back again into single-ness; just the old familiar inexorable sceptical opposition.

His second candle was alight.   Michael spoke, in Russian, and arrested him standing in the middle of the floor with his back to her.   She heard his voice, no longer chippy and staccato as it had been in the midst of their intimate talk down-stairs, but again dim, expressionless, the voice of a man in a dream.   Madame Lintoff had hoisted herself on to the bed. She had put on a little black ulster and a black close-fitting astrakhan cap.   Between them her face shone out suddenly rounded, very pretty and babyish.   From the deep Hebrew eyes gleamed a brilliant vital serenity. An emancipated Jewish girl, solid, compact, a rounded gleaming beauty that made one long to place one's hands upon it; but completely herself, beyond the power of admiration or solicitude; a torch gleaming in the strange void. . . . But so *solidly* small and pretty. It was absurd how pretty she was, how startling the rounded smooth firm blossom of her face between the close dead black of her ulster and little cap. Miriam smiled at her behind the to and fro of dreamy Russian sentences. But she was not looking.

It was glorious that there had been no fussing. No one had even asked her to sit down. She could have sung for relief. She wanted to sing the quivering alien song that was singing itself in the spaces of the room. There was a chair just at hand against the wall, beside a dilapidated wicker laundry basket. But her coffee was where Michael had deposited it, on the chest of drawers at his side. She must recover it, go round in front of Lintoff to get it before she sat down. She did not want the coffee, but she would go round for the joy of moving in the room. She passed him and stood arrested by the talk flowing to and fro between her and her goal. Michael rose and stood with her, still talking. She waited a moment, weaving into his deep emphatic tones the dreamy absent voice of Lintoff.

Michael moved away with a question to Madame Lintoff sitting alone behind them on her bed. She was left standing, turned towards Lintoff, suddenly aware of the tide that flowed from him as he stood, still motionless, in the middle of the room. He stood poised, without stiffness, his narrow height neither drooping nor upright; as if held in place by the surrounding atmosphere. Nothing came to trouble the space between them as she moved towards him, drawn by the powerful tide. She felt she could have walked through him. She was quite near him now, her face lifted towards the strange radiance of the thin white face, the glow of the flaming beard; a man's face, yielded up to her, and free from the least flicker of reminder.

'What do you think? What do you *see*?' she heard herself ask. Words made no break in the tide holding her there at rest.

His words followed hers like a continuation of her phrase:

'Mademoiselle, I see the *People*.' His eyes were on hers, an intense blue light; not concentrated on her; going through her and beyond in a widening radiance. She was caught up through the unresisting eyes; the dreamy voice away behind her. She saw the wide white spaces of Russia; motionless dark forms in troops, waiting. . . .

She was back again, looking into the eyes that were now upon her personally; but not in the Englishman's way. It was a look of remote intense companionship. She sustained it, helpless to protest her unworthiness. He did not know that she had just flown forward from herself out and away; that her faint vision of what he saw as he spoke was the outpost of all her experience. He was waiting to speak with an equal, to share. . . . He had no social behaviour. No screen of adopted voice or manner. There was evil in him; all the evils that were in herself, but unscreened. He was careless of them. She smiled and met his swift answering smile; it was as if he said, 'I know; isn't everything wonderful?' . . . They moved with one accord and stood side by side before the gleaming candles. Across the room the two Russian voices were sounding one against the other; Michael's grudging sceptical bass and the soft weary moaning contralto.

'Do you like Maeterlinck?' she asked, staring anxiously into the flame of the nearest candle. He turned towards her with eager words of assent. She felt his delighted smile shining through the sudden enthusiastic disarray of his features and gazed into the candle summoning up the vision of the old man sitting alone by his lamp. The glow uniting them came from the old man's lamp . . . this young man was a revolutionary and a doctor of philosophy; yet the truth of the inside life was in him, nearer to him than all his strong activities. They could have nothing more to say to each other. It would be destruction to say anything more. She dropped her eyes and he was at once at an immense distance. Behind her closed door she stood alone. Lintoff began to walk about the room. Every time his movements brought him near he stood before her in eager discourse. She caught the drift of the statements he flung out in a more solid, more flexible French, mixed with struggling, stiff, face-stiffening scraps of English. The people, alive and one and the same all over the world, crushed by the half-people, the educated specialists, and by the upper classes dead and dying of their luxury. She agreed and agreed, delighting in the gentleness of his unhampered movements, in his unself-conscious, uncompeting speech. If what he said were true, the people to pity were the specialists and the upper classes; clean sepulchres. . . . How would he take opposition?

'Isn't it weird, étrange,' she cried suddenly into a pause in his struggling discourse, 'that Christians are just the very people who make the most fuss about death?'

He had not understood the idiom. Sunned in his waiting smile she glanced aside to frame a translation.

'N'y a rien de plus drôle,' she began. How cynical it sounded; a cynical French voice striking jests out of the surface of things; neighing them against closed nostrils, with muzzle tight-crinkled in Mephistophelian mirth. She glanced back at him, distracted by the reflection that the contraction of the nostrils for French made *everything* taut. . . .

'Isn't it funny that speaking French banishes the inside of everything; makes you see only *things*?' she said hurriedly, not meaning him to understand; hoping he would not come down to grasp and struggle with the small thought; yet longing to ask him suddenly whether he found it difficult to trim the nails of his right hand with his left.

He was still waiting unchanged. Yet not waiting. There was no waiting in him. There would be, for him, no more dropping down out of life into the humble besogne de la pensée. That was why she felt so near to him, yet alive, keeping the whole of herself, able to say anything, or nothing. She smiled her delight. There was no sheepishness in his answering radiance, no grimace of the lips, not the least trace of any of the ways men had of smiling at women. Yet he was conscious, and enlivened in the consciousness of their being man and woman together. His eyes, without narrowing from that distant vision of his, yet looked at her with the whole range of his being. He had known obliterating partialities, had gone further than she along the pathway they forge away from life, and returned with nothing more than the revelation they grant at the outset; his further travelling had brought him nothing more. They were equals. But the new thing he brought so unobstructively, so humbly identifying and cancelling himself that it might be seen, was his, or was Russian. . . .

Looking at him she was again carried forth, out into the world. Again about the whole of humanity was flung some comprehensive feeling she could not define. It filled her with longing to have begun life in Russia. To have been made and moulded there. Russians seemed to begin, by nature, where the other Europeans left off.

'The educated *specialists*,' she quoted to throw off the spell and assert English justice, 'are the ones who have found out about the people; not the people themselves.' His face dimmed to a mask, dead white Russian face, crisp, savage red beard, opaque china-blue eyes, behind which his remembered troops of thoughts were hurrying to range themselves before her. Michael broke in on them, standing near, glowing with satisfaction, making a melancholy outcry about the last bus. She moved away leaving him with Lintoff and turned to the bedside unprepared with anything to say.

Where could she get a little close-fitting black cap, and an enveloping coat of that deep velvety black, soft, not heavy and tailor-made like an English coat, yet so good in outline, expressive; a dark moulding for face and form that could be worn for years and would retain, no matter what the fashions were, its untroublesome individuality? Not in London. They were Russian things. The Russian woman's way of abolishing the mess and bother of clothes; keeping them close and flat and untrimmed. Shining out from them full of dark energy and indifference. More oppressively than before, stood between them the barrier of Madame Lintoff's indifference. It was not hostility. Not personal at all; nor founded on any test, or any opinion.

In the colourless moaning voice with which she agreed that there was much for her to see in London and that she had many things she wished particularly not to miss, in the way she put

her foreigner's questions, there was an overwhelming indifference. It went right through. She sat there, behind her softly
moulded beauty, dreadfully full of clear hard energy; yet
immobile in perfect indifference. Not expecting speech; yet
filching away the power to be silent. No breath from Lintoff's
wide vistas had ever reached her. She had driven along,
talking, teaching, agitating; had gone through her romance
without once moving away from the dark centre of indifference
where she lay coiled and beautiful. *Her* sympathy with the
proletarians was a fastidious horror of all they suffered. Her
cold clear mind summoned it easily, her logical brain could find
sharp terse phrases to describe it. She cared no more for
them than for the bourgeois people from whom she had fled
with equal horror, and terse phrases, into more desperate
activities than he. He loved and *wanted* the people. He felt
separation from them more as his loss than as theirs. He
wanted the whole vast multitude of humanity. The men
came strolling. Lintoff asked a question. They all flung
sentences in turn, abruptly, in Russian, from unmoved faces.
They were making arrangements for to-morrow.

Lintoff stood flaring in the lamplit porch, speeding them on
their way with abrupt caressing words.

'Well?' said Michael before they were out of hearing.
'Did you like them?'

'Yes or no as the case may be.' Michael's recovered London
manner was a support against the prospect of sustaining a
second meeting to-morrow, with everything already passed
that could ever pass between herself and them.

'You have made an *immense* impression on Bruno Feodoro-
vitch.'

'How do you know?'

'He finds you the type of the Englishwoman. Harmonious.
He said that with such a woman a man could all his life be
perfectly happy. Ah, Miriam, let us at once be married.' His
voice creaked pathetically; waiting for the lash. The urgent
certainty behind it was not his own certainty. Nothing but a
too dim, too intermittent sense of something he gathered in
England. She stood still to laugh aloud. His persistent

childish naughtiness assured her of the future and left her free
to speak.

'You *know* we can't; you *know* how separate we are.   You
have seen it again and again and agreed.   You see it now;
only you are carried away by this man's first impression.
Quite a wrong one.   I know the sort of woman he means.
Who accepts a man's idea and leaves him to go about his work
undisturbed; sure that her attention is distracted from his full
life by practical preoccupations.   It's *perfectly* easy to create
that impression, on any man.   Of bright complacency.   All
the busy married women are creating it all the time, helplessly.
Men see them looking out into the world, practical, responsible,
quite certain about everything, going from thing to thing, too
active amongst things to notice men's wavering self-indulgence,
their slips and shams.   Men lean and feed and are kept going,
and in their moments of gratitude they laud women to the
skies.   At other moments, amongst themselves, they call
them materialists, animals, half-human, imperfectly civilized
creatures of instinct, sacrificed to sex.   And all the time they
have no suspicion of the individual life going on behind the
surface.'   To marry would be actually to become, as far as
the outside world could see, exactly the creature men described.
To go into complete solitude, marked for life as a segregated
female whose whole range of activities was known; in the only
way men have of knowing things.

'Lintoff of course is not quite like that.   But then in these
revolutionary circles men and women live the same lives.   It's
like America in the beginning, where women were as valuable
as men in the outside life.   If the revolution were accomplished they would separate again.'

She backed to the railings behind her, and leant, with a heel
on the low moulding, to steady herself against the tide of
thought, leaving Michael planted in the middle of the
pavement.   A policeman strolled up, narrowly observing
them, and passed on.

'No one on earth knows whether these Russian revolutionaries are right or wrong.   But they have a thing that none of
their sort of people over here have—an effortless sense of

humanity as one group. The *men* have it and are careless about everything else. I believe they think it worth realizing if everybody in the world died at the moment of realization. The women know that humanity is two groups. And they go into revolutions for the freedom from the pressure of this knowledge.'

'Revolution is by no means the sole way of having a complete sense of humanity. But what has all this to do with *us*?'

'It is not that the women are heartless; that is an appearance. It is that they know that there are no *tragedies*. . . .'

'Listen, Mira. You have taught me much. I am also perhaps not so undiscriminating as are some men.'

'In family life, all your Jewish feelings would overtake you. You would slip into dressing-gown and slippers. You have said so yourself. But I am now quite convinced that I shall never marry.' She walked on.

He ran round in front of her, bringing her to a standstill.

'You think you will never marry . . . with *this*'—his ungloved hands moved gently over the outlines of her shoulders. 'Ah—it is most—musical; you do not know.' She thrilled to the impersonal acclamation; yet another of his many defiant tributes to her forgotten material self; always lapsing from her mind, never coming to her aid when she was lost in envious admiration of women she could not like. Yet they contained an impossible idea; the idea of a man being consciously attracted and won by universal physiological facts, rather than by individuals themselves.

If Michael only knew, it was this perpetual continental science of his that had helped to kill their relationship. With him there could never be any shared discovery. She grudged the formal enlightenment he had brought her; filching it from the future. There could never now be a single harmonious development in relation to one person. Unless in relation to him. For an instant, marriage, with him, suggested itself as an accomplished fact. She saw herself married and free of him; set definitely in the bright resounding daylight of marriage . . . free of desires . . . free to rest and give away to the tides of cheerfulness ringing in confinement within her. She saw the world transformed to its old likeness; and walked alone with it, in her old London, as if awakened from a dream. But her vision was disturbed by the sense and sound of his presence and she knew that her response was not to him.

The necessity of breaking with him invaded her from without, a conviction, coming from the radiance on which her eyes were set, and expanding painlessly within her mind. She recognized, with a flush of shame at the continued association of these two separated people, that there was less reality between them now than there had been when they first met. There was none. She was no longer passionately attached to him, but treacherously, since she was hiding it, to someone hidden in the past, or waiting in the future . . . or *any one*; any chance man might be made to apprehend . . . so that when his man's limitations appeared, that past would be there to retreat to.

He had never for a moment shared her sense of endlessness. More sociably minded than she, but not more sociable, more quickly impatient of the cessations made by social occasions, *he* had no visions of waiting people. His personal life was centred on her completely. But the things she threw out to screen her incommunicable blissfulnesses, or to shelter her vacuous intervals from the unendurable sound of his perpetual circling round his set of ideas, no longer reached him. She could silence and awaken him only in those rare moments when she was lifted out of her growing fatigues to where she could grasp and state in all its parts any view of life that was different from his own. Since she could not hold him to these shifting visions, nor drop them and accept his world, they had no longer anything to exchange.

At the best they were like long-married people, living, alone, side by side; meeting only in relation to outside things. Any breaking of the silence into which she retreated while keeping him talking, every pause in her outbursts of irrepressible cheerfulness, immediately brought her beating up against the bars of his vision of life as uniform experience, and gave her a fresh access of longing to cut out of her consciousness the years she had spent in conflict with it.

Always until to-night her longing to escape the unmanageable burden of his Jewishness had been quenched by the pain of the thought of his going off alone into banishment. But to-night the long street they were in shone brightly towards the movement of her thought. Some hidden barrier to their separation had been removed. She waited curbed, incredulous of her freedom to breathe the wide air; unable to close her ears to the morning sounds of the world opening before her as the burden slipped away. Drawing back, she paused to try upon herself the effect of his keenly imagined absence. She was dismantled, chill and empty-handed, returning unchanged to loneliness. But no thrill of pain followed this final test; the unbelievable severance was already made. Even whilst looking for words that would break the shock, she felt she had spoken.

His voice, breaking the silence, came like an echo. She went like a ghost along the anticipated phrases, keenly aware only of those early moments when she had first gathered the shapes and rhythms of his talk.

Freedom; and with it that terrible darkness in his voice. Words must be said; but it was cruel to speak from far away; from the midst of joy. The unburdened years were speeding towards her; she felt their breath; the lifting of the light with the presence, just beyond the passing moments, of the old companionship that for so long had been hers only when she could forget her surrounded state.

His resonant cough brought her again the sound of his voice . . . how could the warm kind voice disappear from her days ? . . . she felt herself quailing in loneliness before the sharp edges of her daily life.

Glancing at him as they passed under a lamp she saw a pale, set face. His will was at work; he was facing his future and making terms with it. He would have a phrase for his loss, as a refuge from pain. That was comforting; but it was a base, social comfort; far away from the truth that was loading her with responsibility. He did not know what he was leaving. There was no conscious thought in him that could grasp and state the reality of his loss; nor what it was in him that even now she could not sever from herself. If he knew, there would be no separation. He had actually moved into his future; taken of his own free will the first step away from the shelter she gave. Perhaps a better, kinder shelter awaited him. Perhaps he was glad in his freedom and his manner was made from his foreigner's sense of what was due to the occasion. He did not know that there would be no more stillness for him.

Yet he *did* dimly know that part of his certainty about her was this mysterious *youth*; the strange everlasting sense of being, even with servants and young children, with *any* child, in the presence of adult cynical social ability, comfortably at home in the world. Perhaps he would be better off without such an isolated, helpless personality in the life he must lead. But letting him go was giving him up to cynicism, or to the fixed blind sentiments of all who were not cynics. No one would live with him in his early childhood, and keep it alive in him. He would leave it with her, without knowing that he left it.

All the things she had made him contemplate would be forgotten. He would plunge into the life he used to call normal. That was jealousy; flaming through her being; pressing on her mind. For a moment she faced the certainty that she would rather annihilate his mind than give up overlooking and modifying his thoughts. Here alone was the root of her long delay. It held no selfless desire for his welfare . . . then he would be better off with *any one*. He and the cynics and the sentimentalists were human and kindly, however blind. They were not cruel, not ready to wreck and destroy in order to impose their own certainties. Even as she gazed into it, she felt herself drawn powerfully away from the abyss of her nature by the pain of anticipating his separated future; the experiences that would obliterate and vanquish her; justifying, as far as he would ever again see, his original outlook. She battled desperately, imploring the power of detachment, and immediately found words for them both.

'It is weak to go on; it will only become more difficult.'

'You are right, it is a weakness'; his voice broke on a gusty breath; 'to-morrow we will spend, as we have promised, the afternoon with Lintoffs. On Monday I will go.'

The street swayed about her. She held on, forcing her limbs; passing into emptiness. The sounds of the world were very far away; but within their muffled faintness she heard her own free voice, and his, cheerful and impersonal, sounding on through life. With the breath of this release she touched the realization that some day, he would meet, along a pathway unknown to her and in a vision different from her own, the same truth. . . . What truth? God? The old male prison, whether men were atheists or believers? . . . The whole of the truth of which her joy and her few certainties were a part, innocently conveyed to him by someone with a character that would win him to attend. Then he would remember the things they had lost in speech. The enlightener would not argue. Conviction would come to him by things taken for granted.

Clear demonstration is at once fooled. All *men* in explanatory speech about *life*, have at once either in the face, or in the unconscious rest of them, a look of shame. Because they are not living, but calculating. Women who are not living ought to spend all their time cracking jokes. In a rotten society women grow witty; making a heaven while they wait.

But if from this far cool place where she now was, she breathed deep and let mirth flow out, he would *never* go.

At the very beginning of the afternoon Miriam was isolated with Madame Lintoff. Forced to walk ahead with her, as if companionably, between the closed shop-fronts and the dismal gutter of Oxford Street, while her real place, at Michael's side, with Lintoff beyond, or side by side with Lintoff, and Michael beyond, was empty, and the two men walked alone, exchanging, without interference, one-sided, masculine views.

She listened to Madame's silence. For all her indifference, she must have had some sort of bright anticipation of her first outing in London. And this was the outing. A walk, along a grey pavement, in raw grey air, under a heavy sky, with an Englishwoman who had no conversation.

Most people began with questions. But there was no

question she wanted to ask Madame Lintoff. She knew her too well. During the short night she had become a familiar part of the picture of life; one of the explanations of the way things went. Yet it was inhospitable to leave her with no companion but the damp motionless air.

Relaxing her attention, to make an attempt at bold friendliness, she swung gaily along, looking independently ahead into the soft grey murk. But hopelessness seized her as a useless topic sprang eagerly into her mind and she felt herself submerged, unable to withstand its private charm. Helplessly she explained, in her mind, to the far-off woman at her side that this bleak day coming suddenly in the midst of July was one of the glorious things in the English weather. Only a few people find English weather glorious. Clever people think it contemptible to mention weather except in jest or with a passing curse. Madame Lintoff would have just that same expression of veiled scorn that means people are being kept from their topics. For a few seconds, as she skirted a passing group, she looked back to an unforgettable thing, that would press for expression, now that she had thought of it, through anything she might try to say . . . a wandering in twilight along a wide empty pavement at the corner of a square of high buildings, shutting out all but the space of sky above the trees. That lovely line about Beatrice, bringing bright, draped, deep-toned figures, with the grave eyes of intensest eternal happiness, and heads bent in an attitude of song, about her in the upper air; the way they had come down, as she had lowered her eyes to the gleaming, wet pavement to listen again and again into the words of the wonderful line; how they had closed about her; a tapestry of intensifying colour, making a little chamber filled with deep light, gathering her into such a forgetfulness that she had found herself going along at a run, and when she had wakened to recall the sense of the day and the season, had looked up and seen November in the thick Bloomsbury mist, the beloved London lamplight glistening on the puddles of the empty street, and spreading a sheen of gold over the wet pavements; the jewelled darkness of the London winter coming about her once more; and then the glorious shock of remembering that August and September were still in hand, waiting hidden beyond the dark weather.

She came back renewed and felt for a moment the strange familiar uneasy sense of being outside and indifferent to the occasion, the feeling that brought again and again, in spite of experience, the illusion that every one was merely playing a part, distracting attention from the realities that persisted within. That all the distortions of speech and action were the whisperings and postures of beings immured in a bright reality they would not or could not reveal. But acting upon this belief always brought the same result. Astonishment, contempt, even affronted dignity, were the results of these sudden outbreaks.

But a Russian idealist would not be shocked, but would be appallingly clever and difficult. All the topics which now came tumbling into her mind shrank back in silence before Madame Lintoff's intellectual oblivion. It was more oppressive than the oblivion of the intellectual English. Theirs was a small, hard, bright circle. Within it they were self-conscious. Hers was an impersonal spreading darkness.

They were nearing Oxford Circus. There were more people strolling along the pavement. For quite a little time they were separated by the passing of two scattered groups, straggling along, with hoarse Cockney shouting, the women yodelling and yelling at everything they saw. The reprieve brought them together again, Miriam felt, with something rescued; a feeling of accomplishment. Madame Lintoff's voice came hurriedly —was she noticing the Salvation Army band, thumping across the circus; or this young man getting into a hansom as if the whole world were watching him being importantly headlong? —mournfully came a rounded little sentence deploring the Sunday closing of the theatres. She would have neatly deplored September. . . . Je trouve cela *triste*, l'automne.

But thrilled by the sudden sounding of the little voice, Miriam tried eagerly to see London through her eyes; to find it a pity that the theatres were not open. She agreed, and turned her mind to the plays that were on at the moment. She could not imagine Madame Lintoff at any one of them. But their

bright week-day names lost meaning in the Sunday atmosphere;
drew back to their own place, and insisted that she should find
a defence for its quiet emptiness. They themselves defended
it, these English theatre names, gathering much of their colour
and brightness from the weekly lull. But the meaning of the
lull lay much deeper than the need for contrast; deeper than
the reasons given by sabbatarians, whom it was a joy to defy,
though they were right. It was something that was as difficult
to defend as the qualities of the English weather.

This Russian woman was also a continental, sharing the awful
continental demand that the week-day things should never
cease; dependent all the time on revolving sets of outside things
. . . and the modern English were getting more and more into
the same state. In a few years Sunday would be 'bright';
full of everyday noise. Unless someone could find words to
explain the thing all these people called *dullness*; what it was
they were so briskly smothering. Without the undiscoverable
words, it could not be spoken of. An imagined attempt
brought mocking laughter and the sound of a Bloomsbury
voice: 'Vous n'savez pas quand vous vous rasez, hein?'
Madame Lintoff would not be vulgar; but she would share
the sentiment.

Miriam turned to her in wrath, feeling an opportunity.
Here, for all her revolutionary opinions, was a representative
of the talkative oblivious world. She would confess to her
that she dared not associate closely with people because of the
universal capacity for being bored, and the *hurry* every one was
in. Her anger began to change into interest as words framed
themselves in her mind. But as she turned to speak she was
shocked by the pathos of the little cloaked figure; the beautifully
moulded, lovely disk of face, shining out clasped by the cap,
above the close black draperies, and withdrew her eyes to
contemplate in silence the individual life of this being; her
moments of solitary dealing with the detail of the day when she
would be forced to think *things*; not thoughts; and did not know
how marvellous things were. That lonely one was the person
to approach, ignoring everything else. She would protest,
make some kind of defence; but if the ground could be held,

they would presently be together in a bright world. But there was not enough *time*, between here and Hyde Park. Then later.

Behind, near or far, the two dry men were keeping their heads, exchanging men's ready-made remarks.

'Est-ce qu'il y a en Angleterre le grand drame psychologique ?' What on earth did she mean?

'Oh, yes; here and there,' said Miriam firmly.

She sang over in her mind the duet of the contrasting voices as she turned in panic to the region within her, that was entrenched against England. Some light on the phrase would be there, if anywhere. Shaw? Were his things great psychological dramas?

'*Galumphing* about like an *ele*phant.' . . . The sudden bright English voice reverberated through her search. Sudermann? She saw eager, unconscious faces, well-off English people, seeing only their English world, translating everything they saw into its language; strayed into Oxford Street to remind her. She wanted to follow them, and go on hearing, within the restricted jargon of their English voices, the answer to questions they never dreamed of putting. The continentals put questions and answered them by theories. These people answered everything in person; and did not know it.

The open spaces of the park allowed them to line up in a row, and for some time they hovered on the outskirts of the crowd gathered nearest to the gates. Michael, in Russian, was delightedly showing off his Hyde Park crowds, obviously renewing his own first impression of these numbers of people casually gathered together—looking for his friends to show that they were impressed in the same way. They were impressed. They stood side by side, looking small and wan; making little sounds of appreciation, their two pairs of so different eyes wide upon the massed people. He could not wait; interrupted their contemplation in his ironic challenging way.

Lintoff answered with an affectionate sideways movement of the head; two short Russian words pouching his red lips in a gesture of denial. But he did not move, as an Englishman would have done after he thought he had settled a debatable point; remaining there gently, accessible and exposed to a further onslaught. He held his truths carelessly, not as a personal possession, to be fought over with every other male.

It was Michael who made the first movement away from his summed-up crowd. They drifted in a row towards the broad pathway lined with seated forms looking small and misty under the high trees, but presently to show clearly, scrappy and inharmonious, shreds of millinery and tailoring, no matter how perfect, reduced to confusion, spoiling the effect of the flower beds brightly flaring under the grey sky and the wide stretch of grass, brilliant emerald until it stopped without horizon where the saffron distances of the mist shut thickly down. She asked Michael what Lintoff had said.

'He says quite simply that these people are not free.'

'Nor are they,' she said, suddenly reminded of a line of thought. 'They are,' she recited, clipping her sentences in advance as they formed, to fit the Russian intonation, with carelessly turned head and Lintoff's pout of denial on her lips, 'docile material; an inexhaustible *supply*. An employer must husband; his horses and machinery; his people he uses up; as-cheaply-as-possible-always-quite-sure-of-*more*.'

'That has been so. But employers begin to understand that it is a sound economic to care for their workers.'

'A few. And that leads only to blue canvas.'

'*What* is this?'

'Wells's hordes of uniformed slaves, living in security, with all sorts of material enjoyments.'

'It surprises me that still you quote this man.'

'He makes phrases and pictures.'

'Of what service are such things from one who is incapable of unprejudiced thought?'

'Everybody is.'

'Pardon me; you are *wrong*.'

'Thought *is* prejudice.'

'That is most-monstrous.'

'Thought is a secondary human faculty, and can't *lead*, *any one*, *anywhere*.'

He turned away to the Lintoffs with a question. His voice

was like a cracked bell. Lintoff's gentle, indifferent tones made
a docile response.

'I suggest we have *tea*,' bellowed Michael softly, facing her
with a cheerful countenance. 'They agree. Is it not a good
idea?'

'Perfectly splendid,' she murmured, smiling her relief. He
could be trusted not to endure, to be tired of an adventure
before it had begun. . . .

'Certainly it is splendid if it bring dimples. Where shall
we go?' He turned eagerly, to draw them back at once to the
park gates, shouting gaily as he broke the group, 'Na, na;
where? What do you think, Miriam?'

'There isn't anything near here,' she objected. She pressed
forward with difficulty, her strength ebbing away behind her.
His impatience was drawing them away from something towards which they had all been moving. It was as if her real
being were still facing the other way.

'No—where really can we go?' In an instant he would
remember the dark little Italian-Swiss café near the Marble
Arch, and its seal would be set on the whole of the afternoon.
The Lintoffs would not be aware of this. They were indifferent
to surroundings in a world that had only one meaning for them.
But the sense of them and their world, already, in the boundless
immensity of Sunday, scattered into the past, would be an
added misery amongst the clerks and shop-girls crowded in
that stuffy little interior where so many of her Sunday after-
noons had died. The place cancelled all her world, put an
end to her efforts to fit Michael into them, led her always
impatiently into the next week for forgetfulness of their recurring, strife-tormented leisure.

Verandas and sunlit sea; small drawing-rooms, made large
by their wandering shapes; spaces of shadow and sunlight
beautifying all their English Sunday contents; windowed
alcoves reflecting the sky; spacious, silken, upstairs tea-rooms
in Bond Street. But these things were hers, now, only through
friends. Here, by herself, as the Lintoffs knew her, she belonged to the resourceless crowd of London workers.

Michael ordered much tea and a lemonade, in a reproachful

aside to the pallid grubby little waiter squeezing his way between the close-set tables with a crowded tray held high.

''Ow many?' he murmured over his shoulder, turning a low-browed anxious face. His tray tilted dangerously, sliding its contents.

'You can count?' said Michael without looking at him.

'Four tea, four limonade,' murmured the poor little man huskily.

'I have ordered *tea*,' thundered Michael. 'You can bring also one bottle limonade.'

The waiter pushed on, righting his noisy trayful. Michael subsided with elbows on the smeary marble table-top, his face propped on his hands, about to speak. The Lintoffs also; their gleaming pale faces set towards the common centre, while their eyes brooded outwards on the crowded little scene. Miriam surveyed them, glad of their engrossment, dizzy with the sense of having left herself outside in the park.

'Shall I tell the Lintoffs that you have dimples?' Michael asked serenely, shifting his bunched face round to smile at her.

She checked him as he leaned across to call their attention. It was in this very room that she had first told him he must choose between her company and violent scenes with waiters. He was utterly unconscious; aware only of his compatriots sitting opposite, himself before them in the pride of an international friendship. Yesterday's compact set aside, quite likely, later on, to be questioned.

The Lintoffs' voices broke out together, chalkily smooth and toneless against the Cockney sounds vibrating in the crowded space, *all* harsh and strident, *all* either facetious or wrangling. Their eyes had come back. But they themselves were absent, set far away, amongst their generalizations. Of the actual life of the passing moment they felt no more than Michael. Itself, its uniqueness, the deep loop it made, did not exist for them. They looked only towards the future. He only at a uniform pattern of humanity.

Yet within the air itself was all the time the something that belonged to everybody; that could be universally recognized; disappearing at once with every outbreak of speech that sought

only for distraction, from embarrassment or from tedium. . . .
She sat lifeless, holding for comfort as she gathered once more,
even with these free Russians, the proof of her perfect social
incompatibility, to the thought that this endurance was the
last. These were the last hours of wandering out of the course
of her being. She felt herself grow pale and paler, sink each
moment more utterly out of life. The pain in her brow pressed
upon her eyelids like a kind of sleep. She must be looking
quite horrible. Was there any one, anywhere, who suffered
quite in this way, felt always and everywhere so utterly
different?

Tea came, bringing the end of the trio of Russian phrases.
Michael began to dispense it, telling the Lintoffs that they had
discovered that the English did not know how to drink tea.
Ardent replies surged at the back of her mind; but speech was
a far-away mystery. She clung to Michael's presence, the
sight of his friendly arm handing the cup she could not drink;
to the remembered perfection of his acceptance of failures and
exhaustions. Mechanically she was speaking French . . .
appearing interested and sincere; caring only for the way the
foreign words gave a quality to the barest statement by placing
it in far-off surroundings, giving it a life apart from its meaning, bearing her into a tide of worldly indifference.

But real impressions living within her own voice came
crowding upon her, overwhelming the forced words, opening
abysses, threatening complete flouting of her surroundings.
She snatched at them as they passed before her, smiled her
vanishing thread of speech into inanity, and sat silent, half
turned towards the leaping reproachful shapes of thought,
inexpressible to these people waiting with faces set only towards swift replies. Madame Lintoff made a fresh departure
in her moaning, sweetly querulous voice . . . a host of replies
belonged to it, all contradicting each other. But there was a
smooth neat way of replying to a thing like that, leading
quickly on to something that would presently cancel it. Quite
simple people. Mrs. Bailey, saying wonderful things without
knowing it.

Answers given knowingly, admitted what they professed to

demolish. She had forfeited her right to speak; disappeared
before their eyes, and must yet stay, vulnerable, held by the
sounds she had woven, false threads between herself and them.
Her head throbbed with pain, a molten globe that seemed to
be expanding to the confines of the room. Michael was inaccessible, carefully explaining to Madame Lintoff, in his way,
why she had said what she had said; set with boyish intentness
towards the business of opening his dreadful green bottle.

Lintoff sat upright with a listening face; the lit, brooding
face of one listening to distant music. He was all lit, all the
time, curiously giving out light that his thinly coloured eyes
and flaming beard helped to flow forth. She could imagine
him speaking to crowds; but he had not the unmistakable
speaker's look, that lifted look and the sense of the audience;
always there, even in converse with intimate friends. But of
course in Russia there were no crowds, none of that machinery
of speaker and audience, except for things that were not going
to end in action. When Michael lifted his glass with a German
toast, Lintoff's smile came without contracting his face, the
light that was in him becoming a person. He was so far away
from the thoughts provoked by speech that he could be met
afresh in each thing that was said; coming down into it whole
and serious from his impersonal distances; but only to go back.
There was no permanent marvel for him in the present. The
room was growing dim. Only Michael's profile was clear,
tilted as he tossed off his dreadful drink at one draught. His
face came round at last, fresh and glowing with the effreves-
cence. He exclaimed, in gulps, at her pallor and ordered
hot milk for her, quietly and courteously from the hovering
waiter. The Lintoffs uttered little condolences most tenderly,
with direct homely simplicity.

Sitting exempted, sipping her milk while the others talked,
lounging, in smooth gentle tones, three forces, curbed to
gentleness, she felt the room about her change from gloom to
a strange blurred brightness, as if she were seeing it through
frosted glass. A party of young men were getting up to go,
stamping their feet and jostling each other as they shook themselves to rights, letting their jeering, jesting voices reach street

level before they got to the door. They filed past. Their faces, browless under evilly flattened cloth caps, or too large under horrible shallow bowlers set too far back, were all the same, set towards the street with the look, even while they jested, of empty finality; choiceless dead faces. They were not really gay. They had not been gay as they sat. Only defiantly noisy, collected together to banish, with their awful ritual of jeers and jests, the closed-in view that was always before their eyes; giving them, even when they were at their rowdiest, that look of lonely awareness of something that would never change. That was *why* they jeered? Why their voices were always defensive and defiant? What else could they do when they could alter nothing and could never get away? The last of the file was different; a dark young man with a club-footed gait. His face was pursed a little with the habit of facetiousness, but not aggressively; the forehead that had just disappeared under his dreadful cap was touched with a radiance, a reflection of some individual state of being, permanently independent of his circumstances; very familiar, reminding her of something glad . . . she found it as she brought her eyes back to the table; the figure of a boy, swinging in clumsy boots along the ill-lit tunnel of that new tube at Finsbury Park on a Saturday night, playing a concertina; a frightful wheezing and jangling of blurred tones, filling the passage, bearing down upon her, increasing in volume, detestable. But she had taken in the leaping unconscious rhythmic swinging of his body and the joy it was to him to march down the long clear passage, and forgiven him before he passed; and then his eyes as he came, rapt and blissfully grave above the hideous clamour.

'Listen, Miriam. Here is something for you.' She awoke to scan the three busy faces. It had not been her fault that she had failed and dropped away from them. Had it been her fault? The time was drawing to an end. Presently they would separate for good. The occasion would have slipped away. With this overwhelming sense of the uniqueness of occasions, she yet forgot every time, that every occasion was unique, and limited in time, and would not recur. She sat up briskly to listen. There was still time in hand. They had been ages together. She was at home. She yawned and caught Lintoff's smiling eye. There was a brightness in this little place; all sorts of things that reflected the light, metal and varnished wood, upright; flat surfaces; the face of the place; its features certainly *sometimes* cleansed, perhaps by whistling waiters in the jocund morning, for her. She did not dust, she could talk and listen, in prepared places, knowing nothing of their preparations. She belonged to the leisure she had been born in, to the beauty of things. The margins of her time would always be glorious.

'Lintoff says that he understands not at all the speech of these young men who were only now here. I have not listened; but it was of course simply Cockney. He declares that one man used repeatedly to the waiter making the bill, one expression, sounding to him like a mixture of Latin and Chinese—*Ava-tse*. I confess that after all these years it means to me absolutely nothing. Can you recognize it?'

She turned the words over in her mind, but could not translate them until she recalled the group of men and the probable voice. Then she recoiled. Lintoff and Michael did not know the horror they were handling with such light amusement.

'I know,' she said, 'it's appalling; fearful'—even to think the words degraded the whole spectacle of life, set all its objects within reach of the transforming power of unconscious distortion.

'Why fearful? It is just the speech of London. Certainly this tame boor was not swearing?' railed Michael. Lintoff's smile was now all personal curiosity.

'It's not Cockney. It's the worst there is. London Essex. He meant *I've; had; two;* buns or something. Isn't it *perfectly* awful?' Again the man appeared horribly before her, his world summarized in speech that must, *did* bring everything within it to the level of its baseness.

'Is it possible?' said Michael with an amused chuckle. Lintoff was murmuring the phrase that meant for him an excursion into the language of the people. He could not see its terrible menace. The uselessness of opposing it. . . .

Revolutionaries would let all these people out to spread over everything. . . . The people themselves would change? But it would be too late to save the language. . . .

'English is being destroyed,' she proclaimed. 'There *is* a relationship between sound and things. . . . If you heard an American reading Tennyson . . . "Come into the goiden, Mahd." But that's different. And in parts of America a very beautiful rich free English is going on; more vivid than ours, and taking things in all the time. It is only in England that deformed speech is increasing—is being *taught*, in schools. It shapes these people's mouths and contracts their throats and makes them hard-eyed.'

'You have no ground *whatever* for these wild statements.'

'They are not wild; they are tame, when you really think of it.' Lintoff was watching tensely; probably deploring wasted emotion.

'Do you think, Lintoff . . .' They moved on in their talk, unapprehensive foreigners, leaving the heart of the problem untouched. It was difficult to keep attached to a conversation that was half Michael's, with the Lintoffs holding back, acquiescing indulgently in his topics. An encyclopaedia making statements to people who were moving in a dream; halting and smiling and producing gestures and kindly echoes. Michael like a rock for most things as they were and had been in the past, yet knowing them only in one way; clear as crystal about ordered knowledge, but never questioning its value.

She wanted, now, to talk again alone with Lintoff . . . anything would do. The opposition that was working within her, not to his vision, but to his theory of it, and of the way it should be realized, would express itself to him through any sort of interchange. Something he brought with him would be challenged by the very sound on the air of the things that would be given her to say, if she could be with him before the mood of forgetful interest should be worn away. She sat waiting for the homeward walk, surrounded by images of the things that had made her; not hers, England's, but which she represented and lived in, through something that had been born with her. If there was any one she had ever met to whom these things could be conveyed without clear speech or definite ideas, it was he. But when they left the restaurant they walked out into heavy rain and went to the place of parting, separated and silent in a crowded bus.

Michael was going to keep his word.

Michael alone. With more than the usual man's helplessness. Getting involved. At the mercy of his inability to read people.

The torment of missing his near warm presence would grow less, but the torment of not knowing what was happening to him would increase.

This stillness creeping out from the corners of the room was the opening of a lifetime of loneliness. It would grow to be far more dreadful than it was to-night. To-night it was alive, between the jolly afternoon with the Lintoffs—*jolly*; the last bit of shared life—and the agony of to-morrow's break with Michael. But a day would come when the silence would be untormented, absolute, for life; echoing to all her movements in the room; waiting to settle as soon as she was still.

She resisted, pitting against it the sound of London. But in the distant voice there was a new note; careless dismissal. The busy sound seemed very far away; like an echo of itself.

She moved quickly at the first sinking of her heart, and drew in her eyes from watching her room, the way its features stood aloof, separate and individual; independent of her presence. In a moment panic would have seized her, leaving no refuge. She asserted herself, involuntarily whistling under her breath, a cheerful sound that called across the night to the mistaken voice of London and blended at once with its song. . . . She would tell Michael he must communicate with her in any dire necessity. . . . Moving about unseeing, she broke up the shape of her room and blurred its features and waited, holding on. Attention to these wise outside threats would drive away something coming confidently towards her, just round the corner of this vast, breathless moment. . . . She paused to wait for it as for a person about to speak aloud in the room, and drew a deep breath sending through her a glow from head to foot . . . it was there; independent, laughing, bubbling up incorrigibly, golden and bright with a radiance that spread all round her; her *profanity* . . . but if incurable profanity was incurable happiness, how could she help believing and trusting it against all other voices? If the last deepest level of her being was joy . . . a hilarity against which *nothing* seemed to be able to prevail . . . able, in spite of herself, in spite of her many solemn eager expeditions in opposition to it, to be always there, not gone; always waiting behind the last door. It was simply *rum*. Her limbs stirred to a dance. How *slowly* he had played that wild Norwegian tune; making it like an old woman singing to a fretful child to cheat it into comfort; a gay quavering.

Its expanded gestures carried her slowly and gently up and down the room, dipping, swaying, with wooden clogs on her feet, her arms swinging to balance the slow movements of her body, the surrounding mountain landscape gleaming in the joy of the festival, defying the passing of the years. She could not keep within the slow rhythm. Her feet flung off the clogs and flew about the room until she was arrested by the flying dust and escaped to the window while it settled behind her on the subdued furniture. A cab whistle was sounding in the street and the voices, coming up through the rain-moist air, of people grouped waiting on a doorstep. Come out into the deep night, out again into endless space, from a room, and still keeping up the sound of carefully modulated speech and laughter. The jingling of a hansom sounded far away in the square. It would be years before it would get to them. They would have to go on fitting things into the shape of their carefully made tones. She was tempted to call down to them to stop; tell them they were not taking any one in.

A puff of wind brought the rain against her face, inviting her to stay with the night and find again, as she had done in the old days of solitude, the strange wide spaces within the darkness. But she was drawn back by a colloquy set in, behind her, in the room. Warmly the little shabby enclosure welcomed her, given back, eager for her to go on keeping her life in it; showing her the time ahead, the circling scenes; all the undeserved,

III—L

unsought, extraordinary wealth of going on being alive. She stood with the rain-drops on her face, tingling from head to foot to know why; why; *why* life should exist. . . .

Going back into the room she found that her movement about it had all its old quality; she was once more in that zone of her being where all the past was with her unobstructed; not recalled, but present, so that she could move into any part and be there as before. She felt her way to sit on the edge of her bed, but gently as she let herself down, the bedstead creaked and gave beneath her, jolting her back into to-day, spreading before her the nothingness of the days she must now pass through, bringing back into her mind the threats and wise sayings. She faced them with arguments, flinching as she recognized this acknowledgment of their power.

Lifelong loneliness is a *phrase*. With no evidence for its meaning, but the things set down in books. . . . People who *record* loneliness, bare their wounds, and ask for pity, are not wholly wounded. For others, no one has any right to speak. What is 'a lonely figure'? If it knows it is lonely it is not altogether lonely. If it does not know, it is not lonely. Books about people are lies from beginning to end. However sincere, they cannot offer any evidence about *life*. Even lifelong loneliness is life; too marvellous to express. Absolutely, of course. But relatively? Relative things are forgotten when you are alone. . . .

The thought, at this moment, of the alternative of any sort of social life with its trampling hurry, made her turn to the simple single sense of her solitude with thankfulness that it was preserved. Social incompatibility, thought of alone, brought a curious boundless promise, a sense of something ahead that she must be alone to meet, or would miss. The condemnation of social incompatibility coming from the voices of the world roused an impatience which could not feel ashamed; an angry demand for time, and behind it a sense of companionship for which there was no name.

Single, detached figures came vividly before her, all women. Each of them had spoken to her with sudden intimacy, on the outskirts of groups from which she had moved away to breathe and rest. They had all confessed their incompatibility; a chosen or accepted loneliness. But it was certain they never felt that human forms about them crushed, with the sets of unconsidered assumptions behind their talk, the very sense of existence. They were either cynical, not only seeing through people, but not caring at all to be alive, never assuming characters in order to share the fun . . . or they were 'misjudged' or 'resigned.' The cynical ones were really alone. They never had any sense of being accompanied by themselves. They had a strange hard strength; unexpected hobbies and interests. Those who were resigned were usually religious. . . . They lived in the company of their idea of Christ . . . but regretfully . . . as if it were a second best. . . . 'And I who hoped for only God, found *thee*.' . . . Mrs Browning could never have realized how fearfully funny that was . . . from a churchwoman. . . . And Protestant churchwomen believe that only men are eligible to associate with God. Thinking of Protestant husbands the idea was suffocating. It made God intolerable; and even heaven simply abscheulich. . . . Buddhism. . . . 'Buddhism is the only faith that offers itself to men and women alike on equal terms . . .' and then, 'women are not encouraged to become priests' . . . *Tibet*. . . . The whole world would be Tibet if the people were evenly distributed. Only the historic centuries had given men their monstrous illusions; only the crowding of the women in towns. But the Church will go on being a Royal Academy of Males. . . .

She called back her thoughts from a contemplation that would lead only to anger, and was again aware of herself waiting, on the edge of her bed, just in time. In spite of her truancy the gay tumult was still seething in her mind; the whole of her past happinesses close about her, drawing her in and out of the years. Fragments of forgotten experience detached themselves, making a bright moving patchwork as she watched, waiting, while she passed from one to another and fresh patches were added, drawing her on. Joy piled up within her; but while she savoured again the quality all these past things had held as she lived them through, she suddenly knew that they were there only because she was on her way to a goal.

Somewhere at the end of this ramble into the past, was a release from wrath. She rallied to the coolness far away within her tingling blood. How astoundingly good life was; generous to the smallest effort. . . . The scenes gathered about her, called her back, acquired backgrounds that spread and spread. She watched single figures going on into lives in which she had no part; into increasing incidents, leaving them, as they had found them, unaware. They never stopped, never dropped their preoccupation with people and the things that happened, to notice the extraordinariness of the world being there and they on it. And so it was, everywhere.

She seemed to be looking with a hundred eyes, multitudinously, seeing each thing from several points at once, while through her mind flitted one after another all the descriptions of humanity she had ever culled. There was no goal here. Only the old familiar business of suspended opinions, the endless battling of thoughts. She turned away. She had gone too far. Now there would be lassitude and the precipice that waited. . . . Her room was clear and hard about her as she moved to take refuge near the friendly gas, the sheeny patch of wall underneath it.

As she stood within the radiance, conscious only of the consoling light, the little strip of mantelshelf and the small cavernous presence of the empty grate, a single scene opened for a moment in the far distance, closing in the empty vista, standing alone, indistinct, at the bottom of her ransacked mind. It was gone. But its disappearance was a gentle touch that lingered, holding her at peace and utterly surprised.

This forgotten thing was the most deeply engraved of all her memories? The most powerful? More than any of the bright remembered things that had seemed so good as they came, suddenly, catching her up and away, each one seeming to be the last her lot would afford?

It was. The strange faint radiance in which it had shone cast a soft grey light within the darkness concealing the future. . . .

Oldfield. It had come about through Dr Salem Oldfield. She could not remember his arrival. Only suddenly realizing him, one evening at dinner when he had been long enough in the house to chaff Mrs Bailey about some imaginary man. Sex-chaff; that was his form of humour; giving him away as a nonconformist. But so handsome, sitting large and square, a fine massive head, well-shaped hair, thick, and dinted with close-cropped waves; talking about himself in the eloquent American way. It was that night he had told the table how he met his fiancée. He was a charlatan, stagy; but there must have been something behind his clever anecdotal American piety. Something remained even after the other doctors' stories about his sharing their sitting-room and books, without sharing expenses; about his laziness and self-indulgence.

Mr Chadband. But why shouldn't people on the way to heaven enjoy buttered toast? A hypocrite is all the time trying to be something, or he wouldn't be a hypocrite. . . . And the story he told was *true*. . . . Dr Winchester knew. It was with his friends at Balham that the girl had been staying. Wonderful. His lonely despair in Uganda; the way he had forced himself in the midst of his darkness to visit the sick convert . . . and found the answer to his trouble in a leaflet hymn at the bedside; and come to London for his furlough and met the authoress in the very first house he visited. Things like that don't happen unless people are real in some way. And the way he had admired Michael; and liked him.

It had been Michael he had taken to the Quaker meeting. But there must have been some talk with him about religion, to lead up to that sudden little interview on the stairs, he holding a book in one large hand and thumping it with the other. . . . 'You'll find the basic realities of religious belief set forth *here*; in this small volume. Your George Fox was a marvellous man.' There was an appealing truth in him at that moment, and humility. But before his footsteps had died away she knew she could not read the book. Even the sight of it suggested his sledge-hammer sentimental piety. Also she had felt that the religious opinions of a politician could not clear up the problems that had baffled Emerson. It was only after she had given back the book that she remembered the other George Fox and the Quaker in *Uncle Tom's Cabin*. But she had said she had read it and that it was wonderful, to silence his evangelistic attacks, and also for the comfort of sharing, with anybody, the admission that there was absolute wonderfulness.

After that there was no memory of him until the Sunday morning when Michael had come panting upstairs to ask her to go to this meeting. He was incoherent, and she had dressed and gone out with them, into the high bright Sunday morning stillness; without knowing whither. Finding out, somewhere on the way, that they were going to see Quakers waiting to be moved by the spirit. . . . A whitewashed room, with people in Quaker dress sitting in a circle? Shocking to break in on them. . . . Startling not to have remembered them in all these years of hoping to meet someone who understood silence; and now to be going to them as a show; because Dr Oldfield admired Michael and, being American, found out the unique things in London.

In amongst the small old shops in St Martin's Lane, gloomy, iron-barred gates, a long bleak corridor, folding doors; and suddenly inside a large room with sloping galleries and a platform, like a concert room, a row of dingy modern people sitting on the platform facing a scattered 'chapel' congregation; men and women sitting on different sides of the room . . . being left standing under the dark gallery, while Dr Oldfield and Michael were escorted to seats amongst the men; slipping into a chair at the back of the women's side; stranded in an atrocious emphasis of sex. But the men were on the *left* . . . and numbers of them; not the few of a church congregation; and young; modern young men in overcoats; really religious, and *not* thinking the women secondary. . . . But there were men also on the women's side; here and there. Married men? Then those across the way were bachelors. . . . That young man's profile; very ordinary and with a *walrus* moustache; but stilled from its maleness, deliberately divested and submitted to silence, redeeming him from his type.

To have been born amongst these people; to know at home and in the church a *shared* religious life. They were in heaven already. Through acting on their belief. Where two or three are gathered together. Nearer than thoughts; nearer than breathing; nearer than hands and feet. The church knew it; but put the cart before the horse; the surface before the reality. The beautiful surroundings, the bridge of music and then, the moment the organ stopped, a booming or nasal voice at top speed, 'T' th' *Lord*our God b'long *mah*cies 'n f'giveness.' . . . Anger and excited discovery and still more time wasted, in glancing across to find Michael, small and exposed at the gangway end, his head decorously bent, the Jew in him paying respect, but looking up and keenly about him from under his bent brows, observing on the only terms he knew, through eye and brain. . . .

Michael was a determinist. . . . But to assume the presence of the holy spirit was also determinism? . . . Beyond him Dr Oldfield, huge and eagerly bowed, conforming to Quaker usages, describing the occasion in his mind as he went. It was just then, turning to get away from his version, that the quality of the silence had made the impression that had come back to her now.

Dr M'Taggart said pure being was nothing. But there is no such thing as nothing . . . being in the silence was being in something alive and positive; at the centre of existence; being there with others made the sense of it stronger than when it was experienced alone. Like lonely silence, it drove away the sense of enclosure. There had been no stuffiness of congregated humanity; the air, breathed in, had held within it a freshness, spreading coolness and strength through the secret passages of the nerves.

It had felt like the beginning of a life that was checked and postponed into the future by the desire to formulate it; and by the nudging of a homesickness for daily life with these people who lived from the centre, admitted, in public, that life brims full all the time, away below thoughts and the loud shapes of things that happen. . . . And just as she had longed for the continuance of the admission, the spell had been broken. Suddenly, not in continuance, not coming out of the stillness, but interrupting it, an urbane, ingratiating voice. Standing up in the corner of the platform, turned towards the congregation, as if he were a lecturer facing an audience, a dapper little man in a new spring suit, with pink cheeks and a pink rose in his buttonhole. . . . Afterwards, it had seemed certain that he had broken the silence because the time was running out. Strangers were present and the spirit must move. . . .

It had been a little address, a thought-out lecture on natural history, addressed by a specialist to people less well informed. He had talked his subject not with, but at them. . . . While his voice went on, the gathering seemed to lose all its religious significance. His informing air; his encouraging demonstrator's smiles; his obvious relish of the array of facts. They fell on the air like lies, losing even their own proper value, astray and intruding in the wrong context. When he sat down, the silence was there again, but within it were the echoes of the urbane, expounding, professorial voice. Then, just afterwards, the breaking forth of that old man's muffled tones; praying; quietly, as if he were alone. No one to be seen; a humbled life-worn old voice, coming out of the heart of the gathering, carrying with it, gently, all the soreness and groaning that might be there. No whining or obsequiousness; no putting on of a special voice; patient endurance and longing; affection and confidence. And, far away within the indistinct aged tones, a clarion note; the warm glow of sunlight; his own strong certainty beating up unchanged beneath the heavy weight of his years. A gentle, clean, clear-eyed old man, with certainly a Whitman beard. Beautiful. For a moment it had been perfectly beautiful.

If he had stopped abruptly. . . . But the voice cleared and swelled. Life dropped away from it; leaving a tiresome old gentleman in full blast; thought coming in, to shape carefully the Biblical phrases describing God, to God. In the end he, too, was lecturing the congregation, praying at them, expressing his judgment. . . . Bleakness spread through the air. It was worse than the little pink man, who partly knew what he was doing, and was ashamed. But this old chap was describing, at awful length, without knowing it, the secret of his own surface misery, the fact that he had never got beyond the angry, jealous, selfish, male God of the patriarchate.

Almost at once after that, the stirring and breaking up; and those glimpses, as people moved and turned towards each other, shaking hands, of the faces of some of the women, bringing back the lost impression. The inner life of the meeting was more fully with the women? It was they who spread the pure, live atmosphere? But they were obviously related. They had a household look, but not narrowly; none of the air of isolation that spread from churchwomen; the look of being used up by men and propping up a man's world with unacknowledged, or simply unpondered, private reservations. Nor any of the jesting air of those women who 'make the best of things.' They looked enviably, deeply, richly alive, on the very edge of the present, representing their faith in their own persons, entirely self-centred and self-controlled; poised and serene and withdrawn, yet not withholding. They had no protesting, competing eagerness, and none of the secret arrogance of churchwomen. Their dignity was not dignified. Seen from behind, they had none of the absurdity of churchwomen, devoutly uppish about the status of an institution which was a standing insult to their very existence. . . . It was they, the shock of the relief, after the revealed weakness of the men, of their perfect poise, their personality, so strong and intense that it seemed to hold the power of reaching forth, impersonally, in any thinkable direction, that had finally confirmed the impression that had been so deep, and that yet had not once come up into her thoughts since the day it was made. . . .

The poorest, least sincere type of Anglican priest had a something that was lacking in Dr Oldfield and the pink man. The absence of it had been the most impressive part of seeing them talking together. He had introduced Michael first. And the feeling of being affronted had quickly changed to thankfulness at representing nothing in the eyes of the suave little man. He had given only half his attention, not taking up the fact that Michael was a Zionist; his eyes wandering about; the proprietary eyes of a churchwarden. . . .

St Pancras clock struck two. But there was no sense of night in the soft wide air; pouring in now more strongly at the open casement, rattling its fastening gently, rhythmically, to and fro, sounding its two little notes. It was the *west* wind.

III—* L

Of *course* she was not tired and there was no sense of night. She hurried to be in bed in the darkness, breathing it in, listening to the little voice at the window. Here was part of the explanation of her evening. Again and again it had happened; the escape into the tireless unchanging centre; when the wind was in the west. Michael had been hurt when she had told him that the west wind brought her perfect happiness and always, like a sort of message, the certainty that she must remain alone. But it was through him that she had discovered that it transformed her. It was an augury for to-morrow. For the way of the wind to-night, its breath passing through her, recalled, seeming exactly to repeat, that wonderful night of restoration when, for the only time, he had been away from London. It was useless to deplore the seeming cruelty. The truth was forced upon her, wafted through her by this air that washed away all the circumstances of her life.

CHAPTER III

SHE was inside the dark little hall, her luggage being set down in the shadows by the brisk silent maid. At the sight of the wide green staircase ascending to the upper world, the incidents of the journey, translated, as she drove to the house, into material for conversation, fell away and vanished.

The thud of the swing door, the flurry of summer skirts threshed by flying footsteps; Alma hurrying to meet her. . . . It was folly; *madness*; to flout the year's fatigue by coming here to stay, instead of going away with friends also tired and seeking holiday.

With the first step on the yielding pile of the stair-carpet, she forgot everything but the escape from noise and gloom and grime. She was going up for four endless weeks into the clean light streaming down from above. This time there should be no brisk beginning. She would act out Alma's promise to accept her as an invalid deaf-mute. There was so much time that fatigue was an asset, the shadow against which all this brightness shone out.

But Alma was not welcoming an invalid. There she stood, at the end of her rush, daintily jigging from foot to foot, in a delicate frilly little dress; heading the perspective of pure white and green, surfaces and angles sharp in the east light coming through the long casement. She checked the bright perspective with the thought in her dress, the careful arrangement of her softly woven pile of bright hair, the afternoon's excitement, from which she had rushed forth, shining through her always newly charming little pointed square face.

'Shall I labour up the rest of the stairs, or sit down here and burst into tears?'

'Oh, come up, dear ole fing,' she cried with tender irony; but *irony*. 'Paw fing. Is it *very* tired?' But her gentle arms and hands were perfectly, wonderfully understanding; though her face withdrawn from her gentle kiss still mocked; always within the limpid brown eyes that belabouring, rallying, mocking spirit. She held her smile radiantly, against a long troubled stare, and then it broke into her abrupt gurgle of laughter.

'*Come* along,' she cried and carried a guest at a run along the passage and through the swing door.

It was the downstairs spare room. . . . Miriam had expected the winding stair, the room upstairs, where all her shorter visits were stored up. She was to be down here at the centre of the house, just behind low casements, right on the garden, touched by the sound of the sea. And within the curtain-shaded sound-bathed green-lit space there was a deeper remoteness than even in the far high room, so weirdly shaped by the burning roof; its orange light always full of a strange listening silence.

'*Alma*. How *perfectly* glorious.' She stood still, turned away, as Alma closed the door, contemplating the screened light falling everywhere on spaces of pure fresh colour, against which the deep tones of single objects shone brightly.

Alma neighed gently and with little gurgles of laughter put her hands about her and gently shook her. 'It *is* rather a duck of a room. It *is* rather a duck of a room.' Another little affectionate, clutching shake. Her face was crinkled, her eyes twinkling with mirth; as if she gave the room a little sportive push that left it bashed amusingly sideways. In just this way had she jested when they walked, wearing long pig-tails, down the Upper Richmond Road. If she could have echoed the words and joined in Alma's laughter, she would have been, in Alma's eyes, suitably launched on her visit. But she couldn't. *Amused* approval was an outrage on some-thing. Yet the kind of woman who would be gravely pleased and presently depart to her own quarters proud and possessive, would also leave everything unexpressed. But that kind of person would not have achieved this kind of room . . . and to Alma the wonder of it was of course inseparable from the adventure of getting it together. It was something in the independent effect of things that was violated by regarding them merely as successful larks. . . . Yet Alma's sense of beauty, her recognition of its unfamiliar forms, was keener, more experienced, more highly wrought than her own.

'I shall spend the whole of my time in here, doing absolutely nothing.'

'You shall! You shall! *Dear* old Mira.' She was laughing again. 'But you 'll come out and have tea. Sometimes. Won't you, for instance, come out and have tea *now*? In a few minutes? There 'll be tea; in *ever* such a few minutes. Wouldn't that be a bright idea?' How dainty she was; how pretty. A Dresden china shepherdess, without the simper; a sturdiness behind her sparkling mirth. If only she would stop trying to liven one up. It seemed always when they were alone, as if she were still brightly in the midst of people keeping things going. . . .

'Tea! Bright idea! Tea!' A little parting shake and a brisk whirling turn and she was sitting away on the side of the bed, meditatively, with both hands, using a small filmy handkerchief, having given up hope of galvanizing; saying gravely, 'Take off your things and tell me really how you are.'

'I 'm at my last gasp,' said Miriam sinking into a chair. It was clear now that she would not be alone with the first expressiveness of the room. Returning later on she would find it changed. The first, already fading, wonderful moment would return, painfully, only when she was packing up to go. After all it was Alma's home. But it was no use trying to fight this monstrous conviction that the things she liked of other people, were more hers than their own. The door opened again upon a servant with her pilgrim baskets.

'I nearly always *am* at my last gasp nowadays.' Clean, strong, neatly cuffed hands setting the dusty London baskets down to rest in the quiet freshness.

Alma spoke formally; her voice a comment on expressiveness in the presence of the maid; and an obliteration of the expressiveness of the room; making it just a square enclosure set about with independent things, each telling, one against the other, a separate history. When the maid was gone the air was parched with silence. Miriam felt suspended; impatient; eager to be out in whatever grouping Alma had come from, to recover there in the open the sense of life that had departed from the sheltering room.

'How is Sarah?' Alma felt the strain. But for her it was the difficulty of finding common ground for interchange with any one whose life was lacking in brilliant features. She was behaving, kindly trying for topics; but also, partly, underlining the featurelessness, as a punishment for bad behaviour.

'Oh—flourishing—I think.' She rose, unpinning her stifling veil. She would have to brace herself to reach out to something with which to break into the questions Alma's kind patience would one by one produce. A catechism leading her thoughts down into a wilderness of unexamined detail that would unfit her for the coming emergence.

'And Harriett?'

'Harriett's simply *splendid*. You know, if she only had a little capital she could take another house. She's sending people away all the time.'

'Oh, yes?' Alma did not want to spend time over Harriett's apartment house, unless it was brightly described. It was too soon for bright descriptions. The item had been dragged in and wasted, out of place. A single distasteful fact. The servants, hidden away beyond the velvet staircase, seemed to be hearing the unsuitable disclosure. She sought about in her mind for something that would hold its own; one of the points of conflict that had cleared, since she was last here, to single unanswerable statements. But Alma forestalled her, attacking the silence with her gayest voice. 'Oh, Miriam, what *do* you think? I saw a Speck; yesterday; on the Grand Esplanade. *Do* you remember the Specks?'

Miriam beamed and agreed, breathing in reminiscences. But they would be endless; and would not satisfy them, or bring them together. She could not, with Alma alone, pretend that those memories were merely amusing. It was a treachery. The mere mention of a name sent her back to the unbearable happiness of that last school summer, a sunlit flower-filled world opening before her, the feeling of being herself a

flower, expanding in the sunlight. She could not regard it
as a past. All that had happened since was a momentary
straying aside, to be forgotten. To that other world she was
still going forward. One day she would suddenly come upon
it, as she did in her dreams. The flower-scented air of it was
in her nostrils as she sat reluctantly rousing herself to take
Alma's cue. 'There were millions of them.' It had never
occurred to her that they were funny. Alma, even then,
outside her set of grave romantic friendships, had seen almost
everything as a comic spectacle and had no desire to go back.
'Yes, *weren't* they innumerable! And so *large*! It was a
large one I saw. The very biggest Speck of all I think it
must have been.'

'I expect it was Belinda.'

'Oh, my *dear*! *Could* you tell them apart?'

'Belinda was one of the middle ones. Absolutely *square*.
I liked her for that and her deep bass voice and her silence.'

'Oh, but, Miriam, such a *heavy* silence.'

'That was *why*. Perhaps because she made me feel sylphlike
and elegant. Me, Susan. . . . Or it might have been *Mehetabel*;
the eldest of the younger ones. I once heard her answer in
class. . . .'

'My *dear*! Could a Speck really speak?'

'Hetta did. In a boo; like the voice of the wind.'

She contemplated her thoughtless simile. It was exactly
true. First a sound, breathy and resonant, and then words
·*blown* on it. . . . Alma's amused laughter was tailing off into
little snickers; repeated while she looked for something else.
But the revived Specks marshalled themselves more and more
clearly, playing their parts in the crowded scene.

'And you know the eldest, Alathea, was quite willowy.
Darker than the others. They were all mid-brown.'

'Oh, Miriam; doesn't that express them?'

'I wonder what they are all doing?'

'Nothing, my dear. Oh, *nothing*. Now *can* you imagine
a Speck doing anything whatever?'

'All sitting about in the big house; going mad; on their
father's money.'

'Yes,' said Alma simply, gathering her face into gravity. 'It's rather terrible, you know.' A black shadow bearing slowly down upon the golden picture. But they were so determined to see women's lives in that way . . . yet there was Miss Lane, and Mildred Gaunt and Eunice Bradley . . . three of their own small group; all gone mad.

'Well,' said Alma rising, her hands moving up to her bright hair, adjusting it, with delicate wreathing movements, 'I'm so glad you've come, old fing.' She hummed herself to the door with a little tune to which Miriam listened standing in the middle of the room in a numb suspension. The door was opened. Alma would be gliding gracefully out. Her song ceased, and she cleared her throat with that little sound that was the sound of her voice in quiet comment.

'Wow. Old brown-study.' She turned to look. Alma's pretty head was thrust back into the room. To shake things off, to make one shake things off. . . . She smiled, groaning in spirit at her accentuated fatigue. One more little amused gurgle, and Alma was gone.

She went into her own room. Next door. Opposite to it was Hypo's room. Opposite to her own door, the door of the bathroom, and just beyond, the swing door leading to the landing and the rooms grouped about it. Outside the low curtained windows was the midst of the garden. She was set down at the heart of the house. Sounds circled about her instead of coming faintly up. . . . She drew back the endmost curtain an inch or two. Bright light fell on her reflection in the long mirror. She was transformed already. It would be impossible to convince any one that she was a tired Londoner. Here was already the self that no one in London knew. The removal of pressure had relaxed the nerves of her face, restoring its contours. Her mushroom hat had crushed the mass of her hair into a good shape. The sharp light called out its bright golds, deepened the colour of her eyes and the clear tints of her skin. The little old washed-out muslin blouse flatly defining her shoulders and arms, pouched softly above the pale-grey skirt. . . . I *do* understand colour . . . that tinge of lavender in such a pale, pale grey; just warming it . . . and

belonging perfectly to Grannie's spidery old Honiton collar.
. . . The whole little toilet was quite good; could be forgotten,
and would keep fresh, bleached by the dry bright air to paler
grey and whiter white, while the notes of bright living colour
in her face and hair intensified from day to day. She hunted
out her handglass and consulted her unknown eyes. It was
true. They were brown; not grey. In the bright light there
was a web, thorny golden brown, round the iris. She gazed
into its tangled depths. So strange. So warm and bright;
her unknown self. The self she was meant to be, living in that
bright, goldy-brown filbert tint, irradiating the grey into which
it merged. It was a discovery. She was a goldy-brown
person, not cold grey. With half a chance, goldy-brown and
rose. And the whites of her eyes were pearly grey-blue. What
a number of strange live colours, warmly asserting themselves;
independently. But only at close quarters.

She followed Alma back through the swing door. Alma
hummed a little song; an overture; its low tones filled the
enclosed space, opened all the doors, showed her the whole of
the interior in one moment and the coming month in an endless
bright panorama passing unbroken from room to room, each
scene enriched by those accumulated behind it, and those
waiting ahead; the whole, for her, perpetually returning upon
its own perfection. Alma paused before a scatter of letters on
the table below the long lattice. Links with their other world;
with things she would hear of, stated and shaped in their way,
revealing a world to which they alone seemed to have an interpreting key; making it hold together; but inacceptable . . .
but the *statement* was for ever fascinating. Through the
leaded panes she caught a glimpse of the upper slope of
the little town. A row of grey seaside boarding-houses slanting uphill. A ramshackle little omnibus rumbling down the
steep road.

'Edna Prout's with us for the week-end.' Alma's social
tone, deliberately clear and level. It made a little scene, the
beginning of a novel, the opening of a play, warning the players
to stand off and make a good shape, smoothly moving without

pause or hitch, playing and saying their parts, always with an eye to the good shape, conscious of a critical audience.   There would be no expansive bright beginning, alone with Alma and Hypo, the centre of their attention.

'Who is Edna Prout?' she demanded jealously.

Alma turned with a little bundle of the letters in her hand, speaking thoughtfully away through the window.   'She writes; rather wonderful stuff.'

Away outside the window stood the wonderful stuff, being written, rolled off; the vague figure of a woman, cleverly dressed, rising, pen in hand, from her work, to be socially brilliant.   Popular.   Divided between mysteriously clever work and successful femineity.   Alma glanced, pausing, and looked away again.

'She has a most amazing sense of the past,' she murmured reflectively.   As if it had just occurred to her.   But it must be the current description.   His description.

'The Stone Age?'

'Oh, *no*, my dear!'   She shrieked gently; wheeling round to share her mirth.   'The Past.   *'Istry*.   The Mediterranean past.'

'Her stones are precious stones.'   From this beginning, to go on looking only at things, ignoring surroundings. . . .

'That's it!   Come along!'   Alma went blithely forward, again humming her tune.   But there was a faint change in her confident manner.   She, too, was conscious of going to meet an ordeal.

Through the still, open-windowed brightness of the brown-green room, out into the naked blaze.   Rocky dryness and sea freshness mingled in the huge air.   The little baked pathway ribboning the level grass, disappearing round the angle of the enclosing edge, the perfect sharp edge, irises feathering along it, sharp green spikes and deep blue hoods of filmy blossom patterned against the paler misty blueness of the sea.   Perfect. Hidden beyond the sharp edge, the pathway winding down the terraced slope of the cliff to the little gate opening from the tangled bottom on to the tamarisk-trimmed sea-road.   Seats set at the angles of the winding path.   The sea glinting at your side between the leaf patterns of the creeper-covered pergola. The little roughstone shelter, trapping the sunblaze. The plain bench along the centre of a piece of pathway, looking straight out to the midmost sea; sun-baked gravel under your feet, clumps of flowers in sight. Somewhere the rockery, its face catching the full blaze of the light, green bosses clumped upon it, with small pure-toned flowers, mauvy pink and tender eastern blue. On the level just below it, a sudden little flat of grass, small-flowered shrubs at its edge towards the sea.

All waiting for to-morrow, for endless to-morrows. For the mornings, when the sunlight poured from the other side of the sky and the face of the cliff was cool and coloured. And the evenings, when the blaze had deepened into sunset and afterglow, making a little Naples of the glimpse of white town, winding street, and curve of blue bay visible in the distance beyond the shoulder of the sidemost clump of shrubs along the end of the sunk lawn.

Alma had halted, just behind, letting her gaze her fill. There was no one to be seen. No sound. Nothing to break the perfect expressiveness.

'We 've taken refuge at the back,' suggested Alma into her arm-stretching groan of contentment. Down across the lawn into the little pathway between the shrubs. There they were, in the cool shadows under the small trees. Large bamboo chairs, a cushioned hammock, tea going on, Hypo rising in the middle of a sentence. Miss Prout sitting opposite, upright, posed, knee over knee, feet shod in peacock blue, one pointing downwards in the air, exactly above the other pointing to the gravel. A wide silky gown, loose; held flat above the chest by brilliant bold embroidery; a broad dark head; short wide tanned face.

The eyes were not brown but wide starry blue; unseeing; contradicting her matronly shape. Now that the arrival was over and Hypo had begun again, she still had the look of waiting, apart. As if she were sitting alone. Yet her clever clothes and all her outlines diffused companionship.

The lizards must have looked perfect, darting and basking on the rockery. But why have his heart won only by the one

that quickly wriggled out of the box? . . . Paying attention
only to the people who were strong enough to fuss all the time.
Not seeing that half their animation was assumed. . . . 'Do
you still' . . . the bells of the blue flowers in the deepest
shadow were like lanterns hung on little trees crowded upon
the brown earth. The sound of grass and flowers in blissful
shade poured into the voices, making agreement, giving them
all the quality of blossoming in the surrounding coolness,
aware of it, aware of the outer huge splintering sunlight that
made it perfect, fled away from, left to itself to prepare another
perfection . . . 'divide people into those who like "The
Reading Girl" and those who prefer the Dresden teapot?'

'*Sudden* Miriam. Miriam, Edna, is . . . is *terrifying*. . . .'
He turned full round to hand the buns, both firm neatly-
moulded hands holding the dish ironically-carefully. The
wide blue eyes looked across. Where was she all the time; so
calm and starry? . . . 'She comes down from London, into
our rustic solitude, primed. . . .'

'She's a fighter,' said Miss Prout roundly, as if she had not
spoken.

'Fighting is too mild for Miriam. She crushes. She de-
molishes. When words fail her,' the lifting, descriptive, out-
lining laughter coming into the husky voice, filling out its
insistence, 'she uses her fists. Then she departs; back to
London; fires off not so much letters as reinforcements of the
prostrating blow.' *Kind* Hypo. Doing his best for her.
Launching her on her holiday with approval; knowing how
little was to be expected of her. . . . Ages already she had
been here, blissful. Getting every moment more blissful.
And this was only the first tea. The four weeks of long days,
each day in four long bright separate pieces, spread out ahead,
enclosed; a long unbroken magic. Poor Miss Prout with her
short week-end. . . . But she went from country house to
country house. Certainly. Her garments, even on this
languid afternoon, were electric with social life. Then hostesses were a necessary part of her equipment. She must fear
them, like a man. She herself could not be imagined as a
hostess. There was no look of strain about her. Only that

look of insulated waiting. Boredom, if her eyes had been the thing-filled eyes of a man, bored in the intervals between meals and talk and events.

'Yes, but *do* you?' Lame. But Hypo turned, accepting, not departing afresh to tone up the talk. The ringed, lightning-quick grey eyes glanced again, as when she had arrived, taking in the detail and the whole of her effect, but this time directly messaging approval. The luminous clouded grey, clear ringed eyes, the voice husky and clear, the strange repellent mouth below the scraggy moustache, kept from weakness only by the perpetually hovering disclaiming ironic smile . . . fascination that could not be defined; that drove its way through all the evidence against it. Married, yet always seeming nearer and more sympathetic than other men. Her cup brimmed over. She saw herself as she had been this morning, in dingy black, pallid, tired to death, hurriedly finishing off at Wimpole Street. And now an accepted harmonious part of this so different scene. But this power of blossoming in response to surroundings was misleading. Beneath it she was utterly weary. To-morrow she would feel wrecked, longing for silence.

'Any more tea, anybody? More *tea*, Miriam?' Alma waved the teapot. The little scene gleamed to the sound of her voice, a bright, intense grouping in the green shade, with the earth thrilling beneath and the sky arching down over its completeness.

'Yes,' said Hypo, on his feet. 'She'll have, just one more cup. Let me see,' he went on, from the tea-table, 'you liked; the Girl. Yes. . . . No. The teapot. I accuse you of the teapot.'

'I liked both.' Not true. But the answer to the wrongness of the division.

'Catholic Miriam. That's quite a feat. Even for you, Miriam, that is, I think . . .'

'But she didn't! She called my teapot messy!'

'It's true. I *do* think Dresden china messy. But I mean that it's possible——' She spoke her argument through his answer, volleyed over his shoulder as he brought back her cup, to a remark from Miss Prout. The next moment he was away in the hammock near Miss Prout's low chair, throwing cushions out on to the grass, gathering up a sheaf of printed leaves; leaving her classed with the teapot people.

'Buoyed up by *tea*, Edna,' he chuckled, flinging away the end of a cigarette; propping the pages against his knee. 'By the way, who is Olga?'

'The eldest Featherstonhaugh.' She spoke carelessly; sat half turned away from him, serenely smoking; a small buff cigarette in a long amber tube; but her voice vibrated.

He was *reading*, in her presence, a book she had written. Those pages were *proofs*. . . . My arrival was an interruption in a companionship that made conversation superfluous. What need for Miss Prout to talk when she could put into his hands, alive and finished, something that she had made; that could bring into his face that look of attention and curiosity? How not sit suspended, and dreaming, through the small break in her tremendous afternoon? Yet he was getting the characters mixed up.

'And Cyril. Do I know Cyril?'

She had put *people* in. . . . People he knew of. They joked about it. Horrible. . . . She gazed, revolted and fascinated, at the bundle of pages. Someone ought to prevent, destroy. This peaceful beauty. Life going so wonderfully on. And people being helplessly picked out and put into books.

'This is the episode of the *greenhouse*!' His voice broke on the word into its utmost wail of amusement.

That was 'writing'; from behind the scenes. People and things from life, a little altered, and described from the author's point of view. Easy; if your life was amongst a great many people and things and you were hard enough to be sceptical and superior. But an impossibly mean advantage . . . a cheap easy way. Cold clever way of making people look seen-through and foolish; to be laughed at, while the authors remained admired, special people, independent, leading easy airy sunlit lives, supposed, by readers who did not know where they got their material, to be *creators*. He was reading on steadily now, the look of amused curiosity gone.

Alma came over with a box of cigarettes and a remark; kindly thinking she might be feeling left; offering distraction. Or wishing to make her behave, launch out, with pretended interest, upon a separate conversation, instead of hanging upon theirs. Of course she was sitting staring, without knowing it. . . . And already she had taken a cigarette and murmured an answer obliviously, and Alma had gone, accepting her engrossment, humming herself about amongst the trees, missing his remarks. Deliberately asserting a separate existence? Really loving her garden and enjoying the chance of being alone? Or because she knew all he had to say about *everything*. She came back and subsided in a low chair near Miss Prout just as he dropped his pages and looked out on to the air with a grave unconscious face. Lost in contemplation. This woman, so feminine and crafty, was a great writer. Extraordinary. Impossible. In a second he had turned to her.

'How do you do it, Edna? You do it. It's *shattering*, that chapter-end.'

Miss Prout was speechless, not smiling. Crushed with joy. Alma, at her side, smiled in delight, genuine sympathetic appreciation.

'I'm done in, Edna,' he wailed, taking up the leaves to go on, 'shan't write another line. And the worst of it is I know you'll keep it up. That I've got to make; before dinner; my—my *via dolorosa*; through your abominably good penultimate and final chapters.'

'Am I allowed to read?' Miriam said rising and going with hands outstretched for the magic leaves.

'Yes,' he chuckled, gathering up and handing. 'Let's try it on Miriam. I warn you she's deadly. And of a voracity. She reads at a gulp; spots everything; *more* than everything; turns on you and lays you out.'

Miriam stood considering him. Happy. He had really noticed and remembered the things she had said from time to time. But they were expecting a response.

'I shan't understand. I know I shan't. May I really take them away?'

'Now don't, Miriam . . .' taking his time, keeping her

arrested before them, with his held-up minatory finger and mocking friendly smile, 'don't underrate your intelligence.'

'May I really take them?' she flounced, ignoring him; holding herself apart with Miss Prout. The air danced between them sunlit from between branches. A fresh perspective opened. She was to meet her. See unfold her before her eyes in the pages of the book.

'Yes, *do*,' she smiled, a swift nice look, not scrutinizing.

'How *alive* they look; much more alive than a book in its suit of neat binding.'

'Are we *all* literary?'

'We're all literary,' joined his quick voice. She blushed with pleasure. Included; with only those ghastly little reviews. Not mocking. Quite gravely. She beamed her gratitude and turned away blissful.

'Is Miriam going?'

'I've got to unpack.' He wanted an audience, an outsider, for the scene of the reading. Alma had disappeared.

'Won't *they* do all that for you?'

'Still I think I'll go. . . . Addio.' She backed along the little pathway watching him seek and find his words, crying each one forth in a thoughtful falsetto, while he turned conversationally towards Miss Prout. The scene was cut off by the bushes, but she could still hear his voice, after the breakdown of his Italian into an ironic squeal, going on in charge of it. She sped across the lawn and up on to the open above the unexplored terraces. They could wait. For the moment, unpeopled, they were nothing. They would be the background of further scenes, all threaded by the sound of Hypo's voice, lit by the innumerable things she would hear him say, obliterating the surroundings, making far-off things seem more real. . . . . Mental liveliness *did* obliterate surroundings, stop their expressiveness. Already the first expressiveness had gone from the garden. She did not want to create it afresh. There was hurry and pressure now in the glances she threw. A wrongness. Something left out. There was something left out, left behind, in his scheme of things. She wandered as far as the horizon row of irises to look out over the sea, chased and pulled back as she went. Until the distant prospect opened and part of the slope of the garden lay at her feet. The light had ripened. The sun no longer towered, but blazed across at her from above the right-most edge of the picture. Short shadows jutted from the feet of every standing thing. The light was deepening in perfect stillness. Wind and rain had left the world for good. *This* was her holiday. Everything behind her broke down into irrelevance. How go back to it ? How not stay and live through the changing of the light in this perfect stillness ?

There was no feeling of Sunday in the house. But when Miriam wandered into her room during the after-breakfast lull, she found it waiting for her; pouring into the room from afar, from all over the world, breaking her march, breaking up the lines of the past and of the future, isolating her with itself. The openings of the long lattice-framed wide strips of morning brilliance between short close-drawn folds of flowered chintz. Everything outside was sharp and near, but changed since yesterday. The flowers stood vivid in the sunlight; very still. The humming of the bees sounded careful and secret; not wishing to disturb. The sea sparkled to itself, refusing to call the eye. Yet outside there, as in the room, something called. She leaned out. Into the enlarged picture the sky poured down. The pure blue moved within itself as you looked, letting you through and up. An unbroken fabric of light, yet opening all over, taking you up into endless light.

Sunday is in the sky.

Hypo, coming round the corner from the terrace, his arms threshing the air to the beat of his swift walk; knitting up the moment, casting kind radiance as he came. Married, but casting radiance. He was making for the house. Then Miss Prout was somewhere down there alone. She hurried to be out, seeking her. On the landing she ran into Hypo.

'Hallo, Miriametta. Going out ?'

'I think so. Where 's everybody ?'

'Everybody, and chairs, is down on the terrace. But you 'll want a *hat*.'

'I shan't.' He had often admired her ability to go without. He had been talking to Miss Prout for the last half hour and was now abstractedly making a shapely thing of a chance meeting with a stranger. His words had carried him to the study door. He began inventing his retort, the unfelt shape of words that would carry him on undisturbed, facing the door with his back to her, hand on the door-knob. The end of it would find him within. She cried out at random into the making of his phrase and escaped into the dining-room to the sound of his voice. In the empty dining-room she found again the listening presence of Sunday and hurried to be through it and away at whatever centre had formed down there in the open. Going down the steps and along the paths she entered the movement of the day, the beginning of the sense of to-morrow, that would strengthen with the slow shifting of the sabbath light. Miss Prout came into view round the first bend, a sunlit figure in a tub chair on the grassy level at the end of the terrace. *She* had no hat. Her dark head was bent over the peak made in her flowing draperies by her crossed knees. She was *sewing*. Here. In public, serenely, the first thing in the morning.

Strolling to join her Miriam saw her as she had been last night, set like a flower, unaccented and harmonious, in her pleated gown of old-rose silk, towards the oval of dinner-table, an island of softly bright silk-shaded radiance in the midst of the twilight room; under the brightest of the central light, filmy flowers massed low in a wide shallow bowl . . . a gentleness about her, touching the easy beginnings of talk, each phrase pearly, catching the light, expanding; expressing a secret joy. Then the gathering and settling of the flow of talk between him and her, lifting, shaking itself out, flashing into sharp clear light; the fabric of words pierced by his wails of amusement as he looked, still talking, at the pictures they drew. . . . People they knew passing to and fro; *all* laughable, all brought to their strange shared judgment. The charm of the scene destroyed by the surrounding vision of a wit-wrecked world.

After dinner, that moment when she had drawn herself up

before him, suddenly young, with radiant eyes; looking like
a flower in her petalled gown.   He had responded standing
very upright, smiling back at her, admiring her deliberate
effect.

The break away across the landing, white and green night
brightness under the switched-on lights, into the dusk of the
study, ready peopled with its own stillness; the last of the
twilight glimmering outside the open windows.   Each figure
changed by the gloom into an invisible, memorable presence.
Hypo moving in and out of the cone of soft light amongst the
shadows at the far end.

'We'll try the contralto laugh on the lady in the window-seat.'

The fear of missing the music in looking for his discovery.
And then, into the waiting stillness, *Bach*.   Of all people.
He had found a contralto laugh in *Bach*.   There were no people,
no women, in Bach.   Looking for the phrase.   Forgetting to
look for it.   The feeling of the twilight expanding within itself.
too small.   The oncoming vast of night held back, swirling,
swept away by broad bright morning light running through
forest tracery.   Shining into a house.   The clean cool poise
of everyday morning.   The sounds of work and voices, separate,
united by surroundings greeted by every one from within.
The secret joy in every one pouring through the close pattern
of life, going on for ever, the end in the first small phrase, every
phrase a fresh end and a beginning.   Going on when the last
chord stood still on the air. . . . And if he liked Bach, how not
believe in people?   How not be certain of God? . . . And
then remarks, breaking thinly against the vast nearness.

'What does the lady in the window think?'

'She's asleep.'   Miss Prout had really thought that. . . .

'Oh, no, she *isn't*.'

Miss Prout looked up as she approached but kept on with
her sewing and held her easy silence as she dropped into one of
the low chairs.   She was working a pattern of bright threads
on a small strip of saffron-coloured silk . . . looking much
older in the blaze of hard light.   But far off, not minding,
sitting there as if enthroned, for the morning, placid and
matronly and indifferent.   The heavenly morning freshness

was still here. But the remarks about the day had all been made on the lawn after breakfast. She admired the close bright work. Miss Prout's voice came at once, a little eagerly, explaining. She was really keen about her lovely work.

She was saying something about Paris. Miriam attended swiftly, not having grasped the beginning, only the fact that she was talking and the curious dry level of her voice. Beginning on something as every one did, ignoring the present, leaving herself sitting there outside life. She made a vague response, hoping to hear about Paris. Only to be startled by the tone and colour of her own voice. Miss Prout would imagine that her life had been full. In any case could not imagine . . .

'How long are you staying?' The question shot across at her. She did not know as she answered whether she had seen the swift hot glance of the blue eyes, or heard it in the voice. But she had found the woman who wrote the searing scenes, the strange abrupt phrases that lashed out from the page.

'To-morrow I shall be grilling in my flat,' went on Miss Prout. Alma's laughter tinkled from above. She was coming this way. Miss Prout's voice hurried on incisive, splitting the air, ending with a rush of low words as Alma appeared round the corner. Miriam watched their little scene, smooth, unbroken by a single pause or hesitation, saw them go away together, still talking.

'My hat!' she murmured to the thrilled surroundings, and again 'My *hat*!' She clutched at the fading reverberations, marvelling at her own imperviousness, at the way the drama had turned, even while it touched her, to a painted scene, leaving her unmoved. Miss Prout's little London eyrie. A distasteful refuge between visits. Had it been a flattering appeal, or an insult?

She is like the characters in her book, direct, swift, ruthless, using any means. . . . She saw me as a fool, offered me the role of one of the negligible minor characters, there to be used by the successful ones. She is one with her work, with her picture of life. But it is not a true picture. The glinting sea, all the influences pouring in from the garden, denied its existence. It was just a fuss, the biggest drama in the world was a fuss in which people competed, gambling, every one losing in the end. Dead, empty loss, on the whole, because there was always the commission to be paid. Life in the world is a vice; to which those who take it up gradually became accustomed. Her eyes clung to the splinters of gold on the rippling blue sea. Dropped them, and she was confined in the hot little rooms of a London flat. If Miss Prout was not enviable, so *feared* her lonely independence, then no one was enviable.

'Hallo, Miriametta! All alone?'

'They 've gone to look at an enormous book; too big to lift.'

'Yes. And what 's Miriam doing?'

'Isn't it a perfect morning?'

'It 's a good day. It 'll be a *corker* later on. Very pleasant here till about lunch-time. You camping here for the morning?' She looked up.

He was standing in profile, listening, with his head inclined; like a person suffering from deafness; and pointing towards her his upheld questioning finger; a German class-master.

'I don't know.'

'Then you will. That 's settled?' She murmured a speculative promise, lazily, a comment on his taut, strung-up bearing. What, to him, if she did or didn't?

'That 's agreed then. You camp here,' he dropped neatly into the chair between hers and Miss Prout's, his face hidden behind the frill of its canopy, 'for the morning.' He looked out and round at her, flushed and grinning. 'I want you to,' he murmured, 'now don't you go and forget.'

'All right,' she beamed . . . the *hours* he was wasting spinning out his mysterious drama . . . 'wild horses shan't move me.' He did not want her society. But it was miles more than wildly interesting enough that he wished to avoid being alone with Miss Prout. But then why not dump her, as he always did guests he had run through, on to Alma? He left her a moment for reflections, wound them up with a husky chuckle, and began on one of his improvisations; paying her in advance, putting in time. She listened withheld, drawing the weft of

his words through the surrounding picture, watching it enlivened, with fresher colours and stronger outlines . . . a
pause, the familiar lifting tone and the drop, into a single
italic phrase; one of his destructive conclusions. His voice
went on, but she had seized the hard glittering thread, rending
it, and watched the developing bright pattern coldly, her
opposition ready phrased for the next break. She could stay
for ever like this, watching his thought; thrusting in remarks,
making him reconsider. But Miss Prout was coming. There
would be a morning of improvisations with no chance of
arresting him. It was only when they were alone that he
would take opposition seriously, not turning it into materials
for spirals of wit, where nobody could stand against him.
The whole morning, hearing him and Miss Prout chant their
duet about people . . . helped out no doubt by the presence
of an apparently uncritical audience. I 'm hanged if I will. . . .

'I must have a book or something. I 'll get a book,' she
said, rising. He peeped out, as if weighing her suggestion.

'All right. . . . Get a book. . . . But come back?'

'Eurasians *are* different,' she said. 'Have you ever *known*
any; really *well*?'

'Never known *anybody*, Miriam. Take back everything I
ever said. Get your book and come out with it.'

On her way back she heard his voice, high; words broken
and carried along by a squeal of laughter. They were at
it already, reducing everything to absurdity. Turning the
corner she found them engrossed, sitting close at right angles,
Miss Prout leaning forward, her embroidery neglected on her
knee. It was monstrous to break in. She wandered up and
down the terrace, staring at the various views, catching his eye
upon her as she went to and fro; almost deciding to depart and
leave him to his fate. If he was engrossed he was engrossed.
If not, he shouldn't pretend to be. When she was at a distance
their voices fell, low short sentences, sounding set and colourless; but *intimate*.

'Found your book, Miriam?' he cried, as she came near.

'No. I couldn't see anything. So I shut my eyes and
whirled round and pointed.'

'Your shameless superstitions, Miriam.'

'I *am*. I 've got a lovely one I hadn't seen.'

'A lovely one. A——'

'I 'm not going to tell you what it is.'

'You 're just going to sit down and munch it up. Miriam 's a paradox. She 's the omnivorous *gourmet*.'

'Can I have a cigarette ?'

'Her authors—we 'll *get* you a cigarette, Miriam, no, all right, here they are—her authors, the only authors she allows, can be counted rather more than twice, on the fingers of one hand.'

She took two cigarettes, lighting one from his neatly struck match and retired to a distant chair.

'You 'll have the sun in your eyes there.'

'I like it.' Their voices began again, his social and expansive, hers clipped and solitary . . . the bank of blazing snapdragon grew prominent, told of nothing but the passing of time. What was the time? How much of the morning had gone ? There was a moment of clear silence. . . .

'Is Miriam there ?'

'She is indeed; very *much* there.' Again silence, filled with the echo of his comprehensive little chuckle. Miss Prout knew now that it was not the stupidity of a fool that had spoiled her morning. But, if she could go so far, why not carry him off to talk unembarrassed, or talk, here, freely, as she wanted to, like those women in her book ?

A servant, coming briskly through the sunlight, stopping half-way along the terrace.

'Mr Simpson.'

'Yes. What have you done with him ?'

'He 's in the study.'

'Fetch him out of the study. Bring him here. And bring, lemonade and things.' But he rose as the maid wheeled round and departed. 'I 'd better get him, I think. He 's Nemesis.'

Miriam rose to escape. 'Now don't you go, Miriam. You stay and see it out. You haven't met Simpson, Edna. I haven't. *No* one has.'

'What is he ?'

'He 's—he 's a postscript. The letter came this morning.

Now don't either of you desert.' He disappeared, leaving the terrace stricken. The rest of the morning, lunch, perhaps the whole day . . . Simpson. His voice returned a moment later, encouraging, as if shepherding an invalid, across the garden and round the angle. A very tall young man, in a blue serge suit, a *pink* collar and a face sunburnt all over, an even red.

He was sitting upright in a headlong silence, holding on to the thoughts with which he had come. But they were being scattered. He had held them through the introductions and Hypo's witty distribution of drinks. But now the bright air rang with the rapid questions, volleyed swiftly upon the beginnings of the young man's meditative answers, and he was sitting alone in the circle in a puzzled embarrassment, listening, but not won by Hypo's picture of Norwich, not joining in the expansion and the laughter, aware only of the scattering of his precious handful of thoughts. Towards lunch-time, Hypo carried him off to the study.

'Exit the postscript,' said Miss Prout. Charmingly . . . dropping back into her pose, but talkatively, a kindliness in the blue eyes gazing out to sea. Again she bemoaned her return to London, but added at once a little picture of her old servant; the woman's gladness at getting her back again.

'Only until the end of the week,' said Miriam seeing the old servant, perpetually left alone, getting older. Sad. Left out. But what an awful way of living in London; alone with one old servant. A brilliant light came into Miss Prout's eyes. She was looking fixedly along the terrace.

'He wouldn't stay to lunch.' Hypo, alone and gay. 'He 's *done* with me. Given me up. Gone away a wise young man.'

'He was *appalling*.'

'You didn't hear him, Miriam.'

'I saw him.'

'You didn't hear him on the subject of his guild.'

'He 's founded a *guild* ?'

'It 's much worse than that. He 's gone about, poor dear, in sublime, in the most *sublime* faith, collecting all the young men in Norfolk, under my banner. I have heard this morning all I might become if I could contrive to be . . . as wooden as he is. Come along. Let's have lunch. You know, Edna, there's a great work to be done on you. *You've* got to be turned into a socialist.' He turned as they walked, to watch her face. She was looking down, smiling, withdrawn, revealing nothing. Seething with anticipation. She would be willing. For the sake of the long conversations. They would sit apart talking, for the rest of her time. There would be long argumentative letters. No. She would not argue. She would be another of those women in the Lycurgan, posing and dressing and consciously shining at soirées. Making havoc and complications. Worse than they. How could he imagine her a socialist with her view of humanity and human motives?

'No. We *won't* make you a socialist, Edna. You're too good as you are.' Beautiful, different; too good for socialism? Then he really thought her wonderful. In some way beyond himself. . . .

Turning just in time to be caught by the sun dipping behind the cliff. Perfect sudden moment. No sunset effects. No radiance. Clean, dull colours. Mealy grey-blue sky, dull gold ball, half hidden, tilted by the slope of the green cliff. Feeling him arrested, compelled to receptive watching; watching a sunset, like any one else. The last third of the disk, going, bent intently, asserting the moment, asserting uniqueness; unanswerable mystery of beauty.

'God, reading a newspaper.'

'The way to see a sunset is to be *indoors*. Oblivious. Then . . . just a ruddy glow, reflected from a bright surface. . . . The indirect method's the method. Old Conrad.'

'Madeleine has no use for this storm-rent sky. She wants untroubled blue, one small pink cloud, and presently, a single star.' Then he must have wanted these things himself once. Why did he try to jest young people into his disillusionment?

Yet to-night the sun had set without comment. With his approval. He was openly sharing the unspoken response to the scene of its magnificent departure.

The reproachful, watching eye of Sunday disappeared,

drawn down over the horizon with the setting sun.   Leaving
a blissful refreshment, the strange unearned sense falling
always somewhere in the space between Sunday and Monday,
of a test survived, leaving one free to go forward to the cheerful
cluster of oncoming days.

The afterglow faded to a bright twilight, deepening in the
garden to a violet dusk.   The sea glimmered in the remaining
light that glared along its further rim like a yawn, holding up
the lid of the sky.   The figures in the chairs had grown dim,
each face a pale disk set towards the falling light.   The talk
died down to small shreds, simple and slow, steeped in the
beauty of the evening, deferring to it, as to a host.

They were still the guests of the evening while they sat
grouped round the lamplit veranda supper-table that turned
the dusk into night.   But the end was coming.   The voices
in the lamplight were growing excited and forgetful.   Indoors
and separation were close at hand.

He was oblivious.   Given up to his jesting . . . she watched
his jesting face, shiny now and a little loose, the pouch of his
lips as he spoke, the animal glimmer of teeth below the scraggy
moustache, repellent, yet part of the fascination of his smile, and
perpetually redeemed by the charm of his talk, the intense
charm of the glancing eyes, seeing and understanding, comforting even when they mistook, and yet all the time withheld,
preoccupied behind their clean rings and filmy sightless grey—
fixed always on the shifting changing mass of obstructive mannish knowledge, always on *science*, the only thing in the world
that could get his full attention.   She felt her voice pouring
out suddenly, violently quenching a flicker of speech.   He
glanced, attentive, healing her despair with his quick interest.
The women awoke from their conspiring trance, alert towards
her, watching.

'Yes.'   His voice followed hers without a break, cool, a
comment on her violence.   He turned, looking into the night.
His shaggy intelligent gaze, the reflective slight lift of his eyebrows, gave him the look of an old man lost.   The rosy scene
was chilled.   Cold light and harsh black shadow, his averted
form in profile, helpless, making empty the deeps of the thing

that was called a summer night. Her desire beat no longer towards the open scene. She hated it. For its sake she had pulled him up, brought down this desolation.

'It's a good night. It's about the human optime in nights. We ought to sleep out.' He turned back to the table, gathering up expressions, radiating his amusement at the disarray caused by his temporary absence.

'Let's sleep out. Miriam will. Unless we lock her in.' He was on his feet, eagerly halted, gathering opinions. His eyes came to rest on Alma. 'Let's be dogs. Be driven, by Miriam, into fresh fields of experience.'

Would it happen? Would she agree? He was impatient, but deferring. Alma sat considering, in the attitude Mr Stoner had called a pretty snap, her elbows meeting on the table, her chin on her slender hands; just its point, resting on the bridge they made laid flatly one upon the other. It was natural in her. But by now she knew that men admired natural poses. *He* was admiring, even through his impatience.

'I didn't suggest it. I've never slept out in my life.'

'You suggested it, Miriam. My death, all our little deaths from exposure, will lie at your door.' The swift personal glance he dealt her from the midst of his watching swept round to Miss Prout and flashed into admiration as he turned, still sideways surveying her, to bend his voice on Alma.

'It's quite manageable, eh, Susan?' Miriam followed his eyes. Miss Prout had risen and was standing away from the table posed like a Gainsborough; challenging head, skirts that draped and spread of themselves, gracefully, from the slenderness of her body. She was waiting, indifferent, interpreting the scene in her way, interpreting the other women for him, united with him in interpreting them. . . .

Alma relaxed and looked up, holding the matter poised, deliberately locating the casting vote before breaking into enthusiasm. He paid tribute, coming round the table companionably to her side, but still looking from face to face, claiming audience.

'We'll break out. Each bring its little mattress and things. After they've retired. Yes, I think, *after* they've retired.'

Why the conspirator's smile? The look of daring? What of the servants? They were bound, anyhow, to know in the morning.

It was glorious to rush about in the lit house, shouting unnecessary remarks. People shouting back. Nobody attending. Shouting and laughing for the sake of the jolly noise. Saying more than could be said in talk. Admitting.

And then just to lie extinguished in the darkness wondering what point there was in sleeping out if you went to sleep at once. All that jolly tumult. And he had been so intent on the adventure that he had let Miss Prout change her mind without protest, *only* crying out towards her open window, from the midst of busily arranging his bed on the lawn. . . . 'Have you seen Miriam's pigtails?'

And suddenly everything was prim; the joy of being out in the night surging in the air, waiting for some form of expression. They didn't *know* how to be joyful; only how to be clever. . . . She hummed a little song and stopped. It wreathed about her, telling off the beauties of the night, a song sung by someone else, heard, understood, a perfect agreement.

'What is she doing?'

'She's sitting up, waving her banana in the air; conducting an orchestra, I think.'

'Tell her to *eat* the banana and lie down.' Alma, Rose Gauntlett, Mrs Perry and me, starting off just after I came, to paddle in the moonlight. . . . 'Don't, *don't* do anything that would make a cabman laugh.' Why not? Why should he always imagine someone waiting to be shocked? Damn the silly cabman if he *did* laugh. Who need care? As soon as her head was on the pillow, nothing visible but the huge night and the stars, she spoke quietly to herself, flouting them. He should see, hear, that it was wicked to simmer stuffily down as if they were in the house. He didn't want to. She was making his sounds for him.

'Tell Miriam this is not a conversazione.'

His voice was actually sleepy. Kindly, long-suffering, but simply wanting to go to sleep. There was to be no time of being out in the night with him. He was too far off. She imagined herself at his side, a little space of grass between. Silent communication, understanding and peace. All the things that were lost, obliterated by his swift speech, communicated to him at leisure, clear in the night. Here under the veranda, with its roof cutting off a part of the sky, they were still attached to the house. Alma had been quietly posed for sleep from the first moment. They were all more separated than in their separate rooms indoors.

The lingering faint light reflected the day, the large open space of misunderstandings, held off the cloak of darkness in which things grew clear. She lay watching for the night to turn to night.

But the light seemed to grow clearer as the stillness went on. The surrounding objects lost their night-time mystery. Teased her mind with their names as she looked from point to point. Drove up her eyes to search for night in the sky. But there was no night there. Only a wide high thinness bringing an expansion of sight that could not be recalled; drawing her out, beyond return, into a wakefulness that was more than day-time wakefulness; a breathless feeling of being poised untethered in the thin blue-lit air, without weight of body; going forward, more and more thinly expanded, into the pale wide space.

There is no night. . . . Compared to this expanse of thin, shadowless, boundless light the sunlit sky is a sort of darkness. Even in a motionless high midday the sky is small, part of it invisible, obliterated by light. After sunset it is hidden by changing colours.

This is the real sky, in full power, stripping away sleep. Time, visible, pouring itself out. Day, not night, is forgetfulness of time. Its movement is a dream. Only in its noise is real silence and peace. This awful stillness is made of sound; the sound of time, *pouring* itself out; ceaselessly winding off short strips of life, each life a strip of sleepless light, so much, no more, lessening all the time.

What rubbish to talk about the stars. Vast suns, at immense distances, and beyond them, more. What then? If you imagine yourself at any point in space or wafting freely about from star to star you are not changed. Like enlarging the circle of your acquaintance. And finding it, in the end, the same circle, yourself. A difference in degree is also a difference in kind? Yes. But the *same* difference. Relations remain the same however much things are changed. Interest in the stars is like interest in your neighbours before you get to know them. A way of running away from yourself.

What is there to do? How know what is any one's best welfare?

To be alive, and to know it, makes a selfless life impossible. Any kind of life accompanied by that stupendous knowledge, is selfish.

Christ? But all the time he was alone with a certainty. To-day thou shalt be with me. . . . He was booked for paradise from the beginning . . . like the man in *No. 5 John Street* going to live in a slum, imagining he was experiencing a slum, with the latchkey of his West End house in his pocket. Now if he had sacrificed paradise. But he couldn't. Then where was selflessness?

Yet if Christ had never been, the sky would look different. A Grecian or a Jewish sky. Awful. If the personal delight that the sky showed to be nothing were put away? Nothing held on to but the endless pouring down of time? Till an answer came. Get up to-morrow showing indifference to everything, refusing to be bewitched. There *is* an answer or there would be no question. Night is torment. That is why people go to sleep. To avoid clear sight and torment.

To-morrow, certainly, gloriously, the day-time scenes, undeserved, uncontributed to, would go forward again in the sunlight. Forgetfulness would come of itself. Even the thought of the bright scenes, the scenes that did not matter and were nothing, spread over the sky the sense of the dawn it would be obliged to bring; the permitted postponement of the problems set by night. Dawn stole into the heart. With a sudden answer. That had no words. An answer that lost itself again in the day. But there would be no dawn; only the pitiless beginning of a day spoiled by the fever of a sleepless night. Torment, for nothing. The sky gazed down mocking at fruitless folly. She turned away. She must, would, sleep. But her eyes were full of the down-bent stars. Condemnation, and the communication that would not speak; stopping short, poised, probing for a memory that was there. . . .

A harsh hissing sigh, far away; gone. The unconscious sea. Coming back. Bringing the morning tide. The sound would increase. The sky would thicken and come near, fill up with increasing blind light, ignoring unanswered pain.

'You can put tea in the bedrooms.'

Alma, folded in her dressing-gown, disappearing into the house. The tumbled empty bed on the lawn, white in the open stare of the morning.

'Edna wants to know how we're getting on.' Duplication in light and darkness, of memories of the night. . . . Their two figures, side by side, silhouetted against dark starry blue. Dismantled voices. His *simplicity*. His sharp turn and toga'd march towards the house. A memory of dawn; a deep of sleep ending in faint light tinting the garden? 'Edna wants to know how we're getting on.' *Then* starlit darkness? Angry sleep leading direct to this open of morning.

Every one in the house had plunged already into new beginnings. Panoplied in advantages; able to feel in strong refreshed bodies the crystal brightness of the morning; not worn out as if by long illness.

It was Miss Prout, coming from her quiet night indoors, who was reaping the adventure. She had some strange conscious power. She knew that it was she who was the symbol of morning. Her look of age was gone. She had dared to come out in a wrapper of mealy white, folded softly; and with bare feet that gleamed against the green of the flat grass. Consciously using the glow of adventure left over from the night to engrave her triumphant effect upon the adventurers; of marvellous youth that was not hers but belonged to some secret living in her stillness. . . . It was not an illusion. He saw it too; let her stand for the morning; was crowning her all the time, preoccupied in everything he said with the business of rendering half-amused approval of her miracle. The talk was hampered, as if, by common consent, prevented from getting far enough to interfere with the set shape of spectacle and spectators; yet easy, its quality heightened by the common recognition of an indelible impression. For a moment it made her power seem almost innocent of its strange horror.

When she had left the day was stricken. Evil had gone from the air, leaving it empty. Everything that happened seemed to be a conspiracy to display emptiness. The daily life of the house came into view, visible as it was, when no guests were there, going bleakly on its way. Hypo appeared and disappeared. Rapt and absent, though still swiftly observant and, between whiles, his unchanged talking self; falling back, with his chuckling unspoken commentary, for lack of kindred brilliance; escaping to his study as if to a waiting guest.

Miriam came to dinner silently raging; invisible, yet compelled to be seen. Reduced to nonentity by his wrongly directed awareness, his everlasting demand for bright fussy intelligence. It was her own fault. The result of having been beguiled by joy into a pretence of conformity. For the rest of the visit she would be roughly herself. To shreds she would tear his twofold vision of women as bright intelligent response or complacently smiling audience. Force him to see the evil in women who made terms with men, the poison there was in the trivial gaiety of those who accepted male definitions of life and the world. Somehow make him aware of the reality that fell, all the time, in the surrounding silence, outside his shapes and classifications.

Sunk away into separation, she found herself gliding into communion with surrounding things, shapes gleaming in the twilight, the intense thrilling beauty of the deep, lessening colours. . . . She passed into association with them, feeling him fade, annihilated, while her eased breathing released the strain of battle. He was spending the seconds of silence that to him were a void, in observation, misinterpretations. The air was full of his momentary patience. She turned smiling and caught his smile halting between amused contemplation of vacuity and despairing sympathy with boredom. He had not heard the shouts of repudiation with which she had plunged down into her silence. He dropped her and let

his testing eye, which he knew she followed, rest on Alma.
Two vacuities . . . watched by empty primitive eyes, savage
eyes, under shaggy brows, staring speculatively out through a
forest of eyelash. Having thus made his statement and
caught Alma's attention he made a little drama of childish
appeal, with plaintive brows, pleading for rescue.

'Let's have some light. We're almost in darkness,' said
Alma.

'We are, we are,' he wailed, and Miriam caught his eyes
flashed upon her to collect her acceptance of his judgment.
The central light Alma had risen to switch on, flashed up over
the silk-clad firm little column of her body winged on either
side by the falling drapery of her extended arms, and revealed
as she sat down the triangle of pendant-weighted necklace on
her white throat, the soft squareness of her face, peaked below
by the delicate sharp chin and above by her piled gold hair.
The day had gone; quenched in the decoration of the night
set there by Alma, like the first scene of a play into whose
speech and movement she was, with untroubled impersonal
bearing, already steadily launched, conscious of the audience,
untroubled by their anticipation.

'It's *awful*. The evenings are already getting short,' cried
Miriam, her voice thrilling in conversation with the outer
living spaces beyond the shut-in play. His swiftly flashed
glance lingered a moment; incredulous of her mental wandering? In stupefaction that was almost interest, over her persistence, after diagnosis, in utter banality?

Alma's voice, strangely free, softly lifted a little above its
usual note, but happy and full, as it was with outsiders with
whom she was at her best, took possession of the set scene.
His voice came in answer, deferring, like that of a delighted
guest. Presently they were all in an enchantment. From
some small point of departure she had carried them off abroad,
into an Italian holiday. He urged her on with his voice, his
eyes returning perpetually from the business of his meal to
rest in admiring delight upon her face. It was lovely, radiant,
full of the joy of the theme she had set in the midst and was
holding there with bright reflective voice, unattained by the little

bursts of laughter, piling up her monologue, laughing her own laughter in its place, leading on little bridges of gay laughter that did not break her speech, to the points of her stories. All absurd. All making the places she described pathetically absurd, and mysterious strangers, square German housewives and hotel people, whom Miriam knew she would for ever remember as they looked in Alma's tales, and love, absurd. But vivid; each place, the look and the sound and the very savour of it, each person. . . .

By the end of dinner, in the midst of eating a peach, Alma was impersonating a fat shiny Italian opera star, flinging out, without losing her dainty charm, a scrap of a rolling cadence, its swift final run up and up in curling trills to leap clear at the end to a single note, terrifically high, just touched and left on the air, the fat singer silent below it, unmoved and more mountainous than before.

Hypo was wholly won by the enchantment she had felt and cast. His face was smooth with the pleasure that wreathed it whenever he passed, listening, from laughter that was not of his own making, to more laughter. He carried Alma off to the study with the bright eagerness he gave to an entertaining guest, but intimately, with his arm through hers.

They sat side by side on the wide settee. There was to be no music. He did not want to go away by himself to the other end of the room and make music. Sitting forward with his hands clasped, towards Alma enthroned, he suddenly improvised a holiday abroad. . . . 'We'll go mad, stark staring mad. Switzerland. Your ironmongery in my rucksack, and off we'll go.'

To go away, not the wonderful eventful holiday life here; to go away, with Alma, was reward and holiday for him. . . . This life, with its pattern of guests was the hard work of every day? These times abroad were the bright points of their long march together? Then if this life and its guests were so little, she was once more near to them. She had shared their times abroad, by first unconsciously kindling them to go. And presently they were deferring to her. It was strange that the fact of having preceded them, created, even with them, the sense of advantage persisting so long after they had outdone in such wide sweeps the scope of her small experience.

She had never deliberately 'gone abroad.' Following necessity, she had found herself in Germany and in Belgium. Pain and joy in equal balance all the time and in memory only joy. So that all going abroad by other people seemed, even while envy rose at the ease and quantity of their expeditions, their rich collection of notorious beauty, somehow slight. Envy was incomplete. She could not by stern reasoning and close effort of imagination persuade herself that they had been so deeply abroad as she. That they had ever utterly lost themselves in foreign things. She forgot perpetually, in this glad moment she again found that she had forgotten, having been abroad. She forgot it when she read and thought by herself of other parts of the world. Yet when, as now, any one reminded her, she was at once alight, weighed down by the sense of accomplishment, of rich deeps of experience that would never leave her. Others were bright and gay about their wanderings. But, even while pining for their free movement, she was beside herself with longing to convey to them the clear deep sense they seemed to lack of what they were doing. The wonder of it. She talked to them about Switzerland, where they had already been. It was for her the unattainable ideal of a holiday. She resented it when he belittled the scenery, gathered it up in a few phrases and offered any good gorge in the Ardennes as an alternative. It was not true. He *was* entranced with Switzerland. It was the protuberance of the back of his head that made him oppose. And his repudiation of any form of expression that did not jest. She sought and found a weapon. To go to Switzerland in the summer was not to go. She had suddenly remembered all she had heard about Swiss winters. Switzerland in the summer was an oleograph. In winter an engraving. That impressed him. And when she had described all she remembered, she had forgotten she had not been. And they had forgotten. They had come into her experience as it looked to herself. Their questions went on, turned to her life in London. She was besieged by things to communicate, going on and on, wondering all the time where the interest lay, in remote people, most of them perceived only once and remembered once as speech, yet feeling it, and knowing that they felt it. There was a clue, some clue to some essential thing, in her mood. Suddenly she awoke to see them sitting propped close against each other, his cheek cushioned on her crown of hair, both of them blinking beseechingly towards her.

'*How* long,' she raged, 'have you been sitting there cursing me?'

'Not been cursing, Miriam. You've been interesting, no end. But there's a thing, Miriam, an awful thing called to-morrow morning.'

'Is it late?' The appalling, the utter and everywhere appalling scrappiness of social life. . . .

'Not for you, Miriam. We're poor things. We envy. We can't compete with your appetite, your disgraceful young appetite for late hours.'

'Things always end just as they're beginning.'

'Things end, Miriam, so that other things may begin.'

She roused herself to give battle. But Alma drifted between, crying gaily that there was to-morrow. A good strong to-morrow. Warranted to stand hard wear.

'And turn; and take a dye when you're tired of the colour.'

He laughed, really amused? Or crediting her with an attempt to talk in a code?

'A to-morrow that will wear for ever and make a petticoat afterwards.'

He laughed again. Quite simply. He had not heard that old jest. Seemed never to have heard the old family jests. Seemed to have grown up without jests. To-morrow, unless no one came, would not be like to-day.

The morning offered a blissful eternity before lunch. She had wakened drowsy with strength and the apprehension of good, and gone through breakfast like a sleepwalker, playing her part without cost, independent of sight and hearing and thought. Successful. Dreamily watching a play, taking a part inaudibly dictated, without effort, seeing it turn into the chief part, more and more turned over to her as she lay still in the hands of the invisible prompter; withdrawn in an exploration of the features of this state of being that nothing could reach or disturb. If, this time, she could discover its secret, she would be launched in it for ever.

Back in her room she prepared swiftly to go out and meet the day in the open; all the world, waiting in the happy garden. Through the house-stillness sounded three single downward-stepping notes . . . the first phrase of the seventh symphony. Perfect. Eternity stating itself in the stillness. He knew it, choosing just this thing to play to himself, alone; living in space alone, at one with everybody, as every one was, the moment life allowed. Beethoven's perfect expression of the perfection of life, first thing in the morning. Morning stillness; single dreaming notes that blossomed in it and left it undisturbed; moved on into a pattern and then stood linked together in a single perfect chord. Another pattern in the same simple notes, and another chord. Dainty little chords bowing to each other; gentle gestures that gradually became an angelic little dance through which presently a song leapt forth, the single opening notes brought back, caught up and swept into song pealing rapturously out.

He was revealing himself as he was when alone, admitting Beethoven's vision of life as well as seeing the marvellous things Beethoven did with his themes? But he liked best the slamming, hee-hawing rollick of the last movement. Because it did so much with a theme that was almost nothing. . . . *Bang*, toodle-oodle-oodle, *Bang*, toodle-*oodle*-oodle, *Bang*, toodle-oodle-oodle-*oo*. A lumpish phrase; a Clementi finger exercise played suddenly in startling fortissimo by an impatient school-boy; smashed out with the full force of the orchestra, taken up, slammed here and there, up and down, by a leaping, plunging, heavy-hoofed pantaloon, approving each variation with loud guffaws. The sly swift dig-in-the-ribs of the sudden pianissimos.

To watch a shape adds interest to listening. But something disappears in listening with the form put first. Hearing only form is a kind of perfect happiness. But in coming back there is a reproach; as if it had been a kind of truancy. . . . People who care only for form think themselves superior. Then there is something wrong with them.

On the landing table, a letter lay waiting for the post. She passed by, gladly not caring to glance. But a tingling in her shoulders drew her back. She had reached the garden door. The music now pouring busily through from the next room urged her forward. But once outside she would have become a party to bright reasonableness, a foolish frontage, caricatured from behind. She fled back along her path to music that was once more the promise of joy . . . to read the address of one of Alma's tradespeople, a distasteful reminder of the wheels of dull work perpetually running under the surface of beauty? But this morning it would not attain her. It was not Alma's hand, but the small running shape like a scroll, each part a tiny perfection. She bent over it. *Miss Edna Prout*. . . . This, then, was what she had come back to find; poison for the day. The house was silent as a desert; empty, swept clear of life. The roomful of music was in another world. Alone in it, he had written to her and then sat down, thinking of her, to his music.

Complications are enlivening. Within the sunlight, in the great spread of glistening sea, in the touch of the free air and the look of the things set down on the bench, there was a lively intensity. A demand for search; for a thought that would obliterate the smear on the blue and gold of the day. The thought had been there even at the moment of shock. The following tumult was the effort to find it. To get round behind the shock and slay it before it could slay. To agree. That was the answer. Not to care. To show how much you care by deliberately not caring? People show disapproval of their own actions by defending them. By deliberately not hiding or defending them, they show off a version of their actions. That they don't themselves accept.

Meantime everything passes. There are always the powerful intervals. Meetings, and then intervals in which other things come up and life speaks directly, to the individual. . . . Except for married people. Who are all a little absurd, to themselves and to all other married people. That is why they always talk so hard when two couples are together? To cover the din of their thoughts. This marriage was a success without being an exception to the rule that all marriages are failures, as he said. Why are they failures? Science, the way of thinking and writing that makes everybody seem small, in all these new books. Biology, *Darwin*. The way men, who have no inner convictions, no self, fasten upon an idea and let it describe life for them. Always a new idea. Always describing and destroying, their ideas filtering down, as time goes on, to quite simple people, poisoning their lives, because men must have a formula. Men are gossips. Science is . . . cosmic scandalmongering.

Science is Cosmic Scandalmongering. Perhaps that might do for the House of Lords. But those old fogies are not particularly scientific. They quote the classics. The same thing. Club gossip. Centuries of unopposed masculine gossip about the universe.

Years ago he said there will be no more him and her, the novels of the future will be clear of all that. Poetry nothing. Religion nothing. Women a biological contrivance. And now. Women still a sort of attachment to life, useful, or delightful . . . the 'civilized women of the future' to be either bright obedient assistants or providers of illusion for times of leisure. Two kinds, neatly arranged, each having only one type of experience, while men have both, *and* their work, into which women can only come as Hindus, obediently carrying out tasks set by men, dressed in uniform, deliberately sexless and deferential. How can any one feel romantic about him? Alma. But that is the real old-fashioned romance of every day, from her girlhood. Hidden through loyalty to his shifting man's ideas? Half convinced by them? How can people be romantic impermanently, just now and again?

Romance is solitary and permanent. Always there. In everybody. That is why the things one hears about people are like stories, not referring to life. Why I always forget them when the people themselves are there. Or believe, when they

talk of their experiences, that they misread them. I can't
believe even now in the reality of any of his experiences. But
then I don't believe in the experiences of any one, except a
few people who have left sayings I know are true. . . . Everything else, all the expressions, history and legend and novels
and science and everybody's talk, seems irrelevant. That's
why I don't want experience, not to be caught into the ways
of doing and being that drive away solitude, the marvellous
quiet sense of life at first hand. . . . But he knows that too.
'Life drags one along by the hair shrieking protests at every
yard.'

'Hullo! What is she doing all alone?'

The surrounding scene that had gradually faded, leaving her
eyes searching in the past for the prospect she could never quite
recall, shone forth again.

'I've got to do a review.'

'What's the book?'

'When you are in France, does a French river look different
to you; *French?*'

'No, Miriam. It—doesn't look different.'

He glanced for a moment shaggily from point to point of the
sunlit scene and sat companionably down, turned towards her
with a smile at her discomfiture. 'What's the book, Miriam?
It's jolly down here. We'll have some chairs. Yes? You
can't write on a bench.'

He was gone. Meaning to come back. In the midst of the
morning; in the midst of his preoccupations, sociably at leisure.
She felt herself sink into indifference. The unique opportunity
was offering itself in vain. He came back just as she had begun
to imagine him caught, up at the house, by a change of impulse. Or perhaps an unexpected guest.

'What's the review?'

'*The House of Lords.*'

'Read it?'

'I can't. It's all post hoc.'

'Then you've read it.'

'I haven't read it. I've only sniffed the first page.'

'That's enough. Glance at the conclusion. Get your

statement, three points; that 'll run you through a thousand words. Look here—shall I write it for you?'

'I 've got *fifty* ideas,' she said, beginning to write.

'That 's too many, Miriam. That 's the trouble with you. You 've got too many ideas. You 're messing up your mind, quite a good mind, with too swift a succession of ideas.' She wrote busily on, drinking in his elaboration of his view of the state of her mind. 'H'm,' he concluded, stopping suddenly; but she read in the sound no intention of breaking away because she had nothing to say to him. He was watching, in some way interested. He sat back in his chair; sympathetically withheld. Actually deferring to her work.

She tore off the finished page and transfixed it on the grass with a hatpin. Her pencil flew. The statement was finished and leading to another. Perhaps he was right about three ideas. A good shape. The last must come from the book. She would have to consult it. No. It should be left till later. Her second page joined the first. It was incredible that he should be sitting there inactive, obliterated by her work.

She tore off the third sheet and dropped her pencil on the grass.

'Finished? Three sheets in less than twenty minutes. How do you do it, Miriam?'

'It 'll do. But I shall have to copy it. I 've resisted the temptation to say what *I* think about the House of Curmudgeons. Trace it back to the First Curmudgeon. Yet it seems somehow wrong to write in the air, so *currently*. The first time I did a review, of a bad little book on Whitman, I spent a fortnight of evenings reading.'

'You began at the creation. Said everything you had to say about the history of mankind.'

'I went nearly mad with responsibility and the awfulness of discovering the way words express almost nothing at all.'

'It 's not quite so bad as that. You 've come on no end though, you know. The last two or three have been astonishingly good. You 're not creative. You 've got a good sound mind, a good style, and a curious intense critical perception.

You 'll be a critic.   But writing, Miriam, should be done with
a pen.   Can't call yourself a writer till you do it *direct*.'

'How can I write with a pen, in bed, on my knee, at midnight
or dawn?'

'A fountain pen?'

'No one can write with a fountain pen.'

'Quite a number of us do.   Quite a number of not altogether
unsuccessful little writers, Miriam.'

'Well, it 's wrong.   How can thought or anything, well,
thought perhaps can, which doesn't matter and nobody really
cares about, wait a minute, nothing *else* can come through a
hand whose fingers are held stiffly apart by a fat slippery barrel.
A writing-machine.   A quill would be the thing, with a fine
flourishing tail.   But it is too important.   It squeaks out an
important sense of *writing*, makes people too objective, so that
it 's as much a man's pen, a mechanical, see life steadily and see
it whole (when nobody knows what life *is*) man's view sort
of implement as a fountain pen.   A pen should be thin, not
disturbing the hand, and the nib flexible and silent, with up
and down strokes.   Fountain-pen writing is like . . . demo-
cracy.'

'Why not go back to clay tablets?'

'Machine-made things are dead things.'

'You came down here by *train*, Miriam.'

'I ought to have flown.'

'You 'll fly yet.   No.   Perhaps you won't.   When your
dead people have solved the problem, you 'll be found weeping
over the rusty skeleton of a locomotive.'

'I don't mean Lilienfeld and Maxim.   I can be fearfully
interested in all that when I think of it.   But to the people who
do not see the beginning of flying it won't seem wonderful.
It won't change anything.'

'It 'll change, Miriam, pretty well everything.   And if you
don't mean Lilienfeld and Maxim what *do* you mean?'

'Well, by inventing the telephone we 've damaged the
chances of telepathy.'

'Nonsense, Miriam.   You 're suffering from too much
Taylor.'

'The most striking thing about Taylor is that he does not want to develop his powers.'

'What powers?'

'The things in him that have made him discover things that you admit are true; that make you interested in his little paper.'

'They 're not right, you know, about their phosphoric bank; energy is not a simple calculable affair.'

'Now here 's a strange thing. That time you met them, the first thing you said when they 'd gone, was "What 's *wrong* with them?" And the next time I met them they said, "There 's something *wrong* with him." The truth is you are polar opposites and have everything to learn from each other.'

'Mary Everest Boole.'

'Yes. And without him no one would have heard of her. No one understood. And now psychology is going absolutely her way. In fifty years' time her books will be as clear as daylight.'

'Damned obstructive classics. That 's what all our books will be. But I 'll give you Mrs Boole. Mrs Boole is a very wonderful lady. She 's the unprecedented.'

'There you are. Then you must admit the Taylors.'

'I 'm not so sure about your little Taylors. There 's nothing to be said, you know, for just going about not doing things.'

'They *are* wonderful. Their atmosphere is the freest I know.'

'I envy you your enthusiasms, Miriam. Even your misplaced enthusiasms.'

'You go there, worn out, at the end of the day, and have to walk, after a long tram-ride through the wrong part of London, along raw new roads, dark little houses on either side, solid, without a single break, darkness, a street-lamp, more darkness, another lamp; and something in the air that lets you down and down. Partly the thought of these streets increasing, all the time, all over London. Yet when someone said walking home after a good evening at the Taylors' that the thought of having to settle down in one of those houses made him feel suicidal, I felt he was wrong; and saw them, from inside, bright and big; people's homes.'

'They 're not big, Miriam. You wanted to marry him.'

'Good heavens. An Adam's apple, sloping shoulders, and a Cockney accent.'

'*I* have a Cockney accent, Miriam.

' . . .'

'Don't go about classifying with your ears. People, you know, are very much alike.'

'They 're utterly different.'

'Your vanity. Go on with your Taylors.'

'They are very much like other people.'

'With *my* Taylors. I 'm interested; really.'

'Well, suddenly you are in their kitchen. White walls and aluminium and a smell of fruit. Do you know the smell of root vegetables cooking slowly in a casserole?'

'I 'll imagine it. Right. Where are the Taylors?'

'You are all standing about. Happy and undisturbed. None of that feeling of darkness and strangeness and the need for a fresh beginning. Tranquillity. As if someone had gone away.'

'The devil; exorcized, poor dear.'

'No, but glorious. Making every one move like a song. And talk. You are all, at once, bursting with talk. All over the flat, in and out of the rooms. George washing up all the time, wandering about with a dish and a cloth, and Dora probably doing her hair in a dressing-gown, and cooking. It 's the only place where I can talk exhausted and starving.'

'What do you talk about?'

'Everything. We find ourselves sitting in the bathroom, engrossed — long speeches — they talk to each other, like strangers talking intimately on a bus. Then something boils over and we all drift back to the kitchen. Left to herself, Dora would go on for ever and sit down to a few walnuts at midnight.'

'Mary.'

'But she is an absolutely perfect cook. An artist. She invents and experiments. But he has a feminine consciousness, though he 's a most manly little man with a head like Beethoven. So he 's practical. Meaning he feels with his nerves and has a perfect sympathetic imagination. So presently we are all sitting down to a meal and the evening begins to look short.

And yet endless. With them everything feels endless; the present I mean. They are so immediately alive. Everything and everybody is abolished. We *do* abolish them, I assure you. And a new world is there. You feel language changing, every word moving, changed, into the new world. *But*, when their friends come in the evening, weird people, real cranks, it disappears. They all seem to be attacking things they don't understand. I gradually become an old-fashioned conservative. But the evening is wonderful. None of these people mind how far or how late they walk. And it goes on till the small hours.'

'You 're getting your college time with these little people.'

'No. I 'm easily the most stupidly cultured person there.'

'Then you 're feeding your vanity.'

'I 'm not. Even the charlatans make me feel ashamed of my sham advantage. No; the thing that is most wonderful about those Tuesdays is waking up utterly worn out, having a breakfast of cold fruit in the cold grey morning, a rush for the train, a last sight of the Taylors as they go off into the London Bridge crowd, and then suddenly feeling utterly refreshed. They do too. It 's an effect we have on each other.'

'How did you come across them ?'

'Michael. Reads *Reynolds's*. A notice of a meeting of London Tolstoyans. We rushed out in the pouring rain to the Edgeware Road and found nothing at the address but a barred-up corner shop-front. Michael wanted to go home. I told him to go and stood staring at the shop waiting for it to turn into the Tolstoyans. I knew it would. It did. Just as Michael was almost screaming in the middle of the road, I turned down a side street and found a doorway, a bead of gas shining inside just showing a stone staircase. We crept up and found a bare room, almost in darkness, a small gas jet, and a few rows of kitchen chairs and a few people sitting scattered about. A young man at a piano picked out a few bars of Grieg and played them over and over again. Then the meeting began. Dora, reading a paper on Tolstoi's ideas. Well, I felt I was hearing the whole truth spoken aloud for the first time. But oh, the discussion. . . . A gaunt man got up and began to rail at everything, going on till George gently asked him to keep to the subject. He raved then about some self-help book he had read. Quite incoherent; and convincing. Then the young man at the piano made a long speech about hitching your wagon to a star and at the end of it a tall woman, so old that she could hardly stand, stood up and chanted, in a deep laughing voice, Wagons and stars. Wagons and stars. To-day I am a wagon. To-morrow a star. I'm reminded of the societies who look after young women. Meet them with a cup of tea, call a cab, put the young woman and the cup of tea into the cab. Am I to watch my brother's blunderings? No. I am his lover. Then he becomes a star. And I am a star. Then an awful man, very broad-shouldered and narrow-hipped, with a low forehead and a sweeping moustache bounded up and shouted: I am a God! You, madam, are a goddess! Tolstoi is over-civilized! That's why he loves the godlike peasant. All metaphysicians, artists, and pious people are sensualists. All living in unnatural excesses. The Zulu is a god. How many women in filthy London can nurse their children? What is a woman? *Children.* What is the glory of man? Un-imaginable to town slaves. They go through life ignorant of manhood, and the metaphysicians wallow in pleasures. Men and women are divine. There is no other divinity. Let them not sell their godhead for filthy food and rotting houses and Moloch factories. What stands in the way? The pious people, the artists, and the metaphysicians. Then a gentleman, in spectacles at the back, quietly said that Tolstoi's ideas were eclectic and could never apply generally. Of course he was right, but it doesn't make Tolstoi any the less true. And you know when I hear all these convincing socialists planning things that really would make the world more comfortable, they always in the end seem ignorant of *humanity*; always behind them I see little Taylor, unanswerable, standing for more difficult deep-rooted individual things. It's *individuals* who must change, one by one.'

'Socialism will give the individual his chance.'

'Yes, I know. I agree in a way. You've shown me all that. I know environment and ways of thinking *do* partly make people. But Taylor makes socialism, even when its arguments floor him, look such a feathery, passing thing.'

'You stand firm, Miriam. Socialism isn't feathery. *You*'re feathery. One thinks you're there, and suddenly finds you playing on the other side of the field.'

'It's the fact that socialism is a *side* that makes it look so shaky. And then there's Reich; an absolute blaze of light . . . on the outside side of things.'

'Not a blaze of anything, my dear Miriam, a poor, hard-working, popular lecturer.'

'Everybody in London is listening. Hearing the most illuminating things.'

'What do they illuminate?'

'Ourselves. The English. Continuing Buckle. He's got a clear cool hard unprejudiced foreign mind.'

'Your foreigners, Miriam. They haven't the monopoly of intelligence.'

'I know. You think the English are *the* people. But so does Reich. Really he would interest you. You *must* let me tell you his idea. Just the shape of it. Badly. He puts it so well that you know he has something up his sleeve. He has. He's a Hungarian patriot. That is his inspiration. That England shall save Europe, and therefore Hungary, from the Germans. You must let me just tell you without interrupting. Two minutes.'

'*I*'m intelligent, Miriam. *You*'re intelligent. You have distinction of mind. But a really surprising lack of expression, you know. You misrepresent yourself most tremendously.'

'You mean I haven't a voice, that way of talking about things that makes one know people don't believe what they say and are thinking most about the way they are talking. Bah.'

'Clear thought makes clear speech.'

'Well. Reich says that history so far is always one thing. The Hellenization of Europe. . . . The Greeks were the first to evolve universal ideals. Which were passed on. Through two channels. Lawgiving Rome. And the Roman Church; Paul, who had made Christianity a universal working scheme. So Europe has been Hellenized. And the Hellenization of the *rest* of the world will be through its Europeanization. The enemy to this is the rude materialistic modern Germany. The only hope, England. Which he calls a nation of ignorant specialists, ignorant of history; believing only in race, which doesn't exist—a blindfold humanitarian giant, utterly unaware that other people are growing up in Europe and have the use of their eyes. The French don't want to do anything outside their large pleasant home. They are the sedentary Greeks; townspeople. The English are Romans, official, just, inartistic. Good colonists, not intrinsically, but because they send so much of their best away from their little home. A child can see that the English and Americans care less for money than any people in the western world, are adventurous and wandering and improvident; the only people with ideals and a sense of the future. Inartistic.

'Geography he calls the ground symphony of history, but nothing more, or Ireland would play first fiddle in Great Britain. The rest is having to fight for your life and being visited by your neighbours. England has attracted thousands of brilliant foreigners, who have made her, including the Scotch, who until they became foreigners in England were nothing. And the foreigner of foreigners is the permanently alien Jew. And the genius of all geniuses Loyola, because he made all his followers permanent aliens. Countries without foreigners are doomed. Like Hungary. Doomed to extinction if England does not beat Germany. That's all.'

'There won't, if we can help it, be any need for England to beat Germany. There are, you know, possibly unobserved by your rather wildly rocketing Reich, a few eyes in England. That war can be written away; by journalists and others, written into absurdity.'

'Oh, I'm so glad. Listening to Reich makes one certain that the things that seem to be happening in the world are illusions and the real result of the unseen present movement of history is war with Germany. I don't like Reich. His idea of making everything begin with Greece. His awful idea that art follows only on pressure and war. Yet it is true that the harassed little seaboard peoples who lived insecurely *did* have their art periods after they had fought for their lives. Then no more wars, no more art. . . . *Well;* perhaps art, like war, is just male ferocity!'

'Nonsense, Miriam.'

'Do you really think the war can be written away? There are so many opinions, and reading keeps one always balanced between different sets of ideas.'

'You 're too omnivorous, Miriam. You get the hang of too many things. You 're scattered.'

'The better you hear a thing put, the more certain you are there 's another view. And then there are *motives.*'

'Ah, now you 're talking. Motives; can be used. Almost any sort of motive can be roped in; and directed. You ought to write up that little meeting by the way. You 're lucky, you know, Miriam, in your opportunities for odd experience. Write it up. Don't forget.'

'You weren't there. It wasn't a joke. I don't want to be facetious about it.'

'You 're too near. But you will. Save it up. You 'll see all these little excursions in perspective when you 're round the next corner.'

'Oh, I *hate* all these written-up things: "Jones always wore a battered cricket cap, a little askew." They simply drive me *mad.* You know the whole thing is going to be lies from beginning to end.'

'You 're a romantic, Miriam.'

'I 'm not. It 's the "always wore." Trying to get at you, just as much as "Iseult the Fair." Just as unreal, just as much in an assumed voice. The amazing thing is the way men go prosing on for ever and ever, admiring each other, never suspecting.'

'You 've got to create an illusion, you know.'

'Why illusion? Life isn't an illusion.'

'We don't know what life is. You don't know what life is. You think too much. Life 's got to be lived. The difference between you and me is that you think to live and I live to think. You 've made a jolly good start. Done things. Come out and got your economic independence. But you 're stuck.'

'Now *there*'s somebody who's writing about life. Who's shown what has been going on from the beginning. Mrs Stetson. It was the happiest day of my life when I read *Women and Economics*.'

'It's no good, you know, that idea of hers. Women have got to specialize. They are specialists from the beginning. They can't run families, and successful careers at the same time.'

'They could, if life were differently arranged. They will. It's not that so much. Though it's a relief to know that homes won't be always a tangle of nerve-racking heavy industries which ought to be done by men. But the blaze of light she brings is by showing that women were social from the first and that *all* history has been the gradual socialization of the male. It is partly complete. But the male world is still savage.'

'The squaw, Miriam, was——'

'Absolutely social and therefore civilized, compared to the hunting male. She went out of herself. Mother and son was society. *He* had no chance. Every one, even his own son, was an enemy and a rival.'

'That's old Ellis's idea. There's *been* a matriarchate all right, Miriam, for your comfort.'

'I don't want comfort, I want truth.'

'Oh, you *don't*, Miriam. One gives you facts and you slide away from them.'

Household life breaks everything up. Comes crashing down on moments that cannot recur. . . . Thought runs on, below the surface to conclusions, arriving distractingly at the wrong moment.

It always seems a deliberate conspiracy to suppress conclusions. Lunch, grinning like a Jack-in-the-box, in a bleak emptiness. People ought not to meet at lunch-time. If the bleakness is overcome, it is only by borrowing from the later hours. And the loan is wasted by the absence of after-time, the business of filling up the afternoon with activities; leaving everything to be begun all over again later on.

How can guests *allow* themselves to arrive to lunch? The

smooth young man had come primed for his visit. Carefully talking in the Wilson way; carefully finding everything in the world amusing. And he was not amused. He was a cold selfish baffled young man, lost in a set. Welcomed here as a favoured emissary from a distant potentate.

And now, with just the same air of reflected brilliance, he was blithely playing tennis. Later on he would have to begin again with his talk; able parroting, screening hard coldness, the hard coldness of the pale yellow-haired Englishman with good features. A blindfold humanitarian giant? Where are Reich's English giants? Blind. Amongst the old-fashioned, conservatives? Gentlepeople with fixed ideas who don't want to change anything? The Lycurgans are not humanitarians. Because they are humanitarians deliberately. Liberals and socialists are humanitarian intellectually, through anger. Humanitarian idealists. The giants are humanitarian unconsciously, through breeding. Reich said the strongest motives, the motives that made history, were *unconscious*. Consciousness is increasing. The battle of unconscious fixed ideas and conscious chosen fixed ideas. Then the conservatives must always win! They make socialists and then absorb them. The socialists give them ideas. Neither of them are quite true. Why doesn't God state truth once and for all and have done with it?

And all the time, all over the western world, life growing more monstrous. The human head growing bigger and bigger. A single scientific fact, threatening humanity. Hypo's *amused* answer to the claims of the feminists. The idea of having infants scooped out early on, and artificially reared. Insane. Science rushing on, more and more clear and mechanical. . . . 'Life becomes more and more a series of surgical operations.' How *can* men contemplate the increasing awfulness of life for women and yet wish it to go on? The awfulness they have created by swaddling women up; regarding them as instruments of pleasure. Liking their cooking. *Stereotyping*, in their fixed mechanical men's way, a standard of deadly cooking that is destroying everybody, teeth first. And they call themselves creators. Knickers or gym skirts. A free stride from the hips, weight forward on toes pointing straight, like orientals. Squatting, like a savage, keeping the pelvis ventilated and elastic instead of sitting, knees politely together, stuffy and compressed and unventilated. All the rules of ladylike deportment ruin the pelvis. Ladies are awful. Deportment and a rigid overheated pelvis. In the kitchen they have to skin rabbits and disembowel fowls. Otherwise no keep. Polite small mouthfuls of squashy food and pyorrhoea. Good middle-aged church people always suggest stuffy bodies and pyorrhoea. Somewhere in the east people can be divorced for flatulence.

But the cranks are so uncultured; cut off from books and the past. Martyrs braving ridicule? The salt of the earth, making here and there a new world, unseen? Their children will not be cranks. . . .

A rose fell at her feet, flung in through the window.

'Come out and play!'

This is joy. To stand back from the court, fall slack, losing sight of the scatter of watching people round the lawn. Nothing but the clasp of the cool air and the firm little weight of the rough-coated ball in a slack hand. The loose-limbed plunge forward to toe the line. One measuring glance and the whole body a taut projectile driving the ball barely clear of the net, to swish furrowing along the ground.

'The lady serves from the cliff and Hartopp volleys from the sky. They're invincible.' The yellow young man was charming the other side of the net. Not yellow. His hair a red-gold blaze when the sun was setting, loose about his pale eager sculptured face; and now dull gold. He had welcomed her wrangling rush to the net after the first set, rushing forward at once, wrangling, without hearing, Hypo coming too, squealing incoherent contributions. And then the young man had done it again, for her, to make a little scene for the onlookers. But the third time it had been a failure and Hypo had filled the gap with witty shoutings. And all the time the tall man with dense features had said not a word, only swung sympathetically about. Yet he was a friend. From the moment he came up through the garden from France with his bag, uninvited, and sat down and murmured gently in response to vociferous greetings. Ill, after a bad crossing. So huge and so gentle that it had been easy to go up to his chair as every one else had done, and say lame things, instead of their bright ones, and get away with a sense of having had an immense conversation. He played the game, thinking of nothing else. Understood the style and rhythm of all the incidental movements. The others were different. They had learned their tennis; could remember a time when they did not play. Playing did not take them back to the beginning of life. Was not pure joy to them.

He was wonderful. He altered the tone. The style and peace of his slow sentences. Half German. The best kind of German. Now *he* could prevent war with Germany, if he could be persuaded to waft to and fro, for Reich's ten years, between the two countries, talking.

He talked through the evening; keeping his hold of the simplest thread of speech with his still voice and bearing. Leaving a large, peaceful space when he paused, into which it was easy to drop any sort of reflection that might have arisen in one's mind. Hypo scarcely spoke except to question him, and the smooth young man, dramatically posed, smoked, in silence. The huge form was a central spectacle, until the light faded and the talk began to die down. Then Alma asked him to play. He rose, gigantic in the half light, and went to the piano murmuring that he would be pleased to improvise a little. Amazing. With all his foreign experience and his serene mind, his musical reflections would be wonderful. But they were not. His gentle playing was colourless. Vague and woolly. And it brought a silence in which his own silence stood out. He seemed to have retired, politely and gently, but definitely, into himself. The darkness surrounding the one small shaded light began to state the joy of the day. Every one was beaming quietly with the sense of a glorious day. The tall man was at ease in stillness. In his large quiet atmosphere communication flowed, following serenely on the cessation of sound. Nun danket alle Gott. . . . How far was he a believer in the old things? His consciousness was the widest in the room; seemed to hold the balance between the old and the new, sympathetically, broad shouldered and rather weary with his burden. Speaking always in a frayed tired voice that would not give in to any single brisk idea. There was room and space and kind shelter in his mind for a woman to state herself, completely, unopposed. But he would not accept conclusions. His mild smooth shape of words would survive anything; persisting. It was his *style*. With it he carried himself through everything, making his way of talking a thing in itself. No ideas, no convictions; but something in him that made a perfect manner. A blow between the eyes, flattening him out, would not break it. There was nothing there to break, nothing hard in him. A made mould, chosen, during his growing, filling itself up from life, but not living . . . a gentleman, of course, that was it. Then there was an abyss beneath. Unstated things that lived in darkness.

But the silence lasted only an instant. Before its test could reveal anything further than the sudden sharp division of the sitters into men and women, Alma made movements to break up the party. Hypo's voice came, enchanting, familiar and new, its qualities renewed by the fresh contacts. The thing to do, he said rising, coming forward into the central light, not in farewell, into a self-made arena, with needless challenging sturdiness from one of the distances of his crowded mind. It would be one of his unanswerable fascinating misapprehensions. The thing to *do* was to go out into the world; leave everything behind, wife, and child, and things; go all over the world and come back; *experienced*.

'And what about the wives?'

'The wives, Miriam, will go to heaven when they die.' He turned on his laugh to the men in the background; and gathered their amused agreement in a swift glance. They had both risen and were standing, exposed by the frankness of their spokesman, silent in polite embarrassment. They *really* thought, these two nice men, that something had been said. The spell of the evening was broken up. The show had been given. Dream picture of moving life. Entertainment and

warm forgetfulness. Every one enchanted and alive. Now
was the time for talk, exchange; beginning with the shattering
of Hypo's silly idea. How could men have experience?
Nothing would make them discover themselves. Either of
them. Perhaps the tall man . . .

'Men as they are,' she began, trusting to the travelling power
of her mental picture of him as an exception, 'might go——'

But her words were lost. Alma had come forward and
was saying her good nights, hurriedly. They were to go, just
as everything was beginning. All chance of truth was caught,
in a social trap. The men were to be left, with their illusions,
to talk their monstrous lies, unchecked. Imagining they were
really talking, because there was no one to contradict. Unfair.

She rose perforce and got through her part. It was idiotic,
a shameful farce. Evening dress and the set scene, so beautifully arranged, were suddenly shameful and useless. Taken
to bits; silly. She seemed to be taking leave of herself, three
separate selves, united in the blessed relief of getting rid of the
women. In the person of the tall man, she strode gracefully
across the room to open the door for Alma and herself, breaking
out, with the two other men, at once, before the door was
closed, with immeasurable relief, into the abrupt chummy
phrases of old friends newly met.

CHAPTER IV

THE tiger stepping down his blue plaque. The one thing in the room that nothing could influence. All the other single beautiful things change. They are beautiful, for a moment, again and again; giving out their expression, and presently frozen stiff, having no expression. The blue plaque, intense fathomless eastern blue, the thick spiky grey-green sharply shaped leaves, going up for ever, the heavy striped beast for ever curving through, his great paw always newly set on the base of the plaque; inexhaustible, never looked at enough; always bringing the same joy. If ever the memory of this room fades away, the blue plaque will remain.

Mr Hancock was coming upstairs. In a moment she would know whether any price had been paid; any invisible appointment irrevocably missed.

'Good morning.' The everyday tone. Not the tone of welcome after a holiday.

'Good morning. I'm so sorry I could not get back yesterday.'

'Yes. I suppose it could not be helped.' He was annoyed. Perhaps even a little suspicious.

'You see, my brother-in-law thought I was still on holiday and free to take my sister home.'

'I trust it is not anything serious.'

'It was just one of her attacks.' Suppose Sarah should have one, at this moment? Suppose it was Sarah who was paying for her escapade? She summoned her despairingly, explaining, saw her instant approval and her private astonishment at the reason for the deceit.

Supported by Sarah she rounded off her story.

'I see,' said Mr Hancock pleasantly; weighing, accepting. She stood before him seeing the incident as he would imagine it. It was growing true in her mind. Presently she would be looking back on it. This was how criminals got themselves mixed up.

'I 'm glad it was not anything serious,' said Mr Hancock gravely, turning to the scatter of letters on his table. He *was* glad. And his kind sympathy was not being fooled. Sarah was always being ill. It was worth a lie to drag her out into the light of his sympathy. A breath of true life, born from a lie.

The incident was at an end, safely through. He was satisfied and believing, gone on into his day. She gathered up his appointment book from under his nose. He was using it, making entries. But he knew this small tyranny was her real apology, a curse for the trouble she had been obliged to give him. While he sat bereft as she took in the items of his day, their silent everyday conversation was knitted up once more. She was there, not failing him. He knew she would always be there as long as he should really need her. She restored the book to its place and stood at his side affectionately watching him tackle his task, detached, aware of her affection, secure in its independence.

They were so utterly far apart, foreigners in each other's worlds. Irreconcilable. But for all these years she had had daily before her eyes the spectacle of his life work; the way and the cost of his undeviating, unsparing work. It must surely be a small comfort to him that there had been an understanding witness to the shapely building of his life.

Understanding speech she could never have, with any one . . . except the Taylors, and she was as incompletely in their world as in his. The joy of being with him was the absence of the need for speech. She whisked herself to the door and went out shutting it behind her with a little slam, a last fling of holiday freedom, her communication to him of the store of joy she had brought back, the ease with which she was shouldering her more and more methodical, irrelevant work.

There was nothing to pay. Then the moment over the telegram *had* been a revelation.

'You ought to see the Grahams. Stay another day and see the Grahams.'

III—N

I might have wired asking for another day. Impossible. The day would have been spoilt by the discomfort of knowing him thinking me ungrateful and insatiable. Only being able to say when I came back that I waited to see a man dying of cancer. He would have thought that morbid. The minute the telegram was sent the feeling of guilt passed away. Whilst Hypo was chuckling over it at the top of the stairs, there was nothing and no one. Only the feeling of having broken through and stepped forward into space. Strong happiness. All the next day was in space; a day taken out of life; standing by itself.

Mr Graham was old-fashioned, and modern too. He seemed to have come from so far back, to see backwards, understanding, and to see ahead the things he had always known. Serene and interested, in absolutely everything. As much in the tiny story of the threepenny bit as in anything else, making it seem worth telling, making me able to tell it. Seeing everything as *real*. Really finding life marvellous in the way no one else seemed to do. Ill as he was he looked up my trains, carefully and thoughtfully. The horror and fear of death was taken away from me while I watched him. Perhaps he had always felt that the marvellousness of there being such a thing as life was the answer to everything. And now that he was dying knew it more completely?

They were both so serene. Everybody was lifted by being with them into that part of life that goes on behind the life that seems to be being lived.

All the time it was as if they had witnessed that past fortnight and made it immaterial, a part of the immaterial *story* of life. . . .

That fortnight had the shape of an arranged story, something playing itself out, with scenes set and times to come in in the right place. Upset by that one little scene that had come in of itself.

The clear days after the two men had gone back to town. The long talks kept undisturbed. All the long history of Gissing.

Gissing's ideal women over-cultivated, self-important creatures, with low-pressure vitality and too little animal. . . . 'You 're rather like that, you know.' . . .

'Men would always rather be made love to than talked at.'

'Your life is a complex system of evasions. You are a mass of *health*, unused. You 're not doing anything with yourself. . . .' '. . . Two kinds of women, the kind that come it over one, tremendously, and nurses.'

'Most good men are something like chimpanzees. The best man in those relationships is the accomplished rake . . . that 's the secret of old Grooge. . . . Yes; you 'd hate him. He 's one of the old school; expert knowledge about women. That 's nonsense of course. There *is* no expert knowledge about women. Men and women are very much alike. But there 's the honest clean red-blooded people and the posers and rotters and anaemic people. And there are for your comfort a few genuine monogamists. Very few.'

'You 're stuck, you know. Stuffed with romantic ignorance. You 're a great chap. A gentleman. That 's an insult, isn't it? You don't exploit yourself.'

'I 'm not sure about you. You 've got an awfully good life up in town, jolly groups; various and interesting. One hesitates to disturb it. . . . But we 're old friends. And there 's this silly barrier between us. There always is between people who evade what is after all only the development of the friendly handshake.'

'She 's a very fine artist. Well, she, my dear Miriam, has lovers. They keep her going. Keep her creative. She 's a woman one can talk to. There 's no tiresome barrier. . . .'

'Your women are a sort of omnibus load.'

'There 's always the box seat.'

'They all grin. Your one idea of women is a grin.'

'There 's a great deal to be said for the cheerful grin. You know, a woman who has the grit to take things into her own hands, take the initiative, is no end of a relief. Women want to. They ought to. They 're inhibited by false ideas. They want, nearly all women want all their corners taken for them.'

'This book 'll be our brat. You 've pulled it together no

end. You ought to chuck your work, have a flat in town. Be general adviser to authors.'

Queer old Professor Bolly, pink and white and loud checks, standing outside the summer-house in the brilliant sun.

'Is this the factory?'

'This is the factory.'

'Does he dictate to you?'

'My *dear* Bolly. . . . Have five minutes; have *half* a minute's conversation with Miss Henderson and then, if you dare, try to imagine *any one* dictating to her.'

Pink and white. Two old flamingos. Pulling the other way. Bringing all the old conservative world into the study . . . sending it forward with their way of looking at the new things. Such a deep life in them that old age and artificial teeth and veined hands did not obscure their youth. Worldly happy religious musical English people.

'The Barrie question turns solely upon the question of romance. You cannot, dear young lady, *hesitate* over Barrie. You must either adore, or detest. With equal virulence. I am one of the adorers. *Romance*, for me, is the ultimate *reality*. . . . Seen through a glass darkly.'

On the other side of the room Mrs Bolly was telling her tales of Bayreuth. There were both untouched by the Wilson atmosphere. Not clever. They brought a glow like fire-light; as if the cold summer hearth were alight, as the scenes from their stories came into the room and stood clear.

The second afternoon, Hypo stretched out on the study lounge, asleep, compact and calm in the sunlight like a crusader on a tomb, till just before they went.

'There's something unconquerable in them.'

'Yes, Miriam. Silliness *is* unconquerable. Poor old Stevenson; went to the Pacific to get away from it. *Died* to get away from it.

'Don't go away. Camp in here. I'm all to bits. You know you're no end of a comfort to me.'

'I can't be. You're hampered all the time I'm here by the silly things I say; the way I spoil your talk.'

'You've no idea how much I like having you about. Like

the sound of your voice; the way your colour takes the sun,
your laughter. I envy you your sudden laughter, Miriam;
You don't know the fine individual things in yourself. You 've
got all sorts of illusions, but you 've no idea where you really
score.'

'Can't get on with anybody.'

'You get on with me all right. But you never tell *me* nice
things about myself. You only laugh at my jokes.'

'I 've never told you a hundredth part. There 's never
any time. But I 'll tell you one nice thing. There 's a way
in which ever since I 've known you, you obliterate other men.
Yes. For me. It 's most tiresome.'

'Oh, my dear! Is that true, Miriam?'

'Oh, yes. From the first time I saw you. There you were.
I can't bear your ideas. But I always find myself testing other
men, better men, by the way, by you.'

'I haven't any ideas, Miriam, and I 'm a reformed character.
There 's heaps of time. You 're here another ten days yet.
You shall camp in here. We 'll talk, devastatingly.'

'If I once began——'

'Begin. We 're going to explore each other's minds.'

'I should bore you to death.'

'You never bore me. Really. It does me good to quarrel
with Miriam. But we 're not going to quarrel. We 're going
to explore each other and stop nowhere. Agreed?'

'I 've seen you *ill* with boredom. You hate silence and you
hate opposition. You always think people's minds are blank
when they are silent. It 's just the other way round. Only
of course there are so many kinds of silence. But the test of
absolutely everything in life is the quality of the in-between
silences. It 's only in silence that you can judge of your
relationship to a person.'

'You shall be silent. You shall deploy a whole regiment of
silences . . . but you 'll fire off an occasional volley of speech?'

'Real speech can only come from complete silence. Incomplete silence is as fussy as deliberate conversation.'

'One has to begin somewhere. Deliberate conversation
leads to real conversation. You *can* talk, you know, Miriam.

You 're not a woman of the world. You don't come off all the time. But when you do, you come off no end.'

If *his* mind could be tackled even though there were no words to answer him with, than any one's mind could be tackled.

Finding him simple and sad, able to be uncertain, took away the spell from the surroundings; leaving only him. Seeing life as he saw it, being forced to admit some of his truths, hard and cruel even if rearranged or differently stated, made the world a nightmare, a hard solid daylight nightmare, the only refuge to be, and stay, with him. Yet the giving up of perpetual opposition brought a falseness. Smiling agreement, with unstated differences and reservations piling up all the time. Drifting on into a false relationship.

The joy of being with him, the thing that made it worth while to flatter by seeming to agree, was more than half the sense of triumphing over other women. Of being able to believe myself as interesting and charming and mysteriously wonderful as all these women we talked about, who lost their wonder as he stated their formula.

By the time the Grimshaws came everything was sad. That is why I was so successful with them. Gay with sadness, easy to talk to, practised in conversation. Without that, they would not have sought me out and carried me off by themselves and shown me their world.

'I 've been through a terrific catechism.'

'You 've impressed them, Miriam. I 'm jealous. They come here; to see me; and go off with Miriam.'

'Bosh. They thought I was intelligent. They don't think so *now*. Besides they really were trying to interview you through me.'

'That 's subtle of you, Miriam. Old James. You 've no idea how you 're coming on. Or coming out. Yes. I think there 's always *been* a subtle leap in Miriam. Without words. A song without words. Good formula for Miriam. What did they interview me about?'

'I refused to be drawn. Suddenly, in the middle of lunch

she asked me in her Cheltenham voice, "What do you do with your leishah?" I think she really wanted statistics; guttersnipe statistics.'

'She 's an enchantress. No end of a lark, really. She runs old Grimshaw. Runs everybody. You 're rather like her, you know. You 've got the elements, with your wrist-watch. What did you say?'

'Nothing. I haven't the faintest idea what I do with my leisure. Besides I can't talk about real things to a bayonet. She *is* fascinating, though.'

'She 's a gipsy. When she looks at one . . . with that *brown* smile . . . one could do anything for her.'

'There you are. Your *smiles* . . . But he 's the most perfect darling. Absolutely sincere. A Breton peasant. I talked to him about some of your definitions. Not as yours. As mine.'

'Never mind. He knew where they came from.'

'Not at all. Only those I thought I agreed with. And he 's given me quite a fresh view of the Lycurgans.'

'Now don't you go and desert.'

'Well, he must be either right or wrong.'

'What a damned silly thing to say. Oh, what a *damned* silly thing to say.'

Chill windy afternoon, grey tamarisks waving in a bleak wind, tea indoors and a fire bringing into the summery daylight the sudden message that summer was at an end. The changed scene chiming together with the plain outspoken anger. Again the enlivening power of anger, the relief of the clean cut, of everything brought to an end, of being once more single and clear, free of every one, homesick for London.

Mr Hancock's showing-out bell sounded in the hall. The long sitting had turned into a short one. No need to go up yet. He 'll come downstairs, pad-pad, flexible hand-made shoes on the thick stair carpet, the sharp turn at the stair-end, the quick little walk along the passage and soft neat clatter of leather heels down the stone stairs to the workshop. Always the same. The same occasion. Which occasion? That used to be so clear and so tremendous.   Confused now, but living on in every sound of his footsteps.

Homesick for London.   For those people whose lives are set in a pattern with mine, leaving its inner edge free to range.

Perhaps the set pattern is enough.   The daily association. The mass of work.   Its results unseen.   At the end it might show as a complete whole, crowded with life.   Life comes in; strikes through.   Everything comes in if you are set in a pattern and always in one place.   Changed circumstances bring quickly, but imperfectly, without a background, the things that would be discovered slowly and perfectly, on a background, in calm daily air.   All lives are the same life.   Only one discovery, coming to everybody.

The little bell on the wall burred gently.   Room free.   No hurry.

I 'll wait till he 's gone downstairs.

'Nice Miriam.   You really are a dear, you know.   You 've a ruddy, blazing temper.   You can sulk too, abominably. Then one discovers an unsuspected streak of sweetness.   You forget.   You have a rare talent for forgetfulness and recovery. You 're suddenly pillowy.   You 've no *idea*, Miriam, what a blessing that is to the creature called man.   It 's womanly you are.   Now don't resent that.   It 's a fine thing to be.   It makes one want you, quite desperately.   The essential deeps of you.   Like an absolution.   I 'm admitting your deeps, Miriam.'

'It 's most inconvenient suddenly to be forgetting you are having a row with a person.   It 's really a weakness.   Suddenly getting interested.'

'Your real weakness is your lack of direction, the instability of your controls.   If I had you on my hands for six months you 'd be no end of a fine chap.   Now don't resent that.   It 's a little crude, I admit.   Perhaps I ought to beg your pardon. I beg your pardon, Miriam.'

'I never think about myself.   I remember once being told that I was too excitable.   It made me stare, for a few minutes. And now you.   I believe it.   But I shall forget again.   And you are all wrong about "controls."   I don't mean mine.

I mean your silly idea of women having feebler controls than men.'

'Not my idea. Tested fact.'

'Damn facts. Those arranged tests and their facts are utterly nothing at all. Women's controls appear to be feebler because they have so much more to control. I don't mean physically. Mentally. By seeing everything simultaneously. Unless they are the kind of woman who has been warped into seeing only one thing at a time. Scientifically. They are freaks. Women see in terms of life. Men in terms of things, because their lives are passed amongst scraps.'

'*Nice* Miriam.'

'Now we can begin to talk. It's easier, you know, to talk hand in hand.'

The touch of his hand bringing a perfect separation. Everything suddenly darkened. Two little people side by side in a darkness. Exactly alike. Hypo gone. His charm, quite gone.

Alma crossing the end of the lawn. There was not any feeling of guilt. Only the sense of her isolation. Companionship with her isolation. Then the shock of his gay voice ringing out to her across the lawn.

'Susan, if you have that day in town, awful things will happen.' Her little pink-clad figure turning for a moment to wave a hand.

'Of course they will! Rather!'

'We're licensed!'

'Susan doesn't like me.'

'She does. She likes you no end. Likes you currently. The way your hair goes back over your ears.'

He misses nothing. That is his charm, his supremacy in charm over all other men. And misinterprets everything. That is his tragedy. The secret of his perpetual disappointments. He spoiled everything by the perpetual shock of his *deliberate* guilt and *deliberate* daring. That was driving me off all the time. The extraordinariness of his idea of frankness! His 'stark talk' is nothing compared to the untroubled outspokenness of the Taylors.

III—* N

The *burden* of his simplicity. No one in the world could be more simple.

He thought my silence meant attention and agreement, when I wanted only to watch the transformation going on all round me. That would have gone on; if he had given me time; not destroyed everything by his sudden trick of masterfulness; the silly application of a silly idea. It's not only that coercion is wrong; that it's far better to die than to be coerced. It's the destructiveness of coercion. How long before men discover that violence drives women utterly away into cold isolation? Never, since the beginning of the world, has a woman been mastered. I'm glad I know why. Why violence defeats itself.

'You don't desert me completely? We're still friends? You'll go on being interested in my work?'

He knew nothing of the life that went on of itself, afterwards. I had driven him away. I felt guilty then. Because I took my decision. And absolved myself. The huge sounding darkness, expanding, turned to a forest of moving green and gold. The feeling of immense deliberate strength going forward, breaking out through life.

If it came again I should absolve myself. But it won't. It is something in him, and in his being an Englishman and not, like Michael, an alien mind.

'*Alma*. I want a slice of life!'

'Of course, my very dear! Take one, Miriam. Take a *large* one. An oat. Not a vote. One woman, one oat. . . .'

'I want an oat *and* a vote. No. I don't want a vote. I want to have one and not use it. Taking sides simply annihilates me.'

'Don't be annihilated, old fing. Take an oat.'

'Give me one.'

'I will. I *do*!'

Alma's revealed splendour . . . lighting and warming the surrounding bleakness. In that moment her amazing gift that would move her so far from me seemed nothing. Herself, everything to me. Alma is a star. Her name should be Stella. But I had already decided that it would not be him. And that marvellous beginning cannot come again.

'Particularly jolly schoolgirls! You 'll like them. They 're free. They mean to be free. Now they, Miriam, *are* the new woman.' Posing, exploiting, deliberately uncatlike cats. *How* could he be taken in? *Why* were all her poses revealed to me? What brought me on the scene just at those moments? Why that strange little series of events placing me, alone, of the whole large party, innocently there just at that moment, to see the origin of his idea of a jolly smile, and how he answers it?

'You looked like a Silenus.'

'That sort of thing always looks foolish from the outside. It was nothing. I beg of you, I entreat you to think no more of it.'

Again the little bell. Clean. A steady little summons. He had not gone downstairs.

He was washing his hands; with an air of communicativeness.

'I 've a piece of news for you. I have decided to leave Mr Orly and set up, elsewhere, on my own account.'

'Really?' The beating of her heart shook the things she was holding in her hands.

'Yes. It 's a decision I 've been approaching for some time. As you know, Mr Leyton is about to be taken into partnership. I have come to the conclusion that it is best on the whole to move and develop my practice along my own lines.'

So calmly handing out desolation. Here was the counterpart of the glorious weeks. Her carelessly-made living was gone; or horribly reduced. The Orlys alone would not be able to give her a hundred a year.

'When is it to be?'

'Of course, whenever I go, I shall want help.'

'*Oh* . . .'

He went on very busily on with his handwashing. She knew exactly how he was smiling, and hidden in her corner smiled back, invisibly, and made unnecessary clatterings to hide the glorious embarrassment. Dismay struck across her joy, revealing the future as a grey, laborious working out of this moment's blind satisfaction. But joy had spoken first and left her no choice. Startling her with the revelation of the way the roots of her being still centred in him. Joy deeper and more powerfully stirring than the joy of the past weeks. They showed now a spread embroidery of sunlit scenes, powerless, fundamentally irrelevant, excursions off the main road of her life. Committed beyond recall, she faced the prospect of unvarying, grinding experience. The truth hidden below the surfaces of life was to yield itself to her slowly, imperceptibly, unpleasurably.

She got through the necessary things at top speed, anyhow, to avoid underlining his need of her, and ran downstairs.

A letter on the hall table, from *Hypo*. . . . *Dear Miriam— I've headed off that affair. You've pulled me out of it. You really have. When can I see you? Just to talk.*

THE TRAP

TO
BRYHER

CHAPTER I

A SHORT by-street paved from side to side. Narrow house-fronts, and the endmost houses, hiding the passage that curved round into the further street, high enough to keep out of sight the neighbouring cubes of model dwellings and to leave, as principal feature in the upper air, the tower of St Pancras church. An old little street. A scrap of old London standing apart, between the Bloomsbury squares and the maze of streets towards the City. The light gleaming from its rain-washed flagstones gave it a provincial air and a freshness unknown to the main streets, between whose buildings lay modern roadways dulled by mud or harsh with grimy dust.

Whenever during all her London years Miriam had passed the spot where it opened into the thoroughfare, the little by-way had drawn her eyes; always stating its sequestered charm. Entering it now for the first time she had a sense of arriving nowhere.

She found her number to the right, just beyond the opening, on a blistered door, whose knocker, a blurred, weather-worn iron face, gazed sadly downwards. Next the door, within a small window screened from the interior by a frayed serge curtain, were ranged small blocks of stone and marble, polished columns, scraps of moulding; and in the centre upon an oblong mount an alabaster finger. A lady's forefinger, fastidiously posed—the nail, smooth joints, and softly curving flesh most delicately carved. Its white cleanliness seemed to rebuke the dust that lay thick upon the other objects and made their welcome quiet and impersonal. It was personal, emotional. Arrogant, calling the eye from the surrounding dusty peace.

Dust lay even upon the large grey cat compactly curled amongst the sharp angles and looking forth with a green eye, glass-clear and startlingly bright in contrast to the dried socket from which its fellow should have shone.

She raised the heavy knocker and tapped. The sounds echoed down the empty court and left a stillness into which flowed her own tremulous stillness. Down the street a black cat came towards her, serene and unnoticing, keeping aloof along the centre of the way.

Yet she was an inhabitant of Flaxman's Court. Up there, on the upper floors of the house that remained so quiet before her claim, were rooms as quiet, her own. Soon she would daily be slipping out into this small brightness, daily coming back to it, turning from strident thoroughfares to enter its sudden peace.

She knocked again, more loudly. If Miss Holland were not there, she was shut out. But certainly the door would open. She knew, so careless was her spirit, that she was not shut out. In a moment there came the sound of boots upon uncarpeted stairs. The door opened; but not upon Miss Holland. There before her was the dark passage that skirted the little shop and led to the staircase, the way up to the quiet, eager, empty rooms, obstructed.

Since he stood aside, welcoming, and greeted her by name, the man could be none other than the landlord. An unconsidered item, appearing at the outset. Not only postponing joy, but enhancing it; for if this meeting were its price, how good must be what lay ahead.

She hoped that during the swift moment of confronting once more his long-forgotten way of being, that she had shown no sign of antipathy. She could not be sure, for in that moment she had been back again in bitter conflict. The shape was a duplicate. The same tall, grey-clad form, neither thin nor solid, the same pale eyes, arrogant and embarrassed, the florid skin, the drooping fair moustache half-hiding the fleshy red lips through which had come the voice familiar and shunned from beyond memory.

She went forward followed by the voice into an air dense with shut-in odours dried brown by stale pipe-smoke. It was as if the door just closed behind her were never set open, and any egress there might be at the back, closely sealed. And here, at the centre of a fog of smells of which the air of the passage was but the fringe, someone was living.

The voice behind her on the stairs rang clear through the murk; a refined voice, musical; they always had good voices.

'I've had thwee buckets of boiling water over the floors, and I'm going to have thwee more.'

Yet another price to pay. This time not intermittent but permanent. How long did scrubbing last?

Though the air cleared as they mounted the stairs, it had now a new smell, meeting and mingling with the thinned odours coming up from below, the smell of long-lying London dust. A staircase window, fast shut, showed a grimy sky. On the first floor were two rooms standing open, their doorways close together at right angles. The window of the large front room gave a blurred view of the house-fronts over the way. The back room was a small square, with a square window. The sky here was fly-blown, but less dim than from the stair-case window, and there were trees, black-stemmed, bearing many-shaped masses of drying leaves. A short flight led up to the second floor. Here were the rooms, two; open doors at right angles as on the floor below. Windows wide, smells banished; clear clean height of air. It was the height of the rooms that made these narrow four-story houses look tall.

'Oh, they're *nice* rooms,' she said.

'They're nice old houses, they've been *good* houses,' he panted plaintively. 'I live next door, with my mother. Come *upstairs*, Miss Henderson. I'm at work up *there*.'

He went on up the narrow flight leading to the attic. When his long form had disappeared, Miriam turned into the large room; a large oblong, its end wall, opposite the broad high window, broken by a door communicating with the back room. Going through it, she found the smaller room dark. There was a pale wash on the walls of the other room, but here a dark old paper absorbed the light without reflection. And the ceiling, of course, would be dark with grime. The ceiling seemed to have looked down at her long ago. Long she had stood, with life gathered richly about her, in the empty window-lit space where she now asked whether really she had seen up there while she welcomed this superfluous second room, the thing that lay reflected in her mind, growing dim, changing to a feeling, a part of the warm sense of life all about her.

'Won't you come up, Miss Henderson? I'm at work up *here*.'

She had forgotten the man and the third room. At this moment, in order not to go up, she would have sacrificed the possession of the third room. On her way out she glanced at the ceiling. It *was* painted. Floating draped figures, garlanded, in dull crimsons, faded rose and blue and gold, dim with grime, set within a moulding shaped to fill the angles of the square and filmed to a yellowish brown.

'This is a nice room.'

The man, a good deal altered by a large white apron, was standing behind his buckets.

'My name's Sheffield. I *told* Miss Holland. Perhaps she didn't tell you?'

The room stated itself, competing with the voice. It was high and airy, its ceiling sloping on all four sides; in the front to a deep lattice, having a wide shelf underneath.

'She's a very nice lady. Nice *quiet* lady. There's not so many about nowadays.'

It was all coming back; the attitude towards life that had so tormented her when she listened unaided by thought. She knew now that it was blasphemy. It is blasphemy, she could say, if this man were equally armed, blasphemy to imagine that each next generation is plunging into an abyss.

'People don't keep themselves to themselves like they did. There's too much running about. Don't you think so, Miss Henderson?'

She was looking out upon the rain-washed parapet a yard away from the window. 'Nice to have a parrypidge in case of fire; plenty of roofs and chimley-pots to walk on.'

'Yes,' she said hastily. 'People run about because they wonder who they are.'

'That's it. Don't know where they are. That's the position of the L.C.C. Money to spend and must find

something to spend it on. Public money. Pitched away. Not
a hayputh o' good out of it.'

The sudden presence in the room of the L.C.C. made him
harmless.

'Officials are strange people. Being officials makes people
strange.' She stood seeking something that had passed word-
lessly through her mind while she snatched this borrowed
thought. Something she ought to say, hidden because she
was being insincere. It remained hidden, and she passed
towards the door, his inferior, having nothing to offer half
so good as his own mistaken convictions.

'You going *down*, Miss Henderson?'

She was at the top of the winding stair before she spoke the
leave-taking that left the room empty, as it would be this
afternoon.

Very gently she went down her stairs. In this clear upper
light, angles and surfaces declared themselves intimately. The
thing she loved was there. Light falling upon the shapes of
things, reflected back, moving through the day, a steadfast
friend, silent and understanding. She had loved it wherever
she was, even in the midst of miseries; and always it had belonged to others. This time it was her own. The breath she
held facing it was a cool stream, bringing strength; joy. Nothing could be better than this. None of the events, none of
the passions of life, better than this sense of light quietly falling.

Coming back in the afternoon, she found Miss Holland
installed, her half of the larger room fully furnished.

From a low camp-bed with a limply frilled Madras muslin
cover, her eyes passed to a wicker wash-stand-table, decked
with a strip of the same muslin and set with chilly, pimpled
white crockery. At its side was a dulled old Windsor chair,
and underneath it a battered zinc footbath propped against
the wall. Above a small shabby chest of drawers a tiny square
of mirror hung by a nail to the strip of wall next the window.
No colour anywhere but in the limp muslin, washed almost
colourless.

But over the whole of the floor, gleaming, without blemish,
was the new linoleum. And soon the dividing curtain would

hang between her and Miss Holland's cheerless things. A
length of cord hung ready, suspended in a deep loop from the
top of the window frame to a hook in the wall above the connecting door, and on the floor beneath the window lay a pile
of material.

She cried out at the sight of it, bringing Miss Holland in
from the next room.

'Yes,' she said disdainfully, 'that is the curtain.'

Though in the course of two meetings Miriam had grown
used to Miss Holland's way of speaking, it was still fruitful of
wonder. She wondered now, hearing it unchanged by the
informality of the occasion, how it had first come into being.
At Wimpole Street it was a familiar tone, common to upper
middle-class folks of the better sort. In men it was disarming;
a contraction of the range of the voice to two or three fluty
notes. In women it was commentary having, even in jest, a
note of distress, deprecation of almost everything under the sun.

She had already discovered the exact amount of constriction
of the throat necessary to its production, and felt it draw the
muscles of her nose and mouth into an expression of faintly
humorous contempt. Heard now, as it were in its dressing-
gown, it gave a clue to the mode of being that would automatically produce it; disdain of life's external processes, of
everything but high ends, any kind of high end, from the
honour of England to the dignity of the speaker and of the
person spoken to, that everything in life must be moulded
to serve.

Once accepted, it would ban any kind of passionate feeling,
even passionate chirpiness. Even mirth would not be allowed
to reach beyond a faint amusement. On the whole, so far,
she had decided against it, decided that it might even be possible to become a sort of châtelaine without the constricted
voice.

But on this occasion the voice showed itself in a new light.
Subtly attractive. For behind Miss Holland's tone was a
smile that beamed the more warmly for the frost through which
it came. It reached and touched like sunlight. Garden sunlight that had been missing through all the wandering years.

Did all these people emanate from high walled gardens, scorning everything that was outside?

In any case, here she was, indefinitely committed to live at close quarters with a scorn she was not sure of being able to share. Must at least beware at the times, this was one of them, when the châtelaine way of taking life went to her head, of treachery to things that stood outside it. Meanwhile the experience would be charming. And to be a little moulded by it would not be atavism. For Miss Holland was more than the châtelaine. She had broken loose, set herself in adventurous circumstances; a châtelaine facing both ways.

'I saw you did not like the idea of sacking, though I think it might have been made quite pretty, painted artistically, as I am sure you could have done it, with a Grecian key pattern or something of the kind, along the border.'

She had spoken standing near the heaped material conciliatingly, and now bent and caught gingerly at an end, as if uncertain of its mood.

'Still, I thought I would get this. It is the new stuff they are calling "casement cloth" in quality rather like a fine "crash." Very durable, and not ruinous in price.'

'Perfect. Tones with the floor and my crocks. But you must let me pay. It's my extravagance.'

'Not at all. I quite like it. I shall certainly contribute my share. Your things are here. They are charming. I perceive that you have excellent taste.'

'Joy, where are they?'

'I had them set down in here. I thought you would prefer to arrange them yourself.'

She threw open the connecting door and stood back, a gracious hostess introducing guests. How tall she was indoors, and big. Heavy in build, yet limber and light-footed; graceful. The grey in the sleek dark mass of hair scarcely showed. Her large eyes, set well apart on either side of her good nose, when there was no street light to show the tired muscles round about them, were really beautiful. Liquid radiant blue, with a darker ring.

'I suddenly,' Miriam said, going into the crowded little

room, 'remembered crockery and went back to Maple's. But there's a tragedy. I forgot an indispensable.'

She was startled by laughter, an abrupt fairy tinkle, affectionate and gay.

'Never mind,' said the voice, unchanged. 'I will obtain one for you.'

'How?'

'Oh, quite easily, I assure you.'

'And, oh Lord, a pail! I forgot a pail.'

'There is no need to invoke the Deity. I have several pails.'

Miriam turned and saw happiness shine from her. Her presence was balm as she stood so lightly there—a momentary stillness poised for help, ready to welcome any confession, shoulder any burden that might be offered—and then turned on a dancing step towards the big room, thoroughly pleased, deep, quite deep, in delight at the prospect of settling down here in intimacy.

And here they were. And it *was* wonderful. Full of a deep refreshment. The experiment was turning to success. But not yet quite fully. Not until the curtain was up and the strips of privacy were secure.

She was not sure that Miss Holland desired a complete privacy. The curtain, for her, was an affair of modesty, a physical not a spiritual covering. Spiritually she had nothing to hide.

She had no back premises. No reservations. And here, at last, no doubt, was the secret of the effortless decorous speech of the 'gentlewoman.' And the secret of its tiresomely unvarying form. The quality it expressed went right through. They not only spoke as they thought, but thought as they spoke, guided and fashioned their thought, even to themselves, in forms of decorous speech. Anything that could not so be moulded was banished. Anything 'unspeakable'—their strongest term of contempt. Thus they were, even when alone, permanently at attention.

For herself, the coming of the curtain would be the moment of dropping the mask of attention, the moment of soaring freely within this new life. Things were going ahead too fast.

Strong impressions succeeding and obliterating each other too swiftly to be absorbed.

'I'll go round for my things. Must find a greengrocer,' she said, looking in on Miss Holland cutting a slice from a substantial bar of plain soap.

'You prefer a greengrocer? I am employing the Church Army myself. They are most useful. And it is quite the least expensive way of moving. The men should now be on their way with the last of my things. They could then, if you like, fetch yours.'

'Ah! Perfect,' said Miriam, and set forth.

Going westwards she met a sky ablaze with fiery rose thrown up behind clouds that hid the drooping sun, and saw, looking back, the London scene transformed; pink houses, grey roofs tinged with madder. The sun had still a good way to drop. The clouds might shift. Coming back she would walk in brilliance.

The Church Army men arrived as she was putting together the last of her things.

They were oppressive. Met in the freedom of a slum they would have been dreadful enough. But with their prison air of sullen shyness, overlaid by an ill-fitting respectability, they were, she felt as she stood telling them what things were to be removed, heart-breaking by reason of their ignorance of the world they now feared. They did not know that the evil that in them had come up and out into action was in everybody.

She wanted to fête them, give them tea, somehow make them cease tiptoeing about the room with that dreadful air of shame. But her voice, which she tried to make casual, sounded rallying, expressive of equality, insulting; she could only wish them to finish and be gone.

Her forgotten book was lying on the table. The book that had suddenly become the centre of her life. Now, with these men here, the very existence of the volume seemed a mockery. She took it in her hands, felt it draw her again with its unique power. The men could, must, manage without supervision. For the second time, during which they stood listening as though she had not spoken before, she pointed out the things which were to be taken, and sat down with the book.

Sitting thus with the book in her hands and her eyes upon the title, set within the golden lines of an upright oblong in letters of gold upon the red cover, she found herself back within the first moment of meeting it. In the little book-shop, a treasure house opened by the so small subscription. Saw again the close-packed ranks of well-known names, names that had until then, whenever she thought of them, stood large along the margin of life, and that seemed now, set minutely down upon neat rows of volumes, suddenly uninteresting, irrelevant to the impulse of her search. And then this book, for all the neutrality of its title and of the author's name, drawing her hands, bringing, as she took it from the shelf and carried it, unexamined, away down the street, the stillness of contentment.

She could, so long as the men remained, get no further. Within the neat red binding lay altogether new happiness. But she was aware only of the sluggishly moving men, of the shelter from whence they had come and whither presently, when she, free and a millionaire, should have been shifted from palace to palace, they would, with their dingy barrow, shamble back.

The men were going downstairs. The last moments in this room that held the whole of her London life were ticking themselves away, appealing in vain for some sadness of farewell. Just round the corner in Flaxman's Court was Miss Holland, expectantly at work. And here she sat with a book open upon her knee, asking only to be left in communion with a style.

She glanced through the pages of its opening chapter, the chapter that was now part of her own experience; set down at last alive, so that the few pages stood in her mind, growing as a single good day will grow, in memory, deep and wide, wider than the year to which it belongs. She was surprised to find, coming back after the interval of disturbed days, how little she had read. Just the opening pages, again and again, not wanting to go forward; wanting the presentation of the two men, talking outside time and space in the hotel bedroom, to go on for ever.

And presently fearing to read further, lest the perfection of satisfaction should cease.

Reading a paragraph here and there, looking out once more the two phrases that had thrilled her more intimately than any others, she found a stirring of strange statements in her mind. A strange clarity that was threatening to change the adventure of reading to a shared disaster. For she remembered now, having hung for a while over Waymarsh's 'sombre glow' and 'his attitude of prolonged impermanence,' that she had already read on into the next chapter, that something had happened, so bitter as to have been pushed from her mind. And yet her mind had been at work upon it. It had happened with the coming of Maria Gostrey, and had culminated, at the dinner-party, in her red neck-band. Disappointing. Yes. Here she was again, drawing on her gloves and being elaborately mysterious.

The thought, too, of reading in the new room, with Miss Holland on the other side of the curtain, changed the proportions of the adventure. Made it almost improper. She imagined herself trying to explain why the phrases that lit the scene were wonderful. And it seemed, thought of as a public matter, ridiculous to have been so excited by the way he conveyed information without coming forward to announce it. But even more disquieting was Miss Holland's reinforcement of the need to confront the author with his own cynicism, to tell him that in every word he came forward with his views, which were the most hopelessly complacent masculine ignorance.

It was only as private, shared by no one else, that the adventure was glorious. Thought of as carried under the eye of a witness, it seemed criminal—'anti-social.' She now for the first time imagined men reading the magic pages, suffering unconsciously their insidious corruption. This man was a monstrous unilluminated pride. And joy in him was a mark of the same corruption. Pride in discovering the secrets of his technique. Pride in watching it labour with the development of the story. The deep attention demanded by this new way of statement was in itself a self-indulgence. Thought of as enjoyed in a world that held Church Army men it was plain wickedness.

But the cold ignorance of this man was unconscious. And therefore innocent. And it was he after all who had achieved the first completely satisfying way of writing a novel. If this were a novel. There *was* something holy about it. Something to make, like Conrad, the heavens rejoice. Perhaps at lunch times, or in rare solitudes, she could go on, get at the whole of the light there was in him. Style was something beyond good and evil. Sacred and innocent.

The new furniture peopled the room with clear reflections. The daylight was dimmed by the street, but it came in generously through the wide high window. And upon the polished surfaces of the little bureau, set down with its back to the curtain, and upon its image, filling the lower part of the full-length strip of mirror hung opposite against the wall, were bright plaques of open sky.

The bureau was experience; seen from any angle it was joy complete. Added to life and independent of it. A little thing that would keep its power through all accidents of mood and circumstance. The inlaid design enclosing the lock of the sloping lid formed a triangle with the small brass candlesticks at either end of the level top, and the brass handles of the three drawers hung below on either side, garlands, completing the decoration.

Pools of light rested on the squat moss-green crockery of the wash-table, set, flanked by clear wall and clear green floor, between the mirror and the end of the small bed which skirted the wall as far as the door opening on to the landing. The unencumbered floor made a green pathway to the window. It was refreshment merely to walk along it, between clean sightly objects. Squalor was banished. No more smell of dust. No more sleepless nights under a roof too hot to grow cool even in the hour before dawn. Here in the mornings there would always be beauty, the profiles of things growing clear on either side of the pathway of morning light, the profiles of flowers, set in a bowl between the sentinel candlesticks.

Miss Holland's voice came unheralded, startlingly out of the silence. She must have come through from the back room in noiseless slippers. Miriam answered that she had forgotten about clothes, and proposed nails in the attic.

'It will be no trouble at all. I have lengths of bamboo and still some yards of green material. We will regard any provision of French wardrobes down here as franking me to use the attic for my charts and other impedimenta. You, I observe, have no debris.'

'Only a few books.'

'You have a goodly store of books. I shall look forward to a treat.'

'There's a book I'm reading now——' She began walking up and down the linoleum path in the excitement of wondering whether Miss Holland could be brought to share the adventure.

'It is in a way the most wonderful I have met. The most real.'

'No doubt you are a connoisseur.'

'I'm not. But I've never got so much out of a novel before. I say, this stuff shows every mark.'

Miss Holland would get nothing from James. She would read patiently for a while and pronounce him 'a little tedious.'

'It will at first. But you need not be concerned about that. I am at home all day, and it will be a very slight matter to keep things more or less in order. Perhaps we can make a little bargain. I for my part will willingly undertake the rooms and the marketing if you will save me from the *palavering*.'

'Will there be any?'

'Well, for example, the rent. The landlord is a most *odious* man. I abhor the thought of tackling him. You, I am sure, will manage anything of that sort better than I. Yes. Most certainly. You have an air.'

A few words weekly seemed a small price to pay for freedom from the mysteries of cleaning and catering, and Miriam agreed to pay the rent, to call next door and pay it; keeping Sheffield away from the house.

Miss Holland went on talking as if to herself.   Expostulating.
It was a mistake, she concluded, to drop domesticity.   She
preferred to keep her hand in, while safeguarding sufficient
leisure for reading and so on.

Miriam saw her keeping house, dressmaking, and yet free
to wander abroad in the sunlight, and to come home, full of
the life and brightness of London, to rest and read, with her
feet up, 'to counteract the strain upon the heart, of the upright
posture,' following the example of 'those sensible Americans
who discuss business with their feet on the mantelshelf.'   She
judged unconventionalities according as they did or did not
serve the cause of hygiene.

'Much,' she finished hurriedly, as if to avoid further postponing anything Miriam might be going to say, '*Much* can
be done with a damp duster.'

Miriam wondered whether, after all, housework might not
hold some strange charm.   Something that was lacking in a
life lived altogether in the world of men; altogether on the
surface of things.   Always, in relation to household women,
she felt herself a man.   Felt that they included her, with a
half-contemptuous indulgence, in the world of men.   Some of
them, those to whom the man's world was still an exciting
mystery, were a little jealous and spiky.

As if encouraged by silence, Miss Holland pursued her theme.

'I have a horror of becoming an *official* woman.   It is, I
think, a most obnoxious type.   It abounds.   In London it is
to be met wherever women are in positions of responsibility.
Real or fancied.   And it is on the increase.   There have, of
course, always been official women.   Even in rural districts,
where, most unfortunately, they have but one sphere of activity.
We used to call them the curates-in-charge.'

Vicarage humour at first hand.   Miriam laughed suitably;
ensconced, an eavesdropper.

'Church workers.'

'They are the bane of a parish.   Work, yes.   That they
most certainly do, to the accompaniment of loud complaints
on the score of other people's inactivity.   Implying, of course,
that they themselves hold a monopoly of intelligence and

efficiency. Whereas the truth is to be found in their inability to attract helpers or to collaborate with those who really desire to take part in the work. These women are actuated solely by personal ambition, the desire to run the parish and to be openly recognized as doing so. Nothing less will content them. Nothing less. It is a *most* perturbing spectacle. And I, for one, have no hesitation in admitting that I am driven to the conclusion that authority is harmful to women. They grow so *hard*. So *coldly* self-important and dictatorial.'

Miriam knew she would want to run the parish, choose the music, edit the vicar's mind, lecture the parishioners.

'In London many of them are social workers. They spend their time on committees. But not in service. They quell.'

She handled her statements as she had handled the pile of green material, pouncing, taking disdainful hold. Her sentences were sallies, each one leaving her voice halted on an interval of deprecating sounds. Her voice came from a height. She must be standing, poised, in her light way, for movement. Talking as if to herself, assuming a lack of interest. Yet the air was full of her shy desire for response.

'They must be holy terrors.'

'I fear,' chuckled Miss Holland, 'that I am not completely convinced of their holiness.'

'I've never met any of these women. Avoid women on the whole. But I dare say I should be that type myself if I weren't too lazy to achieve a position.'

'Believe me, you could never be official. You are much too artistic.'

Miriam was too disappointed to feel flattered. There was no illumination here. Exposing herself before the tribunal, she had been judged in a class of which the judge knew nothing. Compared with Miss Holland, she might perhaps be called artistic. But it was grievous to be supplied already with a false reputation. To be imagined as cultured in a way that was respected in vicarages.

She glanced around upon the poor things that already she loved with an immemorial love whose secret eluded her, whose going forth she knew to be blind and personal. Her eye was at once arrested by a small dark something upon the white coverlet of her bed. A ladybird. Too square. Perfectly square and motionless. Even as she called to Miss Holland to come through and observe, the sight of it thrilled her in every nerve.

A swish of the curtain and Miss Holland was at her side, bent and peering.

'Dear, dear, *dear!*' she moaned. 'I feared, I *feared*. I'll get the dustpan.'

The floor rocked with her swift departure. Miriam stood fascinated. The unspeakable thing had revealed itself, and she was not only calm but curious. A moment ago it had existed only in her mind, an ultimate she could not imagine herself seeing and surviving. It looked like a fragment of an autumn leaf. Miss Holland's voice sounded in the further room. Miriam listened to the low tones for entertainment while she kept watch.

'I feared, I feared,' and then a swift ferreting, drowning the anxious monologue.

Weary of the scene that was holding up her installation, she turned away to the window, half expecting to be leapt upon from behind. She was vitalized by the incident; tingling from head to foot. It was strange that one could recognize at sight an unknown thing; but far stranger that within a moment of pure shock there should be life, the keen sense of living that stood away outside the bounds of everyday life.

What a set of circumstances were these that brought only vermin to give her the pang of immortality? Not a thing one could testify at a dinner-table. Why not?

When Miss Holland came back she would remind her that monkeys were timid, and fearful of small creeping things. Being a Protestant she probably revelled in Evolution—wouldn't see that it left everything more spooky than before.

She was looking straight in at a window of the opposite house. The panes were clean and clear, the curtains on either side a dull dark green, hanging in straight folds. Sombre. Faintly, clearer as she made it out, a thick tall white candle rose

in the midst of the gloom, just inside the window, changing the
aspect of the curtains, making a picture. Just visible, right
and left, were the shoulders of two high-backed chairs. She
imagined them occupied, the beam of the thick white candle
falling on two forms. But in this street what forms? It was
clear that she and Miss Holland were not the only aliens.
Perhaps 'artistic' bachelor women who made a cult of their
diggings, wore sage-green dresses and would emerge to become
a spectacle known by heart, now both together, now one alone,
crying cultured witticisms from the street to the window.
Women standing critically aside from life, hugely amused by
it. But would such have achieved that candle, at once a person
and a piece of furniture? Lamps they would have, with art
shades. Or if candles, still art shades. It might be an an-
chorite. But the company of such a candle was not solitude.
Underneath the window was a cobbler's shop.

'Just look here,' she cried to Miss Holland coming back
preceded by her voice. The things in her own room seemed
to greet, as she turned, the things in the room across the way.
It was a man's room. It had an air of waiting for an untimed
return.

'I hope,' said Miss Holland, through a rapid scrunching of
paper. 'I trust, it was only those Church Army men.'

Miriam watched her go away, with the dustpan at arm's
length, still gravely expostulating.

'It's dreadful,' she said to her returning form, 'but also
fearfully funny, to find the ultimate horror sitting contentedly,
poor little thing, on the end of your bed.'

She tinkled and tinkled at that, woefully crying out through
her laughter, repudiating and agreeing and contradicting.

'But I admire your spirit,' she wailed finally.

'Do look at this huge candle across the way.'

Miss Holland moved to her side and peered anxiously,
frowning in anticipation.

'Very odd,' she said sceptically. 'A ship's candle, something of the kind.'

'Where did they get it? Besides, too tall, it would burn a
cabin roof. Perhaps an altar candle.'

'Very eccentric.' She turned away, busily, skittishly. Pleased about something, but not interested in the candle.

Her light busy footfall was audible upstairs as Miriam faced the boxes and parcels waiting, piled amongst the furniture of the little back room, to be unpacked. With Sunday at hand, it would never occur to Miss Holland to leave it all and go out. But she, too, must be wanting tea. There could be tea, now, amongst the wreckage. Laughter and relaxation.

Yet not to go out now was to miss so much. To go out, leaving behind this treasure of disorder, and sit at leisure in an undisturbed world, would be to reap the full adventure of being installed. Homekeeping people missed that adventure. They slaved on and on, saying how nice it will be when everything is *straight*. And then wondered why it was not nice.

Left to herself, she would now go out, not only for tea but for the whole evening, into a world renewed. There would be one of those incidents that punctually present themselves at such moments, a link in the chain of life as it appears only when one is cut off from fixed circumstances. She would come home lost and refreshed. Laze through Sunday morning. Roam about the rooms amongst things askew as though thrown up by an earthquake, their exposed strata storied with memory and promise. There would be indelible hours of reading and dreaming, of harvesting the lively thought that comes when one is neither here nor there, but poised in bright light between life ended and a life not yet begun. The blissful state would last until dusk deepened towards evening and would leave her filled with a fresh realization of the wonder of being alive and in the midst of life, and with strength to welcome the week slowly turning its unknown bright face towards her through the London night. With great speed, at the eleventh hour, she would get everything roughly in order.

Miss Holland appeared at the sitting-room door, eyeing the disorder.

Miriam groaned her fatigue aloud.

'Let's leave it,' said Miss Holland, contemptuously. 'Oh, let's *leave* it,' she wailed in a protesting falsetto, which averted face and outstretched fingers disgustedly flipping.

'Let's drop everything and go out for tea,' she went on, relaxing, looking into space, while with eyebrows raised disdainfully she stood halted for response.

'Oh, agreed,' said Miriam. 'I'm expiring.'

'We will *not* expire. We will seek tea *immediately*.'

She swung round on one heel and bounded lightly back into the bedroom with her tinkling laugh. The little scene remained in Miriam's eyes, somewhere within it the exchanged glance of delighted understanding that had driven them both to cover which was not cover, for they were immediately together again, and the dividing curtain could not mask the results of their encounter, the quick movements, the duet of cheerful hummings.

Miriam went back into the little room to collect her outdoor things; checking an impulse to eager snatching, steadying herself against the sudden arrival of the personal note.

Under her hat was the red book. The *personal note* repeated itself before her mind's eye, in print. And as she searched for her gloves the note described itself as it were aloud, in a voice speaking urbanely from the surrounding air. Its indubitable descent; its perhaps too great and withal so manifestly, so wellnigh woefully irretrievable precipitancy. Its so charming and, for all she could at the moment and within the straitly beleaguering the so eminently onerous and exciting circumstances assemble of disturbing uncertainty, so brilliantly, so almost *dazzlingly* sunlit height. In simpler words, things were going too fast and too far. An exact and dramatic landscape of thought. Things seen as going too fast and too far, distilled into refinement. Cuyp.

She tried to imagine herself producing phrases for the landlord from a mental landscape of what would be occurring between them in terms of thought. It would certainly make her dignified, and to the landlord, mysterious. It might daunt, reduce him, keep him at a distance. But it was difficult to weave in the word 'rent' the so simple, the so potently humiliating monosyllable that was the immediate, the actual, the dreadfully unavoidable . . . ornate alias. Ah! Clifford Allbutt. James was the art of beautifully elaborating the ornate alias?

Her eyes roamed as she moved about putting on her things.

Seeking up and down the strip of bedroom for a centre, some running together of effects where her spirit could settle and find its known world about it. There seemed to be none, though the light was fading and the aspect of the room as it had been when her things were first set down was already in the past. Each glance produced the same picture; a picture seen and judged long ago and with which her eyes could do nothing. She took refuge with single objects, finding each satisfactory, but nowhere reaching home. Swimming in transparent shallows, unable to touch bottom, stand steady, and see forth. Her life had somehow ceased. Behind her back unawares, while she had flown from newness to newness, its thread had been snapped. The small frayed end remaining in her hand was drawing her ahead across a level that showed no coverts; no deep places to be invaded by unsummoned dreams and their good end in the recreation of familiar things.

Though it was late when they arrived, the club was just as she had seen it on her first solitary visit. The same hush in the large drawing-room, the same low murmuring of conversation between women half hidden in the depths of easy chairs.

Seated in two little high-backed chairs by the central window, they found themselves looking down on the square, a small forest dim in the twilight, asheen where the light poured in from the street lamps. A twilit loveliness at rest. Walked through, the squares were always a new loveliness, but even at a stroll they passed too quickly. There, at last, was one of the best of them arrested for contemplation.

Away behind was a roomful of independent strangers, also aware of the square set ever before their eyes. This was freedom, in company, enriched. The sense of imprisonment she had felt on coming down the street with Miss Holland, the tangible confirmation when Miss Holland, laughter sounding in the tones of her confidently talking voice, suddenly took her arm, of the note struck too soon, and too high, vanished altogether in the freedom of this neutral territory.

Miss Holland was responding formally, in low tones, to her comments on the aspect of the square. Spontaneity, it was evident, was to be shelved just where it might be safely indulged; just where one attained an impersonality as wide as the wide world.

Suddenly she found herself wanting to say outrageous things. The decorous voices sounding all about her seemed to call for violence. With difficulty she kept her tone subdued. Level it refused to be. The gift of the square imparted to every word the sound of exciting news. News upon which the dear, the for-the-first-time-so-comfortably, so-opulently-visible London twilight closed gently in.

It was to a morning and not to Miss Holland she was speaking. The wide deep spaces of a London Sunday morning that showed invariably within the witnessed falling of a Saturday twilight. Miss Holland's responses showed her struggling between charmed appreciation and a sense that audible comments were not quite within the boundaries of club etiquette. Silence fell, and within it Miriam saw the scales of judgment descend equally balanced. She had, it was true, given no thought to her neighbours and only now, in retrospect, heard her lively tones penetrate the murmurings of the gathered ladies. But—she was wearing her lavender-grey, her mushroom hat of silky straw, both still quite able to hold their own, and still conquering fatigue whenever she put them on. While Miss Holland, though clothed in awareness of her surroundings, was not even stylishly dowdy. Piled upon her head was a mass of blue crinoline, not only faded, but dulled with inextricable dust. Beneath its shapelessness wisps of lank hair made fun of her dignified bearing. A black tie, running from neck to waist of the skimped blouse uniting her coat and skirt, fought with the millinery hat. Only her eyes took the light, and they were at a loss, turned unseeing, under faintly frowning brows, upon the prospect beyond the window.

She was uneasy, disapproving equally of silence and of speech that was not smoothly decorous.

Tea came. Lights went up all over the room; brilliant light shone down upon the stately Queen Anne service, shone through the thinness of the shallow flowered cups.

'Tea,' cried Miriam, through the shifting of chairs that

followed the coming of the light, 'should never be drunk from cold white cups.'

Miss Holland laughed her laugh, and began with large, composed movements to pour out. At once her appearance was redeemed. For a moment Miriam sat basking in her manner. Then her eyes were drawn to two tall figures risen together from deep chairs far away.

'One ought,' she went on to lend a casual air to her first inspection of fellow-members, 'to drink down to a pattern.' They were without hats and therefore residents. And unexpectedly impressive.

'Good porcelain,' Miss Holland was saying, 'is certainly a great enhancement of the charm of the tea-table.'

They were most strange. They radiated a definitely familiar quality as they stood there gazing down the room. At nothing. There was no trace of the awareness of exposure that set the faces of the women sitting about within view, large-hatted in deep chairs; awareness or careful unawareness. Yet as they moved, now, slowly along the clear spaces of the room, they were visibly the figures of an ordeal. Stately in their white-robed splendour, they were still piteous. Something was dispelling the conventional charm usually inseparable from the spectacle of beauty, tall and well-clothed, moving slowly through a room.

The depth of her interest inspired Miriam to feed her conversation with Miss Holland and remain at the same time free to watch. The mystery cleared as the figures drew near. They were sisters, the one quite ordinary, fully aware and fitted out with the regulation feminine charm of bearing. Conscious of piled brown hair, of brilliant oval cheeks, of dark and lively eyes. The upturning bow of her mouth was set in a smile. So it would be set, thought Miriam, years ahead, when the nose and the chin began to approach each other. She was the elder. But her few extra years, the ardour of her head and her splendid form, were in leash to the being of the other. She it was who came unseeing and produced the strange effect. Slender, in childish muslin beside her sister's opulent sophisticated lace, she was formidable. Below her dark hair, drawn flat to the

shape of her head, yet set round it like a mist, was the strong
calm face of a healthy child, a mask clear of expression and
colourless but for the eyes that were startling. Life flowed
from her eyes as if it would wither the air before them. Where
was she? Whence, round-faced child, had she gathered her
wealth of suffering? Her beauty was the beauty of a transfiguration. Here, on this plain afternoon, at the Belmont,
amongst friends.

Reluctantly, as they came quite near, Miriam averted her
screened gaze and met the eyes of the other. Here was con-
ciliation, a deprecating fearfulness changing suddenly as she
came in view of Miss Holland.

'My,' she vowed, wide-mouthed for the leisurely vowel,
'it's Miss Halland.'

Americans! Then perhaps the other girl merely had
neuralgia. Miss Holland had turned, and Miriam saw her
swift disclaiming glance and its change into the shy but brightly
charmed and charming smile, accompanying the greeting that
was yet so formal and, in its apologetic disdainfulness, so like
her voice. She was hidden now behind the tall white figures.
Their voices, playing about her and expanding into the room,
killed Miriam's interest. There was, for her, something in the
American voice that robbed its communications of any depth
of meaning. The very ease of their talk, its expressiveness, the
direct swift way they handled their stores of information and
communicated their thoughts, made even the most fascinating
topics fall dead, rifled of essential significance.

Her stranded attention was caught by the sound of blended
voices approaching from the door. Voices in the midst of talk,
having come into the room talking, but not in the least in the
English way of making conversation to cover an entry. They
were in full swing, their sentences overlapping. Obviously
noticing nothing and no one. They were using the club as a
place to talk in, and were one voice. Sisters or cousins. Yet
they had arranged themselves in chairs without breaking their
talk, which went forward so eagerly that they seemed to be
exchanging opinions for the first time. Now where had she
heard, between sisters, exactly that effect? Somewhere

between members of a large family that formed a society in itself?

No, the three Bannerman girls, just three, no more, living in seclusion with their parents, marching about all over Barnes for years, in perpetual conversation in high, rapid voices.

They had suddenly appeared at the church decorations, keeping it up even there, amongst themselves. Speaking to no one else. Being really interested, but somehow conveying their conviction that the people all around them were too stupid even to be noticed. They had accepted work politely, making clever comments without looking at those who instructed them, and then sat there with quickly moving fingers and a ceaseless fretting of voices. Always one shape of tone: beginning on a refined argumentative switchback of sound. Harriett had caught it, taking them off, for days.

'Isn't it verray re*mar*kable, my dear Miriam, that such a singularly tall man as Mr Spiffkins should be a radical?'

'Don't you, my dear Miriam, consider it highly alarming that rain falls *down* instead of *up*?'

She listened. Here, perhaps, as the Bannermans now appeared in her mind for the first time since she left home, would be light upon that long-forgotten mystery. But a question intruded. Why, since their voices followed the same pattern of sound and bore the same suggestion of being at loggerheads with the social order, why had not the Lycurgans recalled the Bannerman girls? Certainly if they were alive and in London, all three were now active members of the Lycurgan society; the amused superiority in their voices added to the Lycurgan tide of amused superiority to everything on earth.

Yet these women who had brought them back, though they had the Lycurgan voice, had nothing of the crisp cocksureness of the socialist intelligentsia. They were unanimously be-labouring someone, hitting out right and left, but within their expressive voices, moulding their lively scorn, animating the unvarying tone-shape of the intelligentsia-in-argument, was *sorrow*.

The coming of their tea brought a pause. With the ceasing

of their voices warmth withdrew from the sound of the room, and returned at the first phrase sounding together with the cheerful gush of tea hurriedly poured.

'Well, I think it's just simply incomprehensible.'

Miriam knew it was not. She half turned, strangely sure that they would welcome her and quite simply state a case. They were not a clique. Something in their voices related them to everybody in the world. They had the selflessness of those who keep an eye everywhere, without discrimination of persons. They would be at once interested, even in herself, and quite blind. She turned and found a group of three, three small women with one face; a face she knew well at Lycurgan meetings and liked, but always with a queer thrill of uncertainty. It was vital, intimately intelligent, and yet alien, seeming at once to light up and to darken its surroundings.

The club, she thought as she turned gladly back to the loneliness created by Miss Holland's surrounded state, was going to get hold of her in a way of which she had never dreamed, since at the outset it had brought her to the edge of the whirlpool of people with whom this dark face was in her mind so richly associated. Set in a row of Lycurgan faces, all screened, more or less, in the English way and not different, in silence, from a row of Primrose League faces, this one face would stand out, a pale, bony oval set with crisp hair; and eyes, under dark brows, richly despairingly intent. The moment the lecture was over it would be visible, now here now there, and always in eager speech.

Small wonder, since it turned out to be three, that she was always seeing it.

'Now Mrs Wilson *is* charming,' said one. 'A far more charming personality than he.'

However indiscreet, the remark was illuminating. Set up thus on a placard, she need have no hesitation in carrying it away, for Hypo. But she must acknowledge the receipt of it. Turning full round, she met a vivid face that boldly smiled, and, smiling, was drowned in a vivid flush. Miriam smiled too, basking for a moment in the charm, glowing so brightly in its role of a prolonged haunting impression come suddenly

to life at her elbow.   But so formidably.   In place of one figure
a whole group, a multiplicity of attraction.   She turned away
to find that Miss Holland's friends had disappeared.

Miss Holland sat, flushed with talk, quietly but quite
evidently summoning composure; as nearly flustered as it was
possible for her to be.

'How tall those women are,' said Miriam, still intent on the
group behind.

'I did not introduce them,' replied Miss Holland, busying
herself, with downcast eyes, amongst the flowered tea-cups.
'I—well—I thought——' Her deprecating tone collapsed into
a murmur and rose again, recovering.   'Yes, they are tall, both
mother and daughter.'

'Astounding.   I thought they were sisters.'

'Their name is Wheeler.   It is a most interesting story.'

Nothing about Americans could be really interesting.   But
Miss Holland, without looking up, was launched upon her
narrative.

'They are from San Antonio in Texas.   The child Estella
is just fifteen years of age.   Yes, it is remarkable.   A warmer
clime, I suppose.   Still it is very remarkable.   Her grand-
mother was Spanish.   And that perhaps may account for her
exceptional temperament.   She is a musician.   The 'cello.
They have travelled to London for her training.   It seems that
her teachers at home were obliged to confess they could do
nothing further for her.'

'Why not Germany?'

'Well, that is just it.   The reason for their coming to
London is the strangest part of the story.   It seems that there
is a Pole, a celebrated 'cellist.   The child heard him once,
years ago, in New York, and has been saying ever since that he
is the only man in the world who can teach her.   He, it appears,
is giving performances in London this winter.   So they have
come.   The child thinks of nothing else.   For the moment
she is at the Philharmonic Academy.   She dislikes it.   I am
sincerely sorry for her mother.   She is most courageous; and
so wise.   Insists on physical culture.   Very wise.   Skipping
and so on.   At a gymnasium.   The great trouble at the moment

is that it now appears that the Pole takes no pupils. Also that they are not too well off. Estella, however, is determined to see him.'

'Has she given concerts?'

'Not so far. But the Academy wishes to bring her out. At the Queen's Hall.'

'Wicked!'

'Certainly she is young.'

Miss Holland hesitated. She was evidently still full of communications about the Wheelers, but suddenly unwilling to continue. She was guarding them. Miriam saw plainly that her interest was not to go too far. That, she felt, was all to the good. Here was the beginning of an understanding that their interests were to be independent. But the possessiveness and the mystery was making her dislike these Wheelers. They had Miss Holland's interest in a way she was sure she would never do, and Miss Holland was admitting it and saying too, with her honest embarrassment, that she believed these wonderful people would not be interested in her fellow-lodger.

She was her fellow-lodger. Now that personal depths had been revealed, that strange fact remained; an achievement.

CHAPTER II

MIRIAM sat through the evening reading by lamplight in the disorderly little room. Unsatisfactorily. Her attention wandered to Miss Holland lecturing in the East End, and to the thoughts in Miss Holland's mind as she stood confronted by the roomful of dilapidated people.

The shaded lamplight left everything in gloom but the page whose words, yesterday so potent, brought to-night only a sense of the gulf between life and the expression of it. She had reached the conclusion that fiction was at worst a highly flavoured drug and at best as much an abstraction as metaphysics, when Miss Holland came back.

She stood in the doorway tall and dim; silent and dubious with fatigue. But when Miriam suggested going out in search of coffee she came to life in horrified resistance, announced her belief in the restorative power of weak tea, and vowed that not on any account would she issue forth without good cause at such an hour.

And out in the blue-lit gloom of the Euston Road, hurrying timidly along, she still protested. But behind her woeful protests was delight. And once they were safely inside the heavily frosted inner doors and the little padrone, as Miriam had predicted, came forward to welcome them and, waving away a hovering waiter, himself found them places and took their small order, she sat back upon her red velvet sofa evidently enjoying the adventure. But beyond a single comprehensive glance, she had not noticed her surroundings. She remarked upon the cleanliness, the cheerful Alpine oleographs. Of all the rest she was unaware.

To have her here, disarmed of her fears, was not enough. But even if they came again and again there would never be more than that. She would never expand to the atmosphere.

Would always sit as she was doing now, upright and insulated, making formal conversation; decorously busy with the small meal.

The place was not crowded. Every one there was distinctly visible—the lonely intent women in gaudy finery, the old men fêting bored, laughing girls who glanced about; the habitués, solitary figures in elderly bondage to the resources of the place.

'Of course,' said Miriam at last, 'there are all sorts of queer people here.'

She sat back, unwilling to go, looking out into the room as if unaware of Miss Holland's preparations to depart, following immediately on her last sip of the excellent coffee. But supposing Miss Holland should even for a moment sit back and contemplate her surroundings? She would see only material for pity or disgust. See only morally. Her interest in individuals would be an uninteresting interest. That young man, with his pose of careful conscious detachment, would not for her be any kind of epitome, but just a young man—'probably some sort of student.'

'It is now,' said Miss Holland, glancing at her wrist-watch, 'well past midnight. This has been a unique experience. And, just for this once, I do not object to it. But it must certainly not be repeated.'

Miriam gazed at her. She was blushing. She had seen all that there was to see. Miriam remembered her own first horror. But that had been alone and in youthful ignorance.

'I'm sorry you don't like my little haunt.'

'It is scarcely that. The place is clean and pleasant, and doubtless a great convenience to many people. But, dear me, dear me, I can only imagine the horror of my chief in beholding me sitting here, and at such an hour.'

Astonishment kept Miriam dumb and passed into resentment. Having delivered her judgment, Miss Holland now sat contemptuously drawing on her gloves. The episode over and escape at hand, she released a scorn that was almost venomous. It lingered about her politely smiling relief, an abominable look of triumph. Of personal triumph.

Miriam clung to her silence. She felt the advantage fall to

her own side as she saw Miss Holland's acceptance of her unspoken thoughts.

'It is different for yourself,' she said in answer to them. 'You are free from the necessity of considering appearances.'

'I'm a guttersnipe, thank heaven,' said Miriam.

Miss Holland laughed. A small sound incapable of reaching the next table. She was really amused.

'You are anything but that. And in certain respects you may consider yourself fortunate.'

Donizetti's had been insulted. At sight of Miss Holland hurrying with bent head, as if weathering a gale of contamination, down the aisle between the rows of little tables, Miriam hated her. Hated her refusal to place herself outside the pale of feminine dignity. The narrow pale. Deep. But were they deep, these people who went about considering their dignity? 'Dignity is absurdity,' she vowed, keeping step with Miss Holland's light swift walk.

There is one thing worse than a dignified man and that is an undignified woman. Chesterton. It sounded so respectful; chivalrous. Made me try to remember to be dignified for a whole day. I tried to crush Hypo by quoting it.

'Just so,' he said. 'Dignity is the privilege of the weak.'

She tried to imagine Miss Holland undignified. Rushing about and babbling inconsequently. Tiresome, men called those women, but were glad of them if they had kind hearts. Mrs Orly has no dignity. But she is neither weak nor tiresome. Her heart is a . . . er . . . domesticated tornado.

Walking home, estranged from Miss Holland, Miriam found her own life, that had stood all day far away and forgotten, all about her again; declaring itself independent of the success or the failure of this new relationship. Like a husband's life . . . the life he goes off into in the morning and can lose himself in, no matter what may be going on at home. If this new arrangement were a success, something would be added to life. If it were a failure, nothing would be taken away.

By the time they reached home she felt free from all interest in Miss Holland and saw their contract as it had at first appeared, a marriage of convenience; a bringing down of expenses that

would allow them both to live more comfortably than they
could alone. Miss Holland no doubt saw it in the same light.
The extremest differences of outlook were neither here nor
there. There would be no need, now that these first disordered
hours were over, for any association beyond what was needed
for the running of their quarters.

She looked forward to getting to bed in the new surroundings,
recapturing singleness and the usual Saturday night's sense of
the spaces of Sunday opening ahead. Fatigue had given way
to the new lease of strength that always came if she stayed up
long enough and, when she found herself safely behind the
curtain, she hoped that Miss Holland, audible on the other side,
was sharing her sense of refreshment. She began to regret
the incident that had reduced their exchange to courteous
formalities, and to wish for an impossible re-establishment of
the inexperience of the earlier part of the day.

Only impossible because of the way people were influenced
by things said and done. She was herself, she knew, but never
quite permanently: never believing that what people thought
themselves to be and thought other people to be, went quite
through. . . . Always certain that underneath was something
else, the same in everybody.

'Of course, I could never feel the same again.' She could
never make up her mind whether it was good or bad not to be
able to make that statement from the heart. Whether it was
good fortune to have access to a region where everything was
forgotten, and within which it was impossible to believe people
were what they represented themselves to be. Yet speaking
or acting suddenly from this region where she lived with herself was always disastrous. And still there remained that
unalterable certainty that invisibly others were exactly what she
thought them, and would suddenly turn into the person she was
seeking all the time in every one . . . the person she knew
was there.

It seemed now, so far off were those first bright early hours,
that Miss Holland and she had been long associated. The first
freshness had gone, or she would not now find herself with her
hand on her own life. But although that was recovered, there

was now also something else. Something going forward even as she moved about slowly, delightfully hindered by new things and the need for new movements that made the process of going to bed a conscious ceremonial.

On the other side of the curtain Miss Holland was moving about in the same leisurely obstructed way. Her things were not new; but she was having to find her way amongst them afresh. This must be bringing all sorts of things into her mind. They were sharing adventure. At the very least, there was that. It was a great deal. From the point of view of the amazingness of life and people, it was everything. And now the strange something was growing clearer. Their prolonged silence was speaking. Of course . . . '*C'est dans le silence que les âmes se révèlent.*'

Miriam tiptoed about, breathlessly listening. Clearly, almost audibly, the silence was knitting up the broken fabric of their intercourse. Thought of now, Miss Holland seemed young and small. She had been, once. Alone with herself, of course, she still was. And at the centre of her consciousness there was an image of her new friend, not as she appeared to be, but as she really was; just as within her own consciousness there was an image of the real Miss Holland.

Miss Holland did not know this. Only one here and there seemed to know it. And those one never came across, except in the street suddenly, walking by themselves. But Miss Holland was feeling the result of the silence. The result of their having been, *à force de préoccupations*, alone in company. Maeterlinck would call them *menus préoccupations*. But a person standing lighting candles and moving about a room is . . . what?

A puff of wind touched the large window, rattling it gently in its frame. Miss Holland muttered to herself.

'I fear that window rattles,' she said at the next sound, but still to herself, a meditative tone.

'Yes,' said Miriam in cheerful conversational voice, and at once felt its irrelevance. She had answered only the tone. In the actual communication there was a fresh source of division. She loved rattling windows; loved, loved them. Anything

the wind could do, especially at night. The window was old.
It would certainly rattle: perhaps bump and bang. It would
be better even than the small squeak, squeak, of the small
lattice at Tansley Street. And with each sound she would be
aware of Miss Holland, disliking it.

'I can't *abide* rattling windows,' said Miss Holland, vin-
dictively.

'I love them.'

'What a strange taste,' said Miss Holland ruefully, and
immediately laughed her tinkling laugh. They laughed together, and began moving more briskly, creating a cheerful
noise to emphasize small jests. Again and again Miss Holland's
laugh sounded. She was happy and pleased. How embarrassing it would have been, Miriam reflected, if the last stage of the
toilet had presented itself without this cover of bright sound.
The trial, once happily over, was over for good.

She sat on her pillow and slid down carefully into the freshness of the new bed. Its compactness was not disturbed.
Her clothes were all out of sight. The room about her was
exactly as it had been when freshly arranged.

'Oh,' she cried, listening to the pleasant bumping of the
window as her body relaxed on the unyielding level of the new
mattress and the low pillow fitted itself to her neck. 'Oh,
" music that softlier on the spirit lies——"'

'I hope you are not alluding to the window,' chuckled Miss
Holland.

'Oh, my bed, my angelic little bed. I thought it might seem
narrow, but it is so hard and flat that I feel as if I were lying on
the plane of the ecliptic with no sides. And I seem so long.
I can see myself like someone laid out.'

'What a very dismal idea!'

'Oh, no. I always think of it when I sleep in beds that don't
let you down. It doesn't depress me a bit. You see, I have
no imagination. But my bed at Tansley Street was all hum-
mocks. There was only one way I could lie at all and I made
no shape. Now I feel like a crusader on a tomb, and utterly
comfortable. And the little light coming through the curtain
from your side makes a quite perfect effect, a green twilight.'

'You shall enjoy the perfect effect for a few moments longer. I am going to wedge that abominable window.'

Something almost like fear took possession of Miriam. Protest was impossible. It was clear Miss Holland must not be tormented. Her mind clung to the wind-sounds, whilst with small exasperated mutterings Miss Holland sought about for something to fit the gap. An immense discomfort settled upon her when the window was finally dumb. Its silence seemed to press upon the air. And though the window was open at the top, the room seemed close. It was as if Miss Holland had robbed her of a companion and as if far away the companion were reproaching her for yielding without protest to the world that keeps a suspicious eye on the doings of the weather, an attitude she hated like an infection. The room seemed now full of Miss Holland; rebuked by her into a dead stillness. That would be there on all the nights. Each one, dumb and dead. The prospect was unnerving. There was something of the atmosphere of the sick-room in this awful calm. Miss Holland's candle was the nightlight, keeping going the hot pressure of the evening. Yet most people probably disliked a rattling window, the sound that made a stillness in the room and in the street. It was bad to be so different and to like being different.

How difficult to sleep in this consciously quiet enclosure. For it was not the quiet of a still night, the kind of night in which you listen to the expanse of space. It was a stillness filled with the coiling emanation of a humanity recognizing only itself, intent only on its own circlings. The darkness when it presently came would be thick with the remainder of the continuous coiling and fret of all those people who live perpetually at war with everything that is not perfectly secure.

Miss Holland's light was out. She was apparently sitting up in bed arranging draperies at great length.

'I have not locked the door,' she said, suddenly: Miriam despaired.

'I think for to-night it does not matter. We can make a point of remembering it in future.'

'I 'm afraid,' said Miriam, 'I should *never* remember it.'

'Have you not been in the habit of locking your door?'

'I never even thought of it.'

'Strange,' said Miss Holland. And Miriam began to suppose that it was strange. She ran over in her mind some of the odd people from time to time sharing her lonely top floor. Foreign waiters when Mrs Bailey was doing well, or queer odd men who could not afford the downstairs rooms. She had never, at night, given them a single thought. But that was not the sort of thought Miss Holland meant, or not consciously. But all this was perfectly horrible. Yet was it foolish, or perhaps unkind, never to have been aware? O'Laughlin, dear O'Laughlin. She had been aware of him. Sorry.

'There was,' she said, 'a drunken Irish journalist who used to come blundering up the stairs at all hours of the night.'

'Horrible, horrible,' breathed Miss Holland.

'His door,' it occurred to her for the first time, 'was at right angles to mine.' Miss Holland was gasping. 'He used to stumble about on the landing, and sometimes, poor dear, be sick.'

'Dear, dear, dear! It was a most extraordinary establishment. But I think the oddest thing is that you should not have made fast the door.'

'I suppose so. But I would trust Tommy O'Laughlin drunk or sober, now I come to think of it. He never paid his bills, poor dear, and he borrowed.'

'He must have been a worthless creature.'

'He was a gentleman, Tommy was, and a dear. Though he once embarrassed me frightfully. It was at dinner. Of course he was intoxicated, though not looking so. In the midst of a long tirade about Home Rule he burst into tears and said if he had only seen Miss Henderson earlier in his life he would have been a different fellow.'

'No doubt he admired you immensely!'

'I'd never spoken to him.'

Miss Holland laughed wisely, but a little scornfully. No châtelaine, of course, would boast of scalps.

'He was married!'

'Dear, dear!' breathed Miss Holland.

'Trying for a divorce.'

'Dear, dear, *dear!*'

Miriam awoke in the darkness abruptly. About her were the images that had filled her mind when Miss Holland's candle had gone out. She regarded them sleepily, wondering what could so soon have called her back. What was calling her now, urgently, out from the thickness of sleep. She stirred and woke completely.

'Are you awake?' Miss Holland's voice coming anxious and reproachful through the stillness was added to the minute, unmistakable irritations.

'Yes, are you?   I mean are you being devoured alive?'

'Indeed, indeed, I *am*,' wailed Miss Holland. 'It is a *disaster*.'

'It's weird,' said Miriam, lunging. 'Where can they all come from?   I'm going to get up.'

'Indeed, that is all we can do. Light candles and make instant warfare.'

'I'm so sleepy.   I think I shall change in the dark.'

'I fear that will be useless,' groaned Miss Holland, striking a match. 'I fear, I fear the worst.'

Out on the green floor and with the two candles cheerfully gleaming. Alone, such an adventure would have been misery.

She grew interested in following Miss Holland's instructions, and was almost disappointed when the white expanse of her bed offered no further prey.

'Seven,' she announced.

'All drowned?' asked Miss Holland suspiciously.

'M'm, poor things.'

'I fear I do not share your solicitude,' chuckled Miss Holland.

'Well, perhaps I associate them with summer.   In a London summer there are always one or two, having their little day. I've tried once or twice to keep still and endure.'

'And then?'

'I shake my nightgown out of the window, but always feel mean.'

'You are *most* tender-hearted.'

'I agree with the Frenchman, "*ce n'est point la piqûre dont je me plains, c'est le promenade.*"'

'You speak French delightfully, toote ah fay kom oon Parisienne.'

'Imitation; I can imitate any sound. But where do all these fleas *come* from?'

'The floor, the floor, I fear.'

'Heaven and earth! We must leave at once.'

'Well, I think perhaps with perchloride in the cracks . . .'

'Meantime?'

'We must do our best.'

'It goes from the brain to the toes.'

'To the *toes*. But only for the unfortunate possessors of thin skins. And them, the wretches seek. If there were in the universe only one flea, it would make straight for me.'

Her voice ended on a childish wail. *Fleee*, she had said, making it innocent and pretty.

'Do you mean to say there are people . . .?'

'I do indeed. During my first period of training in the slums I was amazed at the complete insensibility of many of my fellow-workers. Amazed and, under the circumstances, envious.'

'Oh, I don't envy them a bit. Those people with skins like felt; they miss everything.'

'I agree. At the same time, I think a moderately thick skin is a boon. I see no disadvantage in escaping intolerable discomforts. It is possible to have too thin a skin.'

'For survival, yes. Blond people are dying out, they say.'

'Blondes have not a monopoly of thin skins.'

'No. I have a friend who slums. She loathes the poor.'

'Dear, dear; a most unfortunate qualification for her work.'

'Not their poverty. Their sameness. She is one of the kindest people I know.'

'Strange.'

'They ought to be pensioned.'

'The poor?'

'Everybody. I should love to be pensioned.'

'And remain in idleness and dependence? Oh, no.'

'Not dependence. Interdependence. No compulsion.'

'What would you do?'

'Spend several years staring; and then go round the world.'

'You are delightful! I am not sure that I approve of the years of staring. But to go round the world would, of course, be most enchanting.'

'Yes; but I should not want to improve my mind. I should still stare. If I went. Probably I shouldn't go. Nothing short of dynamite will shift me. I am astounded to find myself shifted here.'

'I fear at the moment you must be wishing yourself back again.'

She had no realization of the adventure it was to be anywhere at all. To her it was not a strange, strange adventure that their two voices should be sounding together in the night, a double thread of sound in a private darkness, making a pattern with all the other sounds in the world. But she had accepted the compliment. There was a vibration in her voice: joyful.

Again and again they were awakened for battle, until their slumber was too deep to be disturbed.

St Pancras bells were cheerfully thumping the air when Miriam got up to wander about in the dark brilliance that filled the room like the presence of a guest, and was so exaggerated that it not only supplied a topic wherewith to start the morning, but an occupation engrossing enough to free her, even in thought, from descent into the detail of the day. It held everything off and yet kept her in happy communion with Miss Holland, moving busily the other side of the curtain.

Yet the night had done its work. A host of statements were plucking at her mind: balancing the quality of life here and life at Tansley Street. At week-ends. Behind them was a would-be disquieting assertion of the now complete remoteness of both her working life and the eventful leisure that had for so long ousted the old-time Tansley Street evenings. It was a bill of costs, flourished; demanding to know what she had done.

But it stood off, powerless to gain the centre of her attention, making no break in her sense of being nowhere; of inhabiting, within a shadowless brilliance, a living peace that held her immensely unoccupied, and ready, whenever things should once more present themselves in detail, to see them all in a fresh light.

For a while it seemed that they could never again so present themselves. The light as she gazed into it was endless, multiplying upon itself; drawing her away from all known things. Life henceforth would more fully attain her, lived as at this moment she knew it could be lived, uncalculating from the deeps of a masked splendour.

It would not last. Already the strange moments were linking themselves with kindred strange moments in the past. But, like them, it set itself while it lasted over against the rest of her experience, with a challenge.

It was growing steadily darker.

'It's a thunderstorm.'

'I think so. The air is most oppressive.'

Miss Holland came and stood at her own half of the window so that they were side by side and visible to each other. Above the curtain screening the lower part of their window, they looked across to the white pillar of candle. A flash of bright daylight lit up the grey street, and soon the wheels of the storm rumbled high up across the sky. Heavy drops fell slowly, increasing until they came in a torrent.

'That will carry it off.'

'Sometimes I don't mind storms. I don't to-day.'

They held their places at the window, watching the pale lightning light the rain, hearing the thunder follow more swiftly. Presently a blinding white fire and a splintering crash just above their heads made them both exclaim.

As the thunder rolled bumping and snarling away across the sky, they saw the figure of a man appear from the darkness beyond the candle and stand pressed close to the window with arms upstretched and laid against the panes. Through the sheets of rain his face was not quite clear. But he was dark and pale and tall and shouting at the storm. So he lived there alone. The storm was a companion. He was alone and aware. Had he seen the new people across the way?

A brilliant flash lit up the white face and its frame of heavy hair. The dark eyes were looking straight across.

Yeats: and he lived *here*. Miriam drew back and sat down on the end of her bed. This queer alley was then the place in all London in which to live. He had found it for himself. Was he dismayed at the sight of Philistines invading the retreat where he lived hidden amongst unseeing villagers? She vowed not again to look across when there was any sign of his presence. He should be invaded without knowing it. She would see him go in and out, see without seeing: screening him even from her own observation. And all the time his presence would cast its light upon their frontage.

'The strange room,' said Miss Holland, who also had left the window, 'has a tenant as eccentric as itself.'

'Do you know who it *is*?' Miriam stole back to the window to learn the disposition of the door of his house. He had disappeared. It was a side door, next to the cobbler's window, like theirs next to the stonemason's.

'It is Yeats. W. B. Yeats . . . the poet.'

'Indeed?' exclaimed Miss Holland delightedly. 'A poet. That is charming. Quite enchanting to feel that poetry is being written so near at hand.'

She was peering out, as if looking for verses on the air between the opposing windows. She had no feeling of shyness in mentioning his work. If unobserved she could catch him at it, she would note his methods. Perhaps he would sit there at work in his window. But the least they could do, having innocently become witnesses of his workshop, would be to stand off and leave him free.

To disperse Miss Holland's concentration, she rushed into speech.

'I've known him by sight for years, wandering about in a black cloak. One night I was strolling along the strip of pavement round one of the square gardens. It was quite dark under the trees between the stretches of lamplight, and there was nobody about. Suddenly in a patch of light I was confronted by a tall figure, also strolling. We both stood quite still, staring into each other's eyes with thoughts far away, each taking in only the fact of an obstruction. Then I realized it was Yeats. I can't remember how we got past each other. One of us must presently have plunged into the gutter. But, looking back, it seems as if we walked through each other.'

Miss Holland produced a series of bird-like sounds, each seeming in turn to refuse to make a word.

The storm was moving on and the strange light, lifting as the sky cleared, left a blankness.

Later in the morning the light from a clear high sky broke up the harmony between the things in the room and set a pallor upon the green pathway to the window. It was the end of a story, the story of the first morning—a single prolonged moment that would last.

It was over, and here she was, conscious of her surroundings.

Something must be swiftly woven into the treasure she held in her hands or she would drop into the crude spaces of this midday light and lose the threads. She heard Miss Holland, as if in response to her need, leave the little back room and go upstairs. It would be in order, the little back room. A room apart, like Mag's and Jan's old sitting-room in Kenneth Street that used to seem such a triumph of elaborate living. Her spirit went forth and nested incredulously within the little back room.

'It will mean growing plump and sedentary. Not wanting to sail forth and see people. Wanting people to come to me, hear the tinkle of my tea-things, sink into the world a bright little afternoon-tea scene makes on Sundays for people who have no centre.'

By Jove, yes. One of the reasons why household people like the odd, homeless sort is that they make them realize their own snugness, by revelling in it.

Miss Holland was audible upstairs rattling saucepan lids. They were to feed up there, kept warm by the ugly oil-cooker, and reserve the back room for elegant life and tea-parties.

Already Miss Holland had made breakfast on the cooker. By means of some mechanism in its interior. Interesting to explore. One day she would explore it. Find out its secret and then, to be quite sure, ask Miss Holland. It stood out, as she thought of it, as the most fascinating thing upstairs, next to the way the light came through the long lattice; and the shadows upon the slopes of the roof.

'You shall teach me,' she heard her own sleepy voice over the welcome tray; 'how to kick——'

'How to kick a cooper!' Miss Holland had trilled without a moment's hesitation, and, after they had laughed: 'Kippers require *very* little in the way of cooking.' A memory of Eleanor: ''Addocks don't 'ardly *need* any cooking, de-er.'

She tipped herself off the little bed that made such an excellent sofa, and strolled into the back room.

It was darker than ever. Round and round she looked, taking in the things. Looking for more, and different, things. Absurdly half believing that the things she saw would change, would somehow become different under her eyes.

Green serge curtains, patched and faded, hung dismally on either side of the window. Two easy chairs covered with faded threadbare cretonne filled, with their huge ugliness, the main part of the floor-space. Between them stood a stained and battered bamboo table and an ancient footstool, worn colourless. Pushed into a corner was a treadle sewing-machine, and at its side a small round table bearing a tarnished lamp. That was all. That was all there would be in their sitting-room.

The worst was that nothing shone. Nothing reflected light. It suddenly struck her as an odd truth that nothing of Miss Holland's reflected light. Even the domed wooden cover of the sewing-machine, which was polished and should have shone, was filmed and dull.

The only suggestion of life in the room would be the backs of the books stacked in piles on the mantelshelf. She found relief for her oppression in the minute gilded titles of some of the books. They gleamed faintly in the gloom, minute threads of gold.

Well, here it was, the lovely little sitting-room. . . .

She moved about in it, still unable quite to exorcize the idea that it would change. With eyes cast down, she made her way from part to part, imagined varnish on the floor. Flowers set about. People, hiding the chairs. It would be pain to bring friends in. Cruelty to ask any one to endure the room for an hour.

There would be no tea-parties.

When her attention returned, Miss Holland's dead belongings had changed a little. They were forgotten and familiar. Here, after all, was a room and a window, and the things were sufficient. Unobtrusive, like dowdy clothes. She remembered how, between whiles, she loved dowdiness. How her heart went forth with mysterious desire to thoroughly dowdy, flat-haired women. Women who had no style but their set of beliefs.

Something of this kind must have drawn her to Miss Holland, even while she saw her only as a possible sharer of expenses.

Miss Holland had been brought by her star. She was moving about on the upstair landing in her heavy, light-footed way, busy and intent. She coughed. Her cough had exactly the sound of her voice.

Would it be possible to go through life in the state of permanent protest expressed by that eloquent cough? For a day perhaps. But a night's sleep plays strange tricks.

Yet the shock of the furniture had confirmed her sense that something was being offered. Low-toned, apparently gloomy, yet having a strange fascination, a *quality*. If she put forth no resistance it might be the most exciting, revealing, adventure she had yet had. It was an offer; an offer of the chance of becoming a postulant châtelaine.

'But you make tea with a *charm*! This is nectar!'

Miriam stood with the teapot in her hand, looking forward to everlasting Sundays of making tea for Miss Holland and charming her with conversation. They had talked all the afternoon without weariness. The day stretched back long and eventful, full of talk and laughter, to the far-off episode of the morning. Filled with memories, the rooms had grown dear. And the evening lay ahead, secure, if they chose to remain shut up here together. Then a week apart. No evenings. Miss Holland coming home late and tired. There would be only the week-ends for the continuation of their talk.

'The fiancée came to tea yesterday,' she said, unawares, and stopped. Miss Holland, surely, must be weary of her stories. 'I must stop,' she said, 'finish my tea and absolutely, really unpack.'

'By no means, mademoiselle, having uttered the fascinating word, you must continue.'

Forcing back a smile, Miriam went on with her story. Marvelling at a world that had left this woman to loneliness. Lonely as she was, she scanned life unenviously, placed herself at once sympathetically within the experience of any one presented to her. It was as if she herself had had vast experience. Yet in her life there were only those two parts: the vicarage home until she was thirty-five, and then this life in London. She had brought with her all the old-fashioned ideas, and yet, without being a socialist, had a forward-going mind, a surer certainty of social transformation than was to be found amongst the Lycurgans.

'I told her I hoped she knew she was marrying the best man in the world.'

'Delightful. You made her very happy.'

'Although extremely strong-minded and in the midst of a successful career, she is a girl, the English girl in the midst of the divine illusion.'

'Why divine *illusion*? So contradictory.'

'Well, illusion because its picture of what life with the beloved will be is mistaken. Divine because it reveals to both the best in themselves and each other, what they really *are*, without knowing it until then.'

'Y . . . es,' said Miss Holland, clasping the edge of the table and gazing out through the window. 'It is unfortunate that it is so frequently doomed to die and inevitably to change.'

'Never. In women, absolutely never, once it 's there.'

'Ah, in *women*.'

'She 's an amazing person. Can fall out of a moving cab

without being hurt.   She said, of course, that she knew.   But
wanted to hear all about him.'

'You were able to render her a charming service.'

'No.   It frightened me for her sake that she wanted to talk
about him.   Of course, she thought me tongue-tied.   I was.
But only because feeling that her best realization was just
that moment with me.   If we had talked, there would have been
a wilderness of detail, and the moment gone without taking its
full effect.'

'Yet it is most natural that she should have wished to talk
of him.'

'It frightened me.   She had a charming white hat.'

Though she went on for a while humouring Miss Holland's
desire for pictures and stories, she now framed her discourse
in ready-made phrases, and was interested in seeing the way
they made effects such as she herself had often gathered up from
overheard conversations, and in discovering how they fitted
a shape of thought about life and led on automatically to other
phrases, little touches that finished them off; till she began to
believe that life was expressible in these forms of thought which
yet she knew left everything untouched.

But the centre of her interest, the thing that was making her
talk grow absent and careless, and consist more and more of
sounds in response to Miss Holland's lingering consideration
of all that had pleased her, was the way that unawares during
their long sitting the room had come to life.   Nothing now
looked dingy.   There was a warm brightness; within the
air.

When their talk had drifted to a pause and she was alone,
she ruefully regarded the day's interchange.   Shadowless only
by being an excursion into a world she had long ago ceased to
inhabit.   By using only materials that would make common
ground, she had woven a fabric of false impressions.

Again and again, as they talked, the set of circumstances
that were the zest of her personal life had risen before her, in
terms such as Miss Holland would use in describing them,
and made a preoccupation that had kept her a bright and
interesting talker.   Yet Miss Holland was aware.   Though in

her eagerness for every word she had shown only awareness of a different reach and different perceptions, she knew, without recognizing its nature, that between them there was a gulf.

To keep back even half-accepted points of view was not fair play. Brought uneasiness. Yet why tell her of things that might not happen?

CHAPTER III

SERENITY had retreated outdoors, and increased there. To-day, in the space between the week's work and the week-end with its pattern ready-set, was serenity immeasurable; given by autumn. Autumn gleaming beyond the park railings through sunlit mist.

Autumn had accumulated unawares. But this meeting with it had begun early this morning in the balmy stillness of the square. Just when the lame old woman had crossed the street. Cheerfully; unhampered by heat or cold or wind.

It had made the happiness of the morning's work, its gaiety and ease. And now at its midday fullness it made the visit of the Brooms—so central as she had sat at her ledgers—retreat into the background. This still air passing into her spirit, the great trees standing in it, thick with coloured leaves upon the spread of misty grass, stamping their image, would remain when the rest of the holiday was forgotten.

Yet the Brooms, both Grace and Florrie, belonged to the unfathomable depth of autumn. Not to its wholeness. To single features. Any single feature contemplated brought them there to look and love. Only in London. They belonged to London from the first. To the heavy, tinted trees. To the first breath of exciting, oncoming cold, distilling the radiance of the sun-warmed earth. To the mauve twilights of fogless November days. To Christmas, and to June with spring and summer together in the scent of sweet brier wafted across their suburban garden; making, in its small green space with masonry visible all about, a sharper sense of summer than was to be found in the open country. They belonged to every feature of the London weather. Taking the sting from the worst and adding brightness to the best.

But this opening, with its view of the short broad path,

belongs to no one. The sight of it is always a stepping forward into nowhere with eyes on the low fence at the end, the gap, the two poplars pluming up on either side, making it a stately portal to the green expanses beyond.

The poplars say:

> Les yeux gris
> Vont au paradis.

And the picture remains after the high railings have come back again. Its message brings more light than there is into the thickets of shrubs and bushes, and takes the suggestion of sadness from the stretches of grass dulled even in sunlight by the thick autumn air.

Les yeux gris; in spring and autumn.

But most clearly in autumn when the air of the park is rich with outbreathed summer. Answering everything with the unanswerable beauty of autumn.

The afternoon streets were bustling with farewells to the week. Out across them went her own glances of farewell, making them newly dear and keeping them still echoing about her when she arrived to be alone by daylight for the first time in the ancient stillness of the house.

She hurried upstairs to take possession and prepare for the coming of the Brooms.

The stillness was absolute. New in her experience and disquieting. Her old room had always greeted her. Had been full at once with the sound and colour of her life.

This stillness was impermeable. Wrapped within it, the rooms disowned her. Maliciously, now that they had her to themselves, they announced the fact behind the charms of the week of settling in. Bereavement. Not only of her self, left behind irrevocably in the old room, but also, now that she surveyed it undisturbed by Miss Holland's supporting presence, of the bright motley of her outside life. Everything had thinned, was going thinly forward without depth of background. Against these ancient rooms she was powerless.

If she were living alone in them? She imagined herself living alone in them, and at once the tide of her life began to rise and flow out and change them. They dropped their ancient preoccupations and turned friendly faces towards her, promising welfare.

But as long as she stayed in them accompanied they would acquire no depth. Their depth was the level of her relationship to Miss Holland. Without her she was lost in them, a moving form whose sounds impinged less surely upon their stillness than the sounds of the mice scampering over the attic floor.

All through the week, in coming home late each evening to the certainty of talk, to hurried sleep in the orderliness created by Miss Holland, there had been a glad sense of life renewed. New, exciting life, bringing at first the surprise of an escape homeward that had left the London years unreal; a tale told busily day by day to drown the voices calling her home. That first sense of home-coming had vanished, lost among the entertainments of unfamiliar ways of living. But it had been at work all the week. All the week, serving as space for continuous talk, the rooms had been changing, growing larger, expanding together with the life lived there, a wealth falling into her hands too swiftly for counting.

Apart from that life they were nothing. They stood defined, mean and dismal, crushing her. And for these mean and dismal rooms, set above a thick ascending darkness where other lives were hemmed and crushed, she had sacrificed the spacious house with its unexplored distances and its perpetual familiar strangeness.

And haunting each room, as in solitude she surveyed it, was the mocking image of Sheffield.

And at this moment Miss Holland, in half-holiday mood, would be buoyantly pacing some chosen part of the glad open wilderness of London. Well had she known what she escaped in refusing to deal with Sheffield. But she did not know that life set to weekly meetings with him was darkened not only because he was 'odious,' but also because the paying of rent tore life up by the roots.

The payment of Mrs Bailey's bills, looked back to now, seemed to be all a single transaction: a chance meeting on the stairs, a hurried handing of money, eye to eye, smiling. A single guilty moment and then a resumption of a relationship not based on money. It had marked, not the passage of time, but its rest, at an unchanging centre. Paying rent to this man would be counting off time; and a weekly reminder of the payment for life going on all over the world. To be obliged at the best moment of each week to face Sheffield, acknowledging another week passed in the world as he saw it, would be to fight without weapons against the mocking reflection in the mirror he held up.

Putting off the ordeal until the last moment, she prepared for the coming of the Brooms. Reflected in the long mirror was her gay carefree self, the self that bore in the eyes watching it from their distant suburb, a charmed life; offering no resting-place for the pity they wanted to bestow. It would remain when they had gone, and would carry off the rent-paying with a high hand.

They were coming. Soon their voices would sound about her in the different rooms.

It was her happiness that had hailed them from afar and summoned them without a thought of how these new quarters would appear in their eyes. In the eyes of Mrs Philps, dressed for an afternoon call and now already on her way.

Unless she said Miss Holland was at home and ill and at once took them to the club, they would come up, through the smells and gloom of the passage and stairway, expecting at least a bright, flowered-chintz flat.

The ordeal of facing Sheffield had now turned into a reprieve. She ran downstairs and knocked peremptorily at his door, which opened immediately upon him shirt-sleeved, his sparse hair in wisps about a preoccupied face. His private face, caught unawares, reflecting thoughts turned upon detail. After all, he had a personal life, perplexities. There was nothing in the poor thing to dread. It was idiotic to hold him in mind as waiting there behind the door for her coming.

His eager, inattentive voice, bidding her upstairs, sounded about her as she stated her errand. She went up the uncarpeted stairs to set the rapid tapping of her shoes against the influences brooding in the ancient gloom.

'My *mother* is upstairs,' he said from behind, in his mocking sing-song. Hearing it again, Miriam thought of it as a silence, with mocking speech extending before and after; the uniform sound of his mind. A good mind, ill-fed and circling. Recognizable English prejudices, soured.

'*This* is Miss Henderson,' he cried gleefully closing the door behind her, the door of a room already, with its coffee-coloured lace curtains keeping out the shadowed light of the court, in a heavy twilight. The same voice, feebler, but deeper and flexibly rumbling, came from a mass risen up at the fireside, a mass of draperies about a tall form unsteadily bowing and capped with ponderous lace.

The voice rumbled on while Sheffield put a chair for her, and it seemed at the end of a few minutes that she had been sitting there indefinitely, listening to a flow of speech that communicated nothing but its tone. Yet she had spoken. She remembered the sound of her own voice in the room, the voice of all her family. And there was the semblance of conversation, Sheffield standing by, chanting refrains, presiding. Triumphantly, as if he had purposely brought her to face and be overwhelmed by their united voices.

She braced herself to resist the influence of this life-stuff seething bitterly in its corner. But it cast shadow everywhere. Sitting smiling and inattentive, she heard the continuation backwards through the years, through all the years she had known and further back into those differently lovely years her parents had known, of these bitter life-shadowing voices. They went forward too, shadowing the future, until death should silence them.

Opposition would be futile. Her words would fly like chaff before the wind of their large bitterness, a general arraignment, she gathered, growing used to the angry sing-song, of everything in the world.

She thought of the autumn sunlight, held it in her mind, thought of it as existing in their minds and in the minds of every one in London to-day; the hint of an answer, the moment one paused to look at it, to every problem in the world. But these two were not perceiving the sunlight in her mind.

III—P

Aware of her submissive attention, they were growing more explicit, going into detail, one against the other. Mother and son, bitterness embodied, thought out, added to, grown old behind a close hedge of contempt for everything *new*.

They had a sort of clear-sighted observation. Humanity, they would say if they had the words, doesn't change *essentially*. But to get anywhere with that conviction they ought to be religious. To be in a group. They were cut off from the religion that goes with the attitude. An amateur church, self-ended. They were the offshoots of the worst kind of Protestantism. Protestant enlightenment in a vacuum.

Sadness grew in her with the sense of the utter absence in herself of anything wherewith to stem the bitter flood. The refuge was she taking in apparent acceptance was a condemnation. Leaving her less than they.

When at last the rent was paid and she was free to go, such a length of life had been passed in the sad room, so much unfamiliar experience lived through, that the parting was like a parting with old friends. Unawares, she found herself voicing regret for her forced departure and promising to come again. She felt her future divided between the two houses set so closely side by side. They smiled, pleased. Stood close, flattering and fondling her with their voices. They had had a happy hour. The old woman came to the top of the stairs to speed her on her way. Standing on the landing with escape at hand, she had a moment of hesitation. Voicelessly she cancelled her compliance, stood free and remote and felt as she went how their scorn followed her, scorn of anything that could not ring against their hardness any hardness of its own.

Outside in the court, she paced to and fro between her door and the entrance to the main street, waiting in the free air of her own world for the coming of her friends. But no oblivion could draw out the bitterness folded into her memory. And though the voices of the friends would drown the sound of that murderous chanting, the thing behind it, the thing she had recognized in Sheffield a week ago, was something ultimate. Inexorable; a flourishing part of the world's life not hitherto clearly known to her, all the time taking effect in the sum total. Life being hated, seen only as material for bitter laughter.

She looked up at the neat respectable house-front, the best in the court, at the shrouded windows of the room where still her spirit lingered. Next week she would stand firm and pay the rent at the door. Better still, the inspiration came together with the sound of the Brooms' voices behind her, slip it into the letter-box. The Sheffields were banished. The scene ahead held now no shadow but the weekly call of the raucous-voiced, knocker-slamming men from the Snow-white Laundry that had for so long impersonally fetched and returned her things, losing nothing, and now turning out to be linked to its delighted clients not, as she had imagined, by some fresh, kindly, middle-aged woman, but by grubby cigarette-smoking, impatient men with the voices of mutinous slaves.

It was not only Mrs Philps who was dumb. The girls, too, came up in pensive amazement through the darkness and smells of the lower floors to arrive silent on the bleak top landing. Miriam displayed the rooms, making much, as they stood about gathering up with trained eyes the mournful details, of the general loftiness, the large windows, the many doors. On the way up to the attic she remembered that she had not shown the painted ceiling.

Since the first shock of Miss Holland's furniture she had forgotten the existence of the ancient splendour brooding above. Each going into the little room had brought the hope of finding it changed, less gloomy, less dull and lifeless. Until, accepting, she had ceased to see anything but the light travelling through the square window to die. Reappearing now in her mind, the faded ceiling restored her first vision of the rooms. The way they had seemed porous to the sound and sunlight of the open.

Her visitors stood in the doorway of the attic looking in vain for something upon which their eyes might rest. In her half of the bedroom, kept till the last, they would find what they sought, feel radiating there the more brightly for their coming, something of what it was that held her life entranced and held them to herself. She, too, would feel it; the incommunicable quality that crept sooner or later into her surroundings, deep

and central within the air.   It was there waiting for every one,
within their own surroundings.   But so many seemed to ignore
it, and others, chafing, imagined it elsewhere, far off.

The girls made straight for the bureau, admiring, repeating
phrases of warm admiration in tones whose relief voiced all
their earlier embarrassment.

'Pretty,' said Mrs Philps, who had come down the room to
look.   'Imitation Chippendale.'

Glancing round, she brought her eyes quickly back to the
bureau, at which the girls were gazing as if afraid to look elsewhere.   Joining them near the window, to which presently all
three had turned as if in the hope of finding material for comment outside, Miriam remembered Yeats.   Yeats would en-
lighten them.   The sight of his chosen dwelling-place would
bring them, nearer than anything she might try to say, a vision
of her world not as a thing pitiful compared to the world they
knew, but as something differently real.

'Across the way,' she said lightly, 'in rooms exactly matching
these, is a poet, a great poet.'   She watched Mrs Philps glance
across to the opposite house.

'He might have an *office* there perhaps,' said Mrs Philps with
an expression Miriam had seen on the faces of gentlewomen
doing distasteful kitchen jobs, lips held in, the upper lip drawn
slightly back showing the teeth.

She hurried them off to the club.

Out in the street, the three were at once acting upon her in
their old way, revealing the power built up in their sheltered
lives.   How far, with their untaxed strength, they outdid her
in swiftness of observation.   How well they knew and how
warmly they cherished every stock and stone upon the highways
of London.   They had due knowledge.   But it was knowledge
enclosed, multiplying only upon itself.

Vainly as they carried her along, surrounding her, accustomed
to her silence and unresentful, she sought for a clear centre
where these old friends and the friends with whom her life
was now involved, might meet and understand each other.
Philistia.   The mental immobility of Philistines.   But Philistines, within their own world, were rich and racy.   Their

critics, in failing to savour the essence of middle-class life, missed the essence of all life whatsoever. They feared the *power* of the Philistines. Their power of stifling freedom. Freedom for what? Freedom, unless people became samurai, slid down into a pit. Perhaps these clever scornful ones, the moderns and the Lycurgans, were all escaped Philistines?

Hearing the life in their voices, she loved them as they were, unchangeable. Through Philistinism lay perhaps one of the ways of salvation. No. In the midst of the happiness they brought there was always a lurking shadow. The shadow of incompatibility; of the impossibility of being at once bound and free. The garden breeds a longing for the wild; the wild a homesickness for the garden. Is there no way of life where the two can meet?

And here, she realized as they went up the wide staircase, the broad way leading easily to the destruction of home-made ideas, was a small beginning of such a way of life. Within it the Brooms were small and helpless. Travellers in an unknown land, not yet able to take their bearings. They would recover. Later on, at home, they might make their severe comments, but unawares the range of their vision would have been enlarged. Gleefully she felt their irrevocable experience as they stood ranged just as they had been at the door of her sitting-room, in the doorway of the club smoking-room looking in upon women, unmistakable gentlewomen, lounging insouciantly. Representing not names and families but selves in their own right.

The drawing-room was again crowded, and again there was one free table near a window looking out upon the stately autumn trees and, upon it, tea set ready, waiting for them as the result of the order they had not seen her give in the hall. It was a perfect moment. Here they were at last after all the years, her guests at a table of her own. And they were much more than at home and happy. They were at court, in the heart of splendours. The girls admired openly. And Mrs Philps, whose affection for her had flourished upon a background of pity and half-indulgent disapproval, withdrew all

their past battlings in one glance, arch, bridling, altogether
delighted and approving.

But in the perfect moment a light had gone up that showed
Miriam a new self and a new world.　It was she, not they, who
was abroad in a strange land.　She who was travelling ahead
beyond recall.　The decoration bestowed upon her by Mrs
Philps was already askew, not suiting her, not desired.　The
understanding exchanged between them was of a pact she would
never willingly fulfil.　The women's pact.　And while dispensing tea, talking as they liked her to talk, making a little
drama for their delight, she privately thanked life for turning
on this light in the presence of friends, who, cherishing her
smallest expressiveness, left her free to survey this new aspect
of things whilst the light was still at its first brilliance.

A disquieting brilliance.　For her initiation as a hostess was
so slight.　To sit thus, irresponsibly dispensing club fare, was
the merest hint and shadow of hostess-ship.　Yet it had been
enough to make the world anew.

To feel charming, to want to be charming, to join for a
moment the great army of hostesses as an equal, was proud
experience.　But it was also a sort of death.　For it included
letting everything in the world go by.　Feeling ready to do or
say anything that would contribute to the comfort and happiness of one's guests.　In Mrs Philps's smile there had been,
unknown to Mrs Philps, the recognition of another victim
joining the conspiracy of the regiment.　And she had recognized
aright.

For here, complete and full-grown within herself, was one
alert to avoid anything leading to discord.　Aware of convictions and points of view, personal feelings, everything that
made one's own intimate vision of life, shelved; receding and
falling as if shamed, into the loneliest background of consciousness.　If all this and much more, things revealed and sliding
away too swiftly be caught and examined, were the price of
merely entertaining friends at a club, what of the *real* hostess ?
What of the millions of women serving life sentences ? Hostesses
not only to friends but to households, willing or unwilling
humbugs for life.

Yet the game is enchanting. And brings, within an immense loneliness, a sort of freedom. That was there distinctly. A sort of enforced freedom. To have nothing oneself. To seek only the being of others regardless of their quality as persons; feel only their weight as mere humanity. Humanity seen thus as guests without distinction brought back the wonder of life renewed. Pitiful and splendid. If these strange large beings taking tea were thieves and murderers, the joy of tending them would be the same. Perhaps greater. It was more thrilling to wait upon Florrie and Mrs Philps, whose lives she shared only imaginatively, than upon Grace, with whom she had a sort of identity.

CHAPTER IV

SWAGGERING along the middle of the empty pavement, the long cape of his short overcoat swinging like the cloak of a stage villain. With bent head he is playing his part to an imagined audience. He knows nothing of the contrast between the small figure and the big arrogance.

He swung round into Flaxman's Court, and Miriam, following, paused for joy, mentally summoning heralds to precede and a brass band to follow him, so stately with head held high and plunging gait controlled to a military strut, was his entry into the humble street. He stopped just as she moved aside to gain her door, swung right about and bore down upon her, bowing, slouch hat in hand.

'*Allow* me!'—a deep hollow stage voice.

She halted surprised. He was close by her side, his hat replaced with a flourishing movement that released from his person the thick odour of stale smoke, the permanent smell of the ground floor. The grotesque figure, now crouching, all dilapidated cape and battered sombrero, over the keyhole, was the owner of the windowful of stone and marble.

'Enter, madam,' he declaimed, flinging open the door. Thanking him, she moved into the passage and was going on towards the stairs, but the hollow tones broke forth again, reverberating in the narrow space made dark by the closing of the door.

'I am greatly honoured,' he was saying, 'by this event.'

She turned perforce. He was again profoundly bowing. She could just discern the dim outlines, the cape winged out by his deep obsequiousness.

'You will, I trust'—the voice was meditative, suggesting words ahead to be delivered with care—'not deem me intrewsive in expressing in your gracious presence'—indeed, Miriam felt, her

456

presence was gracious compared to this exhalation of concentrated odours, stifling and making her long to be away and up the stairs—'my respect, and, furthermore the great and happy en'ancement arriving upon this house by your coming, with your lady friend, *also* most gracious, to abide beneath the roof that shelters my spouse and myself.'

'We like being here,' said Miriam, politely, smiling into the darkness.

'Lady, I thank you for your graciousness.'

'Not at all,' she said, and felt him silent for an instant before an evidently unexpected lapse from gracious ladyhood.

This was all most dreadful. His tone had been deep and broken; touching. Behind his bombast was something genuine, making high demands upon her, including her with Miss Holland, crowning her as a châtelaine. She had undeceived him, spoken brusquely, revealed her different state.

'I am glad,' she added quickly, in Miss Holland's most stately manner, reflecting that a gracious aloofness was an excellent protection, 'that you find us pleasant neighbours.'

'More than that,' came the low broken voice, and her eyes, used now to the dim light, saw that he bowed more deeply than ever. 'No poor words of mine could avail to express the felicity experienced in the presence of beauty and graciousness. I would have you to know'—he reared his head and spoke upwards to the staircase—'that I am a repairer of statoos.'

Ah, here was the secret, the real origin of the attack. But it was interesting. A queer trade.

'You have made all those things in your window?' she said to encourage him, and standing a little nearer to the stairs composed herself to endure and listen.

'I am a repairer of statoos. But let not that mislead you. These hands,' he upheld and waved them in the air, 'recall to pristine loveliness *only* the classic. In preference, the *Greek*.' He was breathing quickly, angrily. Poor man, without an audience. In his whole circumstances, no audience. Her interest in his work changed to a desire to give him freedom from minding.

'It would be dreadful to waste your time repairing rubbish,' she said quickly and added, suddenly feeling that he was strong enough for an attempted truth, 'only people sometimes love rubbish *very* much. For them it is not rubbish.'

'Let them love their rubbish, gracious lady, let them love—mistake me not. I have no quarrel with love. The love of the Saviour, the greatest of all lovers, redeems the statoos badly made to honour it. But not to Perrance, not to *Perrance* let them come if their rubbish be broken. The classical, the Greek, that alone of the work of man's hands can command the love of Perrance.

'So great a love that he has'—he drew a deep breath—'it may surprise you but it is nevertheless trew, he has mastered the characters of the Greek tongue it*self*.'

'Greek is very difficult,' said Miriam.

'He can, in the rendering of an account for 'Ermes repaired, equally as well use the original *Greek*.' He threw open the door leading to his little shop, but with no air of inviting her to enter. He wanted to provide a clearer light for her contemplation of the marvel he represented?

The light revealed weakness. Large watery eyes fierce with self-conceit, grown old in unchallenged self-conceit. An angry mouth, tremulous beneath branching buccaneer moustachios. He was waiting for responsive wonder, ready, the moment it should be spoken, to break forth again. His violence calmed her pity. He was proof against the whole world. Determined to escape, she smiled approval and remarked, in the voice of departure, on the amount of industry represented by the house as a whole.

'Stay,' he cried, 'yet one moment,' and disappeared into the shop, to return in an instant with some small object clasped, hidden by his cape, to his breast.

'I have here,' he patted his breast with a free hand, 'a small work, a work of my own hands, dedicated, as is seeming and suitable, to *womankind*. Deign, gracious lady, to accept the same as a token of gratitude and esteem for your presence under this roof.' With a deft movement he flung back the cape and presented the hidden object. It was the alabaster finger.

'Oh, no!' Miriam cried. 'You must not give me *that*.'

But he was embarrassed, holding it forth, his head bent, his voice once more low and broken.

'Take, take,' he said, 'I will not sell it and I shall find no recipient more worthy. Take, I beg you.'

The heavy little block came into her hands. She gazed at it murmuring appreciations, trying to thank him in the way he wanted to be thanked. His eloquence was at an end. He bowed silently at each phrase, saying only, when at last she turned to go, 'Lady, I thank you.'

He had said his say.

But what of the future chance meetings? What could she give in return for the burden of this gift, so much heavier than its weight in her hands?

On her way upstairs, pondering this disquieting confirmation of her half-hearted candidature for the estate of dignified lady-hood, she saw that the first-floor rooms were open and the luggage disappeared from the landing. Passing the door of the front room, she caught a glimpse of a young woman, her head pillowed on arms outstretched upon a small bare table, talking and sobbing in a strangled Cockney voice. The light from the large window fell bright amongst the coiled masses of her brown hair, shone through their upper fluffiness, making a nimbus. She was young and slight; an air of refinement in the set of her black dress. Come to live *here*. Seeking now, of course, stranded alone in two rooms of this dingy aged house, her old self, life as she had known it before she was isolated with him. The absent him she was so fully revealing.

This was marriage, thought Miriam, going on up the stairs, a bright young couple welcomed by Sheffield for being so nice and respectable. Tragedy; the beginnings, before its dry-eyed acceptance, of womanly tragedy, the loss of self in the procession of unfamiliar unwanted things. In the company of a partner already re-immersed in his own familiar life.

There was weakness in such public careless abandonment. And subject for the mirth of cynics. But strength, too, strength of which cynics, comfortable well-fed people in arm-chairs, had no inkling. The strength was broken for a moment against the walls of a man's massive unconsciousness. Upon that the woman would be avenged; breaking fiercely through in her search for something in the world about her to respond to her known self with its all-embracing radiance. That strange indestructible *radiance*, discoverable in all women, even in those who professed the utmost callousness.

How bright, how unfairly upon a gay and sunlit peak seemed the lives on the top floor compared to those being lived below! How mean it seemed to be going eagerly up to talk to Miss Holland, with an evening ahead full of varied enchantments. Miss Holland to come back to when it was over; for more talk.

The door of her room stood open, twilight within. Miss Holland was at home. In the sitting-room. There would be lamplight, heralding the brighter radiances ahead.

The sitting-room was almost dark. The light of a guttering candle set on a chair struck dimly upwards over Miss Holland in her flannel dressing-gown; mending an ancient skirt. Her hair in wisps round a face harshly lit from below, and heavy with shadows. The reek of spilt paraffin came from the small stove in the fireplace. It was only an instant's vision, rapidly erased by Miss Holland's surprised greeting and eager re-arrangements. But the picture of her intense private concentration on gloomy economies had added itself to the scene downstairs.

While Miss Holland cleared away, Miriam retreated to her bedroom and set Perrance's gift down in several places in turn. Everywhere it refused to harmonize. The delicate elegant finger suggested a life moving in refined paths towards extinction; an effigy of that conscious refinement that speaks more clearly than anything else of the ugliness of dissolution. In this room so warm with life there was no place for a hint from the tomb.

'Ah, mon enfant, tout cela *pourrira*.'

'Oui, mon père, mais ce n'est pas encore pourri.'

She went back to the gloomy sitting-room eager to communicate to Miss Holland the newly revealed life of the household.

'M'no,' said Miss Holland, 'the man Perrance I have not so far seen. His wife I fear is a poor thing. A countrywoman from Devonshire. London conditions, though I gather she has lived here ever since her marriage, are too much for her. And it is only too evident that she does not recognize the necessity for hygiene. Everything in their quarters is, I fear, most unwholesome. And to make matters worse, they keep, like so many childless Londoners of that class, innumerable *cats*. I fear she rarely bestirs herself. He, I understand, brings in all foods. And requires a great deal of cookery. She complains in a mopy, resigned way, about *that*. I fear they do not agree any too well. There are, very frequently, loud discussions going on when I come in at night.'

She spoke with disdainful rapidity, as if eager to make way for other themes.

'He's a freak, from a circus, the perfect mountebank. But there's something, as there always is in a charlatan.'

'I fear I'm no psychologist. I've not seen the man as yet, but I fear, I *fear* his voice sounds suspiciously *thick*. M——you've seen him?'

'He's given me that finger from the window. I suppose it's a paper-weight.'

Miss Holland was transformed. Flushed and frowning with incredulous approval.

'But what a *charming* tribute!' she cried. '*Indeed*, I am surprised. Most certainly I should not have credited Perrance with so much perception.'

'I wish he hadn't. *I* can't live up to graceful attentions.'

'No need, no need.' She was speaking meditatively towards the shaded lamp. 'You have the secret of charm, an enchanting possession. Is it not enough?'

'That's an illusion. I haven't.' She described the scene on the first floor.

'Yes, yes, dear, dear,' interrupted Miss Holland, waving it away. 'We are in *strange* surroundings. Those poor things are *not* married. That odious Sheffield who made their arrival an excuse for calling on me—I did not tell you. Eh, he is odious,' she shook her head, childishly screwing up her features, '*odious*—believes, of course, that they *are*. They are both hotel employees. It is one of those unfortunate cases. And they are *quite* without circumspection, talking loudly, with open doors. The young man is a presentable fellow, nice-looking and respectful in manner. He intends, I gather, to marry her. There is, of course, an infant on the way.' Without waiting for response she waved her glasses towards the mantelshelf.

'I have been looking at your books. That Shoppenore is an abominable fellow.'

'Oh, those old essays——'

'He permits himself the most unpardonable insolences.'

The châtelaine's response to Schopenhauer. Yet since she had not simply cut him and turned away, since she had read on and been disturbed, he was not quite disposed of. Evidently, even for her, the bare fact of his being no gentleman was not enough. She had thrown an indignant glance and was waiting.

What would she do, if he were sturdily defended? wondered Miriam, smiling at the thought of herself as champion of this man whose very name brought a pang out of the past. For years she had forgotten him, together with the reflections that had exorcized him. It would be a weary business to recall the steps of that furious battle.

'He was most frightfully sincere.'

Miss Holland's face turned a dull red. She had really suffered, then, under the lash of those rhythmic phrases; a little believing. This was an abyss. Here indeed was the worst Schopenhauer could do. His least pardonable outrage. She felt the shock of it reflected along her own nerves. It roused her to battle.

But as she felt her way back to the centre of the fray she found herself once more siding with the man, fearing and hating the mere semblance of woman. Its soft feebleness, its helpless blind strength in keeping life going. Felt again all her old horror and loathing of femininity, still faintly persisting. What *was* the answer to Schopenhauer? Swiftly seeking she passed again the point where she had first realized the collapse of the Lady, the absurdity, in the face of ordered thought, of oblivious dignity and refinement.

'He was a Weary Willy. That is to say a pessimist. A man

who attends—by the way, the schoolboy was right—only to the *feet*. Feet being, of course, always of clay. He saw life for everybody, going from gold to black, no escape, and each generation in turn fooled by nature, through woman, into going on.'

'How beautiful upon the mountains,' whispered Miss Holland, 'are the feet——'

'Peace. Yes. But the staggering thing about all these men, the Hamlets and the Schopenhauers, is that they don't notice that people are *miserable* about being miserable. And uncomfortable, in varying degrees, in wrong-doing. When they make up their philosophies of life they leave out *themselves*. Like the people who talk of the vastness of space and the ant-like smallness of humanity. If *one* man, say Schopenhauer, *sees* quite clearly all the misery of life, and that it ends, for everybody, in disease and pain and death, then there is something in mankind that is not corruption.

'Then again all these thought-system people must have an illogical as well as a logical side. A side where they don't believe their own systems. If they quite believed, instead of making a living out of their bitterness they would make an end of *themselves*. But you know it's popular. There are lots of people who revel in it. Men particularly. It makes them feel superior.

'And there's another thing in these people. By the way, they generally have long *thin* noses. Perhaps they don't breathe properly. But the great thing is that you must consider life *obscene*. You must look at it from the outside, as shapes, helplessly writhing in the dark. If you *see* all this, and Schopenhauer did, you grin and snort and stand aside. Women, he proves, don't see it. And so they *are* obscenity, blind servants of obscenity, for ever.'

'Horrible. Horrible.'

'That doesn't matter. It isn't true. It's words. Nothing can ever be expressed in words.'

CHAPTER V

EVERY friend to tea at the club is an event. Never-to-be-forgotten. What each one says is written in my memory. And all of them are more real there than on their own backgrounds. Simpler.

They are overwhelming, bringing both life and themselves; at large. Shining; so that I want not to talk to them, but to keep them there in place and contemplate them.

But for them it is dull. Perhaps embarrassing. They find me empty-minded, distraite. And do not know why I am distraite. When they go, there is no reason for asking them to come again, but my desire to contemplate them.

Except Mrs Orly.

Every moment in her presence is realization. She babbles. Has no ideas. No self. Knows nothing about any one. But redeems every one. God can't be worse than Mrs Orly. And if she were on the judgment-seat, every one would be recklessly forgiven. With a flushed little face and flashing eyes she would spank. Flare and scold. And then, pitiful helping hands. Unscrupulously covering.

Having no self, she brings every one a rich sense of self.

Most people, all the time, in every relationship, seek only themselves. Past selves, if they are old.

Affection is joy in things past or things to come? Bereavement is losing one's deposits? That would explain why old people always think the past, the world of their own time, better than the one that is developing under their eyes. We can take only what we have. Even from genius. The accepting party must have within himself the same genius. Otherwise, no taking what is given. There comes a new way of thinking; a new world. But ultimately the changed world is

464

the action of one's own spirit. The only sureness in things is the action of one's own spirit. Egoism? But egoism carried far enough.

Whoso would save his life must lose it. But not for the sake of saving it. And first he must have a life he loves well enough to make it worth losing. Perhaps all those big sayings of Christ are dangerous for small people. So the Catholics won't trust them with the Bible. The Bible let loose means a crowd of uncultured little churches; fighting each other.

Insufficient egoism keeps people plaintive. That's another line of thought, but it joins. Egoism must be huge. Free from self.

Then I am the smallest thing I know. Caring only for the come and go of days, and the promise of more days. There is not a soul I would sacrifice myself for. Not even Michael, in his helplessness. When I felt that the world must stop to prevent his going to the Russian war, it was myself I feared to lose. Otherwise I should want to stop the world for all who go to be killed on battlefields. I do; a little. But that may be fear.

'You were a lovely person in your blue gown.' A lovely person in your blue gown.

'You were a lovely person in your blue gown.'

For that moment, walking across the empty spaces of the large high room full of blazing lights—that was when it was I felt him looking, and felt myself not there but looking on, with his eyes—I was a lovely person in a blue gown.

'You were a lovely person in your blue gown. Again you surprise me with a new aspect. I've seen you look charming, in Miriam's quiet way. Didn't know you could be splendid. Don't fly out. It's all right. I'm staying friends. Honour bright. For the present.'

That was written in the study in some luminous interval, eyes on a person crossing a room in a blue gown. Written on his principle of the niceness of saying nice things and having them said. . . . He is right. It works.

'You were a lovely person. . . .'

Yet there is something wrong in his way of wanting effects, illusions. Seeing through them even while he goes under to them. Outline and surface, the lines of flowing draperies, carriage, the shape of a skull, he sees as fine because he sees them emerging from a fire-mist and a planet. Pitiful, and passing in their turn towards other forms. Yet those he singles out are at once in a solemn compulsion. Comically conse-crated. Set somewhere between heaven and earth.

But for a while it is a real state . . . changing you.

What a difference it made to the sitting here in the club smoking-room, waiting for people to arrive. This might have been shivering loneliness, nervous anticipation of coming guests. Instead, there was calm, easy anticipation and forget-fulness. Yet even now he might be moving forward to some fresh beginning that would set her definitely in the past.

Meanwhile she was launched in a tide flowing brightly to music. Launched with her own hands still steering the fragile barque . . . how to continue the metaphor? . . . the bright firelight was intruding another. The launched barque was best, suggesting cool freedom and movement. If it stayed in mind, it would serve to shape the letter to be written to-day or to-morrow. To-morrow it must be, with the full evening ahead to be followed by the disappearance of the secret life in the companionship of Miss Holland.

To-morrow at Wimpole Street, where perhaps already another letter would have arrived.

The fragile barque; ships that pass in the Night. In sun-light. There is no night. For those who are alive there is no darkness. Meetings and meetings and meetings, and every time a new setting.

'You are being made. You 've no idea how you are growing.'

Better to find out for oneself and be grateful. But he must always be instructing. Yet there was joy apart from him. Joy that had lived so long in secret, flowing out now across the strange world of people and events.

She blessed the club. Its gift, at the moment when solitude

had departed from her home-life, of a new solitude; strange
lives surrounding her without pressure, and sometimes granting
these large quiet moments.

The door opened upon Miss Holland.

Miss Holland at an immense distance. And somehow
changed; coming in like a visitor. She was dressed, what she
called *twollettay*, and evidently at the height of her social form.
Free for the evening and looking in here on her way almost as
if she knew how supporting would be her familiar figure,
ceremonially transformed, at this moment of first launching
out as an evening hostess.

Miriam watched her come largely down the empty room.
Ah, hers was splendour, par exemple! How well she bore the
high spaciousness. Hers was an effectiveness that made its
own terms, in advance.

'They 've made you an enchanting table,' said Miss Holland,
reaching the fireplace to stand sideways, firm hand on the
mantelpiece and well-shod foot extended to the blaze.

Miriam had given no thought to the table. She gazed
admiringly. What nobility of form and outline.

The large shady hat hid the limp hair and gave the eyes more
than their usual depth. They were alight altogether, hesitating. She was communing with herself, eager to communicate. What? Something about Flaxman's? No, or she
would be frowning. And this high social moment was not for
such things.

Miriam plunged into the story of her visit to Dr Densley,
compressing it to a few phrases, and throwing up her hands
with the despairing gesture of the correct hostess off duty,
told how he had invited himself to her party as an awkward
fifth.

'But he gave you good news, or you would not look so
bonny and happy.'

'Said Densleyish things. A number of old saws. Over-
work, late hours, heading for a crash. Said that for a New
Woman I am disquietingly sane, and that my criminal carelessness about things that most women are in a reasonable
hurry over, may possibly mean that I'm in for a long life.'

'A most ingenious theory!'

'I don't know. He's been reading Shaw. Can't believe that women really think about anything but capturing a man; for life. He wound up by imploring me not to miss marriage, and what of all things do you think is his idea, or at least the idea that most appeals to him in marriage? The famous "conflict for supremacy"!'

'Indeed an unfortunate definition of matrimony.'

'Yes, but wait. That's not all. Talk about women getting hypnotized by ideas! His mind, his so scientific mind—is putty. With immense solemnity he informed me, "*No* woman, dear girl, is truly happy until she is the loser in that supreme conflict."'

'Dear, dear! An essentially pagan view.'

'It's the view of a man who knows he would lose.'

'I trust you did not tell the poor thing that!'

'Oh, but I did. I know it's begging the question. But I say things like that on principle. Anything to break up addlepated masculine complacency. Not that it matters a toss to women, but because it's all over everything in the world like a fungus, hiding the revelations waiting on every bush.'

'What was his response?'

'He looked very sick for a moment, and then laughed his laugh and began repeating himself. Went back to his saws about wasting youth.'

'Indeed, indeed, many are doomed to that. There, at least, he is right. Though most certainly not in regard to yourself. A propos, I am dining here, with the Wheelers. The child is in great trouble. The Polish 'cellist, it seems, is not after all to be in London this season. She is in despair.

'Of course, after coming across the world to see him.'

'In despair. They must now, if they can raise sufficient funds, go to Poland. It seems that there is a lady, high up in the social scale and a patroness of musicians in general, who might be willing to help, provided that the 'cellist is willing to see the child and to make an exception to his rule of not taking pupils. It is therefore imperative to communicate with him

by *letter*. I have been wondering whether your Russian
friend . . .'

'Michael. Of course. I'll ask him to-night. What is he
to say?'

Miss Holland was flurried, transfigured; but still polite.
Managing to phrase her decorous thanks before she hurried,
almost running, away down the room. She returned in an
instant, radiant.

'The Wheelers are *delighted*.'

But she was blushing. Evidently the Wheelers were in the
next room. Could easily be brought in to state their needs.
She wanted to keep them to herself. Be all in all to their
stranded helplessness. And when a moment later a maid
announced Dr Densley, she made at once for the door, where
she was held up for a moment by his entry, and so escaped
back to the tremendous consultation.

Hands outstretched, he had made his smiling rush down the
room and taken her lightly by the shoulders when the door
opened to admit Michael. Summoning Densley from the
hearthrug to the bright central light, she introduced them.
They stood in a strange little silence. Densley, robbed of his
usual soft-voiced flow of words and laughter by the spectacle
of Michael, of whom he had heard so much, was taking a
moment for contemplation, sure no doubt that she, like all the
women of his world, would immediately emit suitable remarks.
She ignored the obligation, flouted a suddenly realized desire
to please him by filling up the measure of his large admiration,
for the sake of watching these two old friends for the first time
confronted.

It made them strangers to herself, people seen for the first
time. Divested of their relationship to her, they were at once
diminished and enlarged. Large and separate, each set in the
stream of his own life. And small; small figures in a moving
crowd.

It was Michael who broke the silence, announcing with stern
shyness and courteously bent head that the profession of medicine was arduous and at the same time most fascinatink.
Miriam saw the other man, as he stood listening with a dawning

smile to the slow stately English, read Michael's gentle spirit and hand him on the spot a protective affection. They stood talking. Michael bowing to punctuate his phrases but with a pleased smile shining behind his pale features, ready to emerge when the gravity he thought fitting to the occasion should have had its due. Densley, below a brow grave and thoughtful as Michael's but without its sadness, smiled his smile that was laughter, the laughter of his everlasting enchantment.

She left them to spy from the landing for any sign of the arrival of the Taylors. The silent empty hall brought her a vision of Dora, hurrying home to dress, meeting a friend on an island in the midst of traffic, one of those encounters that occur whenever one is in a hurry, and to which Dora would give herself as if space and time had no existence.

The gong rang out and residents became audible descending from the upper rooms.

She went back to summon the men and warn Densley that he had committed himself to a meal prepared in honour of the Taylors, without meat. Also that he would hear from Mrs Taylor all about the medical profession. His to-and-fro gust of laughter left him open-mouthed like a mask of Comedy, silently gazing at her his assurance of his readiness for all her friends might do.

Through the open door she heard the continuous rustling descent of residents. All the tables would be full. So much the better, in case her oddly assorted party should produce long silences. She felt no desire for conversation and wondered, as she led the way downstairs, whether hostesses in general suffered the indifference that now held her in its grip. And if they did, why the business of entertainment was not abolished. She remembered how porous to the onlooking eye were people gathered talking at a feast. To be merely a silent guest was troublesome enough, but it was nothing to the burden of being obliged to produce, before the assembled eyes of the twenty residents, even the semblance of a dinner-party.

The dining-room was full of sound as she went in followed by the two men, held a little in the rear by the backward sweep of her long gown; a fabric of sound unbroken at any point in the rows of tables set against the walls, and all, even the one she had selected, fully occupied. All heads were averted, intent towards centres.

Gentlewomen. Yes; but those were just the people who saw without looking.

Here was the secretary at her elbow, smilingly indicating. Miss Holland was right, there in the central pool of light, well away from the serried ranks of small square tables, was the club's settlement of the problem of five diners, a round table, gleaming with silver and glass and festive with bowls of flowers.

As they took their places, falling accidentally into the best distribution for her serenity, herself facing away from the main wall and its unbroken row of diners, Michael on her right giving them his impressive profile, and Densley across the way, his fine easy presence set full towards them, a servant announced the arrival of the Taylors. She left her party begun, with Densley, grave and kindly, set towards Michael to draw from him, and cherish, just anything it might occur to him to say.

Dora and George, unbelievably there, brought to the decorous hall its furthest reach of odd experience. They came from so much further than the long distance they had travelled across London to spend an evening in the land that to them was not even Philistia, but just Bedlam. The Bedlam of an illusion so monstrous as to be comic—for all observers but those who toiled helplessly at its provisioning: George's 'under-dog.'

They stood face to face, not seeing her. George in the half-light and against the dark ancient furniture, looking more than ever like the young Beethoven, his searching eyes bent beneath a frowning brow upon Dora's serene face of an intellectual Madonna upturned in absent-minded protest, while he explained, certainly not for the first time, exactly where, in their passage across London, they had missed their way. For an instant Miriam watched them, the beauty that together they made standing there in perfect physical contrast, a rare pure balance, as rare as their unmistakable equality of spirit. She rejoiced in the thought of them set down with Michael and Densley. Four widely separated worlds met together.

When actually they were so set down, George on her left

and Dora all delicately harmonious colour between Michael's and Densley's black and white, the enchantment was so strong that she felt it must radiate to the four corners of the room. It served to support her in face of the absence in her thoughts of anything that could form a starting-point for general conversation.

She took refuge with Dora. Dora's was the mind that could enclose all the others, and gaze over each of their territories in turn. She began at once by accusing Dora. Making her the culprit of the wandering pilgrimage.

Delicately flushing, her limpid absent eyes aware of the presence about her of disturbed people waiting for conversational openings, aware also of the restraining influence of her own serene beauty, Dora defended herself in the leisurely dimpling way that showed her armed for no matter what conflict. Dora was at her best. Densley hung towards her, delighted at once.

Here in strange garb and unfamiliar bearing was yet, he was assuming, the woman he understood, the woman existing in such numbers in his own set, and vocal, until Miriam had revolted and silenced her, in all his conversation; the woman who professes to be either amused or shocked by sexual allusions, disguised in commonplace remarks, and jests back, or tactfully heads off. How far, she wondered, would Dora, with her hobby of endless cool sampling of humanity, go out to meet this naïve masculinity? So far she sat screened, gently glowing, harmless.

If she held to this mood, went on turning upon him her lovely mild eyes, and Densley's warm-hearted worldliness took the field, then it was George, indulgent to Dora's adventure, who would be the enclosing, contemplating mind. Already, amidst the jests that carried them through the first courses, he was gathering fuel for the sole recreation afforded him by chance social festivities. For mirth over the spectacle of evasions. To-night the spectacle was all about him, all over the room, rampant and unconscious, distracting him almost completely.

By the time the sweets appeared there were two groups at the table: Dora and Densley, averted towards each other in animated talk; George and Michael responding to everything Miriam offered, usually both at once, refusing to blend. Here, already, at her first party, was the English separation. No general conversation. Not even the English alternative, the duel between two men; the prize-fight. The party had fallen to bits. But it was worth while. For on the far side of the table, Dora's sweet mezzo was dominating Densley's baritone. She had tackled him. It was his opportunity, perhaps his utmost chance of being lifted outside his complacent dogmas.

It was presently evident that he was remaining impermeable. Though still listening and responding, he had lost interest, discovered that she failed, for all her soft appeal, to fall into any one of the classes he thought he understood, into the fascinating, the maternal, or the saintly. His mind gave her its ear, but his eyes with their everlasting message went again and again to a far corner of the room. Which of the disdainful club residents had become his chosen companion?

Dora was questioning him now, collecting physiology. Her voice penetrated the subdued, rapidly thinning talk coming from the small tables. Glancing round as if in search of an attendant, Miriam discovered the long row of diners, lingering over their coffee, one and all intent upon the centre table. And in the far corner that was drawing Densley's glances, Mrs Wheeler, talking with Miss Holland and her daughter, both with their backs to the room and unable to see the distant bourne of her eyes, dark and gleaming above the heightened flush upon her cheeks as she sat there, mutely wise, telling him a plain tale of gallant endeavour.

The women at the table near the fireside were now openly staring.

As if by arrangement, by some operation of the fascinated attention of these two listeners, there was a sudden silence all over the room.

'Of course,' said Dora's voice into the midst of it, dreamy as her pose, elbow on table, hand supporting chin, brow lifted in thought above eyes gazing into space, 'we shan't get parthenogenesis until we want it.'

The silence ended in abrupt risings and departures.

'Not in our time,' Densley had said, encircling the departing ladies with a smile that was not only homage and benediction, but glee. Private glee over the addition, to his store of anecdotes, of such a fine new specimen. He, at least, thought Miriam, as they rose from the table, would not regret the evening spent outside his world.

Michael, half risen, bowing towards the centre of the group, had something to say. One of his generalizations. The party was united at last.

'These speculations,' he announced, to the group Miriam rejoiced to see not only arrested by the inevitable topic but charmed by his gentleness, feeling the pull of him in their midst, 'are most-interestink. There are it is sure in these matters no absolute certainties, but what is sure *is*, that the realization of this idea would be, not advance, but retrogression.'

'Hear, hear,' said Densley, in his smoothest girlish falsetto.

As they all went down Fleet Street on their way to the Lycurgan meeting, Miriam wondered whether she would be asked to resign from the club. But much more pressing than this question was the feeling that her party had, in bringing together three of her worlds, shown her more clearly than she had known it before, that there was no place for her in any one of them. So clearly that she now wished it could end and leave her to go to the meeting alone.

There was in Lycurgan meetings some sort of reality, either coming from the platform or, more often, from irrelevant things rising in her own mind as she sat surrounded by so many speculative minds.

But to-night she would not reach unconsciousness of her surroundings. And the ideas coming from the platform would be severely tested by these alien presences. Already in advance, these ideas looked like a mere caprice of her leisure hours, a more or less congenial background of thought upon which presently might emerge a sudden enlargement of her own life. More and more lately they had been growing to mean things shared with Hypo, bright with life because they were his, and for the same reason suspect, suspect because of his unrivalled

expressiveness, a faculty that might be turned with equal conviction in a quite opposite direction.

And once they were in the hall, and she was sitting with the
serene worlds of Michael and Densley and the Taylors close to
her, the urgency of all the Lycurgans stood for grew immediately less. This world of clear ideas summoning mankind to
follow like an army, seemed again, as when she had first met it,
to contain a trick, to be too clear, too, hard, too logical to embrace the rich fabric of life. She experimented in unthinking
it; and a silence fell on many of the flagrant cruelties of civilization. They lost their voice. Their only educated, instructed voice. The Lycurgans were a league to arrest cruelties.
But a cold, cynical, jesting league, cold and hard as thought,
cynical as paganism and cultivating a wit that left mankind small
and bleak, in a darkness where there was no hope but in intelligent scheming. Even the women. The Lycurgan women
were all either as hopelessly logical as men, or methodically
pink. And the men; the everlasting prize-fight, the perfect
unsociability underlying their cold ideas. Except for one or
two. And they were idealists, blind with the illusion that
humanity moves with one accord.

Each one moves singly. To join the movements of others
is harmful until you have moved yourself. Movement is with
the whole of you. Ideas come afterwards.

How much time had passed? Only a moment or two. The
chairman was still bleating. And they had not noticed her
inattention.

They were sitting in a row at the back of the hall. The
proceedings seemed very far away. Held off by their nearness
to each other, by the way after one short hour and in spite of
their incompatibilities, they were, when placed amongst
strangers, in touch with each other.

It was worth while. Worth while to miss the intensities.
To be happily surrounded. And this way, the social and
domestic way of meeting things, the cool easy way of normal
people, was perhaps the best way. It robbed things of all but
their obvious surfaces, the practical data of life. Reduced them
to the terms of what could be said about them and handed

round from one to the other. Small wonder that reformers tended to become tub-thumpers, so immense must be the resistance offered by people living, as nearly every one did, in groups, closely related and drawn this way and that by perpetual single instances.

Less wonder that most people assumed the fact of life, took it without amazement, for granted, so thinly of necessity was spread their awareness of anything whatever.

She gave herself up to joy in her party, in being linked with them in profane, mirthful detachment from all that was going forward, shockingly accompanied by the crackling of Michael's disgraceful bag of hardbake. Was it her fault that they were so detached? The result of some demoralizing influence at work behind her imagined interest in socialism? She felt it was not. They were all on a moral holiday, not only from their own worlds, but from any world whatsoever. Happy in being together, passing through an uncalculated interval, a strange small time that they would remember with pleasure.

Going homewards through the spring evening with Densley she felt the world even further off; thin, irrelevant. That was his influence. For him the world was something against which every one was fighting with weapons feeble or stout. Single people, the individual battle, that was the centre of his preoccupation. His interest in Mrs Wheeler was his sense that she was making a good fight, sturdily, perhaps unscrupulously . . . that she was what he would call a real woman. Herself he regarded as so far unreal, good material for reality, holding back.

His wide, varied experience of humanity seemed all about them, as they wandered at truce arm-in-arm through the darkened evening streets. And she found herself, as always, leaning upon his ordered knowledge and yet repudiating it, so entirely did it imply an incomplete conception of life. Every symbol he used called up the image of life as process, never in any direction as completeness.

Faced alone, it appeared to him as bitterly sad, and the last disaster of an unhappy fate.

Faced in groups as he knew it best, it showed in his eyes only as material for comedy. It was of the comedy he was always trying to convince her. In life itself, the bare fact of life, there seemed for him to be no splendour. For men there was ambition, hard work, and kindly deeds by the way. And for women motherhood. Sacred. The way to it pure comedy; but once attained, life for the mother in a mansion of the spirit unknown to men, closed against them and for ever inaccessible. The attainment of full womanhood was farewell, a lonely treading of a temple, surrounded by outcasts.

He stood, it was true, to some extent within the lives of women, but witnessed again and again the farewell, saw the man lessened, left behind for ever on the threshold of magnificence, the woman left in a loneliness mitigated only by the fireside companionship.

The strange thing was that seeming to value her for what he called the intellectual heights that had kept her uncorrupted by petty social life, he yet wanted her to come down from them and join the crowd. That if even for one moment she could show any unguarded feeling, anything free from criticism, even deliberately freed from criticism, he was ready to become the gay priest of initiation into the comedy whose every dramatic possibility he knew by heart.

CHAPTER VI

THE morning lays cool fingers on my heart and stands there an intensity of light all about me and there is no weight or tiredness. When I open my eyes there is a certain amount of light —much less than I felt before I opened them—and things that make, before I see them clearly, an interesting pattern of dark shapes; holding worlds and worlds, all the many lives ahead. And I lie wandering within them, a different person every moment. Until some small thing seen very clearly brings back the present life and I find a head too heavy to lift from the pillow and weariness in all my frame, that is unwilling to endure the burden of work to be done before the evening can come again bringing strength.

Yet what ease of mind I have now. What riches and criminal ease, exemptions and riches. Everything is done for me and I am petted and screened from details. Secretly she plans my comfort, saying nothing.

And at Wimpole Street it is the same. And there also it is the work of a woman. The fiancée, who has altered so many tiresome things, lifted off so many burdens.

'You ought not to carry those heavy ledgers up and down stairs. You are killing yourself.' Perhaps it was the heavy ledgers. Anyhow there is now always this fearful weariness side by side with the happiness.

Life flowed in a new way. Many of the old shadows were gone; apprehensions about the future had disappeared. Side by side with the weariness, and with nothing to explain its confidence, was the apprehension of joy.

Wearily she tumbled her happy self out of bed, feeling, as her feet touched the floor, the thrill of the coming day send a small current of strength through her nerves. If only she could preserve it. But everything nowadays came headlong and smiling, everything and everybody. No enemies, no difficulties. With every hour glad tidings calling. Calling from yesterday. Crowding to-day so closely that much must be missed, joy scamped and missed and waiting and pouring over into to-morrow that would bring yet more things.

Why me? What have I done? Why is it that something seems to be looking after me?

One can't change one's nature, which is one's fate. Yet there is a sense of guilt in finding everything so easy.

Perhaps I shall have an awful old age? No, from forty to sixty is the best of life. I shall go on getting happier and happier. Because it takes almost nothing to make me as happy as I can bear.

But there is this terrible tiredness. Densley may be right. But one can't marry just to escape fatigue. 'Have you noticed, dear girl, that we have spent a whole evening together without argument?'

'I never argue, bless you.'

'You give me your blessing?'

'What need have you?'

'My dear girl.'

'I'm neither dear nor in the least girlish.'

'You're a girl, my dear, unspoiled by worldly women, the dearest I know—with a man's mind.'

'It's your fashionable patients, parasites, helpless parasites, I'm not blaming them, who make you think women are all cats.'

'My dear golden girl, all grace and charm if only she chose, when do I see you again?'

The milk boiled over and Miss Holland laughed from her bed. Again it had made a frightful mess on the oil-stove. Nearly every day Miss Holland had somehow to make that mess disappear. Yet she always laughed. Was now gaily getting up to the accompaniment of her usual jests on the catastrophe.

It seemed enough for her that she lived in the glow of another life. For that she seemed willing to pay any price in unseen labour.

'Did you speak to your friend about writing to the musician?'

'No.'

'Indeed?' What a strange, sharp note.

'Not last night. I shall see him to-day probably, or to-morrow.'

Miriam could feel wrath coming through the curtain.

Miss Holland was speechless, her large frame, moving now impatiently about, a boiling wrath. Evidently she had undertaken; would now have to explain to these cherished friends. But what a turmoil! How easy to find words for them and carry them along a little. Was the whole world to be stopped for their letter?

She was glad she had spoken with serene indifference. Evidently her evening, the shape of her evening entertaining friends, was nothing. Her usefulness, to these wonderful acquaintances, all she was worth. It was careless, of course, to have forgotten. But she was glad now that she had forgotten. Glad to see for how little Miss Holland could adopt a tone of frigid annoyance. Damn, she thought, I've undertaken it. I'll do it in my own time.

Almost immediately on the heels of her own words and preceded by little sounds expressing the depth of impatient scorn, came Miss Holland's most fastidious voice:

'Had it been made to a *man*, your promise would at once have been carried out.'

Miriam forgot her anger in amazement at the spectacle of a châtelaine with a volcanic temper and a spiteful tongue. She searched her memory in vain for anything to equal the venom of this attack.

'After that, you count upon my asking him?' she said, feeling herself adream, lost in pity before the revelation of the importance to Miss Holland of these club acquaintances.

For herself, the little idyll in the rooms was at an end. That could be marked off at once, at the cost of a small pang that turned, even as she wondered in what form, short of an instant withdrawal of herself and her belongings, the insult could be wiped out, to an indrawn breath of freedom. But side by side with the thought of vengeance, came forgiveness. It was all simply pitiful.

The answer to her quiet question, reaching her as she passed into the next room, was a burst of weeping. She paused for a moment to be sure of the astonishing sound and fled from it, closing the connecting door. This, she felt, was the last depth of shame, to be involved, to have been subject to, this meanest of all abandonments.

She and Miss Holland were separated now, utterly. The principle at stake was before her like a sanction, holding her at peace. She dressed serenely, her thoughts browsing far away. The milk, boiled afresh, made a tea more excellent than usual. The two biscuits were a pleasant feast. The dreadful little room seemed for the first time to establish a direct relationship with herself.

With never a backward thought, she went out into the spring sunshine, five letters, found waiting in the box, rich in her hand. One from him. There might be another on her table at Wimpole Street. But the letters, even for to-day, his letter, stood away, waiting friends around her spellbound calm. It was not, she told herself, the calm of mere indifference. It was the calm of perfect opposition to a certain form of baseness. It brought peace and strength.

In beatific mood she sat down at her table and wrote to Miss Holland that on the terms set by her this morning she must decline to discuss anything whatever. The moment her letter was dispatched, anger seized her. She hoped Miss Holland would suffer all she could in anxiety over the success of her project.

Miss Holland, it was clear, despised her and had found, in wishing to make her look small in her own eyes, crushing eloquence. And what she had said was true, in a general way. Often and often, memory told her, she had sacrificed women for men, baldly, visibly. But then there had always seemed to be something at stake. Now there seemed to be nothing at stake. She wanted nothing so much as to be charmed and charming. And that she was so, or her thoughtless happiness mysteriously made her so, things multiplied perpetually around her to declare. Apart from the menace of devastating fatigue, she swam in joy, felt even dark things turn to joy within her mind.

The old life and death struggle between conflicting ideas had died down. She could see the self who had lived so long upon that battle ground, far off; annoying, when thought of as suffered by others. But it was not without a pang that she looked back at that retiring figure. It had been, at least, with all its blindness, desperately sincere. She was growing worldly now, capable of concealments in the interest of social joys, worse, capable of assumed cynicism for the sake of advertising her readiness for larks she was not quite sure of wishing to share. And thought was still there, a guilty secret, quiet as a rule. Sometimes inconveniently obtrusive at moments when she most wished to approximate to the approved pattern of charming femininity.

Fearful of really forgetting her commission, she wrote at once to Michael and floated off into her day, her mind away in the bright pattern of life, the scenes of the many dramas being played out all round her, of the new worlds into which unawares her obscure career had led her, secure in the knowledge that while she lived thus sunnily, all difficulties in the daily routine would solve themselves under her hand.

A charm, the charm that came over the leads where the birds hopped, and into the conservatory-office in the spring sunshine, lay over everything. Shadows were there. The shadow of Nietzsche, the problem of free-love, the challenge of Weiniger, the triple tangle of art, sex, and religion. Poverty and Henry George. But she was out in the dance of youth, within hearing of all that was happening along the rim of life as it pressed forward into a future that was to be free of much that had darkened the being of those who went before, and had freed her already from the fear of isolation and resourcelessness. She was ready now to drop all props and wander forth.

Lo here, lo there. But the kingdom of heaven is within. Communist colonies were not a solution of anything.

Yet the kingdom within is a little grey and lonely. Marriage is no solution, only a postponement. A part solution for some people.

I am a greedy butterfly flitting in sunlight. Enviable, despicable. But approval of my way of being speaks in me, a secret voice that knows no tribunals. The joy and ease of this evening-lit life is a presage because it is a fulfilment. Man never is, but always to be blest. But I *am* blest. *Alles ist relativ*. I am blessed beyond anything I ever dreamed of, within these inexorable circumstances.

The happiness that came when they were even bleaker was a presage. Of what? Someone says there is nothing meaner than making the best of things. But happiness is incurable. A thing you can't help. Perhaps it is the result of being a woman. One of Wells's crawling cabs waiting to be hailed? Bosh. If I wait for any one, it is for one who will show himself to have been hailed by the same kind of happiness.

Mrs Cameron, running singing up the stairs, pushed open the door and stood tall, a bright questing figure; determinedly bright, a deliberately cheerful blue overall covering all but the sleeves of her multi-coloured gown; hanging from her arm a great basket of primroses.

'Good morning,' she laughed. 'How is 't with thee?'

Miriam delighted in the gaiety of colour she made standing there in the flood of top-light; in the heroic tilt of her head, in everything but the deliberately rousing, deliberately gloom-flouting ring of her laugh, which yet, so frequently breaking forth, was the thing that compelled her tired eyes, tired bright hair, and thin face into harmony with the gay colours of her house and clothing.

She smiled from her place at the table, made room for Mrs Cameron in her mind, and prepared to squander, in seeing life with her, a bit more of the morning hour. Mrs Cameron came in pleased, and began at once with her legends. Miriam read off in her own thoughts legends to match. It was a clear shape, deliberate. A way of ignoring all but the shining surfaces. Of setting everything, even the old woman dying penniless in the mews, in a light that made surfaces shine.

But her way of denying gloom brought gloom in the end. Spread it everywhere. Miriam felt herself drooping, was glad when she rose, spindling up to her full gay height and settling herself on her feet with a little spring that made the primrose bunches jostle each other in the basket.

'I'm off to kirk with Donald. A special service. There's a call,' for the first time her face clouded, 'a need abroad in the air for intercession, Mr Groat says, a *wonderful* turning for help and guidance. *Such* a hopeful sign.'

'Yes,' said Miriam sympathetically, 'certainly it is.' But her mind was arguing that there is nothing in the world that is not a hopeful sign.

'The state of *society*,' breathed Mrs Cameron, eagerly dropping her voice. But Miriam had left her. The whole day would not be long enough for the enterprise of getting Mrs Cameron down to underlying things. She wanted the bright figure to stay, gathering the beams of the spring sunlight before her eyes, but Mrs Cameron had read the opposition in her face.

'Fare thee well, lassie,' she chanted in hillside voice and flung, as she went, a bunch of primroses on to the table. Miriam pursued her for a word of thanks. From half-way down the stairs she turned with her piercing smile, and sang out:

'It's your *life* you are living here, lassie, and flowers are for all.'

Miriam turned back. The small bunch lying upon the scatter of charts and letters was there to brighten her life that was spending itself, had spent itself for the ten years since she left home, the years that are called 'the best.' So Mrs Cameron saw it. So perhaps every one would see it. She herself the only blind spectator. It was true. This scene that she persisted in seeing as a background, stationary, not moving on, *was* her life, *was* counting off years. The unlimited future she meted out for the life she was one day to lead appeared to Mrs Cameron defined, a short span.

A tap at the door and Eve coming in with the mid-morning soup and her look of adoring care. She moved in the room with a restrained eagerness. Taking her time. Never still, yet waiting, savouring, as Miriam was savouring, their perfect interchange, the sudden lift into happiness that came to them in each other's presence. Miriam stood motionless, suddenly conscious of herself as standing considering Mrs Cameron's judgment with bent head, and then as utterly relieved of it by Eve who passed to and fro close by her as if she were not there, and was gone with a light click of the gently closing door. And there had been an endless moment of communion, a moment for both of them, of oblivion and renewal in the presence of a lover.

It was part of Eve's wonderfulness that she should have come in just then, to answer Mrs Cameron. Miriam held the image of her in her mind, her gently rounded, ever so little stocky and stumpy figure; the deep rose flush on her cheeks over which the cloudy black hair cast a margin of shadow; the pure serenity that radiated from her, that was independent and ultimate. Past accounting for, and independent of knowledge. That was itself knowledge.

And ever since, a year ago, she had first appeared in the house, she had come punctually, at bad moments, into the room. And had grown shyly and quite silently to know how near she was and how precious. She had come so unobtrusively, replacing the jaunty careless Ellen, gone away with the Orlys. It was strange, one of those strange hints life brought, that she should have appeared at the very time of the other Eve's unbearable death, bearing not only her name, but her gentle certainties. And her way of gathering all spears to her own breast.

Miss Holland's reply came by hand at teatime. Victorian hand-writing, with a difference. Something of rounded warmth in the longish uprights. She strongly deprecated the unfriendly tone of Miriam's note. In after-teatime mood, her mind flooded with the bright light of the evening ahead, Miriam faced the distasteful problem. Clearly Miss Holland wanted her to admit that they had both been foolish and to suggest that the incident should be forgotten and a fresh beginning made. But the balance was not equal between a deadly insult and an unfriendly tone. Or was it?

Was passionate anger better than cool reason? Perhaps Miss Holland was right all through. Be that as it might, it was impossible to countenance emotional scenes or run any risk of a touching reconciliation. Still less any bright amiable forgiveness with its wicked life-insulting suggestion of 'fresh beginnings.'

To-morrow, perhaps, in far-away mood after the evening's revels, something would come in words that would straighten things out without offence. There is a straightening-out process going on in life itself, if left alone. Already it was possible to smile at the whole occurrence, at both parties.

'I can't,' she wrote at top speed, 'be a party to the way of settling differences that is known as feminine. Can't play any part in scenes. Can't face explanations, apologize or be apologized to. So there we are. My friend has been written to and will probably act without delay. There for me the matter ends. Any further consideration of it would induce a regrettable attack of profanity.'

CHAPTER VII

THE enclosed golden light of a party. People transformed. All wearing the air of festival. All wandering about with happy eyes, expectant; the eyes of the beginning of a party. All but a few. At every party there were those few.

And at this party, very soon almost all were like the few. For a while they had gone in and out of the three rooms as if looking for something that was about to reveal itself. Something they know is there and are always seeking.

Something very joyous. The joy of a party is the newness of people to each other, renewed strikingness of humanity. They love each other, to distraction. Really to distraction. Before they fall into conversation and separate.

A large party. More than large enough and varied enough, as the crowd thickens, to represent the world. Whatever that is. And because, at least by sight, all are known to each other, each one's quality already tested, expectation is baffled. A few go on seeking, will go on all the evening, looking forth from themselves as if sooner or later the gathering would assume a single shape and perform a miracle.

This must be true of all gatherings, of all except religious meetings. The strangeness, and the hopes aroused by strangeness, are illusions. Mirages arising wherever people gather expectantly together. The few who at parties have not the glint of expectation in their eyes are those who know this. Some are cynical. Some enduring. One or two ignore people as persons. See them only as parts of a process.

It is true, then, though town life hides the fact, that individual life cannot begin until the illusion of wonderful people presently to be met is vanquished. The whole world, all the scattered people brought together and made known to each other, would soon be like this party, each tested and placed. Even the best of them known as limited.

487

Then domestic life, troglodyte life, is the severest test of quality. The coming to the end of the charm of strangeness. Of exogamy. The making terms and going on, or the hard work of silently discovering near things afresh. Re-thinking them. Keeping them near, as strange things are at first near, and, like strange things, beloved.

'What have I to do with thee?' Yes. But that was a man who had a message for every one in the world and very little time to get round with it. Not the voice of one who is weary of the near in space and time and hopes to find the distant more appreciative.

Yet even he demanded a personal allegiance. 'If ye love me, keep my commandments.' What is love? Who can interpret commandments? They all stood round adoring, begging for explanations and instructions. Perhaps he meant, 'You admire what I am. Take my hints. You will find out the rest.'

Wandering eyes were growing rarer, though still new-comers arrived and toured hopefully. Groups were forming of people masked, or visibly bored, sustaining the familiar. Wit, surrounded, was hard at work. Here and there rival theorists were audible, disarmed by the occasion and affably wrangling. And every one, even the schemers circulating girt and keen, or wearing the veil of nonchalance, waited now for the gathering to do something of itself. For here, for good or ill, in the circling Lycurgan year, was a party, and every one counting on at least a moment's distraction.

How intolerable with its challenge, its throwing back the self empty on to the self, and its revelation of the weariness of selves, would be the whole spectacle, but for here and there a figure of sincerity bearing the burdens of the rest, drawing nerve-poisoning influences from the air.

Full, the rooms were now. A moving bright maze of people and amongst them many strangers, guests. A leaven of the unthinking world, as the Lycurgans were the leaven that was to drive through the world of thought. But the strangers were not the zest of the meeting. Now that they were here, with their bearing of eager curiosity or amused polite deference, being introduced, talked to, some already the centres of arguing groups, it was through the familiar figures that life seemed most strongly to flow. Again as in family life; the quality of the familiar showing clearest under the beam of an alien light.

Densley, hurrying from far away with arms outstretched.

With the sense of coming down through space, that held her still, yet welcoming, with a welcome not for him, but for the strange journeying, his and hers, she reached level in time to rise and greet him as he seized her hands. For a moment he surveyed her through his laugh. Then they were off, arms linked, on a tour of the rooms.

Eyes gleamed at him as he went debonair, talking, not listening, needing no response but her radiance and abandon to his guiding arm. Solace at once; a rebuilding of strength to face this crowd that now stood off, no longer impinging, no longer eloquent except of a friendly indifference. Life, through all happenings, could pass like this. Happenings would be disarmed, bright strangeness rooted in an unexamined sameness. There would be solace for all the wounds of thought in his unconsciousness. But no companionship. For a long while nothing at all of profound experience and then, perhaps, her whole being arranged round a new centre and reality once more accessible, but in a loneliness beside which the loneliness of the single life was nothing.

He would never know this. A listening radiance, and superficial statements and activities, would satisfy him. Yet he suspected a rival and respected, while contesting, its power. Offered, as a substitute, his own secret life of faith in humankind, his shining love. For him all these special people gathered here represented not a determined movement to arrest Juggernaut, but material for joyous existence.

Is civilization Juggernaut? Are there not within it as many, and more, of those who promote its best qualities as there are of socialists attacking its defects? And of those like Densley, who work consciously for the increase of human happiness, how many there are and how much kindlier than these people, most of whom seem so little kind, so much merely the jealous custodians of ideas.

III—* Q

'Ideas are such chancy things. We not only can't get along without them. There 's no escaping them, and they are all figures of speech.'

'*Homo sapiens*, eh? Well, so long as he has a good figure . . .' Kind imbecile, imbecile, but kind. 'But ideas, my dear girl, are not the greatest thing in the world. And they easily take one too far away from life.'

'That wouldn't matter. But while they last they keep you on a monorail. All specialists are on monorails.'

'Monomaniacs, eh? Now tell me who is the lassie in the white smock?'

'That 's a djibbêh. And her name is Nora Beaworthy. Keep your pun. Although I dare say in the end she will. All those pink people will be worthy when they 're grey. Anyhow it 's no good. Having had a thoroughly vivid time and made a number of hurried young men take up socialism, she 's now engaged.'

'She leaves me heart-whole, my dear. But I saw her on the way here, running at top speed down Pall Mall in her white gown, the spirit of spring.'

His glance was wandering as it always would, gathering up and delighting in bright youth, in the appearance of animation; utterly blind to all the tricks of conscious attractiveness. Blind, too, to cattish subtleties. He was wax in the hands of his mondaines.

She looked round for people upon whom he might exercise his social graces. Who would give him what he needed to keep him at his glowing best. But there were none here of his kind. None who rushed thoughtlessly through ready-made evolutions. Refusal to accept these evolutions at their surface value he would see only as uncharitableness.

Alone together, he and she might make terms. But in his ready-made social surroundings they would at once be antagonists. The so much less sociable, so much more discriminating socialists became suddenly dear, the salt of the earth. They were, after all, little as she knew them, her own people. She thought with them, was ready to act with them. They, and not those others, were her family.

She chose a group of young women and set him in the midst of their ready smiles and swift replies. Saw them sum him up.

Dancing was beginning in the end room. The first dancing she had seen since she left home. It held her eyes. People transfigured, circling, lit from above. But only for a moment. It was memory that had put the happy haze about them. They were clear and cold, not lost in their dancing. Not even those whose heads gleamed with youth. They danced with a difference. They were the new generation.

She longed to dance and drop the years. And here, as if in ironic commentary, was old Hayle-Vernon, handsome in smooth evening dress, stepping elegantly towards her. With a light in his young dark eyes. He too felt his youth beckon and come close.

'Shall we dance?' His pallor was flushed. With boyish uncertainty. With the distance he came in ignoring that they were strangers.

To him her twenty-eight years were infancy. He was saying so with his smile. Knew, besides, no more of their number than of her. She felt her youth rise to lead him back to his, and his gratitude for the gift vibrating in his smooth voice as he began, the moment they swung in amongst the dancers, by remarking that it was pleasing to see Lycurgans as ready to hop as they were to hope. On and on as they circled—the tails of djibbêhs beating about them, every couple vocal, some straining away from each other as they danced, to argue more effectually—his voice persisted. Her scraps of reply, though he bent his head for them until his beard brushed her cheek, did not get through his slight deafness. But all they had in common, known to them both, was speaking between them, making a sadness; making them hate each other for apprehending. Never again would they attract each other from afar, nor ever, now that they had spoken, want to speak again. Unless presently they could meet in some mental difference. She gathered as his voice went on, emerging suavely above the primitive swinging pressure of his body and theorizing now, about art in the socialist state, material for discussion when presently they should be seated.

But on their sofa in the alcove they were immediately joined by Arnold Englehart who stood before them deferentially, yet like a threat; equally oblivious of Hayle-Vernon's deep-seated indifference to socialism and of the sacredness of sitting-out couples, pouring out his newest plan to bring about socialism in a fortnight.

Englehart was real, and his plans burned as enthusiastically as upon his bent head his hair, lit from behind and standing out like a bush above his unseeing face. Hayle-Vernon was alight in pursuance of his hobby of pulling a thread of thought through shapeless assertions. But in every word he spoke sounded his central unbelief. Prominent Lycurgans. Good men. Keeping an eye on injustices. Trying, from whatever motive, to reform the world. One chasing an abstraction called humanity, and the other an abstraction called intelligence.

It seemed that the air grew icy about them. It was a relief to catch sight of Densley, beaming with social happiness. Through the rising tide of Englehart's talk she watched him afar. Tall and lean and swiftly graceful in all his movements. Yet padded. A lean tall firmly-padded baby. The slight rotundity of his slenderness, like his bantering man-of-the-world society talk, was the radiation of his substantially nourished mind. His mind spoke from his broad unconscious brow. Serene and attentive between his frivolous words and friendly curling hair. A Harley Street brow. Calm where all these Lycurgans were irritable. And in his shapely nose, slightly blunted, like so many professional noses, was the cause, or the expression, of his interest in philosophy. Flirtatious interest, in the intervals of listening for the ever-changing gossip of science and accepting, because they bore out his own kindly experience, the statements of evangelistic religion.

'Multiple shops, proliferating'—she glanced in time to catch Hayle-Vernon's flicker of amusement—'like a cancerous growth.' But Englehart's adoration of Wells was a charming décor, taking nothing from his individuality. He had so much intensity that it blazed, like paraffin, a little wildly, but never with the wind. That was the great thing about the Lycurgans. That they thought. They were not impressionists further than every one, merely by being alive and not sure of the whence and the whither, must be helplessly impressionist.

The accumulations of two years of attention to Lycurgan thought, the images fashioned by their more articulate intelligentsia to express their sense of the destruction of modern civilization by disorderly forces grown out of that civilization, were again uppermost as she returned to the thought of Densley and his indiscriminate social happiness. His friendship, for instance, with little Mr Taunton. Perhaps that was inevitable. Poor little Taunton, shocked into worldly wisdom by his experience at the hands of Eleanor, flying, from his refuge under the tiles with his Plato, into marriage, must now have visitors. And doctors and clergy and lawyers must hang together. And their wives support the fabric. 'A *charming* little woman,' said Densley, 'she listened while her man and I discussed the sacraments.' Meaning that Densley and Taunton, putting their heads together about religion, were swimming in waters beyond her depth; that she, being not only a woman, but charming, that is to say an apparently uncritical listener, sat respectfully by and earned in due course the indulgent lowering of the conversation to matters she could understand. But would they have talked so busily, kept on for so long their amicable duel, without an audience? And would they have been so serene if they had seen into her thoughts, seen her read them as she watched their play?

Conversation of this type, comfortably fed and arm-chaired men discussing in the presence of deferential wives, was the recreation of his less frivolous leisure. And for the rest, fashionable dinner-parties, opinions about the latest plays and the latest novels, scandals, the comparing of notes about foreign travel, hotels and so on—always the same world, always shut in however far away, with the same assumptions, not about life, for these people never thought about the fact of life, only about the details of living, and about behaviour. His world was ready-made, and clearly now as she watched him for the first time from afar and socially surrounded, she saw that if she went into that world she would fail him; fail just where a rising doctor's wife must be a tower of strength.

The sadness of farewell, bringing with it in equal companion-ship a humiliating annoyance, was shallow; farewell to a selfish coveting, doomed all along by its heartlessness. Yet even as she saw him cut off, going his own bright way, it stirred within her, asserting a depth she had not guessed; prompting to reck-lessness, reminding her with a long backward glance how clearly, through all the years she had known him, 'fate' had been at work throwing them together in solitude, carefully not revealing him in association with grouped humanity until now. To draw back now was to reduce their common past, from the moment of his coming, bounding lightly at mid-night into Eleanor Dear's garret, an abrupt tired man, prescribing a sleeping draught and thankful to get away as soon as he knew there was someone prepared to stay all night and not afraid to go out and ring up a chemist, to waste of time.

Waste of time in an alcove—a comfortable alcove inviting waste of time by being there and being unable to protest. Waste of time; except for the gathered knowledge of his good-ness? Perhaps Hayle-Vernon, whose elegant sophistries had at last broken the tide of Englehart's talk and left him standing, still eager, aware that his ardour had miscarried, and though not actually looking about him, yet already on the look-out for another listener, had gathered, in the time Englehart had wasted with him, a knowledge of Englehart's unconscious goodness?

Wilkins the author, gesticulating greetings, came up and hooked Englehart away by the arm.

With Englehart gone, Hayle-Vernon was left in a void, statuesque, draped only with his manner of a prominent Lycur-gan. He had joined the society for the sake of self-realization, consciously contributing his proud talent for straightening out the statements of those who, in so far as they were driven by feelings that were clearer than their thoughts, were careless about language? Separated from passionate conviction he was inoperative. Perhaps, identifying me with the new group of young Lycurgans, he credits me with passionate convictions? And here I sit—while from far away in the cold centre where he formulates his criticisms, facing cessation, he is coming back to make suitable remarks—equally stranded, in a perfect equality of inoperativeness.

'You are going to write for *The New Order*?'

'Not in *The New Order*. I write about socialism in an anarchist paper.'

'The Impossibility of Anarchy?'

'No. That anarchy and socialism are the same in spirit. Only that socialists think they can define the future and anarchists know they can't.'

'That's very amusing. But, I think, scarcely true. To begin with, anarchy, as defined——'

Densley, swinging about on his tall stride, halting for a moment with head turned, near at hand; seeing her sitting at the feet of a distinguished-looking elderly Lycurgan, moving clear of groups, keeping himself free to come forward when the next dance should begin. Sounding through Hayle-Vernon's undulating vocalization came her own thoughts, as if he were speaking them.

Farewell to Densley is farewell to my one chance of launching into life as my people have lived it. I am left with these strangers—people without traditions, without local references, and who despise marriage, or on principle disapprove of it. And in my mind I agree. Yet affairs not ending in marriage are even more objectionable than marriage. And celibates, outside religion, though acceptable when thought of as alone, are always, socially, a little absurd. Then I must be absurd. Growing absurd. To others, I am already absurd.

There is no one on earth who knows the right and wrong of these things. There are only prejudices. Where do they come from? People are prejudices. Life is a prejudice. Or it wouldn't go on. Your life is the prejudices you are born with. That is determinism. But something must be determined. By their prejudices ye shall know them. Not by anything acquired. By instincts. Which are judgments ready-made.

Free-lovers seem all in some indefinable way shoddy. Born shoddy. Men as well as women. Marriage is not an institution, it is an intuition. Marriage, or sooner or later absurdity. Free-love is better than absurdity. . . .

Yet the free-lovers dancing there seemed both sadness and mockery. Dancing is shimmer. Satin and silk and white slippers. Rooms white and gold. Massed flowers. Rapt faces to whom problems and socialism are unknown. Youth, and an audience of elderly parents and friends. It seems mockery for these people with their brains full of ideas and their bodies decked in protests, to dance. Dancing brings an endlessness in which nothing matters but to go on dancing—in a room, till the walls disappear—in the open, till the sky, moving as you dance, seems to cleave and let you through.

People from South Place, gravely circling.

'That's not dancing, it's the Ethical Movement.'

Shaw. The darling. Religiously enduring. Coming to Lycurgan gatherings as others go to church.

The ring, made by those who remained, extended when their linked hands were stretched at arm's length, all the way round the large room. These people were part of the crowd that had stood shouting the refrains of the folk-songs led by the woman on the estrade with the determined voice. Seen thus they had seemed threatening, inhuman; an édition de luxe of the noisy elements in a street crowd. And more threatening, because they were driven by ideas. The massed effect of djibbêhs and tweeds and dress-suits, bellowing, was of a wilful culture banded together in defiance of a world it could not see.

But now, standing ringed round the room with linked hands they were charming. Innocent; children linked for a game, dependent on each other. In the midst of them, somehow in the centre to which all their faces were turned, was something beyond the reach of socialism. It sounded even in the dismal notes of *Auld Lang Syne* with its suggestion of mournful survival from a golden past. To stand thus linked and singing was to lose the weight of individuality and keep its essence, its queer power of being one with every one alive.

But it was also embarrassing. Made an embarrassment that every one had to share. For the thread of song was stronger than any one there. Even those who, meeting known eyes above an unusually opened mouth, or imagining themselves to be objects of hilarious scrutiny, tried to be individually funny, were presently overwhelmed and drawn along. The thin beginning on a few voices had swelled to a unison of varying octaves and strengths. She heard her own voice within it and felt as she sang how short and wavering and shapeless was her life, and short and wavering even the most shapely lives about her.

As the dismal refrain was lifting its third monotonous howl there came from behind her, where a door opened on to a cloakroom, a woman's voice, angry, deep, and emphatic, like an ox roaring at a gate. Her hand was torn from her nearest companion's and the newcomer was in the ring singing with stern lustiness below a hat askew. The last words of the song echoed round the room upon the might of her voice.

CHAPTER VIII

ANOTHER spring vanished. . . .

A sheet of crocuses singing along the grass alley. White, under trees still bare. Crocuses dotting the open grass with June gold. . . .

Suddenly a mist of green on the trees, as quiet as thought. Small leaves in broad daylight, magic reality, silent at midday amidst the noise of traffic.

Then full spring for three days. Holding life still, when the dawn mists drew off the sea and garden and revealed their colour.

Every one had loved it, independent of other loves. Become for a while single. Wanting and trying and failing to utter its beauty. Every one had had those moments of reality in forgetfulness. Quickly passing. Growing afterwards longer than other moments, spreading out over the whole season; representing it in memory.

CHAPTER IX

THE room is still in midnight darkness and full of the feeling of midnight. There must have been a sudden sound—perhaps a wild squealing of cats, too soon after I fell asleep. In a minute it will begin again; a low yowling, just beneath the window, growing louder. Then a scuffle and piercing shrieks. Silence; and more shrieks, at a comfortable distance.

Savage night-life of cats. Welcome, heard far off making shrill streaks of light in the darkness and suggesting daytime; all the friendly little cats of London.

There is no sound. Not a breath. In spite of the wide open window the air is stifling. And though there is no breeze, the reek of cats comes up and in. All the summer it has come in. It is part of the air of the room.

Yet the nights in here have been paradise. Cool sleep. Escape from the night-sounds of the court. Escape from Miss Holland's obliviousness of the sounds of the court.

She is dull not to hear. Or strong? Dull strength in not hearing.

Noisy home-comings in the spring. Strident, hideous voices in a reeling procession along the court and dying away in the distance. Drunken monologues. Every sound echoing near and clear in the narrow court. And she heard *nothing*. The cobbler, noisily taking down his shutters in the early light, had called her from sleep, not from feverish dreams. And when the summer came and sounds filled the court till dawn, still she heard nothing.

Why is all this saying itself over so freshly? At some moment every night before I go down into sleep, it says itself. And now I have come back from half-way to sleep it is all there is in my mind. Because I am always trying to ignore it. Never thinking of it by day. And here it is, belonging to me. Closer than anything that happened yesterday.

Hoarse-voiced lovers lingering on after the roistering has died down. Men and women coming in quarrelling from the main street. Voices that had once been gentle for each other, madly seeking lost gentleness in curses. Curses and blows dying down to a panting stillness; out there, in the dismal court.

Night-long, through open windows, thick, distorted voices in strife. Shut in, maddened. Maddened confined men. Women despairingly mocking. Worst of all, children's voices sane and sweet in protest, shrilling up, driven by fear, beyond the constriction of malformed throats, into sweetness.

And she had heard *nothing*.

But this same thickness or dullness had kept her unaware of what it was that in the end had turned this stuffy little back room into a refuge.

She did not know that there were sounds more intolerable than those coming in from the street. The street sounds varied. Were sometimes obliterated by wind and rain, and were at their worst only at the height of the summer. And even at their worst they were life, fierce and coarse, driving off sleep; but real, exciting. Only unendurable because there was no hope during their lifetimes of any alteration in the circumstances within which all these people were confined.

But those other sounds never varied. And spoke of death. That was the worst, that they filled the room with the sense of death and the end.

They cast a long shadow backwards over the whole of life, mocking it.

Night after night they had to be anticipated and then lived through. One by one. To come home late was not to escape them. They were all there collected in the quiet room. Centring in the imagined spectacle of the teeth waiting in their saucer for the morning.

To sleep early was to wake to the splutter of a match and see the glare of candlelight come through the porous curtain. To hear, with senses sharpened by sleep, the leisurely preparations, the slow careful sipping, the weary sighing, muttered prayers, the slow removal of the many unlovely garments, the prolonged swishing and dripping of the dismal sponge. All heralding and leading at last to the dreadful numb rattle of vulcanite in the basin.

Yet the worst to bear was the discovery of the hatred these innocent sounds could inspire. Still there unchanged, pure helpless hatred, rising up as it had risen in childhood, against forced association with unalterable personal habits. . . .

But the shock of discovering that hatred anew, finding I have not moved on, only been lulled into good humour by solitude, did not lessen the first joy of the little back room. For a while, in spite of the ugly things in it, and the never-ending reek streaming in through the window, the joy remained. There was that night when I sat writing until morning. Once more able to expand and think. And the air seemed as pure as if it had come in over the countryside.

And something of the first joy has remained. A lower tone. But still here. In the quietude. In the certainty of deep sleep and a happy mood in the morning.

To-night, with Miss Holland away, there is a double stillness. Perhaps I woke because she is away? For some *reason*, I woke. Something to say itself. And all these thoughts, bringing back the joy of the little room anew, are getting in the way. Idling along, going round and round. Me, gossiping with myself.

And all the time something is waiting. Just at hand. Behind the things in my mind. And now, with me more awake, here come the remains of yesterday. Crowding in to be looked at. Taking me back to stand and look again to find out what remains; what really meant something to me, if I could find out what it meant.

Strangeness of London on Bank Holiday. Its underside turned uppermost and spread over the whole surface. Daily London grown invisible, incredible. Never to come back.

I'm glad I've spent one Bank Holiday in London. Seen and heard its reality. I'm glad it's over. It's like being separated from a lover. The blank feeling, at the end of the afternoon, that it is for ever.

The certainty that this wild tumult of people is the reality and the rest a sham. I almost feared to look at them lest they should see me wondering *why* they all go back. Why they don't know their power and end the system that holds them. I fear them. And to-morrow, with my lover back again, I shall feel more glad of that than sorry at the thought of all these people who keep London what it is to me, gagged again, and chained. Taken out of my sight. Toiling, out of my sight.

Mean. Fear of losing small comforts and accustomed dreams. Like a timid elderly man of fixed habits settling comfortably in the autumn into his usual chair at the club. The peacefully noisy streets. Kept clean. Unconsciousness in the lulling song of the traffic.

Why should I wander in bliss while they toil in grime and darkness ?

In the evening, *Yeats*. Far away from the tumult; hidden, untroubled in his green room. Sitting in the window-space, not giving a thought to the rampant multitudes. Not minding, not giving a thought to them. Yet they threatened him as he sat there. Made his joy small and absurd. Even while it was balm to see his unconsidered detachment. To see him, poor and outcast, a king for the evening, throned in his shadowy little kingdom in the security of the London night. If he had given a thought to the unleashed thousands, or to any one watching, in some way his face would have changed. But he was aware only of his poetry and the sounding-board, the green-robed woman sitting low in the opposite chair. Radiant and composed. But not only listening, not as he thought, just listening. She, like him, was special, lived in his world, as an appreciator. But besides hearing, seeing what he saw, feeling as he felt, she saw him. Saw, far away within the form turned towards her alone—declaiming from the book held sideways so that he could see her face and make towards her delighted hand-swayings for the passages that pleased him most—the halting, half man's half woman's adoration he gave to the world he saw, his only reality.

And while she admired, she pitied.

And fifty yards away the toilers raged. The sound of them made the two engrossed figures, softly lit by the high presiding candle, a little absurd. Irrelevant and insecure. As if they might topple. Ought to topple. Ought to listen and topple down.

Gerald and Harriett. Drawn, driven, washed about by tides they do not see. Flung on rocks, washed off and flung forward. Their unaware faces. Strength of unawareness; pushing on. That was my comfort—that they did not know. And because they did not know, I would not. Clung only to the things they saw and got away without realization. Yet I realized it all. Here it is, tormenting me.

There is no choice of what one shall see on waking by accident. Things are there, set out clearly, stating their essence. What they meant when I passed through them feeling only the movement, from behind closed doors, of *le sort*. Not thinking, because they were long prepared and there was nothing to be done. But there is always, when *le sort* moves, a sense of guilt. Of having brought things about; let things happen that need not have happened. That is why, when they happen, one does not think. The fear of being crippled by condemnation. Yet it is all written in the book of consciousness.

Written indelibly. Because one can look to and fro, from one thing to another, and each remains in place, presenting always one face, like a photograph.

Gerald and Harriett and Elspeth starting for Canada. Without good-bye. None of us dared to say good-bye. Outside the gaslit compartment there seemed to be nothing but whirling darkness and cruel laughter. We jested without a gap. Annoying Elspeth, who longed only for the train to start and the relations, who kept attention from centring on herself, to be gone. The sound of her childish complaints was one with the laughter of the outer darkness. She stood on the seat, a shining little figure in the harsh gaslight, clutching the doll Sarah had found time, on that awful last day, to dress. Beneath her unconscious feet was the machinery that would carry her into exile.

There they were in the imprisoning carriage. And then gone. It was a death. Something buried alive. I dared not feel. There was relief afterwards in walking down the platform with Gerald's sister, a stranger just met, in knowing by the hard clutch of her hand that she, too, was not daring to feel. We both knew we had witnessed a crime.

'Can you get home?'

'Yes.' Our voices were rough and shuddering.

'We'll meet again.'

We unclasped our hands and parted abruptly, our faces distorted with not weeping.

I came home and read the *Punch* Gerald had left behind.

Michael's telegram. Once more the presence of him in the early morning, plunging along across the wide shadow of St Pancras Church, his voice at my side and again the discomfort of hearing unknown people lightly and swiftly described as they appeared to him: delocalized, people in a void. The things he said about her told me nothing but that she was courting him and he had no idea of it. And I let him go in ignorance. Pushed him into the arms of a stranger.

'Take flowers. One always takes flowers to people when they are ill. And stay long enough to tell her all she wants to know about the congress.'

And I knew when he told me of the engagement that he was uneasy, neither happy nor confident. And it was broken. Broken by him. And no one will ever know why, and the obstinate little gentleman can't see that it casts a greater shadow on her than if he spoke out and that if he can't speak out he should invent. There she goes, back into her life with a shadow, cast by Michael.

'Methodical culture, my dear young lady, yes. But with plenty of revolution.'

Raymond wanted me to look at the programme and I told him crossly that I wanted the music first and didn't believe in methodical culture. That was before I noticed the man in the cloak on my right, watching us.

'And now it's over, by way of methodical culture, I'll look.'

Raymond was genuine and the strange man was genuine. I was more pleased by his manner than by the truth in either of them. I held both their views. But wanted to impress both of them. Partly for the sake of the truth. Men are either-or,

all the time.   But what I liked best was peacocking out of the
hall with both of them talking, one in each ear.

Strangeness of the seaside at Christmas time.   Sunlit frost
on the morning grass.   Green garden in full sunlight.   Blaze
of blue sea and blue transparent sky.   Blue and green and gold
of summer, and warmth in the tingling air.

All the things of an old-fashioned Christmas except religion.
Deliberate Christmasing, without belief.

And she came to midday dinner in an old woollen tam, held
in place by a grubby motor-veil tied under her chin.

'She gets *one* good, annihilating dress.   Devastates about
in it.   On occasions.   For the rest of the time she allows her
things . . . to accumulate atmosphere.'

He thought her a bit of a charlatan.   'No end of a rogue
really.   But when she smiles that *brown* smile—she's a gipsy,
you know, a certain amount of grime sets her off—one would
do *anything* for her.'

He's always complaining that women don't do anything,
and when they do, and make others do, he's at once ready with
some belittling explanation.

And I hated them both.   Was surly behind politeness till
she had gone.   When at once I forgot she was still in the
world.   There's stupidity.   Enough to exclude one from the
élite of all worlds.

Yet Selina Holland is afraid of losing me.

Selina has no doubt that death will transfer her into the
presence of God.   Yet she wants, for the time that remains
to her, wide circumstances, ease.   Is willing, for the sake of
the ease and space she sees so clearly, to go to the ends of the
earth.   '*Wide* sky; unstinted air; *room* to move,' exactly in the
voice she uses for '*Good* Bermaline.'

A religious woman, living on prayer; blossoming, in middle
age, into splendid health on the power of prayer and teaspoons-
ful of Listerine.   Ready to give up her work amongst the poor
and systematically seek wealth and comfort.

Perhaps in the end she will actually go; to California.   Make
her way.   Master hotel-keeping as she has mastered hygiene

and midwifery, and confectionery.   Leave London as coolly
as years ago she came.   And contrive her transference just as
she had contrived this holiday to Edinburgh.   Ingeniously.
Horrible ingenuity of genteel poverty: two coats and skirts,
one on the top of the other, and a little handbag.   By the
midnight train.

She despises the world, yet uses it.   Is using it now to
accumulate money.   The being here with me is now altogether
an affair of economy.   But if I were religious, it would not be.
I should be the centre of her personal life.   She would try to
get me to California.   'Would you like to come?' and then
answering herself before I had time to speak: 'No; you are too
cultured.'   But that was long ago.   Whilst there was still the
sense of being her great adventure.   Before the trouble about
the letter.   Before Miss Trevelyan came to tea.   Badly dressed,
with a cold in her head.   Tall, like Miss Holland.   Two tall
figures sitting upright in front of the little fire, not lounging,
sitting as if they were just going to move.   Both looking into
the fire, Miss Holland with a pleased smile, Miss Trevelyan
stolidly, as she told without a break and almost without questions from Miss Holland everything that had happened to her
family and friends during the year.   She had Miss Holland's
indifference to surroundings and her obliviousness of differences
in the quality of experience.   Assumed that everything affected
every one in the same way.

'Miss Brown has married and gone to live in Birmingham.'

To hear them talk was to feel that one person was making
remarks aloud; talking to herself of shadows in a dream.   I
began to understand why Miss Holland found me lively and
charming.

And then, when they had formally said good-bye and Miss
Trevelyan had gone out into the rain in her cloak: 'A per-
fectly happy year together.   We would both gladly repeat it.'
I can see their year.   A peaceful association of two workers.
Both disciplined and incessantly active.   Sharing disapprovals.
Living as if in a siege; enclosed and conspiratorial and happy.
Prayers and puns and loyally exchanged services.   A life of
perfect agreement untroubled by thought.   And I am jealous.

Perhaps it was then, knowing that if she still desired a renewal of life with Trevelyan, I was only second-best, that I really moved away from her. Feeling inferior as well as superior to Miss Trevelyan. Feeling hidden in them both something I cannot reach. That I shall reach one day and meet them suddenly, when they have both passed out of my life. Something they have given without knowing it.

It is since then that she has more and more effaced herself and no longer courted every opportunity of standing, if only for a moment and deprecatingly, at fresh angles of vision. Miss Trevelyan reinforced her. But she still thinks there ought to be personal affection between us. Doesn't notice that I can't call her Selina.

Failing with her, leaves other successes shadowed.

To and fro, linked by their common quality of condemnation, went small forgotten incidents of the year, covering it. There was nothing else. The central things standing so brightly in her daytime consciousness were nothing. Unfounded. Mirage of youth. Sunlit reflections on the sea within whose depths she would presently be lost. Life was being spent in watching the glint of sunlight upon waves, believing it her own sunlight and permanent, while all the time it was light created by others, by millions of lives in the past, by all the labour that now kept the world going. And while she had watched the penalty had been piling up.

I am left in a corner with death. But it is I who am left, and not dead. Only out of my own element in which, if I were alone, even death would look quite different.

And far away below evidence and the clear speech of events, even now something was answering. Suddenly like a blow bringing her sharply awake, it came: refusal. Surging up and out over everything, clearing the air, bringing a touch of coolness in the stifling air.

Profanity. My everlasting profanity.

She listened guiltily, glad of its imperiousness. Everything had been thought out. There was nothing appearing behind it. There was in the depths of her nothing but this single nowledge that she was going away from this corner where

she had been dying by inches. No consideration of right or
wrong. No feeling for persons; either Miss Holland or those
people downstairs, or those of her own she had been able to
help by this cheaper way of living.

She sighed in pure sadness as she faced this deeper self.
For it was clear now for ever that to be good was not all in all
to her. To endure, suffer long, and be kind was not her aim.
She had never been quite sure whether it was not the hidden
secret of all her decisions, born in her, independent of thought.
Now and then hearing commendation of endurances that did
not bring bitterness, she had been tempted to feel that there
must be, since she had endured much and not become bitter,
in her own character the things called sweetness and
fortitude.

It had always been a strange moment. Two impressions
side by side. The certainty that conscious fortitude and
sweetness could not persist in their own right, and the uncertainty of approving of these things in their unconscious
simplicity; a dislike of being discovered in a state of helpless
merit.

Greater than the sadness of not being good, more thrilling,
was the joy of feeling ready to take responsibility for oneself.

I must create my life. Life is creation. Self and circumstances the raw material. But so many lives I can't create.
And in going off to create my own I must leave behind un-
created lives. Lives set in motionless circumstances.

A voice sounded in the hot darkness. Just outside the
window. Almost in the room.

'I'll do you *in*. If I get you, I'll do you *in*.' Sound of
furniture violently collided with. Perrance. Mrs Perrance.

And I'm sitting up trembling. This, the beginning of this,
was what woke me a few moments ago. The end of their
Bank Holiday.

Again a crash.

I'm full of horror. Too full of horror for pity. It is *my*
voice this time that must sound that awful cry from a window.

With her feet on the floor and her hands feeling for garments,
she listened. Perrance was in monologue. Perhaps he was

helpless. Probably more drunk than Mrs Perrance. Perhaps he would talk himself out. Poor man. Poor woman.

This is life. However far I go away, this will go on. To go away is only to get mental oblivion of it. Yet that is just what I am planning. Here in the midst of it is the hope that my lucky star, the star that keeps even my sympathies clear of being actively involved, will carry me through this, too, without bringing it into my hands.

The voice of Perrance was growing high and thin. Lying down once more in the darkness she could hear each word wailing out into the night. He was chanting his loathing of the mystery of womanhood, cursing it, its physical manifestations, cursing them to heaven in the vile den created by his ignorance and helpless poverty. The den where lived the despair of his isolated mind. Miriam felt its dailiness. Seemed to be within it and to breathe its thick odours as she listened. And to rebel and curse with him. In his soul was light. Something he felt his wife fought against with her dark, silent ways. Why did he not murder her?

And the woman was there with her youth. Before her eyes, pictures of Devonshire. In her mind, wonder at the way things had slipped down and down, to this; and fear, of this maddened stranger who desired only her death.

Well, they adore each other, they adore each other, muttered Miriam as quietness fell. It is terrifying to me because I 'm not accustomed.

A shriek brought her to the middle of the floor feeling cool and strong. 'Stop! stop!' she shouted down out of the window. 'I 'm coming.' But her voice was drowned in the tumult below. A blazing lamp crashed out into the garden and then came the man's voice feeble and sane:

'We mighta been killed. We mighta been before our Maker, Maria.' And a sobbing. Mrs Perrance sobbing in serene despair. Without fear.

Away. Away. . . .